DARK LIGHT OF MINE

OVERWORLD CHRONICLES BOOK TWO

JOHN CORWIN

RAVEN HOUSE

HELLHOUNDS ATE MY PANTS

Justin won Elyssa's heart and saved his dad from rogue vampires, but just when he thinks he can ride off into the sunset on a white horse, trouble not only knocks on his door, it plows through it with hellhounds.

Spawn relatives with their own agendas, vampires running amok, and his father marked for death, it seems there's no end to the kinds of monsters out to make Justin's life miserable. It's almost enough to make him long for the days of man boobs, Kings and Castles, and nerd status. With a list of impossible quests growing faster than he can keep up, tracking down the deadliest assassin in the world may prove easier than winning the approval of Elyssa's parents.

The clock ticking, and dark forces on his heels, Justin gets a crash course in the mysteries and dangers of the Overworld. But with Elyssa by his side and his growing menagerie of friends, impossible odds suddenly seem possible again.

ACKNOWLEDGMENTS

To my wonderful support group:

Alana Rock, Barbara Kuhl, Becky Hammer, Chelle Magliozzi, Dana Prestridge, Hazel Godwin, Karla Ileana, Keren Hall, Karen Stansbury, Nicole Passante Nita Banks, Pat Owens, Sheri Feikert, Terri Thomas and Jennifer Smith.

My amazing editors:
Annetta Ribken
Jennifer Wingard

My awesome cover artist:
Regina Wamba

You guys rock!

BOOKS BY JOHN CORWIN:

THE OVERWORLD CHRONICLES

Sweet Blood of Mine

Dark Light of Mine

Fallen Angel of Mine

Dread Nemesis of Mine

Twisted Sister of Mine

Dearest Mother of Mine

Infernal Father of Mine

Sinister Seraphim of Mine

Wicked War of Mine

Dire Destiny of Ours

Aetherial Annihilation

Baleful Betrayal

Ominous Odyssey

Insidious Insurrection

Utopia Undone

Overworld Apocalypse

Assignment Zero (An Elyssa Short Story)

OVERWORLD UNDERGROUND

Possessed By You

Demonicus

Coming Soon: Infernal Blade

OVERWORLD ARCANUM

For the latest on new releases, free ebooks, and more, join John Corwin's Newsletter at www.johncorwin.net!

CHAPTER 1

I answered my cell phone on the fourth ring, and a voice I hadn't heard in a long time said, "Justin, you have to leave your father, and you have to do it now."

A cup in my hand fell from nerveless fingers, clattering on the floor and spraying water everywhere. "Mom?" My legs turned to jelly. I staggered into the den and fell onto the ugly plaid sofa in front of the television.

Elyssa emerged from my bedroom, her face still pale from blood loss, and dark circles underscoring her eyes. She looked as tired as I felt. My father had been captured by a rogue vampire, Maximus, and our rescue mission last night had nearly killed the two of us. Somehow, we'd made it out alive with my father, but my brain felt like mush. A call from my mother was the last thing I'd expected. Elyssa gave me one look and furrowed her brow in concern.

"Yes, it's me," Mom said.

I clenched my phone. A fine line ran down the glass and joined two other stress cracks. "You abandon me a day before my birthday without anything but a crummy letter, and now you're calling me and telling me to abandon the parent who didn't leave?" My voice rose to a shout by the end of the sentence.

"Justin, I couldn't explain everything in the letter. If the wrong people discovered our secret—"

"You mean Ivy?"

She paused for the briefest of seconds before answering. "Yes, like the existence of your sister. I couldn't let your father's family find out about her."

"But it's fine if they know about me?"

"No, it's not. You were kept a secret too. Apparently, when your abilities bloomed, you caught the attention of someone in the supernatural community."

Something ripped. I looked down and realized my fingers had gouged the fabric of the sofa as they balled into fists. "Oh, so it's my fault."

"I'm not saying that at all." Her breath caught. "I don't have much time. Get out of the house. And whatever you do, don't—"

"Mom? Mom?" No answer. The line went dead.

"Is she okay?" Elyssa asked.

I shoved the phone in my pocket and turned to her. "I—I hope so." My forehead crumpled. I took deep breaths to keep the tears at bay. I couldn't afford to wimp out right in front of my tough ninja-dhampyr and all-around badass girlfriend.

She encircled me with her arms and pressed herself against me, soft, warm, and oh-so amazing. "Everything will be okay."

I pressed a stray lock of her raven-black hair behind her ear and pecked a kiss on her nose. "She told me to leave Dad."

Her left eyebrow quirked a notch. "Leave your Dad? After we just rescued him from a gang of rogue vampires? Why?"

"She didn't say. We were cut off."

"That's not good."

I shook my head. "Nope. But I don't know what to do. I can't just leave Dad."

The front door burst open and Dad bolted inside. "Justin, you have to leave now." His face looked pale and frightened.

I pulled away from Elyssa. "What the hell is going on? First Mom and now you?"

He drew in a sharp breath. "Your mother contacted you?"

"She just called and told me to leave you."

He streaked inhumanly fast across the kitchen, into the den, and took my shoulders in his hands. "Did she say where she is?" Hope and agony warred on his features.

"No, Dad." I repeated the conversation and each word seemed to dim the light of hope in his eyes.

He slumped to the couch. "She's right, son. You need to get out of here immediately. Pack light and leave."

I sat down on the easy chair and stared at him. "I'm not going anywhere until you tell me what's going on."

"My family is coming."

"Is that bad?" My stomach clenched. It apparently knew the answer.

Elyssa shuddered. "Worse than you can imagine."

I looked from her to Dad. "You're coming with me, right?"

"I can't. Someone tagged me with a tracking spell and told my family where to find me."

My chin dropped a fraction. "A what? Who would do that? The vampires?"

He shook his head. "It must have been the sorcerer who tried to capture us."

"Shelton? But he just helped us rescue you."

"The tracker wasn't there yesterday, and I haven't been around any other sorcerers lately." He pulled down the collar of his shirt and revealed a tiny red and gold tattoo in the shape of a hummingbird on the back of his neck. The skin around it was slightly red. "Blasted thing itches."

I leaned over and examined it. A hummingbird seemed like a girly thing for a guy to have, and I wondered if maybe he'd gotten drunk, woken up with it, and was too embarrassed to admit the truth. "Uh, Dad, this is a tattoo. Shelton never had the chance to touch you much less ink your skin. Are you sure the vampires who kidnapped you didn't do this?"

"Sorcerers don't need to touch you to tattoo you," Elyssa said, her

3

eyes growing cold and hard. "They only need to be close enough to see where they want the tracker to reside."

"But it's a stinking tattoo. Why don't they make it invisible if they're gonna track you?"

Dad sighed. "I don't know. Maybe it requires more power." He scratched the tattoo and scowled. "In any case, there's no telling how long this thing will last. My family has the scent now and they'll find me wherever I run."

I pressed a hand to my forehead as if it might help me soak in the onslaught of revelations. "Didn't you tell me this house is on a magical ley line? I thought all the energy confused magical tracking."

"It does, but since they know where we live now, they don't need the tracker, just a GPS. If I run, then the tracker will make it just as easy to find me. I might as well wait for them here."

"Are you kidding me?" I grunted in frustration. "What about a backup plan? With all the money you and Mom have in the bank, surely you bought a backup house somewhere on another ley line."

"We have—had two others."

"Why didn't you say so? Let's go!"

He slammed a fist on the couch armrest. "They're already compromised. I checked them out and both places were trashed. That means this house is next on the list."

"Son of a—" I paced the room, wracking my brain for answers.

"Justin, you have to go. Now."

"I just got you back, Dad. I'm not leaving you again."

He groaned in frustration. "Then both of us should pack." With that, he stalked into his bedroom.

"Maybe Shelton can help," Elyssa said.

"And what if he's the one who tagged him?" I thought back to the fight with the vampires when they'd kidnapped Dad. Had Shelton tossed a tracker on him then and not told me? Or had he possibly put one on Dad when we rescued him? It would have been the perfect time. Shelton had driven me, Dad, and Elyssa to my house. I'd been exhausted and barely able to think straight. If Shelton had marked Dad before the vampires took him, maybe that's how he knew where they were keeping him. If that were the case, I wouldn't be as ticked off. But if he'd put it on after the rescue, Shelton wasn't getting away from me without a mouth full of broken teeth.

Elyssa put her hands on my neck, tugging down my collar.

"What are you doing?"

"Checking you for tattoos."

A chill ran through me. It would be really, really bad if we were both tagged. "I didn't even think about that."

"It's a good thing I'm around, then."

The touch of her warm hands on my back and neck were almost enough to make me forget the oncoming danger. I'd had such high hopes for the day. We'd snuggled down and watched the Princess Bride, made out a little, and planned to grab some Chinese food for dinner. In the back of my mind I'd even envisioned what would happen later. How I'd kiss her, unclothe her, and we'd lose our virginity together, the way it was meant to be. She was The One.

"What are you thinking about?" Elyssa said in a low voice.

I realized how strongly my body was reacting to the fantasy playing out in my head, and my face burned with embarrassment.

"Just you."

Elyssa smiled and kissed me on the cheek. "You should pack."

"Yeah." My voice was hoarse at the thought of leaving home with my demon spawn relatives hot on our tails. But I had to face reality. I dashed into my room. Grabbed my large green duffel bag and shoved underwear, socks, shirts, and anything else I could fit inside. Elyssa came from the bathroom with my toiletries kit packed full to bursting and shoved it inside the duffel. I was zipping it up when another thought occurred to me. I sat down in my closet, removed a panel of drywall, and grabbed the stacks of money behind it.

"Did you rob a bank?"

"My parents." It had been their rainy-day fund before Mom left either to rescue my little sister, Ivy, from her parents, the Conroys, or to join them. I had a feeling she'd joined them, though not by choice—or so I hoped. I shoved the money into the duffel and reached back inside the wall for one more thing—a flash drive. I'd copied some files off my mom's computer a few days ago and forgotten all about them. The files looked mostly like gibberish and some kind of programming code when I'd opened them in a text viewer, but at some point I intended to sit down and go through them thoroughly. I dropped the flash drive in the duffel and zipped it shut.

Dad emerged from his room, a stuffed backpack slung over his shoulders.

I looked at the tennis shoes he'd put on instead of the casual sandals he usually wore. "You're coming with us, right?"

He shook his head. "I'm heading away from you. Whatever happens, I won't let them take you."

"Let's go to Shelton first. Maybe he can remove the tracker."

"And if he can't, I'll be a sitting duck along with him and you."

"I'll protect you."

Dad chuckled wryly. "You have no idea how powerful my family is."

"I'll be there too," Elyssa said.

I looked at her like I'd just seen a miniature Elvis break-dancing on her head. "No way, babe. In case you forgot, those vamplings almost killed you last night. You need to go home and rest up."

Fire danced in her violet eyes. "I'll do no such thing. You just try and make me leave, Justin."

Yeah, right. She'd have me on my knees begging for mercy in two seconds if I tried to make her do anything. "Fine. We'll all go."

"But—" Dad said.

"I said *all* of us, Dad. I refuse to lose you again. Or maybe you forgot I almost killed the girl I love to save you and nearly died in the process myself."

"I've forgotten nothing," he growled.

"Good." I pulled out my cell and dialed Shelton.

Several rings later, he answered in a voice thick with sleep. "Damn, kiddo. Can't a guy get some shuteye around here?"

"Did you put a tracker on my dad?"

"Blunt and right to the point, eh?" He yawned loudly. "Sounds like you could use some sleep yourself."

"Shelton, I don't have time for your crap right now. Tell me if you tagged him and if you can remove it."

The phone went silent for a moment. "No, I didn't tag him. As for disenchanting the tracker, I'd have to see it first."

"We have an emergency situation right now. Tell me how to get to you."

"Oh, no you don't. You're not coming to my place with a tracker."

I suppressed the urge to yell. "Where then?"

"Downtown. Centennial Olympic Park. It's a nice public place. When you get there, find a secluded spot and make a circle around your dad."

My thoughts flashed to the last time he'd used one of his fancy magic circles on my dad. "Won't that imprison him?"

"No, you don't know how to make those kinds of circles. But this will block him off from outside magic and, depending on what kind of tracker he has, it might confuse or cut off the signal. "

"Why don't I just make a circle here and you come to us?"

Shelton sighed. "If the tracker is a strong one, a circle might not block it. It's best if we meet somewhere with lots of people in case they do track you. At least that way they won't try anything overt."

The park was about fifteen minutes away by car. "Okay, we're headed out now." I shoved the phone in my pocket and glanced around for the car keys.

Elyssa hiked up the black gym shorts I'd let her borrow since her clothing had been ripped and spattered with gore during Dad's rescue. She strapped a black knife sheath to each of her fair, muscular thighs. Our swords had been lost somewhere, probably in the crypts where the vampires had imprisoned my dad, but subtlety was probably better. People would frantically speed dial nine-one-one the moment they saw Conan the Barbarian and his sword-wielding pals dashing around outside.

My girlfriend produced a piece of chalk from the bloody knapsack still reeking of rotted vamplings, the zombie-like remains of people who failed to turn into vampires. They'd almost killed us in the crypt beneath the old building the vampires called home. "You'll need this to draw a circle." She wrinkled her nose at the bag. "You have some Lysol?"

I grabbed a pink can from under the kitchen sink. Tossed it to her. She doused the small knapsack, fumigating the kitchen. I snagged my keys off the counter. "Let's go."

I had my hand on the doorknob when a soft knock sounded upon it. My hand almost opened the door on reflex, only to have survival instinct slap me in the face and remind me bad people might be waiting on the other side. At least they were polite enough to knock. I checked the peephole. Jade green eyes peered back. I pulled back. Looked again. The green eyes belonged to Katie Johnson, a classmate and former crush of mine. What in the world was she doing here? I thought about the last time I'd seen her and gulped. Elyssa would castrate me if she knew what we'd done.

A black limousine pulled to the curb at the end of the sidewalk behind Katie. My heart skipped a few beats and sped up. My neighborhood was not the sort of place limousines frequented unless it was prom. And it most definitely was not that time of the year.

"Who is it?" Elyssa asked, drawing a silver knife from her thigh sheath.

My breath hitched as the limo driver got out. Big and burly, he sported a black suit and wraparound shades. Then he straightened up, all seven feet of him. He wasn't big and burly. He was monstrous.

Katie knocked on the door again. "Justin? We need to talk. Are you in there? I can hear someone."

"You've got to be kidding me." Elyssa growled. "Get rid of her."

"We've got bigger problems," I said, my wide eyes locked on the massive man coming up behind the unsuspecting Katie.

And no time to solve them.

CHAPTER 2

I pulled open the door and jerked Katie inside in one smooth motion. She shrieked as her momentum carried her into Elyssa. I caught a glimpse of flame-red hair emerging from the other side of the limo as I slammed the door shut.

Katie stared at Elyssa. At the knife in her hand. Her gaze travelled over the duffel bags and the tension carved in Dad's forehead. "Are you going on a trip?" She glared at Elyssa. "And what's she doing here?"

"I don't have time to explain," I said. I looked at Dad. "They're here. We need to go out the back. *Now.*"

"What about her?" Elyssa said.

"We can't leave her here. She'll just have to come along."

Dad raced to the back sliding glass door and opened it. I gripped Katie by the hand and started for the door. She dug in, trying to stop me, but I wasn't hanging around a moment longer.

"Justin? What's going on? Stop pulling me!" She slapped at my hand as her feet slid along the kitchen floor.

I stopped, resisting the desire to toss her over my shoulder and carry her bodily out of there. "There are some very bad people about to come through that front door. Unless we get out of here right now, something bad is going down."

Her eyes flared wide with fear. "Why? Who would—"

"I'll answer your questions later. Let's go."

Elyssa's eyes burned with murderous intent when I turned to face her. It quickly vanished behind a neutral gaze. "Can't you just toss her over someone's fence? I think the neighbors have a pool she might land in if you want me to do it."

"I'm not willing to take the chance the Slades won't harm her."

"The Slades?" Katie asked.

"My dad's family," I said.

"Hurry up!" Dad shouted as he vaulted the tall wooden fence between our yard and the neighbors' to the back.

Katie gaped. "Did he just jump over a six-foot fence?"

"Get on my back," I said, handing my duffel bag to Elyssa.

Thankfully, Katie was too shocked to pelt me with more questions and hopped on my back just as a tremendous crash sounded from inside the house. I turned to look at the shower of splinters from the front door frame spraying into the foyer.

Katie wasn't exactly light as a feather on my back, but my newly acquired supernatural strength hardly noticed her except for the frantic grip she had on my neck. I ran for the fence and leapt over it. Katie shrieked as we landed with a jolt, nearly bursting my eardrums.

"Hold on tight and don't bite your tongue," I said.

Her grip went from tight to absolutely manic.

Elyssa and Dad cleared another backyard fence, and I followed, using the roof of the house to avoid whacking Katie on the head with a low-hanging tree branch. I streaked after Dad and Elyssa as they crossed a residential street and made for a three-story colonial house on the other side. Dodging around a blue sedan parked on the side of the road, I cast a quick glance around to make sure there weren't any noms witnessing our supernatural displays of athleticism. The last thing I needed was to whip the neighbors into hysteria.

I'd just made it into a thicket of woods across the road when I heard it—a low rumbling growl. I looked back expecting to see a dog. Instead, I saw the limo driver. He hadn't leapt the fence. He'd run *through* it, leaving a splintered mess behind. And the noise he emitted wasn't human in the slightest. I expected him to leap the car. Instead, he plowed into it, knocking it to the side like a toy. Katie turned her head and saw the car tumbling, sparking, and screeching down the road on its roof. Her body tightened even more as a ragged scream escaped her throat.

Right then I thanked Coach Burgundy and Coach Wise for blackmailing me into playing football. When I'd first grown into my abilities I couldn't run two feet at super speed without tripping and busting my butt. I was going to need every trick in the book to get away from this guy—thing—oh, whatever the hell he was.

"Can you go any faster?" Katie asked, her ragged breathing quickening with fear.

Something silver flashed past me. I whipped my head back and saw one of Elyssa's knives strike my pursuer point-first full in the chest. It bounced off.

Panic thudded in my heart. "Oh, crap. Oh, crap!"

Elyssa cursed and threw another knife. This one went straight for the limo driver's eye. He swatted it from the air before it hit.

"Aren't those things silver?" I gasped as I caught up with her and Dad.

"Of course they are."

"Maybe you should upgrade to uranium."

We cleared the woods and trampled through an ornate rose garden some retirees had obviously spent their golden years cultivating. Thorns tore at my clothes. Katie gasped. An elderly man sitting on the front porch raised his fist and shook it. "You rotten kids!"

The limo driver ripped through the garden a few seconds later. The rose thorns must have caught in his black suit, because some of them came up by the roots. The old man's apoplectic shouts faded into the distance as we cut right and made for the busy road intersecting this one, our feet blurring with speed.

"I don't think he's as fast as we are," Elyssa said, her words coming between pants.

I spared a look back and saw we were indeed gaining distance as we sped down the straightaway. "Yeah, but how much longer can we keep this up?"

"Oh, I'm fine. Then again, I'm not carrying a bimbo on my back."

"Who are you calling a bimbo?" Katie said, apparently forgetting all about the mortal peril we were in, her voice jolting with every step I took.

I looked ahead at the busy intersection and groaned. Cars jammed the road. "What are we going to do about that?"

Elyssa cast a glance back at our pursuer. "If he punches through those cars, he might kill someone."

I imagined a trail of crushed and smoking cars as the Incredible Hulk's white brother plowed through them like the Kool-Aid man.

"Look." Dad pointed toward some high-voltage power lines to our left. A swath of green clearing ran underneath them, vanishing over a hill in the distance. It wasn't a road, but we could avoid automobile carnage and earn the gratitude of insurance claims adjustors everywhere.

I sucked in a breath and veered in that direction. "Let's go."

We made it up the long hill and dashed left into some woods, hoping to lose our follower while we were out of his line of sight. After what seemed an eternity of backyards, playgrounds, and even a nature trail, we emerged from the woods near a park and a familiar overpass. I tried to get my bearings, panting and looking behind us to make sure we'd really lost the guy.

Katie groaned and almost fell off my back. Dad helped her down. She staggered. I caught her and held her up until she stood on her own feet. "I can't take this anymore," she said. "I feel like I just got off a bull. My legs are killing me."

"You should be safe now. Call someone to pick you up and take you home."

"I'm going to look for a bus stop," Dad said, and jogged toward the four-lane road nearby.

"Where are we?" Katie asked, casting her gaze at our surroundings.

I glanced at the nearby Atlanta skyline. "Somewhere near Freedom Parkway."

"Maybe big tough Brad can pick you up on his Harley," Elyssa said.

Katie narrowed her eyes. "Justin is my boyfriend now, thank you very much."

Fire glinted in Elyssa's eyes. "Since when?"

Katie took my arm. "Since the football game he won for us, right, sweetie?"

The look in Elyssa's eyes could have melted steel. I felt myself withering under her gaze as I separated myself from Katie. "No. We're not."

"What? But, Justin, we slept together. How could you do this to me?"

"You what?" Elyssa shouted, striding towards us, death and destruction carving a scowl on her face.

"We didn't!" I said, backing away from both of them and holding out my hands. "I swear to you, Elyssa, we didn't."

"I may have been drunk," Katie said, "but you were going for my panties and I had my hand on your—"

"Shut up!" I said, heart pounding from fear as much as exertion. "We didn't sleep together. We just made out."

"How convenient," Elyssa said in a snarl. "What happened to losing our virginity together? True love? The Princess Bride?" Tears glistened in her eyes.

"I love that movie," Katie said.

A lump lodged in my throat at the hurt in Elyssa's eyes. "Elyssa, I swear to you on all that is holy in this world I did not sleep with Katie. Besides, you weren't even talking to me then. You hated me."

"That doesn't excuse anything."

My inner nerd chose that moment to remind me just how crazy women were, and also the fact Elyssa probably knew a hundred different ways to cause me immense pain, being a trained fighter for the Templars and all. Unfortunately, he didn't have any brilliant suggestions for handling this situation.

"Justin didn't sleep with her," Dad said from behind me. I almost jumped ten feet straight up.

"How do you know?" Elyssa said.

"Because I jerked him off her and slammed him into the wall while they were both fully clothed. Didn't you see the dent in the drywall?"

13

A smile lit her face. It grew even bigger when she saw embarrassment turning Katie's face a brilliant hue of red. "Good."

My own face felt like it was burning by that point. "Can we lay off talking about my sex life and figure out what to do next?"

Katie crossed her arms and sniffed. "I'm not going another step until you tell me what you are. I've never seen anyone move so fast or jump fences like that. It's not normal!"

I looked at Dad. He looked at me. I looked at Elyssa. She rolled her eyes.

"What's the protocol here?" I asked, not wanting to break the Overworld secrecy code, or any other pact for that matter. I was the supernatural newb of the group and still had a lot to learn about, well, everything.

"Katie, we've involved you in something very dangerous you shouldn't know anything about," Dad said. "Believe me when I tell you it's for the best if you go home right now."

"Oh, no you don't." She pursed her lips. "I'm sticking with Justin."

"Elyssa is my girlfriend," I said. "I'm sorry to be harsh, but I love her, and you sticking around isn't going to change anything."

Tears pooled in her eyes. "I really screwed up, didn't I?" She slumped against a tree as sobs shook her body. "I was such a total bitch to you."

I felt horrible all of a sudden. What was it about women and crying that made me feel like crap? *They must have guilt pheromones in their tears.* I knelt next to her and put a hand on her shoulder. "It'll be okay. You'll find a really great guy one day." This was one speech I never in a million years would have pictured me giving to Katie Johnson. I'd crushed on her so hard at one point I'd actually thought she was the one for me. And then I'd met Elyssa and found out what real love was.

"We've got to get going," Dad said. "The tracker will lead them to us at any moment."

"Who or what is this guy chasing us?" I said. "The way he just knocked a car around like it was a toy is impossible, even for spawn."

"And my knives didn't even faze him," Elyssa added, her gaze meeting Dad's.

"Is he spawn like you?"

Dad shook his head. "No." He ran a hand through his tangled brown hair and glanced at the snarled traffic on the highway leading downtown. "I'm not sure, not a hundred percent, anyway, but I think they're hellhounds."

My jaw went slack. "What? Why are they so hell-bent on catching you anyway? Are you really such a disappointment to the family?"

"I have a lot to answer for in their eyes," Dad said, his lips going tight. "Marrying your mother, a human, was just the first slap in their faces. There's a lot you don't know about our kind, Justin. They're obsessed with social order and ranking. I broke all those rules and they despise me for it."

A cold lump formed in my chest. "Are they going to kill you for it?"

He sighed. "I honestly don't know."

Katie lifted her tear-streaked face. "Will someone please tell me what's going on?"

I glanced at the darkening sky. Night would settle in soon, and I couldn't just leave Katie in this part of town to fend for herself. "Hop on my back if you want answers." *Did I really just say that?*

Apparently I had because she climbed wearily onto my back.

"This is a mistake," Elyssa said. "You're going to get her hurt, killed, or worse."

"What could be worse than dying?" I asked.

"After all you've seen, do you really have to ask?"

I thought back to the vamplings, those half-zombie, half-vampire creatures and shuddered. "I guess not." I blew out a breath. "Let's just find her a cab."

Car tires shrieked behind us. I spun and saw the limo bounce to a halt against the curb. The front two doors sprang open as the massive driver and his slightly shorter twin leapt out. Company had arrived.

And they looked pissed.

CHAPTER 3

I think someone shouted, "Run!" at the top of their lungs. It might have been me, but I was way past rational thought when I saw we had *two* of those crazy mofos after us. I streaked toward downtown, using the tallest skyscraper as a beacon. Dad and Elyssa pulled up alongside me, faces strained with exertion.

"Just how bad," I said, taking a deep breath, "are hellhounds?" I panted.

"Worse than you can imagine," Dad said. "They won't stop hunting us." He glanced back. "Even if we cut off the tracking spell with a circle, they could sniff us out anywhere so long as we leave a trail. We need a car, something to keep our scent off the road. Otherwise we'll drop from exhaustion long before they give up."

If only I had a bottle of Axe Body Spray to dump on the ground. If such a concentration of manly odor didn't confuse their canine noses, nothing would. The men behind us obviously didn't look like dogs, but I was too out of breath to ask more questions. We reached a huge apartment complex. Leapt the razor-wire atop the chain-link fence. We'd already gained some distance on the hellhound dudes, but I didn't expect our lead to last long, if what Dad said about their tracking abilities was true. The apartments were five-story, flat-roofed affairs with a courtyard in the center and two parking decks flanking each side of the complex.

Elyssa motioned us to follow her inside the nearest parking deck. "You said we needed a car?"

"You know how to hotwire one?" I said, impressed.

She shook her head. "No, but with any luck we can carjack someone."

Before I could offer a morally outraged response, she raced around the garage and up the ramps, her gaze sweeping the area for a target. But we reached the roof without finding a victim.

Elyssa looked across the apartments to the other parking deck. "We'll have to take our chances in the next one."

"How are we supposed to get there?" I said. "Jump?"

She offered a brief smile before racing across the deck and launching herself across the wide gap between the deck and the roof of the next apartment building over. Dad followed. My guts knotted tight. It was one thing vaulting backyard fences with Katie on my back and quite another to risk a five-story plunge which would hurt me like hell and probably kill Katie.

Her grip tightened as I contemplated the edge. A whimper escaped her throat and I felt her face press against my back. I hoped to god she had a strong bladder.

"Just get off and hide," I said. "You shouldn't be involved in this." Plus I really wanted the extra load off. I was pooped.

"You'll make it. I trust you."

I sighed. "Why are you doing this? I told you I love Elyssa."

"I want you, Justin, but if I can't have you, I want to know what in the world is going on here. You're like superheroes or something. Just like the ones my little brother reads about in his comic books."

I chuckled. "Hardly." If anything, I was the villain. Demon spawn weren't heroes in anyone's book.

Elyssa and Dad waved me over, their faces tight with urgency. I took a deep breath. Ran at the ledge. Jumped. Katie shrieked as we cleared the gap. I couldn't help but look down at the hard concrete sidewalk far, far below. My feet hit the roof. I stumbled as Katie's weight shifted, but managed to stay upright. A mournful howl gripped the chilly air. Dad cursed. Elyssa gasped. I spun and saw our pursuers staring from across the parking deck roof at us. One of the men reared his head back and loosed a chilling inhuman howl which about made me wet my pants. It was a howl of despair and hopelessness. *Resistance is futile*, it seemed to say. No matter how hard or fast we ran, they would catch us. Besides, why run? We had nowhere to go.

Dad grabbed my arm and wrenched me around. "Ignore the howls, Justin. Shut them out of your mind. Don't let them control you."

Katie's grip loosened on my neck. Sobs shook her body. "We're going to die. It's useless. Life is pointless."

Elyssa dropped to her knees as tears poured from her face. "He's dead," she said. "And it's all my fault." My duffel bag slid from her shoulder and thumped on the roof.

"What the hell is going on?" I asked, shaking off the melancholy mood as both the men continued to howl while they slowly advanced across the parking deck roof for us.

"Their howls kill hope," Dad said. "They bring back our worst memories and nightmares. Thankfully, we spawn are not as easily influenced." He dragged Elyssa to her feet, tried to shake her out of her misery, but it didn't help.

Katie dropped off my back like a sack of potatoes, bawling her eyes out.

"Dad, they're coming. We have to carry the girls."

He glared at our pursuers, his eyes glowing ice-white with fatigue. Mine probably matched his. I wanted to find a nice quiet spot, go to sleep, and dream about kittens. "Justin, if they corner us while we're this tired, we may spawn."

"We'll manifest into our demon forms?"

He gave me a sideways look. "If that happens, we won't be able to control ourselves. We might rampage. People could die."

"What do we do?"

He took a deep breath and picked up Katie, slung her over his shoulder. "We're almost downtown. No matter where we go for miles in any direction we'll run into densely populated areas."

"So, our only chance is to outrun them."

He nodded. "Yeah." The answer sounded dry in his throat.

I looked back at the hounds. "Why aren't they running?"

"I don't think they can howl and run at the same time. They probably think we're immobilized."

"On three?" I scooped up Elyssa and slung her over a shoulder, grabbed my duffel with a spare hand.

Dad gave me a lopsided smile. "One. Two. Three."

We bolted. The howls ceased. Elyssa and Katie bounced against our backs with each long stride, and flopped with each leap. We cleared six rooftops and leapt to the parking deck roof. The hounds leapt each gap with high, graceful jumps belying their huge lumbering forms. I spotted an old tire leaning against the parking deck wall. Dropped my duffel. Gripped the inside of the tire with my free hand. Spun and launched it as the hounds leapt the next-to-last roof. It caught one square in the chest as he hit the apex of his jump. He yelped, sounding like a wounded dog, and vanished between the buildings. His comrade ignored him and came at us, face snarling, his unnaturally long tongue flapping and slavering.

Dad paused at the top of the ramp when he realized I wasn't right behind him. I retrieved my duffel, sprinted to him, and we made our way down the ramp and into the parking deck. Shouting echoed from ahead. A man stood outside his white crew-cab pickup examining the side where a woman in a blue Toyota must have hit him. The woman cowered in fear as he screamed obscenities in her face. Fury rode a rising tide of hot anger in my chest.

"You stupid, blind idiot!" the man shouted. "How could you possibly miss seeing me when I backed out? Women drivers are all brain-dead. Shouldn't even be allowed behind the wheel of a car!" The man's eyes widened with shock the moment he saw us rushing down the ramp, girls slung over our shoulders like a couple of cavemen.

I lengthened my stride, reached him, and punched him square in the nose. He staggered in a wobbling half-circle before face-planting on the concrete. I grabbed him with my free hand and dragged him against the opposite wall, out of the way. "We have an emergency," I told the shocked woman with the blue Toyota. "Tell him he can get his precious

pickup later." I glanced back up the ramp. "Now get out of here and hide!"

She bolted like a crazed jackrabbit.

Dad and I slung the girls into the back seats of the crew cab, not bothering to buckle them in as the panting of the hound grew louder. I unslung the duffel from my shoulder, tossed it to Dad, and hopped in the driver's seat. The truck peeled out under my desperate guidance while Dad turned around and tried to buckle the dazed girls in.

"What—what happened?" Elyssa asked, seeming to recover her wits. She buckled herself in before Dad could finish securing Katie's grief-stricken form.

"Hellhound howls," Dad said. "I'd have thought Templars might know how to protect against those."

"I've never encountered them." Elyssa squeezed her temples. "My head's killing me."

"It'll pass."

"Okay, so they howl, pant, slobber, and yelp, but they still look like men," I said. "Are they shifters like Stacey?"

"The reverse," he replied.

"Huh?"

"Stacey is a felycan—a human who can shift into feline form. Hell-hounds are huge mindlessly-devoted creatures who can shift into human or other forms as a sort of camouflage."

I drifted around the parking deck ramp, tires squealing as I wrestled the big truck under control. A car pulled out a few slots ahead, but my preternatural senses and reflexes guided me around it without a second thought.

"No wonder Edward was such a crazy driver," I muttered.

"Who's Edward?" Elyssa asked.

"You know, from Twilight."

Katie perked up all of a sudden, her eyes red and puffy. "I love Edward."

Elyssa groaned.

I screeched to a halt at the parking deck exit and cursed. A steel gate barred the way, and it looked too solid to smash through. "Crap. What now?"

Elyssa reached between the seats and jerked a gray fob off the keychain dangling from the truck's ignition. "Scan it." She pointed to a pad on a console outside the window.

I rolled the window down and thrust the fob at the pad. It dinged and a light turned green. The steel shutter slid up. Slowly. Like old-man-crossing-the-street-with-a-walker slow. Tires squealed. Metal crunched. Glass shattered. I looked past Dad through the passenger window. A car at the corner of the ramp bounced and rolled, sparks flying before smashing into a Bentley across the driveway as the hound burst around the corner. In mid-stride, the man morphed into a huge ebony dog, fangs bared and tongue lolling. A yellow glow pulsed from within its eyes.

The shutter wasn't halfway up yet, its bottom about level with the middle of the truck's windshield. Dad rolled down his window and crawled into the narrow space between concrete wall and truck. He reached for the bottom of the shutter. Cursed. Jerked it up. The metal groaned. Something gave a metallic pop and the shutter sprang up, slamming into the stops at the end of the rails overhead.

The second Dad had his body back through the window, I gunned it. Katie screamed. I looked left in time to see the other hound, still in human form, bolt down the sidewalk. It was too late to get away. The truck shuddered with the brute's impact, and agony shot into my arm as the door imploded on me. A screech of rubber and the scream of torn metal sounded for an instant. Then silence followed as the truck flipped sideways through the air. Time seemed to slow in my head as my reflexes shot into overdrive. Glass flew sideways. Katie and Elyssa's hair hit the ceiling as the truck went upside down some ten feet off the ground.

Dad's eyes met mine. He didn't have to say what I was thinking. If the truck landed on its roof, this was going to hurt. He, Elyssa, and I might survive, but not Katie. I tore my seatbelt off. Dove into the back seat. Gripped the top and bottom of Katie's seat tight and pressed her hard against the cushions, forming a shield around her. Elyssa gave me a look of concern mixed with something else—jealousy? Sadness?

The truck slammed into the ground before I had a chance to figure it out. Metal met asphalt as the roof crunched. The roof buckled but somehow didn't cave in completely. Then the truck rolled onto the side Katie and I were on and slid down the hill toward a busy intersection at the bottom. The remaining windows shattered, spraying us with safety glass. Agony ripped into the skin on my back as my flesh kissed the rough surface of the road, searing it as we slid.

I cried out in pain, trying to force myself up. Elyssa gripped Katie and pulled her off me just enough so I could get the leverage to end the pain. Tires screeched as the truck reached the intersection and frightened drivers swerved to avoid us. I saw a van rushing our way from the sideways angle where the front windshield used to be.

"Oh crap!" I yelled as the van's tires smoked with the effort to stop it. It still slammed into the pickup. For a moment, we toppled on two wheels. Then another car rear-ended the van with a crunch, slamming the pickup and bouncing it back onto all four tires. I slithered into the driver's seat. Somehow, the engine was still running. I looked up the hill and saw the hounds, now both in human form, tearing down the hill after us. But they weren't running at superhuman speeds anymore. Maybe they were under orders to avoid exposing noms to their existence. I didn't know. Didn't care. I slammed the accelerator down and got the hell out of there.

"Take a right," Dad said. He directed me through several more turns as we ran red lights and dodged traffic for several blocks, the truck's engine rattling like spray-paint cans. He had me stop outside the huge curving structure of the Georgia Aquarium, where I parked in a no-parking zone.

My door was jammed shut from the hound's earlier impact and I didn't want to kick it off the hinges in front of all the tourists jamming the sidewalks, so I crawled out the window and almost face-planted on the sidewalk. Elyssa pulled me to my feet. Dad helped Katie out the other side. A huge crowd of people loitered around the outdoors ice-skating rink Centennial Olympic Park hosted during the colder months.

A few of them stared wide-eyed at the ravaged pickup truck with steam billowing from beneath its hood. Maybe the poor woman with the blue Toyota would be off the hook for damages.

I drew in a sharp breath. "Dad, the woman in the parking garage—do you think the hounds hurt her?"

"They probably ignored her." he said as he set a very dazed Katie back on her feet. "Once given an assignment, they're single-minded to a fault."

I hoped he was right. If he was, it meant we could safely let Katie go around here where she could vanish into the crowd.

Elyssa pressed her palm against my slowly healing back. She gripped me and pulled me in for a quick but passionate kiss. "You just can't help it can you?"

"Help what?" I said, feeling a bit flustered and bone weary.

She smiled and shook her head. "Sometimes I don't know if I want to punch you or kiss you. You don't think half the time, you just react and it scares me half to death."

I gripped her hand and shrugged. "Life hasn't given me much time to think lately." I looked up and saw Shelton sitting on a bench fiddling around with something in his hand. He'd probably expected us a lot sooner. I'd expected a boring drive through traffic, not a fox hunt followed by a demolition derby.

We rushed across the plaza to him. He pointed urgently at a chalk circle on the brick pavers. Dad stepped inside without batting an eyelash. Shelton pressed a thumb to the circle and closed it with a word. A slight hum and crackle popped in the air.

"Christ, people. What the hell took you so long?" He looked me up and down, saw the bloody rags remaining of the back of my t-shirt, Katie's wide eyes, and Elyssa's frazzled hair. Shelton sat back on the bench and chuckled. "All right. What happened?"

"Hellhounds," Dad said. He turned his back to Shelton and pointed to the tattoo. "Can you get rid of this?"

Shelton cursed and jumped off the bench. "You're running from hellhounds? Even if I remove the tracker they'll just sniff their way to you.'

"We lost them."

23

"Are you sure? I didn't think it was possible to shake a hellhound."

Dad nodded. "I've done it before."

"A spawn trick?"

"Only if you consider driving a pickup truck very fast through Atlanta traffic a spawn trick," Dad said with a grim smile.

Shelton laughed and looked at me. "I swear, Justin. You just can't keep out of trouble, can you?"

I dropped onto the bench next to Katie. Elyssa dropped down between us. "Shelton, trouble likes me." I scanned the crowd for any sign of the hounds but saw nothing but normal humans, goodness bless them, each and every one. The hounds were so tall and huge they'd stand out like a pimple on a fashion model's nose.

A dog yipped and I almost took off a passing Chihuahua's head as his owner led him by. A sheepish look crossed Elyssa's face as she slid a knife back into the sheath under her shorts.

"Guess I'm a bit jumpy," she said.

"You and me both."

"Who's this character?" Katie asked, looking Shelton up and down. He was wearing jeans, a Teenage Mutant Ninja Turtles T-shirt, cowboy boots, and his well-worn leather duster. While he didn't exactly look odd, he did somewhat resemble someone out of an old western movie, thankfully, sans the cowboy hat.

"This is Shelton. He's going to remove the tracker from my dad."

Katie glared at me. "When is someone going to tell me what in the hell is going on, Justin?"

I shrugged. "It's not up to me." I nodded at Elyssa. "If anyone knows how much we can tell you, it'd be Elyssa."

Katie narrowed her eyes and pursed her lips. "What makes you so special?"

Elyssa smiled, showing her teeth. "Just shut up and stay on my good side."

"Don't tell me you've dragged another civilian into the Overworld," Shelton said with a groan.

"I didn't drag the other one, in case you've forgotten," I said. "The rogue vam—uh, you-know-whats did that."

"Oh, yeah. Guess you're right."

"Are you going to look at the tracker?" Dad said, obviously losing patience.

Shelton turned back to him. "Yeah, yeah." He stared at the humming-bird tattoo for a moment, his eyes seeming to lose focus. A split second later, he cursed and jumped backward.

"What?" I asked, searching the area for danger.

Shelton sank onto the bench, his face white. "This isn't good," he said, voice hoarse.

Ice locked my heart in mid-beat. "What?"

"This is no ordinary tracker on your dad. It's a death mark."

CHAPTER 4

The shock in Dad's eyes said it all as his hand raced for the tattooed spot on the back of his neck. "A death mark? You're certain?"

"It gets worse."

"How can it be any worse?" Dad said, eyebrows pinching together.

"Worse how?" I asked, jumping to my feet and staring at Dad.

Shelton stood up and motioned Elyssa over. "The Templars train you to recognize marks?"

Her face went very pale as she stood and nodded. "I know most of them, yes."

"You can be my second opinion."

"Templars?" Katie said. "Like from Indiana Jones?"

I put a finger to my mouth to shush her.

She huffed like a spoiled brat. "When are you going to tell me what in the world is going on?"

Elyssa stared at the mark for a moment before shaking her head. "It doesn't look like a mark at all."

"What does it look like to you?"

"A red and gold hummingbird."

Shelton snapped his fingers. "Ah, dammit, that's right. Hold still." He pulled out his smartphone and consulted something for a moment before stepping in front of her. "I'm going to modulate the air right here." He traced a small square in the air in front of her nose. "So don't move."

"Modulate?" she asked, jerking her head back.

He pshawed. "Jeez, woman, no need to freak out. It's so you can see the mark."

"I can see it just fine."

"You see the disguised mark. The real one doesn't show itself until, uh, the job is done."

"You mean when I'm dead," Dad said. "No need to sugar-coat it, Shelton."

"Whatever, old man." Shelton turned back to Elyssa. "Now hold still."

Elyssa gave him a sharp look but did as he told her. Shelton stared at the air in front of Elyssa's nose for a moment before mumbling something I couldn't quite make out. Then he stepped to the side. Elyssa gasped.

Shelton nodded, looking pleased as punch. "You see it?"

I walked next to Elyssa, stooping down a little to place my eyes level with hers. Instead of a hummingbird, I saw a skeletal hand reaching up from a mound of earth, the bony fingers clenching and opening. It was so vivid it no longer looked like a tattoo, but a three-dimensional hologram projected from Dad's skin.

"This is Underborn's mark," Elyssa said. "Underborn from the Devoted."

"Like I said, this ain't no ordinary death mark."

"Since when is any death mark ordinary?" I asked. "What makes this one so special?"

Shelton took a seat next to Katie and gave her a lopsided smirk. "Ready for your first lesson, cupcake?"

"Is this guy supposed to be your friend?" Katie asked. "He's kind of a jerk."

I gave the sigh of the long-suffering and said, "He's a special kind of jerk."

Shelton chuckled and leaned against the backrest of the bench. "Most death marks are handed out by the Brotherhood of Assassins—"

"Assassins Guild," Elyssa said. "They're equal opportunity now, remember?"

"Whatever," he said, waving her comment off as if it were a pesky fly. "That's how I learned it. They're not an above-ground organization so to speak, so you don't hear much about them. Fact is most of the so-called Brotherhood-related deaths are false alarms and rumors."

"Because they're so expensive," Elyssa said. "And anyone caught dealing with the Brotherhood answers to the Templars."

Shelton stared at her for a moment. "You gonna let me finish?"

Elyssa looked up as though praying for heavenly intervention to keep her from pummeling Shelton into the dirt. I was about ready to strangle him myself. From the short time I'd known him, Shelton wasn't the easiest guy to get along with, and his "charming" personality didn't help matters much.

"Now, as I was saying," Shelton continued, tossing a wink at Katie, "The *Brotherhood* is deep, mysterious, and very expensive to hire. They're made up of all sorts—sorcerers with a taste for the dark side, vampires, werewolves, and some kinds of supers I ain't never heard of before."

Katie's eyebrows launched into low orbit. "What are you talking about?" She looked around at each of us, her eyes wide. "You don't even look surprised, Justin. Justin?"

My knowledge of the Overworld barely scratched the surface, but I found myself surprised by very little after discovering I was demon spawn—an incubus who could seduce women and who needed to feed off emotions. Oh yeah, and finding out my dad was also an incubus, my Mom was a sorceress, and that her parents had stolen my baby sister, Ivy, from us shortly after birth. There were loads more I could only guess at, but I probably wouldn't have been surprised if Shelton told me he had a pet yeti waiting at home.

I offered her a wan smile. "I know it's a lot to take in, Katie."

"A lot to take in?" She stood up and backed away. "Are you saying you're not all world-class athletes? You're a bunch of vampires?"

Elyssa smiled broadly as her canines lengthened into sharp, slightly curved fangs. "Sorry to disappoint, but I'm the only vampire here."

Katie gawked at Elyssa. I expected her to bolt screaming at any moment. Instead, she drew closer and inspected the fangs. "Does that hurt? Do you ever accidentally bite yourself?"

A frown replaced Elyssa's smile. "Seriously? You're not even going to run? Or scream?"

"Are you going to suck my blood?"

"As a general rule, I don't suck blood from people." She bored her gaze into Katie's and leaned in until her face was within an inch of the other girl's nose. "But if you touch my boyfriend again I might make an exception."

"What are you, Justin?" She cast a glance at Shelton. "And you?"

Shelton sighed heavily. "Can I finish my blasted story? We'll get to supernatural kindergarten later."

"Just sit down, Katie," I said, motioning to the bench. "Nobody here will hurt you."

She cast a slightly worried gaze at Elyssa before sitting down again, but with a bit more space on the bench between her and Shelton.

"Finally," Shelton said with a frustrated look heavenward. "The Devoted are the cream of the assassin crop. Some say they lead the Brotherhood. Others say they're independent." He shrugged. "I don't know and it really doesn't matter. What I can tell you is anyone can afford their fee, but most won't be willing to pay it."

"So someone very determined wants Dad dead," I said. "But why? What did he ever do to anyone?"

"That," Shelton said, turning his head to gaze at Dad, "is a very good question. Someone would have to *really* hate your dad to pay the fee for a Devoted hit."

"Who put the bounty on me, Shelton?" Dad asked. "I looked at the Conclave website but it didn't say."

Shelton shook his head. "I don't know. I assumed it was the Conroys. They weren't too happy with you sending normal investigators to poke into their business."

Dad's face flushed crimson and his lips curled back in a snarl. "They have my wife and daughter. What do they expect me to do? Send them a thank you card?"

"Whoa, cowboy. Don't take it out on me."

"I have a feeling you know a lot more than you let on," I said to Shelton. "As you told me before—you're a detective. And I know you're not stupid. If you found out where we live, then I'll bet you know exactly who put the bounty out on us."

"I told you, I don't know."

In a flash, I gripped Shelton's duster by the collar and jerked him off the bench. "You're lying."

Eyes glaring into mine, Shelton tightened his jaw and said, "Even if I knew, I wouldn't tell you."

I resisted the urge to launch him across the plaza and into the fountain.

Elyssa's hand touched my arm. "Let him go, Justin."

"He knows something. He knows who wants my father dead, too, I'll bet."

Shelton snorted. "If I knew do you think I'd be helping you right now?"

"Someone threatened him," Elyssa said. "That's why he's not talking."

My grip went slack, dropping Shelton on his feet. He brushed off his duster and took a seat on the bench. I turned to Elyssa. "What—how do you know this?"

"I've built up some instincts over the years, helping my family round up the law breakers." She cast a glance at Shelton. "I think he knows exactly who put the bounty out. And they know he knows, so they told him to keep his mouth shut."

Shelton crossed his arms and narrowed his eyes. "Listen to the girl, ace."

"All you care about is your own hide, isn't it, Shelton? Why did you even bother to help us today? You had to know a tracker meant someone was hunting for my dad." My mouth dropped as the truth hit me. I slapped my forehead. It took all my willpower not to body slam Shelton through the wooden bench. "You thought you'd collect the bounty. I'll bet you figured whoever wanted him would follow us here and you'd have my dad all locked up in a circle by then."

Shelton bolted up from the bench. "Now you're just plain wrong, boy."

"Oh, are you back to calling me 'boy' or 'kid' again? Can't face the fact I see through your games?" I paced away from him, fists clenched and teeth aching from the tightness in my jaw. I faced him. "What was your angle when you supposedly helped me rescue my dad from the rogue vampires? Were you hoping to bag him?"

"If I'd wanted to do that, I could've done it any time. You were exhausted. Your dad and lady Sherlock there were passed out." He stepped toward me. "I could have slipped a pair of sleepers on you. Dumped the both of you on the Conclave's doorstep, collected a hundred grand in bounty for you and your dad, and been outta there."

"But Stacey would have found out and gone after you," I said, my mind clutching wildly for some reason he wouldn't have done exactly as he said. Elyssa might never have recovered if I hadn't given her some of my blood that night, so she wouldn't have been able to go after Shelton if he'd betrayed us.

"The felycan?" He snorted. "You gotta be kidding me. The day I'm afraid of a felycan is the day I go back to wearing diapers."

Dad's voice cut through my thoughts. "Justin, I don't think he has anything to do with this."

"But it makes sense!"

Dad shook his head. "No. He's right. He could've taken us anytime he wanted after you saved me. And if he can't or won't tell us who put out the bounty, there's nothing we can do about it."

I turned back to Shelton. "Can you at least remove the mark?"

He belted out a laugh brimming with disbelief. "You go from blaming me for all your problems to asking for my help again?"

"Well, can you?" I asked.

He ran a hand down his face, grumbling under his breath. "I don't know. A tracker is one thing. A death mark, especially one from the Devoted, is another matter altogether."

"It might be rigged," Elyssa said.

My chest tightened. "It'll kill him if we try to remove it?"

"It might."

"Why bother with the mark? Why not just kill him when they had the chance? If they can mark him, surely they could have just finished the job." I shuddered at the logic. They could have taken my dad at any time. But they hadn't.

"The marks are usually a warning of what's to come," Shelton said. "They give the marked time to put his affairs in order and say goodbye to loved ones. They're also used to strike fear of the Brotherhood into the community and remind everyone they are very real and not to be forgotten."

"So right now there's a timer counting down my dad's life?"

Shelton nodded. "Yeah, that's about the short of it."

My legs felt like jelly. I sank onto a bench, gripping my head with both hands and staring at the ground. How could this be happening to us? The backs of my eyes burned as though they were trying to release tears. But I had no more tears to give. That had been the soft old version of me. Now I had strength and power. I could stop this Underborn guy if only I knew where to find him. But what about my mom and sister? I'd planned to go after them next and rescue them from the Conroys, the maternal grandparents I'd never met. Obviously, I'd have to put those plans on hold and deal with this first. It wouldn't do me much good to reunite my family if Dad died.

"How long do we have?" I asked.

Shelton stared at the tattoo again. "A couple of weeks. Maybe three. The tattoo usually indicates the time unless the client instructs the assassin otherwise. Then the timer might be false just to play tricks with the target's mind before the end."

Something occurred to me. I looked at Dad. "Mom called me and told me to leave just before you got home and told me about the tracker. Do you think the Conroys know about it? Is that why Mom called?"

Dad shook his head. "Anything is possible with them. One of my contacts told me they were keeping an eye out for me."

"Wait just a minute." In my head, I played back the minutes after

Mom's phone call and glared at Dad. "You came from outside the house. You were out looking for Mom again weren't you?"

"Now, son—"

"Don't you 'now, son' me, Dad. I'll bet someone tagged you while you were out." I thought back to when I'd pulled Dad's weak form from the crypt where the rogue vampires had kept him. I had strapped him onto a moggy's back, facedown. His neck would've been visible and I would have noticed such a strange tattoo. "When did you leave home?"

Dad looked away from me. "Right after you went into your bedroom." He looked up, met my eyes. "I can't stop looking, Justin. I'll never stop. Assassins can go to hell for all I care. I'm going to find Alice and Ivy and bring them back. Your mother and sister need me."

"Bring them back to what? Your family knows where we live now. You might be dead in a few days. Whatever you're doing to find them isn't working."

A siren wailed in the distance. I looked up and saw uniformed officers questioning people near the skating rink. One of the people pointed in our general direction. They looked at us and I knew we were running out of time.

CHAPTER 5

I looked back at Dad. "You can't go chasing after Mom anymore. You're a marked man. Your family, the Slades, can find you, and god only knows who or what else is looking for you now." I turned back to Shelton. "Can you cut off the signal?"

"Maybe." He sighed. "I'll need some time, though."

I motioned my head at the cops as they stopped to talk to someone else. "We don't have much time. We need to do something and we need to do it now."

Shelton looked at the cops and chuckled. "You don't do anything without raising a ruckus, do you?"

"If people would just leave us alone—"

"Believe me, I know the feeling." He gave me a meaningful look before pulling out his smartphone again and looked for something. I sidled up to him and watched as he scrolled through a list of files before opening one called *Disruptor 5.0*. Computer code of some sort filled the screen. It looked vaguely familiar although a lot of the symbols on the screen didn't exist on any keyboard I knew of. "I hate to use this," he said. "But it's all I got on short notice."

"What's going to happen?" I asked.

"Just don't try to use your cell phone until I tell you otherwise."

"Should I power it off?"

"Nah. Just don't make any calls." He stepped up to the circle where Dad stood. "Once I break the circle, the tracking spell on the death mark will be able to transmit again. I'm gonna need you to stay real still while I arm this disruption spell."

Dad nodded, turned, and dropped to one knee to give Shelton a better angle on his neck. "Ready when you are."

I stayed at Shelton's side, curious to see what was going to happen. He gave me pained look. "You gonna stay glued to my side or something?"

"I want to see what you're doing."

"Fine. Then you rub out the circle so I can run the spell."

I nodded and stepped up to the chalk outline. "Ready?"

He nodded.

"Go." I wiped part of the circle out with my shoe. A rush of magical energy whispered past my ears like static as it was freed from the circle. Some of it seemed to soak into my skin, leaving goose bumps and standing hairs on end.

Shelton aimed his phone's infrared port at the tattoo and pressed the *Execute* symbol on the screen of the phone as he concentrated his full gaze on the offending ink. The phone beeped and flashed *Processed* in big red letters. A man sauntered past, chatting away on his phone while he walked his dog. Shelton's phone flashed, *Complete*. The man with the dog yelled in surprise as a burst of static roared from his cell phone. More cries of alarm sprang up all over the park as radios and phones burst into high-pitched wails and static. The man's phone smoked where the speaker was before the screen on the phone cracked and died.

"What in the hell did you do?" I asked.

"Told you I hated to use this spell. It's for emergencies only, but this qualifies, wouldn't you say? The spell distorts and overpowers all wavelengths for a period of time."

"But why would a cell phone signal have anything to do with a magical one?"

"I don't know what frequency the tracker is operating on. It could be

35

using anything." He motioned for us to follow. "We gotta get out of here fast, though. The spell uses a lot of power and won't last long."

I glanced back at the cops frantically dancing about as they tore smoking and sparking radios off their belts and threw them to the ground. "Where are we going?"

"I know just the place," Shelton said.

Katie stared dumbfounded as people all over the park tossed their screeching, hissing smartphones on the ground, running from them like they were live grenades. A Pomeranian dog yapped at his master's phone until it made a loud popping noise, then yelped and ran in circles until his leash wrapped so tightly around his owner's legs, the guy toppled over. I tapped Katie on the shoulder to get her attention.

"We're moving out."

She nodded and followed behind me wordlessly.

Elyssa fell into stride next to me. "I know this is a bad time, but, well, I'm starving."

"Blood?"

She nodded.

"I need some sustenance myself." My legs were still weak and trembling from our long run. The demonic source supplying my supernatural abilities howled for relief. My throat felt parched and my stomach growled over and over again. I'd been too hyped with worry to think about it until now.

I glanced at Elyssa. "How will you, uh…you know?"

"My parents have packs. I know of a few other places I can get them, but…" She trailed off.

"But what?"

"I don't want to leave you. You'll probably get killed without my help."

I laughed. "You're such an optimist." I looked at Shelton's back as he led us out of the park and into an alleyway across the street. "Can we trust him?"

"You want my professional opinion?"

"You're obviously a better judge of character than I am."

A smile lit her face. "I think we can trust him to an extent. But

Shelton looks out for Shelton. Don't expect him to deliver more than he can."

"Then why is he helping us?"

"I have a feeling we'll find out."

My stomach clenched at the thought.

After a twenty-minute walk through a warren of narrow service roads, alleyways, and pot-holed streets in a bad part of the city, Shelton stopped in a narrow alley and examined an iron door set into the side of an old red-brick building. It might have been a storehouse at some point. A dozen or more identical doors lined this alley and the next one over, but I didn't see what made this one different. The front of the building faced a cracked and rutted one-way street across from a graffiti-covered convenience store with more bars on the windows than the state penitentiary. A bum in a cardboard hut groaned and rolled onto the filthy alley floor. An empty alcohol bottle rolled from his fingers and into the gutter. In front of the convenience store I saw a group of men laugh raucously, drinking from containers covered with brown paper bags. I almost wished I could hear them swap stories—probably about killing people in prison.

"Nice neighborhood," I said.

He smirked. "Quaint, ain't it?"

The inside didn't look much better. Dust covered a bare concrete floor. A filthy mattress with stains I didn't care to identify occupied a corner of the room. "You're keeping Dad here?" I asked, horrified at the prospect of anyone sleeping on that mattress.

"First-class all the way," Shelton said waving his arms grandly around the room. He pulled out a familiar ebony stick—his wand—mumbled something, and pointed at the floor. A section of the floor dropped down, the concrete turning to stairs as it did.

"That's so cool," Katie said, eyes wide with wonder.

"Not bad, eh, green eyes?"

"Does this mean Harry Potter really exists?" she asked.

"You're looking at him," I said, nodding toward Shelton. "He wears contacts now."

"Ha, ha, real funny," Shelton said as he went down the stairs.

"Why are you so mean to him, Justin?" Katie asked as we filed down the stairs.

I grunted. "He deserves it."

"You seem really ungrateful for all he's doing."

"You don't know Shelton."

"And you do?"

I tossed a glance over my shoulder at her. "Better than you."

"You can be really obtuse." She rolled her eyes.

"Did you miss the entire conversation I had with him in the park?"

Her brow furrowed. "You mean the one where you accused him of being the bad guy and then suddenly changed your mind?"

"Oh, whatever."

Katie's eyes narrowed. "If Shelton is a magician and Elyssa is a vampire—"

"Dhampyr, actually," Elyssa said. "I'm half human and half vampire."

"That sounds totally made up."

"Google it." Elyssa bared her fangs with a cold smile.

"I'll take your word for it, thank you very much." Katie turned her eyes back to me. "What I really want to know is, what are you, Justin?"

"Oh, she's gonna love this," Elyssa said, an amused glint in her eyes.

I looked away from Katie, remembering all the hell I'd gone through for this girl. How much I'd thought I'd loved her. But anything I felt for her was a lit match in a tornado compared to the blaze of love I felt for Elyssa. So telling her what I was even if it made her fear and hate me shouldn't matter. Except being half demon spawn and half human was something I'd sooner nobody knew. Being a vampire sounded a lot sexier, especially considering how many teeny-boppers loved what they saw on TV and in the movies. Demon spawn, on the other hand, had a pretty bad reputation.

Katie tugged my sleeve. "Are you going to tell me?"

Elyssa's concerned eyes met mine and narrowed as if she were trying to figure out what was bothering me. I tried to smile but it faltered.

We stepped out of the narrow confines of a gray concrete tunnel and into what looked like a perfectly normal two-bedroom apartment with a big-screen TV, a kitchen, and all the amenities. Our surprise at coming upon this place saved me from having to respond to Katie's question.

"Back here," Shelton said, leading Dad into a fair-sized room with a bed in the middle of a metallic-looking circle set in the floor.

"I don't like the look of that," I said, unslinging my duffel bag and dropping it on the floor. "Why would you put a bed in the center of a circle?"

Dad stepped inside it anyway and took a seat on the bed. Shelton pressed his thumb to the circle, made a little wiggling movement with it, and the air snapped and crackled.

Shelton stood up, looking tired all of a sudden. "He should be safe for now."

"You plan to keep him cooped up in there?"

"This is a one-way circle," he said, sinking into a wooden chair and pinching the bridge of his nose. "Nothing gets in."

"He's trapped?" I tested the air above the circle and met a hard unyielding shield of shimmering air wherever my hands touched.

"He can get out, but nothing can get in except me."

"It's that easy to throw up one of these things?"

Shelton shook his head. "I had this one primed in case I ever needed it."

"Nice hideaway you've got," Elyssa said. "But what if he needs to use the bathroom?"

"Or feed?" I added.

"The entire apartment is warded with spells that should keep the tracker from sending anything out," Shelton said. "But for now, I want him completely locked down until I have time to check all the wards and make sure it can't leak. Then he can sleep in the bathroom for all I care."

"He'll need to feed soon."

"I'll make him a bowl of cereal," Katie said, pointing to a box of Cheerios sitting on the counter.

Elyssa smirked. "Not that kind of feeding."

A shudder ran through Katie's shoulders. "Oh, gross. I get it."

No, she really didn't, I thought. But maybe that was a good thing.

Shelton went over to the computer desk and moved the mouse until the screen lit up. He double-clicked a program and scrolled through what appeared to be more spell files. "I've got some spells a lot more discreet than the disruptor I used. Once I fine-tune them a bit, he'll have a limited amount of time to get out and do his business."

I stood over his shoulder, watching with fascination at the sheer number of files he had. "Are these what pass for magic scrolls nowadays?"

He smiled and waved a hand at a large wooden chest sitting in the corner of the room. "I have a whole collection of them."

"Scrolls?"

He nodded. "Good for backup in case of emergency."

"Do they look like computer code?"

He shook his head. "Nah, they're written in Cyrinthian, the base language."

"Base language?"

Shelton huffed. "Look, I know you're curious, but I'm trying to dig through a disorganized mess of scriptlets until I find the code that'll help your dad."

I backed off. "Sorry."

Elyssa sidled up next to me, taking my hand in hers and resting her head on my shoulder as we both stared at the code springing up on the screen. "And I thought computer class was confusing," she said.

"It looks so familiar." I tilted my head. "I took a course in programming, and never saw anything like this. Even so, I think I've seen this sort of thing before." And then it occurred to me where I'd seen it. I unzipped my duffel and withdrew the flash drive. "Shelton, can you take a look at this?"

"For crying out loud, man, do you want me to get anything done here or not?"

"This is really important."

He sighed long and loud as he slipped the flash drive into his computer. The files popped up on the screen after a few seconds.

"Copy them over to your computer," I said, not wanting to part with my only copy.

He did as I requested before opening the folder named *Copy of hash codes*. "What the heck?" he said, opening one of the files. Instead of code mixed with gibberish, it came back as better organized code with question marks scattered throughout.

"It's a spell, right?" I said.

"This must be your mom's work," he said, voice full of admiration and maybe a bit of jealousy. "I've never seen such graceful code for nested arcane loops and functions."

Whatever that meant. "So what does it do?"

"Hang on a minute." He ran his finger down the code, pausing at the question marks. After a few more minutes of silence, he finally answered. "This code is missing a lot of custom runes."

"Define, 'rune', Shelton. You know I'm not familiar with this stuff."

"A rune would be the programming equivalent of a variable. Each question mark is a place where ACC is missing the variable or rune definition." He glanced up at me. "ACC stands for Arcane Code Crafter, the program most in the arcane community use for making complicated spells."

"This is nothing like Harry Potter," Katie said. "In fact, it sucks. Who'd want to have to use a computer to make spells?"

Shelton chuckled. "Lemme tell you, sunshine." He held out his hand and a tiny ball of light materialized, hovering just above his hand. "This is easy." Another ball of light appeared and the two rotated slowly around each other. "Still easy," he said. More glowing globes appeared, multiplying and popping out of each other until a galaxy of them filled the space above our heads, some globes forming little solar systems of their own, others gliding serenely around the space, doing their own thing, while others grew larger, forming suns, planets, and other heavenly bodies.

Katie's eyes were wide with wonder. "It's beautiful."

I stared at the amazing sight, my own mouth dropping open a fraction.

"This is hard," Shelton said, strain evident on his face for a few seconds before the galaxy flickered and winked out.

"Can you do it again?" Katie said. "It was so pretty."

"Sure thing, cupcake." He pulled out his smartphone, looked for a moment, and then pressed the screen. Again, the globes popped into existence, multiplying and spreading, except this time they turned into a much larger galaxy complete with realistic colors, nebulae and an amazing array of minute detail.

Gasps escaped our lips as we looked upon the wonders of Shelton's little homemade universe. Then I spotted something very familiar and walked over to look at it. A war raged between tiny spaceships, bright lasers and balls of green and red light exploding before my eyes.

"Those are Klingon and Federation ships," I said. "You're a nerd, Shelton, but, holy crap, do I love this."

Shelton's grin almost split his face. "You should watch the whole thing, man, it's sweet." A frown creased his face. "Except we're getting a little diverted here." He touched his phone and the display vanished.

Katie blinked her eyes as though coming from a trance. "How did you do that?"

"A script I wrote," he said. "I can do some things more easily with my mind, but when it comes to complicated spells with a lot of conditions and variables and parallel actions, it's a lot better just to script it out instead of going old-school and spending a day or so chanting out the entire thing."

"You can do any spell just by programming it?" I asked.

"Not exactly. Some spells require blood or bits of DNA, depending on what you're doing. And rituals usually have to be done the long way."

"Is the death mark something you could do with a scripted spell?"

He shrugged. "Not sure. I'll have to study it and see if I can reverse engineer it." Shelton pointed at the code on the screen. "Without the variables for your mom's spells, I won't be able to figure them out. Not without a lot of time and effort."

"And you have no idea what they do?"

"Actually, I think I know what this one does." He traced the last line in the code where a line of unfamiliar words were on the screen. "This spell is designed for mass murder."

CHAPTER 6

J staggered back a step, feeling an almost physical blow in my chest. My mom wanted to kill people? I couldn't imagine it being even remotely possible. My mom would never kill anyone, would she?

"What are you talking about in there?" Dad asked from the other room.

"Looking for some spells to help you out," I said, not wanting him to know about this just yet. I didn't want to have this particular conversation in front of the others. I leaned down to look at the computer screen again. "Can you find out what the missing runes are?"

Shelton shook his head. "Reverse engineering runes is a skill in and of itself. I have a friend who could do it, given enough time. And he might also be able to help me with the death mark."

"Will he help?"

"Oh, he loves this kind of stuff." Shelton emailed the guy's name and address to me. "Just make sure you tell him TP sent you." His face reddened slightly.

"TP?"

"Don't ask. I would call him and tell him you're coming except he doesn't use email or a cell phone."

I glanced at the guy's name, Mr. Smith. *How original.* "How does he communicate with anyone?"

"By mouth. He's kind of a conspiracy nut, but don't let that scare you off."

I laughed. By my new standards, conspiracy nuts ranked pretty low on the scary scale. "You sure he's still at this address?"

"Oh, that's not his home address. That's where he goes to buy comic books. A place called Trader Mike's."

"Are you telling me to wait around a comic book store until he shows?"

"Yeah. Just look for a medium-sized guy, dark hair, pale skin, about my age." Shelton pulled up a webpage and ran his finger down a schedule. "The latest edition of *Clubfoot* comes out tomorrow, so he'll be there. Back in the day he used to show up first thing in the morning and wait until they opened shop so he could snag a copy."

"*Clubfoot* doesn't sound like a very interesting comic book superhero."

"The main character is more of an anti-hero, truth be told."

"As in, he's kind of a jackass?"

"More like he murders people for sport."

I grimaced. "I guess there's no accounting for taste."

"You got that right."

Shelton pulled my mom's files back up and looked at them. I scanned through the lines of code. A few symbols repeated regularly along with a bunch of if-then statements. "Tell me this, Shelton. Could anyone take your smartphone and execute a spell on it? Make it work?"

"I really should put you through some lessons. Maybe it'd stop you from asking stupid questions."

"For crying out loud. Can't you just answer my question?"

He sighed and swiveled the computer chair to face me. "Smartphones aren't magic. Wands and staffs aren't magic. They're just focal points for the magic to work through. When I execute a spell, I have to run magic through the focus with my will and intent to make it do anything. I built micro-generators for my foci that can amp up the magical juice. And before you ask, no, the micro-generators don't make normal power—they generate and compound magical energy using the Law of Thaumodynamics." He quirked an eyebrow, probably waiting for the inevitable follow-up question.

Except I realized all I would do was pester him with questions until he got pissed off and ignored me. "When can we start lessons?"

"Whenever you want." He closed Mom's spells and crossed his arms. "Start out by contacting Smith. We'll decode this mess and maybe you'll pick up a thing or two along the way."

"What about my dad?"

"The tattoo on his neck is a rune as well. I'll email a picture of it you can show Smith. If you believe in fairy tales, he might just know how to get rid of it."

"Why don't you come with us? Wouldn't it be easier if he sees you?"

"I need to make sure the wards here are stable and find a mobile blocking spell so your dad can leave the circle. I can't be everywhere at once."

Elyssa took my arm. "We should locate the comic book store and scope it out first." She leaned into my ear and whispered the next part. "And I need to feed. Now."

My tummy erupted with a loud groan of agreement. I looked at Katie. "You ready to go home? I'll pay for a cab."

She looked away from the computer screen, her green eyes curious and bright. "You aren't planning to erase my memories are you?"

I chuckled. "No. But Shelton might have to send you to the supernatural rehab program the Arcane Council runs."

"You kidding me?" Shelton said with a snort. "This girl's taking it like a champ. Poor Linda is gonna be scarred for life."

Linda was the woman who'd had the misfortune to be kidnapped as a source of food for Dad when he'd been taken by the vampires. "I can't blame her."

"That's horrible," Katie said. "Does your program teach people about supernatural things?"

A wry smile worked its way onto Shelton's face. "More or less. Heck, maybe you should take it. Justin could probably benefit from it, too, seeing how he don't know squat about the Overworld."

"Fine," I said. "Give me the time and location and I'll take her for orientation."

"That's the spirit." He laughed with genuine delight and I wondered just what I was getting myself into.

"I guess I should get home," Katie said. "My parents are probably wondering why I'm not home yet. And we have school tomorrow."

I groaned. "I don't see a reason why I should bother going back."

"Because people will wonder," Elyssa said. "Questions will be asked." Her eyes grew very serious. "And you have unfinished business with certain elements."

"You mean Coach Burgundy and his promise to hurt my friends if I don't keep playing football." What had started out as punishment for me had morphed into a nightmare thanks to Burgundy and his good old boys club members: the sheriff and the chief of police. Thanks to my supernatural abilities—which they didn't know about—I had an unfair advantage on the field. I'd already helped my hopelessly bad team win one game. The coach and his buddies were counting on me to increase the winning streak and put more money in their pockets.

"That would be it," Elyssa said, her mouth set in a grim line.

"They made you play football by threatening you?" Katie said, eyes worried. "You should tell the police."

I blew out a sigh. "If only it were so easy." Especially since the local law had a hand in the pot. I looked at Dad's room. "I'm gonna tell him what's up and then we should go."

Elyssa touched me with a trembling hand. "Let's make it soon." Her face was sickly pale from hunger. I wasn't feeling that great myself.

I said goodbye to Dad, told him Shelton would fill him in on the plan, but we needed to feed.

Dad nodded. "Be careful, son. Soon as Shelton fixes this issue, I'm going to find the bastard responsible."

I wanted to tell him to sit tight because all his activities so far had only caused more problems. Either messing with the Conroys was really dangerous business or he had more enemies out there than he knew.

Shelton did his magic to make the stairs leading out of the place appear again and told me to email or call him if I needed to get back in. Then Elyssa, Katie, and I made our way out through the abandoned buildings and into the dark streets. We had to walk several blocks, past trudging bums, a few likely drug dealers, and a lot of empty, boarded up houses before finding a cab. We all hopped in and had the driver take us to downtown Decatur where Elyssa and I disembarked.

After I handed the cabby enough money to cover Katie's fare home, she got out and gave me a tight hug. "I'll see you at school tomorrow?"

I gave her a resigned look. "I guess so."

She smiled at Elyssa. "Thanks so much."

Confusion spread over Elyssa's face. "For what?"

"For the most interesting day of my entire life."

Elyssa stared at the cab as it vanished into the distance. "That girl is messed in the head if she thinks today was interesting."

I hugged her tight against me and kissed her cheek. "You have to admit she took it all really well."

"Yeah. I guess." Her body quaked for several seconds before growing still.

"Are you okay?"

She shook her head. "I'm at the verge of losing control. I can't hold on much longer." She gazed at me with eyes the black of night as her pupils dilated, erasing the violet irises.

I jerked back, surprised by the sudden change. I did *not* want to find out what happened when she lost control. "Where can we get you blood?"

"There are places throughout the city the Templars have set up, but I haven't seen my parents since we rescued your Dad yesterday. I need to go home before they send out search parties."

"Where do you live?"

Another tremor shook her body. "You can't come, Justin."

"I'm coming."

"No the hell you aren't. Are you crazy?" Her legs gave out and I barely managed to keep her upright.

"Tell me where, Elyssa. We need to get you blood now. You might not make it on your own."

47

She gave me an address a mile from my house. In fact, I knew exactly where it was because I'd passed the place dozens of times, never once knowing she lived there. I flagged a taxi and barked out the directions, giving him a hundred dollars to get us there fast. I think the guy must've been a rickshaw racer in his native country because he drove like a champ and dropped us off at the gates of the Big Creek Ranch, a horse ranch that somehow managed to survive the urban explosion on the edges of Decatur.

The wide metal gate was closed and locked, but the whitewashed ranch-rail fence wasn't much of a barrier so we climbed over it and trudged down the long asphalt driveway. Thick woods separated the edge of the ranch from the highway on our right. To the left stretched open pastures. The occasional whicker of a horse reached my ears. Antique-styled lamps lined the way, providing dim yellow light. We hadn't gone more than a few feet when I sensed someone approaching.

"Please don't say anything, Justin," Elyssa said, her muscles tense, her face even paler than before.

Up until that point I'd felt pretty confident. Right about then my nerves decided to use my stomach as a punching bag. Also, I was famished. It was foolish coming to this place without a full demon belly or whatever stored the psychic essence I stole from people. I considered turning tail and running, but ego and the desire to keep whatever shreds of manliness I had in Elyssa's eyes powered my legs onward, toward whatever was about to meet us.

A guy who looked to be Shelton's age appeared from the shadows in the woods, his black outfit similar to what Elyssa had worn during our little jaunt against the vampires, perfect camouflage. He held a katana at the ready in one hand. Once his eyes settled on Elyssa, the sword vanished with a *snick* as he slid it expertly back into its sheath. He wore his thick dark hair slicked back. Long mutton-chop sideburns ran down his face, making him look older than he really was, not to mention a lot more redneck.

"Where have you been?" he asked, running to Elyssa and putting his hands on her shoulders. His voice was low and rough, with a southern drawl.

She gave him a weary smile. "I'm fine, Ryland. I need some food. That's all."

Ryland gave me a wary look, eyes narrow and full of suspicion. 'Who's this?" He sniffed the air as if testing my deodorant, which had probably failed by this point.

The guy looked so familiar to me that I opened my mouth to blurt my name in automatic response.

"He's a friend," she said, cutting me off before I made such a stupid mistake. "Please, just get me a pack. I'm on the verge."

His eyes widened as he took in her eyes. "Good lord, sugah. How in the world did you hold off the hunger?" He shook his head. "I'll be right back." With that, he blurred away into the darkness, heading for a tall manor-style house on the slight rise at the end of the driveway.

Elyssa stumbled and almost fell before I caught her in my aching arms. The day's activities were catching up to me, although I wasn't nearly in as bad a state as Elyssa. She'd already been peaked after nearly dying during my Dad's rescue the night before. I should have sent her home the first chance we'd had. What was I thinking, letting her run around like she was in full health?

But she hadn't complained a bit. Hadn't once tried to leave me. Wouldn't even let me send her away. My heart swelled with love for my raven-haired goddess. I couldn't imagine life without her. I looked toward the house and a sense of dread whittled away at me. First, I had to win over her family. Considering how much Elyssa had despised me when she'd first found out I was an incubus, I couldn't imagine how much harder it would be to get her parents to like me, or at the very least accept the fact I loved their daughter.

Elyssa's love for me had won out over her hatred for incubi. But if she'd never had the chance to befriend me before discovering I wasn't entirely human, she might never have loved me or given me a chance to even be near her. This was the challenge her parents posed. They didn't know squat about me, well, except her mom had cut my hair before knowing I was demon spawn.

Awkward!

Ryland sped from the pitch of night, several hospital blood packs in his hands. Elyssa took one, her eyes groggy and unfocused. He pulled the top off and tilted it into her mouth as she sucked greedily. I forced back my gag reflex but kept my eyes glued on her. Drinking blood was so gross, but it was part of her life and I had to get used to it.

"You're a friend, yeah?" Ryland said giving me a once over as Elyssa polished off a second blood pack. "What's your name?" He sniffed again. "And *what* are you? I'd think twice before lying."

I returned his little once-over, taking him in. I could sense something in him that was different than what I sensed with Elyssa or normal vampires. He felt a lot more like Stacey than anything else. Underneath his human shell lurked something not quite human. And I couldn't shake the feeling I'd seen this guy somewhere before.

"Well?" he said again, his rough voice laced with impatience. "I can smell the fear on you."

I suddenly knew exactly who he reminded me of. The mutton-chop sideburns should've been a dead giveaway. "Are you trying to look like Wolverine?"

An embarrassed look crossed his face before his serious demeanor recovered. "What's it to you?"

"Either you're a werewolf or a really big X-Men fan."

He grinned, baring his teeth and exposing canines that were definitely a bit longer than normal humans. At this point, I figured anyone with disproportionate canines had to be supernatural, although mine were normal and boring.

"You're an observant one, stranger." He stepped toward me until his face was inches from mine. "Now, how about you tell me who and what you are before I give you a taste of what I am and what I can do."

Elyssa's arms pressed between us, shoving us apart. I noticed with relief her skin had regained its usual fair hue and her eyes blazed vividly in the dim light from the lamps along the driveway. "Ryland, he's with me, so take your questions and shove 'em."

Ryland laughed, low and harsh. "No need to get mean about it."

"Actually, she's being really sweet right now," I said. "I've seen her mean side and it isn't pretty."

He bared his teeth in a full-on wolf smile. "If you're still alive after that, she must have plans for you."

Oh yeah. She had plans for me all right.

Elyssa rolled her eyes. "Leave us for a minute, Ryland?"

"Sure." He wandered off, though I was sure he could hear anything we said.

"You should go now, Justin. I'm fine and you need to eat."

I stared at the house, my instincts screaming at me to get the hell outta Dodge while my heart told me although the timing wasn't exactly ideal, I should do the whole "meet the parents" thing and see just how bad it was. Elyssa seemed to sense what I was thinking.

"Don't even try," she said her lips pressed tight.

"I have to meet your parents," I said gently. "I love you. I'd do anything for you. Surely me and your parents can get over our differences."

"You don't know my dad."

"Exactly." I took her hand and looked her in the eyes. "I have so many family problems I don't know where to begin. But if I don't at least try to talk to your father, I won't respect myself, and he won't respect me either."

"You're taking a page out of a romance novel, Justin." She placed her other hand on my cheek and her fiery eyes grew soft. "I love you for that and for your big heart. You want things to work out like they do in the movies. I wish they did." Her eyes drifted to the house. "But they don't. My dad has grown to accept some things over the years but he has a special hatred for spawn."

"I'm so sick of people judging me based on what I am!" I growled and clenched my fists. "First you, and now your family. Why can't they judge me by my actions instead of other spawn I've never even met?"

"I don't know his reasons, Justin. I'm sorry it took me so long to get past everything he beat into my head over the years." She kissed me on the lips, and pulled away, her eyes pleading. "Let this wait for another day. Please. Let me talk with him first."

"And make it look like I'm using you to get him to like me?"

"It's not like that."

"Elyssa, just let me talk with him. Give me the chance to do that."

"This is a horrible idea."

"I don't know about that, daughter," said a commanding voice from out of the darkness. A figure stepped into the dim light, all six-and-a-half feet of it, muscles bulging beneath a dark long-sleeved T-shirt. The man looked about my dad's age, though his black hair was peppered with gray. "I think right now is a splendid time to settle this." He stared at me with fiery eyes and I knew exactly where Elyssa had gotten her stern looks.

CHAPTER 7

*J*choked on whatever words had been about to rise from my throat and looked at Mr., um, whatever Elyssa's dad's last name was. I found it hard to believe I didn't even know that tidbit of information. Her father's glare seemed to cut right through me, as though he was staring at my very center and judging me. From the scowl on his face, I could tell he'd already found me unworthy.

"Hi," I said, barely squeaking it out. Elyssa had told me the last time a guy tried to take her out on a date, he left before she could even get down the stairs. The reason, she'd told me, was because her dad had just looked at the guy. Now I knew how the poor schmuck had felt. *Buck up you idiot! You're certainly not impressing him now.*

I stiffened my spine and walked toward him, holding my hand out in greeting. He spared a glance at my hand before crossing his arms and returning his gaze back at my eyes. It took all my might not to look away.

"Sir, I'd like to talk to you about your daughter."

He said nothing.

"Dad," Elyssa said.

He held up a hand to silence her. She gritted her teeth but didn't say anything else.

I waited for his response, but he didn't seem in a hurry to give me one. I sensed another presence join us and looked over, expecting Ryland to return. Instead, I saw Leia, Elyssa's mom.

"There you are," she said, hugging Elyssa while shooting a glare at me over her daughter's shoulder. "I see you've brought company."

"Unwelcome company," Elyssa's father said.

Anger sparked in my chest but I beat it back and took a deep breath. "Hello, Leia," I said. "It's nice to see you again."

She narrowed her eyes. "I can't say the same, I'm afraid."

"Why is that?"

"Oh, I don't know…perhaps because you've somehow, despite all her training, tricked our daughter into caring for you."

Elyssa pulled away from Leia. "He didn't trick—"

"You will be silent," her father said in a low steady voice. He looked at Leia. "I thought this issue was solved."

"Elyssa assured me she was done with him."

"And here I'd thought our daughter was past this foolishness," he said, returning his gaze to me. "It appears we need to solve it once again."

"Maybe we could sit down somewhere and discuss things like rational human beings. I'm sure I could put all your fears to rest," I said, my voice trembling slightly from a battle between anger and taut nerves.

"Your lack of humanity makes that impossible," Elyssa's dad said.

"Thomas, why don't I leave you two to finish this untidy business?" Leia said, gripping Elyssa by the arm and directing her toward the house.

So her dad's name was Thomas. I'd been expecting something like Hardass McGee or Terminator T1000, considering his attitude.

"I'm not going anywhere," Elyssa said, jerking free and coming to stand by me. "Justin did not trick me into loving him. I knew him before he changed and I know him now. He's trying to be honorable, but all you're doing is throwing insults in his face."

"I will not be spoken to that way, young lady," Thomas said.

"Well you don't deserve any better for talking to Justin like this."

Leia crossed her arms. "You do not speak to your father like that. Go inside right this instant while we take care of *it*." Her lip rose into a snarl as she regarded me.

"So, now you're calling me an 'it'?" I said, incredulous. "What's wrong with you people? Are you stuck back in the fifties or something?"

"We know your kind," Thomas said, grinding out his words in a low threatening voice. "I have found some redeeming qualities in most of the major races. But yours lacks anything that could change my mind. You will never have anything to do with my daughter again."

"Dad!" Elyssa shouted. "Just listen to him!"

"No. I've heard enough of its lies." He slammed the bottom of his fist against the other palm. "Didn't I teach you how spawn operate? How they gain your trust before betraying you?" He glared at me. "Oh, they might look and act human. But they're demon spawn, girl. Hellborn and tainted by evil."

"I'd like to think I'm a nice guy," I said. "Obviously a spawn did something really mean to you when you were a kid." I shrugged. "Maybe stole your lunch money or made fun of you. I don't know. I don't care. I love your daughter. That's the simple truth. I would never do anything to harm her and I would do anything for her. Put me through a Templar lying test if you don't believe me."

"I'm through with this farce," Thomas said. "Elyssa, get inside this instant. You," he said, pointing at me, "get off our property before I have you hauled off."

Elyssa put herself in front of me, hands splayed protectively. "Don't you dare, Father." Tears trickled down her cheeks. "You keep your hands off him."

"Or what, *daughter*? Will you attack your own father to protect this filth?"

"Think sense, child," Leia said. "Haven't we taught you better?" She wiped a tear away, her face shifting from anger to grief-stricken. "He's spawn! Where did we go wrong in explaining what they are?"

"It's not a trick," Elyssa said, shaking her head. "It's not!"

Her mom's face softened as she looked at her. "Sweetheart, that's what they do. That's how they infiltrate your very soul and steal it from you."

Elyssa shook her head as tears dripped from her cheeks. "No, Mom. I *know* him. I love him."

My heart ached so much for her right then I couldn't stand it. But I didn't know what to do. I loved her and this situation was tearing her apart. What if my dad had told me the same thing about dhampyrs? What if he'd hated Elyssa? The thought sent a shard of ice stabbing into my chest.

"Please, stop," I said, standing in front of Elyssa. I turned to face her. "You were right. This was a horrible idea." The backs of my eyes felt as though they were floating in hot salty pools, but I didn't dare cry in front of these people. "I can't get through to them," I said in a low voice as I shook my head sadly. "I love you and can't stand seeing you so conflicted."

She pressed her hands to my cheeks, sniffing through her tear-reddened nose. "I told you, Justin. I tried to make you see. They thought I'd ended it. Now that they know I didn't, I'm afraid for us. For our future."

I gripped her hand tight. "We'll make it work. You're my Buttercup and I'm your Westley. I'll become the Dread Pirate Roberts if that's what it takes to win them over."

She smiled through the tears and kissed me. Her mother hissed in displeasure. Strong hands gripped my shirt and slung me away. I hit the ground hard and rolled in the grass before coming to a rest next to a fence. It seemed oddly reminiscent of the time Elyssa had tossed me across a gravel parking lot when she'd figured out what I was.

I rose unsteadily and held up my hands in surrender in the harsh glare of her father. "I'm leaving. Thanks ever so much for the grand hospitality."

Elyssa looked at me, tears sparkling from the violet light in her eyes. "I love you."

"I love you," I said, and then turned and walked back down the long asphalt drive, my hands trembling with anger, my heart thudding in agony. I wanted to punch her father in the face. "Well, that could have gone so much better," I grumbled as I reached the perimeter fence and climbed over it. My legs faltered with fatigue and hunger. I had to feed. Now.

A presence closed in on me. I turned, praying to god I wasn't about to have to fight my way free. Thomas would make mincemeat out of me. Instead, Ryland appeared, a smirk on his face.

"The demon boy who could love," he said in a mocking voice.

"I'd toss you a Milk-Bone but I'm all out," I said, turning away from him.

He blurred in front of me, his face so close I could smell the coffee on his breath. "Funny thing is I know you're telling the truth."

I threw my hands in the air. "Great. The wolf-man believes me. All my problems are solved."

"It took me a long while to gain the trust of Thomas Borathen. Believe you me, it was not a fun process."

"Does he hate lycans too?"

"Nah, I wouldn't say he hates so much as he doesn't trust anyone until they've proven themselves." He shrugged and the corner of his mouth lifted in a half-smile. "Except for spawn. He definitely hates your kind."

"What happened? Obviously one of my dear relatives did something horrible to him."

"I only heard rumors about what really happened. About Thunder Rock. "

"Thunder Rock? That sounds like the name of a really bad boy band. Did a group of teenage demon spawn make his ears bleed with love ballads?"

He chuckled. "Nah, Thunder Rock is a place. Unfortunately, there ain't anyone who will talk about it."

"Why? Because Thomas Borathen would beat the snot out of them?"

Ryland shook his head. "No. Because they're dead."

I sighed long and deep. I needed a good sigh right about then. "And yet again, someone hates me for something I have no control over."

"I hate to say it, but I feel for you." Then he howled with laughter.

I slapped my forehead. I was hopeless as ever. Trying to take charge of my life seemed to backfire on me no matter what I did. "Whatever," I said, and walked toward the road, hoping I could find a nice crowded restaurant where I could sit down and recharge.

Ryland followed.

I spun on him. "Don't you have guard duty or a nice big bowl of Kibbles-n-Bits to go munch on?"

He bared his teeth. "Don't mock me, spawn."

"Are you just making sure I clear the premises?"

"I'm here to escort you home, wherever that may be."

"Argh!" I threw my hands up in the air again and tossed in an eye-roll just to be sure the universe understood I was frustrated as hell. "Fine. Tag along if you want, but I have a couple of pit stops to make."

The first place I went was a Waffle House. I looked like crap with my torn shirt and grass-stained jeans but I figured their clientele wouldn't much care. After polishing off breakfast for dinner while feeding off the emotions of an animated couple who were discussing their plans to win the lottery, I felt much better—or at least as well as I could considering mine and Elyssa's doomed love. *I really need to lay off the melodrama.*

"Do you think Thomas will keep her from going to school?" I asked Ryland as he tore into a very rare, very bloody steak.

He finished chewing, wiped his mouth, and shrugged. "He's an unpredictable man. Then again, he's been around since this nation was born, so I imagine he knows the value of never broadcasting his intent until it's too late."

"We're talking high school here, not war."

"Ah, to Thomas Borathen, everything is tactics and war. And you might be a war he wasn't prepared to fight."

I groaned. "I'm only eighteen and now I have to worry about a lunatic warlord father coming after me?"

Ryland's fist slammed on the table, shaking the syrup and knocking over the sugar. The restaurant grew silent as everyone stopped what they were doing and stared. Ryland didn't seem to care. He leaned toward me. "Thomas Borathen is a great man. Do not dishonor him with such name-calling."

I held out my hands in surrender. "Calm down, man. Jeez, it's not like me calling him names is gonna hurt anyone."

Ryland shoved another piece of steak in his mouth, though his eyes remained suspicious. I drank some water and stared out the window, trying to decide what my next move should be. I didn't want Ryland following me back to Shelton's place. I might be able to outrun him, but seeing as how he was the first werewolf I'd met, I had no idea if he could sniff out my trail even if I outdistanced him.

"Why do you think I'm telling the truth about my feelings for Elyssa?"

Ryland grinned. "I smell the truth, friend."

"Are you sure it's not just my deodorant?"

He finished his steak and sat back in his seat. "My old pack leader told me I had the best nose of anyone."

I sat up straight. "You were in a wolf pack?"

He nodded. "For a time."

"What happened?"

"What do you think happened?" he said, as though the answer should be obvious.

I guessed almost immediately. "A woman."

"Isn't it always?" he said, laughing softly. "She was the one our Alpha wanted, but she liked me." He sighed and jabbed a thumb at his chest. "Wolf politics and human sensibilities do not make a good mix."

"Wolves have to beat the crap out of each other for that, right?"

"I'm afraid so."

"Did you like the girl too?"

He shrugged. "She was very attractive and her scent...it was delicious." His eyes grew troubled. "But I didn't think she was worth the cost to our pack. Unfortunately she chose to push the issue when I rejected her and left me and my Alpha no choice but to decide matters."

"So the Alpha kicked your butt and you left?"

He winced and looked down at the bare bone where his steak had been. "He was my best friend."

I felt for the guy. My supposedly best friends had turned on me. "That sucks, man. I'm sorry."

"I almost killed him," Ryland said, staring at the plate. "I could always beat him, but I never wanted to lead the pack. I left him bloody and near death after our fight. The others demanded I take over as Alpha." A haunted look crossed his face. "But I couldn't do it. I had to get out of there."

"I didn't realize werewolves could die so easily."

His face hardened. "Easy? You've never seen werewolves fight. We aren't weaklings."

"Stop getting ticked at me. I hardly know squat as it is so I'm bound to jump to conclusions."

"Your family never taught you about the Overworld?"

"Dude, I just found out I'm a spawn maybe two weeks ago. My dad told me a little bit but otherwise I'm a total newbie."

"How interesting."

"Yeah. That's one way to put it." I dropped some cash on the table to pay for my food. I wasn't about to pick up Ryland's tab, considering he'd gone through two rare steaks and an order of bacon. That guy could shovel it down like nobody's business.

He paid and we left. I really wanted to go back to Shelton's hideout, but I needed to ditch wolf-man first. I hated to do it, but the best course of action seemed to be figuring out how to lose him. He had an amazing nose, apparently, which meant I'd have to cover myself in rabbit feces or something to make him lose the trail. Or, I could take him someplace he might not want to be anyway.

"Are you a big Wolverine fan?" I asked him as we hiked down a dark road.

He stroked one of his mutton chops. "Yep."

"He's pretty cool." I found a road sign and got my bearings. "You ready to do some running?"

Ryland showed his teeth and stretched his arms. "I thought you'd never ask."

It was dark and nobody was in sight. I zipped away, looking behind me to see how far he was lagging behind. I heard a chuckle and looked to my left. He was pacing me without breaking a sweat. I could've gone faster but I didn't want to waste the energy. After winding our way down some back streets, we flashed down a ragged asphalt road and to an abandoned property with warehouses. I stopped and stared at the place the warehouses should have been. At the place where Stacey lived.

All I found was rubble, flame, and smoke.

CHAPTER 8

*R*yland stared at the destruction and wrinkled his nose. "Sulfur."

I tested the air and caught a faint whiff as well. "What does that mean?"

"Surely you've heard of brimstone."

"Like the stuff from Hell?"

He nodded. "This sulfur odor is not natural."

I couldn't tell the difference. It all smelled like rotten eggs to me. I saw a small form on the ground and ran to it. A pile of concrete had crushed a calico cat. A quick glance around revealed more tiny bodies strewn about. "Oh no." I looked around frantically for the body of a woman or a large cat, my heart aching at the thought of Stacey being hurt or killed. "Stacey?" I called. "Stacey!"

No answer.

Flames flickered in the ruins of several buildings, casting an eerie glow across the shadowy mounds. My blue-tinged night vision kicked on and off as I stared at them.

"You know someone who lives here?" Ryland said.

"Yeah. A friend."

"All I smell is sulfur and felines."

"Dead felines?"

He drew in a whiff. "It's too soon to tell. This happened very recently."

"What's the deal with brimstone and sulfur? You know who did it?"

He raised an eyebrow. "You really don't know anything, do you?"

"Obviously."

"Sulfur usually means demons. Since demons can't just waltz into this realm without a lot of fuss and bother, that would mean manifested demon spawn or their ilk were here." His silvery eyes glinted as orange flames licked and consumed a large wooden beam.

Ryland knelt and examined a shoe print. "I'll survey the perimeter."

"Thanks." After he left, I stared at the rubble and took deep breaths. I hadn't known Stacey long, but I considered her a friend, even if we had met because she was trying to feed off me. Worry settled a hard knot into my stomach and I couldn't just sit around and do nothing. So I grabbed a large chunk of mortar and tossed it onto a patch of bare ground twenty feet away. I grabbed more bricks and tossed them in the same spot. Soon I'd cleared a little of the area where one of the ware-houses had stood, but it'd take a while before I put much of a dent in it.

On the other side of me lay the bodies of several cats I'd pulled from the wreckage, all of them crushed when they'd been caught in the avalanche of bricks, wood, and metal. Some of their remains consisted of little more than bloody, furry goo, but I knew Stacey would mourn them all and want bodies to bury. Ryland rejoined me a moment later.

"Hellhounds," he said grimly. "At least three of them."

"Those sons of bitches," I said crushing a brick in my hand to dust.

"These things ain't got mothers," Ryland replied with a tight grin.

"They were chasing us earlier today. My dad's family, the Slades, wanted us."

"Were they trying to kill you? Or retrieve you?"

"I have no idea." The thought of one of those monsters retrieving me like a stick was unsettling. I pulled a huge wooden beam from the mess and threw it angrily at the stack of debris. "Why would they come here? How could they possibly know about Stacey?"

"Have you been here recently?"

My knees went weak once I realized the meaning behind his question. I'd been here only a day or two ago, asking Stacey to help me rescue my father. "They followed my scent from my house to here."

Ryland nodded. "I thought I smelled you by that building over there," he said, pointing to what remained of the building where I'd last met Stacey.

I raced to the rubble heap where it had stood and searched frantically for a flash of blonde hair or the hint of fair skin among the debris. My stomach clenched as visions of Stacey's broken bloody body flashed into my head. But I found nothing.

"How can I help?" Ryland asked as he looked into my worried eyes.

"I need to find Stacey. Cute blonde with fair skin." I stared at the mountain of rubble. "She might be somewhere in there."

"I'll need to change," Ryland said, removing his clothes. "So don't be alarmed."

"Thanks," I said, my mind too worried to even think of feeling awkward as he removed the last article of clothing from his body. Thick black hair covered his chest and legs, though he didn't have a field of monkey hair on his back. His body was well-muscled but lean and lithe. A long scar ran from one shoulder to the opposite side of his abdomen. A puckered scar covered the joint of his right shoulder. I wondered how a creature with supernatural healing could have scars. Then again, lycans might heal differently for all I knew.

Ryland took a deep breath and stretched his arms wide, then toppled toward the ground. Before he hit, his body seemed to melt. Thick black fur erupted from his skin. His arms and legs folded smoothly, paws forming from feet and hands, joints twisting forward, while his face shifted into a long lean muzzle. Within seconds, a massive black wolf, his shoulders higher than my waist, regarded me with huge silver eyes and a big wolf grin. Ever since my growth spurt, I'd crossed the six-foot line, meaning this wolf was the biggest one I'd ever seen. A horse could ride him.

"Wow," I said, staring at the magnificent beast. I'd been expecting a lot of the nauseating bone-popping and crunching, not to mention yowling that accompanied one of Stacey's transformations. Ryland made it look effortless.

The wolf lowered his muzzle to the ground and sniffed. Ears perked, he stared at some point in the darkness for a second. I wondered if he'd seen a squirrel. He circled the rubble, nose to the ground for several minutes before he looked at me and made a yipping noise. I followed him into the gloom away from the rubble. As we drew closer to the edge of the warehouses, my night vision picked up the hint of something wet amongst the leaves. I touched a finger to it and sniffed. The coppery odor of blood tingled in my nose.

Ryland picked up the pace then stopped in his tracks, ears pointed like radar dishes and alert. With a low growl, he stared back across the destroyed warehouses, ears flattening. He looked at me and pawed the ground, evidently wanting me to wait there. I sniffed the air as well, but caught nothing unusual. Ryland flashed away, his black fur camouflaging him perfectly against the wrecked buildings.

Leaves rustled behind me. I spun, arms cocked and at the ready. A young girl with long black hair cowered at the edge of the woods. I took a deep breath. She was naked as a newborn, her small breasts reacting predictably to the chilly weather. I had never seen her before and wondered briefly if Stacey could alter her human appearance, or if she had a felycan friend she'd neglected to tell me about. The girl's dark olive skin was smooth and flawless. Bright green eyes with a slight slant peered at me with curiosity.

"Is that you, Stacey?" I asked.

She smiled shyly and shook her head.

"Who are you?"

Her silent gaze was the only response. After a moment, she took a cautious step toward me. I stayed perfectly still, wondering if she was going to sprout fangs and eat me, or if she was as harmless as she looked. She came within a foot and stopped, her breath fogging the air between us. Her petite hands reached for my face. I resisted the reflexive urge to jerk away and remained perfectly still as she touched my face, my lips, my ears, and ran a hand through my hair, her body shivering slightly. She was a little more than a head shorter than me, and beautiful in an exotic way. She smelled slightly of ginger and flowers in a warm spring breeze.

I heard a howl in the distance and my blood froze. She heard it too. But instead of fear, her eyes reflected anger and a cute scowl settled onto her face.

"Do you know where Stacey is?"

She looked back at me, her head tilted to the side.

"Stacey. Where is she?"

Her eyes widened in understanding and she motioned me to follow. More howls rang out in the night air. I couldn't tell if they were wolf howls or hellhounds, and my blood felt like liquid nitrogen in my veins.

The girl stopped next to a tree. I looked down and saw blonde hair and fair skin peeking from behind a black shredded skirt, similar to the one Stacey had worn while helping me rescue my dad.

"Stacey!" I dropped to my knees and turned her on her back. She was breathing, but barely. A huge bite wound festered on her thigh. One of her arms had a deep scratch with a foul-smelling white fluid pooling in it. "What's wrong with her?" I said, looking up at the girl. Except she was gone. I looked around, heart racing as more howls pierced the air. I shook Stacey, trying to wake her up, but it was no good. Carrying her like an infant cradled in my arms, I ran from the woods, not knowing what else to do.

A loud yelp echoed nearby. Massive shadows flickered against a brick wall that had somehow remained standing. I raced toward it and spotted a massive black hound battling with Ryland, its yellow eyes glowing like pools of irradiated urine. The two seemed evenly matched, though the hellhound was missing a large chunk of one ear and had a limp. Ryland looked no worse for the wear.

The hound growled, its sharp blackened teeth bared. It lunged. Ryland dodged with ease. His jaws opened wide. He lunged. Sharp teeth snapped onto the hellhound's neck and bit down with a savage crunch. The hound loosed a strangled yelp before its body went limp and thick black blood pooled on the ground beneath its mouth. The suffocating odor of sulfur suffused the air, causing me to gag. Ryland backed away, shaking the hound's neck from his mouth and sneezing viciously.

He pawed at his mouth, finally chewing on a mound of nearby grass until he threw up. I gagged again and turned away.

"Good god, those things are foul," Ryland said from behind me, his nakedness hidden behind a broken stack of bricks. He spat a glob of dark saliva at the hound and trotted away, returning a moment later, fully clothed again, but still spitting. "I need a damned beer."

"You and me both," I said.

He inspected Stacey, checking the two wounds on her. "This isn't good." He touched the wound on her thigh. Stacey moaned but didn't wake up.

"Why isn't she healing?"

Ryland frowned. "Hellhound wounds don't heal easily. They usually fester and kill a person, even if they're a fast healer."

Panic gripped me. I couldn't lose Stacey. True, she was a pain in the butt, but I cared for her all the same. "Someone must be able to help her."

He nodded. "I know someone."

I glanced back at the woods. "There was a girl who showed me where she was. Black hair, short, kind of Asian—oh, and naked."

"Where is she now?"

"She vanished. I didn't have time to look for her."

He sighed. "We don't have time to look for her if we're going to help your friend. Was the girl hurt?"

I shook my head. "She looked healthy, but I hate to just leave her out here."

"Did she have leaves in her hair? Did her fingernails look like polished wood?"

"What kind of question is that?"

"Just tell me."

I thought back and remembered leaves, but whether they were in her hair or not, I couldn't recall. "I think. Maybe."

"Might be one of the woodlanders who helped you."

"A who—what?"

"Nature guardians. There aren't many left, but a few remain to fight the war against civilization."

"Like a tree nymph?"

He chuckled. "No such thing as those, I'm afraid." He saw my expression and grinned. "Don't worry. I was just as disappointed as you. I always wanted to see what one of them would be like in the sack."

"Are we talking Greenpeace?" I said, following Ryland as he made his way across a shallow ditch and back onto the main road.

"They aren't human," he said, looking back over his shoulder at me. "They're something else. Not sure if they're spirit or flesh, to be honest."

"She sure was cute."

"Sounds like it. You got to meet a sexy lady of the forest. All I got was a mouthful of hellhound blood." He spat.

"Are we headed toward a supernatural hospital?" I asked, looking around for a clue as to our direction.

"Not exactly."

"You're sure we're going someplace that can help?" The only other person I could think of that might be able to help was Shelton. Maybe he knew some healing spells.

He stopped and gave the unconscious woman in my arms a wary gaze. "Can you run?"

I nodded.

"Whatever you do, let me do the talking."

"Why?"

"She's a Templar and might not be happy with me if she finds out you're spawn."

I cursed. "Why couldn't I have been something nicer? Like maybe a unicorn?"

He laughed. "Once you find out more about your kind, you'll probably understand why they have such a terrible rep."

"I've heard that one before."

We took off down the road, whizzing past abandoned buildings and through quiet residential neighborhoods until we reached a small house in the Druid Hills area near Emory. Small houses lined the winding road as it curved around hilly terrain cloaked by a dense canopy of trees. It looked like a nightmarish place to drive if the roads ever iced up.

Ryland approached the quaint house with its gray-stone chimney and a red-painted wooden door, the kind that curved at the top and had black-banded metal hinges. The back yard, what little there was, curved sharply downward and into a wooded valley. I remembered going on a bike ride with my family through here, years ago. Or had it been something else?

A woman stands outside the house, speaking with Mom in a heated voice. A young girl standing to the side of the house waves and smiles. The air flickers. Darkens. A deep boom vibrates the air. Wind whips against my tiny body, pulling it, dragging me toward a gaping black hole in the side of the house. The front door slams in a blur of red. A girl screams. The door opens and a wave of green malevolent energy pours outside. The door opens and shuts. Opens and shuts. Blood streaks down the sidewalk as if an invisible painter is dragging a brush. The door is red. The door is red. The door is red.

Someone shook me. Called my name from a long way away. A sharp pain stung my cheek and I stared into silver eyes.

"Justin? Are you okay?"

"Ryland?"

A young woman stood behind him, her blue eyes narrowed in concern. "What's wrong with him?"

"I don't know, he was fine a minute ago, and then he looked at your house and froze."

"I'm fine," I said, the fog in my brain lifting. I looked at the injured female in my arms and was glad I hadn't toppled over during whatever the heck had just happened to me.

"Why were you saying, 'The door is red' over and over again?" Ryland asked.

"Uh, it's red, right?" I looked at the red-painted door in front of me. I glanced at the sidewalk and felt a stab of fear in my stomach. *It was here. I was here.*

"Let's get her inside," the woman said. "Hurry."

The woman looked oddly familiar. So familiar, in fact, a name came into my head and I blurted it out. "Meghan?"

Ryland's eyes widened. "You know her?"

Her eyes flicked to me. "He didn't know my name?"

"No."

I shrugged. "You just look really familiar. I don't know why."

She looked at me for a moment before motioning me to set Stacey down on a cot near the fireplace. The inside of the house was open. Only a few articles of furniture took up space, among them a leather couch against a wall, two cots, and a large wooden table which looked solid enough to support a car. Light pastels colored the drywall and a set of stone stairs led up near the back. I spotted a small kitchen to the right of the small foyer.

Meghan inspected Stacey's wounds for a moment before giving a grim shake of her head. "I can't do anything for her."

My heart tightened painfully. "What do you mean?"

"Was she a friend of yours?"

A knot formed in my throat at her use of past tense. "Yes. She *is* a friend."

Meghan put her hand over mine, her blue eyes sad. "I'm so very sorry. I suggest you say your goodbyes because she'll be dead very soon."

CHAPTER 9

I glared at Ryland. "I thought you told me she could help!" The sorrow gripping my throat turned to anger. "We wasted all this time coming here and she's just giving up?" I pressed a hand to Stacey's feverish brow. The only other place I could think to take her was Shelton's.

"Why can't you help, Meghan?" Ryland asked.

"It's a hellhound bite, Ryland, and it's well past the point where I can clean the wounds and stop the infection from spreading."

"C'mon," he said. "You've got to have a spell somewhere that can do the trick."

"You're a sorceress?" I asked.

"More or less." She looked at Stacey. "I'm an arcane healer."

"There's got to be some spell that can work."

"At this stage of the infection, all I can do is postpone the inevitable. The only thing that would help is a willing..." Her voice trailed off and she shuddered. "No, it's too late."

"A willing what?" I asked. Good god, all she had to do was name it and I'd get it for her. "Tell me, dammit. Whatever you need I *will* find it."

"I doubt you'll be able to get this."

I resisted the urge to grab her and shake her. Stacey moaned and cried out, her body arching in pain. I braced her shoulders to keep her from falling off the cot. Hot feverish flesh met mine. Her face was pale, bloodless. Dark yellow lines ran in her veins, looking ghastly against her skin. A low moan rose in the back of her throat, and her hands curled and clenched so tight blood welled where her fingernails pierced the skin.

Tears burned in my eyes. "Please, Meghan. Tell me what you need."

She looked at me, her face soft with tenderness and regret. "Spawn blood."

I smiled. A hysterical laugh leapt from my mouth and did a jig. "That's it? That's all you need?"

She looked confused. "Do you have some?"

I nodded and held out my wrist. "I have all you need pumping right here."

Her eyes hardened as she backed away. "Is this a joke?"

Ryland's lips pressed together tight. "He's spawn, Meghan."

Fear blazed in Meghan's wide eyes to the point I thought she might pass out. Instead, she whipped out a pale rod and said a word. Pain tore through me as though my blood had turned to razors and was trying to slice its way free of my veins. I fell to the floor writhing in blind agony. My muscles locked and knotted so tight I couldn't breathe. Gray clouds gathered at the edges of my vision, and my view of the gaily-colored rug on the floor faded.

Ryland shouted. Meghan screamed back at him and then the pain abruptly vanished. I lay panting on the floor, my muscles aching from the spasms as my eyesight returned along with the oxygen to my brain. A yellow bird, one of many woven into the thick wool area rug underneath my face, gave me a cheerful look. I pushed myself to my knees and gazed warily at Meghan. Ryland had her wand in one hand and was saying something to her in a low voice, his tone fierce.

"Get it out of my house," Meghan shouted. "Get it out of here!"

I walked over to her, my body flushed with warm endorphins after the excruciating agony flooding it the moment before. "I'll leave after you heal my friend."

"Do it, Meghan," Ryland said, his voice soft. "I promise you he's not like the others."

I dropped to my knees in front of her. She recoiled, her face filled with loathing. "Please help me," I said. "Please." I felt a tear trickle down my cheek.

She stared at my cheek, her eyes filled with confusion. "It can cry?"

"Spawn can cry, sugah," Ryland said in his southern drawl. "And you know my sense of smell. I tell you that tear is as genuine as it gets."

She reached a cautious hand toward my face and stopped. Then she went to a pouch at her side and retrieved a tiny corked vial. Held it to my cheek and retrieved the tear, stoppering the tiny glass container and putting it back in her pouch. *Women. Crazy. God love them, they're all insane.*

"This procedure will not be painless," she said after a moment. 'In fact, you might die." She gazed at Stacey's moaning form. "This late in the infection will require a lot of blood."

I held out my wrist. "Do what you need to do." I gave Ryland a look. "If something happens, will you…" I faltered as Elyssa's sweet smile and fierce violet eyes filled my thoughts. "Please tell Elyssa I love her."

Ryland gripped my hand and stared at me. "I will."

"Move that cot closer," Meghan said, pointing at the other cot across the room.

I did as she directed while she consulted a thin tablet computer with the picture of an orange on the back of it and gathered some surgical tools which looked more akin to torture devices. My heart thudded as I lay down next to Stacey.

"Tie him down, Ryland," Meghan said, handing him thin silvery twine.

"I don't think that'll hold me," I said. "And even if it did, this cot would give out first."

"You can't break diamond fiber." She nodded at the cot. "And it's made of the same material. Do you think I'd be using flimsy garbage when I treat beings with such strength on a regular basis?"

I felt dumb, but that was nothing new. "I don't know much yet. I'm the new kid on the block."

A very tiny smile crept on her face until she seemed to realize it was there and replaced it with a grimace. Ryland wrapped the diamond fiber tight around my chest, arms, and feet, touching the areas where he wanted it to knot and watching as the thin twine seemed to weld itself together. I tested the bonds and found myself fully immobilized. The urge to panic crested like a silent scream in the back of my throat but I beat it back, trying to calm myself by thinking of Elyssa.

"I can only put you in a light trance," Meghan said, pointing her wand at me. "Anything more will make this harder than it needs to be."

I flinched reflexively as the wand pointed in my direction. She said a word and peace settled over me. Her face and the room around me dimmed to gray. I blinked a few times and light returned to the world. I stood in a bright green meadow. Sheep bleated and tore grass from the fresh-smelling earth, chewing it while giving me somewhat indifferent looks. A lamb, his wool snow white and fluffy, ran up to me, his cute little legs still wobbly. He rubbed against my knee, bleating happily.

"Hey there, little guy," I said bending down and scratching his ears.

More lambs joined him, their adorable little fluffy bodies rubbing against my legs, like wooly cats. A chirp sounded in my ear and I turned to see a bright yellow sparrow on my shoulder. It cocked its head at me and warbled out a sweet song. A group of squirrels ran to the end of a long tree limb and stopped a few feet from my nose, chittering and dancing with each other. Pure joy lifted my heart and the tingle of magic sparkled in the air. I opened my mouth to sing when a dark gray cloud blotted out the sun.

The lambs scattered, their bleats frightened and panicked. The squirrels vanished into the tree, and the little bird flashed away in a streak of yellow.

A jagged bolt of white lightning stabbed from the cloud, nailing the bird in midair and reducing it to a puff of burnt feathers. Another fork of lightning engulfed the large oak tree where the squirrels had gone. It flashed into bright sickly green flames. Blazing squirrels leapt from the tree, their tiny bodies sizzling and frying to a crisp as the air filled with the odor of burnt fur.

"No!" I yelled as I looked at the next targets of the malicious cloud. "Leave the poor little lambs alone!"

Thunder rumbled like a mocking laugh and hundreds of tiny tongues of electrical energy stabbed earthward, toward the lambs.

I shouted a word. It was one I had never heard before, sounding something like "Rathi-Da". A sparkling wave of blue energy seemed to shoot from my mouth, its force drawing the jagged bolts of lightning like magnets. It absorbed them all and settled into the earth in a shimmering sheet of azure electricity.

I stared for a moment wondering what in the hell I'd done. Then it occurred to me to wonder where in the hell I was. I didn't remember coming here. This place wasn't familiar in the slightest. I'd been helping Stacey and then—ah, that was it. Meghan. The trance. I was asleep, sort of. I glared up at the now oily-black cloud and extended my middle finger.

"My dream, my rules." I willed the cloud to vanish but nothing happened. Another noise caught my attention far into the distance. I turned, but nothing was there. A charge filled the air, the feel much different than the lightning. My hair crackled with static. My clothes stuck to my body. Pinpricks touched me everywhere.

And then there was agony.

Every cell in my body seemed to erupt at once. Shimmering red globules emerged from the pores on my skin, each one crackling and sparking like tiny red planets. I screamed for what seemed an eternity, my body arching, bones cracking and popping with the strain. My mind tried to blank out, but it couldn't. Something held it awake. The black cloud vanished, sucked away by some invisible vacuum cleaner. The tree and green meadow went next along with the bodies of the unfortunate squirrels and the frightened sheep and lambs I'd saved from ghastly deaths.

A gray blankness settled in, coating my mindscape in a dull layer of fog.

"You filthy monster," Elyssa said, her blade pressed against my throat as she pinned my arms to the ground with her knees. Blood trickled down my neck and all I could see was her tear-stained face and the starry sky of night to either side.

"Get it out of here," Leia said, appearing to Elyssa's left.

"Kill it," said Thomas, as he emerged from her right.

"I'll always love you, son," Mom said, appearing behind Thomas. He grunted and stumbled forward before falling flat on his face, a bloody dagger protruding from his back. Leia and Elyssa didn't seem to notice. Mom pulled an intricately curved wand and touched it to Leia. The flesh melted from her face and body like ice in a sauna, leaving a bloody red slush and a bleached skeleton standing where she'd been.

Mom came behind Elyssa, whose eyes were still locked onto me.

"No," I said. "Mom, no, I love her. Don't hurt her."

"We will stop them," Mom said. "David, it's the only way." She touched the wand to Elyssa.

I screamed as my true love's body exploded into flames, the heat searing my chest as she toppled onto me. Blood and ashes filled my view.

I stood outside the door. Outside the red door. Red streaks ran down the sidewalk. All the way to the street. I spun and saw a woman. Her legs were gone below the thigh, trailing bone and sinew and so much blood it painted the ground red. I raced to her and knelt.

"What happened? Where's mommy?" I pressed a hand to my throat and found it smaller than it should be. My hands were tiny. What had happened to me?

"They must be stopped," she said. "But the others don't want to stop them. They don't want to..." Her blue eyes glazed over and the last bit of color drained from her face. As the light of life left her eyes, the world faded to black around me. I stood and stared as a plastic sword appeared in my hand.

A baby screamed from far away and I was home, standing in the same familiar hallway I'd walked a million times, except now it was impossibly long. Pitch black waited at one end, bright light at the other. I ran for the light, for the screaming baby. My sister.

Justin, you're going the wrong way.

I spun, my toy sword clutched tight as if I could fight an army with it, eyes searching for the source of the voice. "Who said that?" My voice sounded tiny and childlike. I looked at the light. A dark shadow passed over it. The outline of a man with a top hat, his hands reaching for something, cast a sinister figure. A woman's screams drowned out the baby's wails.

The dark holds salvation.

"My sister is in the light!" I screamed. "Save her!"

The dark holds the light.

"You're crazy!" I ran for the light. The hallway stretched before me. The blurry family pictures lining the walls fell as I ran past, the glass in their frames shattering and cracking. I looked back. The hallway disintegrated behind me as a black void raced at my heels. I screamed and ran for all I was worth. My legs wobbled. I staggered. Excruciating pain lanced into every molecule of my body, but I couldn't let it slow me down. I had to save Ivy, my sister. I had to keep the Conroys from taking her.

But I couldn't.

A burning itching sensation caught fire in my feet and spread in a wave over my entire body. I fell. Turned on my back and stared at the vortex of oblivion churning up the hall behind me. And then it sucked me into its maw and I was falling, falling into blackness so deep I might as well have been blind.

After what seemed an eternity of floating, my body blazing and itching like I'd just rolled naked through poison ivy and then coated myself with iodine, the pain vanished. This place was silent. Not even the sound of my breathing punctuated the stillness. I tried to speak, but my attempts met only the absence of sound.

A bright light pierced the dark. It streaked from above, slowing as it grew closer, a heaven-sent beacon in the dark hells of oblivion. As it grew nearer I expected to see wings unfurl and a beautiful angel reach for my hand to guide me from this place. Instead, a familiar face smiled at me from the brightness, her beautiful eyes ablaze with love. I tried to rise but couldn't. She came to me, the brightness shimmering around her like a halo.

"I am your light in the dark," she said, her voice sounding in my mind without her lips moving. "Your dark light. And I will be there for you when the time comes."

Elyssa bent down and kissed me, her lips soft and soothing to my feverish sweaty skin.

I tried to speak but she shook her head gently and held my hand. "I will be with you until the end, my love." Her lips brushed my ear. "Four, three, one, one. Remember."

Warmth filled my body as I gazed into the eyes of an angel. My angel. I looked at my true love until the light faded from my eyes and the pain and weight of life unburdened my body as it lifted away.

CHAPTER 10 - ELYSSA

*E*lyssa woke with a start. She hadn't even realized sleep had taken her. Sweat drenched the tank top and Soffe shorts she'd lain down in. Her pillow was soaked as well. She touched her face and felt the salty damp residue of tears. She couldn't have been asleep for long, she reasoned, because the tears hadn't dried. Or had she been crying in her sleep?

What had awoken her?

The ache of loss formed a hollow spot in her midsection, the feeling that nothing she put there could fill it up. Only Justin could. Only the touch of his hands on her face and his lips against hers could fill this gaping maw. How had this happened? How had she fallen for a guy after growing up without a worry or thinking twice about what another person thought of her?

It had happened so suddenly, so unexpectedly she'd just let it happen, thinking nothing would come of it as usual. Father would scare him off or she'd drive him away by showing him just how little she needed anyone to take care of her. This couldn't be happening. Not to her.

God, it hurt so bad. She punched her pillow. Punched it again. Picked it up and threw it against the wall where it hit with a muted thud. Elyssa got out of bed and paced the room wanting to smash the simple wooden furniture to pieces and scream and rage until the agony in her heart went away and left her alone. How could she do this? How could she let another person take a part of her soul with her wherever he went?

"Justin," she said, and fresh tears leaked from her eyes.

She growled and punched the wooden-paneled wall, cracking it down the center. She punched it again and again until her fists were raw and bleeding.

"Go away. Go away!" She said it over and over as if it would dissipate her feelings. As if she had the power to command love into oblivion.

An image of brilliant light flashed into her mind and she stopped mid-punch. Her fists healed, the skin sealing up and pushing out the splinters in her knuckles. Elyssa barely noticed. The dream was coming back to her. The one that had woken her. The one that made her cry in her sleep. Justin was dying, or dead in the dream. She'd floated to him on a brilliant cloud of light and held his hand until he left her.

Panic welled in her throat and she choked back a scream. No, it hadn't happened. Had it? It was just a dream. But it had felt so real. His skin, the touch of his lips still lingered on hers and she could smell him and the overpowering Axe deodorant he used. She really needed to get him to switch to Old Spice.

Deep breaths didn't make her panic go away. If anything, more images came into her mind. An old crone, toothless and cackling at her. Telling her four-three-one-one was the magic number. Then she'd vanished, replaced by glowing light. It felt as though something had possessed her then, the way dreams usually operated. Except it had seemed frighteningly real.

The bedroom door cracked open and Leia poked in her head. Elyssa hardly ever called her mother anymore. In fact, she'd been trained to call her parents by their first names for years now. Family ties would earn her no leeway in training or any other aspect of Templar business. If anything, having a commander who was also your father made things worse. Ryland's training, from the way he told it, was a cakewalk compared to the things she'd had to endure. But it didn't anger her or make her love her parents any less. If anything, it increased her respect for their standards.

"What's going on in here?" Leia asked, stepping inside, the black soft-soled boots she wore making little sound. The silver ends of two short swords protruded diagonally from sheaths across her back, and the tight black Templar night camouflage she wore pressed tight against her curves.

"Nothing." Elyssa turned her back to her mother and stared out the window.

The door clicked shut. "I can't believe you're being so unreasonable about that—that thing. What part of your lessons don't you remember? Maybe we should send you back to your history teacher and have him fill in the blanks again."

"I remember everything, *Mother*. But I'm smart enough to realize not every individual is a clone of every other of their kind." She turned to face her. "How many dhampyrs have we arrested or put down over the years? I haven't even been on active duty that long and I can list three of them."

"That's different and you know it."

"Different? Tell me how."

"A tiny minority broke the law. Some are serving time at Lazaro while the others resisted and paid with their lives."

"And what makes them different from spawn? I don't remember ever apprehending a spawn. The last time one of them broke Covenant, they turned themselves in."

"Because their house made them do it."

"You can't accept it, can you? Whatever harm spawn did to Thomas is no reason to hate the entire race. Especially not Justin. He's not even full spawn."

"Don't be foolish, girl."

Elyssa bristled, fists clenched and eyes narrowed.

"That's right. You're being a stupid girl, Elyssa. Thomas and I have talked and decided you're of no use to us in a normal school any longer. You're to be reassigned to boarding school with others of your kind."

"You're sending me to Westbury?" It was the only supernatural school close enough to be a candidate.

She nodded. "We wanted you to adapt to a normal human way of life so you'd blend in better should we need you to go undercover once you achieved the Cho'kai. Instead, you let yourself be fooled by spawn and seem so brainwashed we see no way you'll be able to take the trials this year."

Elyssa felt her bottom lip drop in disbelief. "You know I'm ready. Give me the trials right now and I'll prove it to you."

"Oh, you have plenty to prove, *girl*." Leia shook her head. "You could have been the youngest to pass the Cho'kai and the first female in decades to move up to full guardian status."

"Gee, I don't know who's more disappointed. Me or Commander Borathen. All he cares about is that he trained me. I'm not his daughter, I'm an achievement. Just like Jack and Michael before me." Elyssa jerked open her closet doors so hard, the hinges squealed. She grabbed her night camo, stripped, and slid it on. The clingy material felt cool against her clammy skin. She had to get out of there. Had to find Justin.

"What do you think you're doing? We made it very clear you're suspended from duty until we decide what to do with you."

"You can take your duty and shove it."

"That's no way to speak to your mother! You will show me respect."

"Well you're not showing respect for choices I've made or even my opinion, so I don't see how you deserve any respect from me." She sucked in an angry breath to fight back the salty tidal wave threatening to break past her eyes. "If you think you trained me so well, then give me the damned right to choose who my friends are and who I love. Otherwise it's meaningless. All of it!" The last part came out as a shout. Elyssa panted as anger and grief pressed hard against her emotional barriers, the ones she'd spent years building up only to find them torn down the moment she went all gaga for a boy.

Leia stared with wide accusing eyes, her mouth set in a deep scowl. "It's our fault," she said in a restrained voice. "We take the full blame for failing you, child. But we'll set things aright. Don't worry." She sighed.

"In the meantime, you're grounded to your quarters. If you try to escape, we'll put you in the brig. Don't think we won't."

A bitter laugh escaped Elyssa's mouth. "Why should I doubt you? I've already spent more time in there than most of the real criminals."

"Don't force me to—" Leia's voice cut off abruptly as Elyssa blurred to her, feinted with a low kick, spun, and caught her with a hard chop to the throat to keep her from yelling out an alarm.

Elyssa whipped her torso the other way, sending a vicious elbow to Leia's temple. The other woman collapsed, unconscious for at least... Elyssa checked the tiny watch she wore and calculated she had one or two minutes before her mother's supernatural healing kicked in and woke her up. Not much time, but enough to get a head start. She grabbed a small knapsack from underneath her bed where she'd put it after filling it with fresh clothes and toiletries.

The bedroom windows were spelled and warded against use, so she'd have to make her way downstairs and through the front door since using any other door at this time of night would trip an alarm ward and have the entire compound of Templars on her back. She slipped the uniform's hood over her head. It wasn't unusual for Templars to wear them like this indoors, but there weren't many females on site and that might make things tricky. Breasts were hard to hide.

The downstairs hallway was empty. Most agents were out on duty, patrolling the streets or going on raids, away from the prying eyes of the noms—a term many used to refer to normal humans. Some agents would come back for a couple hours of sleep and then go to day jobs, blending in with the noms and keeping ears open for signs of unusual activity. Her mother ran a hair salon of all things. The absurdity of that woman styling hair made Elyssa shake her head at times, though she ran the place almost as strictly as she did her squad of Templar agents.

The house's large foyer was also empty, though Elyssa thought she heard a noise from the kitchen. The manor house served meals to the agents, but the time for eating was long past. She crept past the large entryway into the kitchen and looked inside. Nobody. She removed her knapsack and eased open the walk-in freezer. Wax-coated cardboard boxes lined the shelves along one wall. She opened the nearest and stuffed an empty compartment of the knapsack with enough blood packs to last her for a while. There were other Templar posts around the city supplying blood, but after her escape, they'd all be on the lookout for her.

She fastened the pack on her back and slipped out the front door. Crouching in the darkness, she opened her senses to the environment. A horse whickered and stomped its hoof. A dog barked in the distance. Two sentries moved along the perimeter of the ranch fence, nearly invisible but for their body heat which stood out to her against the chill night air.

Thirty, she thought as her internal timer counted down the seconds. She'd averaged her mother's unconscious state out to ninety seconds and was closing in fast on zero. Time to get away before the alarm went off. She masked her psychic presence, slowed her heart so as to decrease her body heat, and set off down the asphalt driveway at a quick stroll. Thanks to the wards and runes along the perimeter, she had little choice in her exit strategy.

When the heat signature of the sentries faded in the distance to be almost undetectable, she was about halfway down the driveway. Still, the alarm had not been raised, making her curious and very wary. *Fear destroys logic*, she remembered, thinking back to the lessons her Art of War instructor had beaten into her head. *Panic defies reason. Act with reason and logic.* Easy things to remember, but very hard to put into practice during the heat of battle or the cold fear of discovery during an escape. She'd learned the hard way when vamplings had nearly killed her and Justin during their attempt to rescue his father from rogue vampires.

Things had worked out, amazingly, although Justin had done something when he'd saved her. She could almost feel him at times and wondered if she was truly in love with him, or if maybe he had done something to her when he'd pushed life back into her.

"Of course I love him," she said aloud. She'd loved him even before their first kiss. From the way he respected her as an equal to the way he sometimes told her in no uncertain terms he would do something and did.

He could be headstrong, but he'd taught her to stop being so stubborn all the time and to listen to her heart. He'd been such a silly boy at first but had grown into a man—one who would stand up to bullies for his friends and never hesitate to protect those he loved. Maybe he wasn't the best planner in the world, but his heart was always in the right place. And he had a great ass.

A smile touched her lips.

Who wouldn't love a man like that? *Stop questioning your heart. He almost sacrificed his life's blood for you. Treasure him.*

She reached the end of the driveway and listened. No alarm. No rustle of leaves or encroaching body heat to indicate Leia had finally come to and given the order to bring in her rebellious daughter. Worry stabbed Elyssa. Had she miscalculated and hurt her mom? Really injured her badly enough she might be dying right now? Elyssa knew how to hit properly. She could disable a person, completely incapacitate them, or kill if need be. She'd hit her mother just right, she felt certain of it. But the one percent of doubt multiplied in her head.

Doubt kills hope. Hope is the light that leads to victory against all odds. Her Art of War instructor, Victor Mazin, an old one-eyed human was full of crap like that. Then again, that crap usually helped her through times like this and filled her with the resolve to move forward.

The urge to turn around and go back nearly halted her forward progress but she forced herself onward, reciting mantra in her head. She'd set out on this path and now it was her duty to complete it. Finding Justin was the first order of things. He should be back at Shelton's by now. She pulled out her smartphone and retrieved the GPS coordinates for his hideaway. Listened for a moment more to see if she was being followed. When she heard nothing, she zipped down the road a mile, stopping at an abandoned gas station and entering the garage through a broken back door.

Vandals had broken most of the glass from the windows but none of them had been strong enough to lift the metal plate over the oil-changing pit underneath the car lifts or bright enough to find where she'd relocated the button to the hydraulic lift. She leapt up to the rafters and reached inside a vent, pressing the "Up" button on the control she'd fastened there. One of the lifts rumbled into action, hydraulic pumps thrumming as the unit ascended, taking a thick metal plate with it. Once it was fully up, Elyssa dropped to the floor and entered the pit. She picked up the long ten by twelve piece of lumber stowed there and propped it against the lip of the pit.

The old Harley she'd hidden here had half a tank of fuel left and started on the first try. She'd ridden it almost a month ago, so no surprise there. She guided it up the wooden ramp and parked it, the new muffler on it making only the slightest of rumbles. Some would call it sacrilege to silence a Harley, but her brother Michael had helped her with it, agreeing one could still ride in perfect style without all the noise.

After closing the oil pit, Elyssa hopped on the motorcycle and guided it through the broken down back door on the garage. She activated the GPS on her phone and took off for Shelton's place. Soon she'd be back with Justin and the world would feel right again.

CHAPTER 11

I heard screaming. Roaring. Growling. The first image I saw was a wooden-beamed ceiling. Or at least it looked like a ceiling. My eyesight was blurry, like looking through a filthy window only muddying the view worse when you try to wipe it clean with a sleeve. The roaring grew louder. Something wooden crashed against a solid object and glass shattered.

"My house!" a female cried out.

I tried to move but found my arms and legs completely immobile. I could barely lift my head. It felt like a lead weight and resisted, but I finally raised it enough to peer between my feet. A massive black wolf growled at something. A huge ebony paw lashed out at the wolf's muzzle but it ducked away, its silvery eyes locked onto whatever was assailing it.

Ryland. That's Ryland. My thoughts churned like dirty water, but I slowly recalled who and what the large wolf was. Why was I tied down? A creature yowled. Claws scrabbled across a hard surface. A thud and another yowl followed, and a sleek black figure appeared, slipping and sliding, before crashing into the frame holding me tight.

The world cartwheeled. My face missed the floor by inches before the cot came to rest at an odd angle against the wall, giving me a view of the destruction. The quaint room was a mess. Splintered wood littered the floor. A large area rug woven with birds, trees, and a cheerful outdoors scene lay shredded and tattered. Deep claw marks marred the hardwood floors.

The reason for the carnage was clear. A huge panther prowled the perimeter of the room while Ryland in wolf form watched it with wary silver eyes. The panther coiled and leapt with lightning speed, so fast my slowly improving eyesight could hardly follow the streak of black. Ryland dodged at the last moment, his huge jaws widening and closing down as razor claws caught him in the back.

Blood oozed from his right shoulder, but he had the prize. The panther's throat was in his grasp.

"No!" I wheezed, sounding like an old man on his last minutes of life.

The wolf's ears perked up and a pretty young woman stepped into view from the shelter of a doorway across the room.

"He's awake!" she said. "My god, he survived."

The panther screamed, its claws striking blindly at the wolf, some shredding furrows of fur from his coat, but Ryland rotated, keeping his teeth clamped firmly across the panther's throat until it screamed one last time and went limp. The horrid sound of cracking, popping bones and rearranging flesh filled the room. The panther's fur melted away into fair skin, and its sleek muzzle melted into a human face with a mane of grungy blonde hair.

Ryland released his hold on Stacey as she lay sobbing on the floor. Then he howled, triumphant.

I couldn't keep my eyes open a second longer and the darkness claimed me.

SOMETHING WARM PRESSED AGAINST ME. Soft sweetness pressed against my lips. Elyssa? She was here. My dark light. My hands reached around the soft curves of her body and I hugged her close, pressing her lips to mine and drawing in her scent. Except…the familiar scent wasn't Elyssa.

I opened my eyes and stared into amber ones as Stacey pulled back, a gentle smile on her lips.

"You're awake, my sweet," she said, her British accent thick as honey. "Oh, Justin, my knight, my hero. You saved me."

I tried to sit up, but my muscles screamed with burning agony. The diamond fiber was gone. "It worked," I said. "Meghan was able to cure you."

"I awoke after the queerest dream." Stacey grabbed a nearly destroyed pillow from the floor and fluffed it before propping up my head. "And I was in a strange place. Thinking I had been captured, I immediately shifted."

"And fought Ryland." A feather drifted toward my nose, a casualty of the war-torn pillow. I blew at it before it made me sneeze. Considering how terrible I felt, a sneeze would probably put me in a coma.

"Yes, the bloody stinking wolf." She shuddered. "Disgusting creatures."

"Hey, he helped me save you."

She glared across the room where Ryland and Meghan sat at a circular wooden table that had somehow survived the battle. "How in the world did you end up in his company?"

"He's a Templar."

"How can you be so bloody daft, Justin?" Stacey peppered my cheeks with kisses. "And still so delicious?" She sighed. "A girl can't even get a tiny bit of rest without you dragging her off into danger."

"What happened?" I asked. "When we found you, the entire place was destroyed."

She shrugged. "These very foul-smelling men appeared, sniffing the ground like animals. And then they shifted into the largest dogs I've ever seen." She gasped. "Oh dear." Tears welled in her eyes. "Oh no. Marmalade and Dots. Those creatures killed them."

Marmalade and Dots were the moggies Stacey had created to help me rescue my dad. They looked like massive alley cats and were insanely strong. But those black hounds were something else. "They were hellhounds, Stacey. And they were looking for me."

"Those wretched things actually exist?"

I nodded. "My dad's side of the family sent them. Either to kill or capture us."

"Well, which is it?"

I tried to shrug but fire raced up my neck when I did. "I don't know." I told her about Dad's death mark and the little we'd done so far. I jerked as memory kicked in a detail I'd forgotten and my muscles spasmed. "What time is it? Is it morning yet?"

She glanced toward a window. "No, it's still before dawn."

"I have to get to Trader Mike's and find Mr. Smith."

"You're not going anywhere for a day at least," Meghan said, coming across the room with a steaming cup of something minty in one hand.

"I have to. It's to help my dad." *And to find out what my mom is up to with those deadly spells of hers*, I thought.

"That's not the entire truth," Ryland said, his nose wrinkling.

"No, it's a guess. I have my doubts about this guy, but I hope he can help."

"You stink like rubbish," Stacey said, her imperious Victorian-era British accent lashing out at Ryland like a whip.

"You smell rather nice," Ryland said with a wolfish grin. "And you taste even better."

Stacey sniffed and looked away from him, nose held high. "Stinking dogs. Why don't you go sit like a good boy, preferably far from me?"

Ryland's grin grew even larger. "You got it, kitten."

Stacey sniffed again.

"You're going to pull a nose muscle if you keep sniffing like that," I told her. "And stop being such a bitch to him."

Her eyes grew wide. "A *bitch*? How could you insult me so?"

"Give it a rest. He helped me save your life. He killed one of the hellhounds."

Disbelief narrowed her eyes. "I find that rather hard to believe."

"How did they get you?" I asked. "Couldn't you outrun them?"

"They demolished the building right out from beneath me before I could recover from the shock of seeing them murder Marmalade and Dots. I was dazed but managed to morph as they came in for the attack." Tears pooled and ran down her cheeks. "One of them had me by the throat. But it didn't kill me, Justin. It was as if the vicious creature wanted me to suffer from my wounds before I died."

Anger built inside me, pounding against my ribcage and demanding revenge on these things for hurting her. But I felt so weak a mouse could probably whip my tail in a fair fight. I looked up at Meghan. A battle raged in her eyes and I could tell she wasn't over her hatred for my kind. She still didn't like having me here. Maybe I could use her disgust to my advantage.

"Can you at least get me on my feet?" I asked her. "I'll get out of your house and your life. I promise."

She remained silent for a moment, her eyes seeming to search my face for something. "You said a lot while you were under, including some things I couldn't believe. But now that I look at you, I see your mother's spirit burning bright in those eyes of yours. She was never one to let the threat of death stop her from anything."

"Everyone tells me I look more like my dad."

She gave a nod. "True. But inside, you're like Alice. Determined. Stubborn. But she's a planner. She would never rush into danger, especially not weak like you are now."

"It's not exactly danger. It's a nerd who likes comic books who may also be able to decipher something for me."

"Danger seems to enjoy following you from what I've heard."

How did she know my mom so well? Her face sparked a sudden onslaught of memories.

A young girl opens the red door. A woman screams. A roar. Crimson-streaked concrete. Blood soaking into the earth. A woman draws ragged breaths as her life's blood leaks from torn and shredded legs. "They must be stopped. But the others don't want to stop them," a female voice whispers in my ear.

I squeezed my eyes shut as the images faded and understanding replaced my confusion. "My mom used to bring me here sometimes," I said. "I was little and so were you."

She nodded, her face a careful mask. "Are you remembering too?"

"Yes. Something hurt your mother badly."

"Killed her." A tear broke through her brave façade. "And your mother would never tell me why. Only that she would set things right."

"Why didn't I remember this until now?"

"She blocked your memories. Blurred them from your mind. You were too young to understand and she didn't wish you to be scarred with such pain."

"Your father?"

"He died two years before my mom."

"Who raised you? Why do you still live in this place?"

"My aunt. She's dead now, too." Meghan knelt by my side, her lips trembling. "They all die, I'm afraid." She reached the flat of her palm for my forehead, her face grimacing with what might be revulsion. When she touched me, she flinched, as if expecting to feel the slimy skin of an eel. "I'll help you remember."

White light flashed before my eyes and a dozen scrambled scenes ran backwards through the theater of my mind. Colors, sounds, and my sense of touch ran together in a churning mess. I couldn't make heads or tails of anything. Then a hand seemed to wave across my face, clearing my unfocused senses like windshield wipers across foggy glass.

Someone held my hand. I looked up into the blue eyes of my mom as she towered over me like a giant. She focused on the red door ahead. Walked to it and knocked. A girl a few years old than me answered.

"Hello, Meghan. Your mother is expecting me."

"Yes, of course, Mistress Conroy."

"Meghan, you are to never call me that. I am Ms. Case. Do you understand?"

"My apologies Mistress—Ms. Case."

"Thanks, sweetie."

"Alice," said a woman's voice from within. "Is it true?"

Mom stepped inside as she replied. "Yes, Sandy. I'm pregnant." The door shut behind her, leaving me outside. I stooped to inspect a toad as it appeared from under a rotted tree stump in the front yard.

"That's Alfred," Meghan said, squatting next to me. "His family lives in there."

"I like toads. I wish I could hop like a toad," I said.

"You can!" Meghan's eyes lit up. She held out a hand. "Here, take my hand."

I followed her to the side of the house to a large trampoline beneath a huge tree. I'd never jumped on one before and excitement raced through me. Meghan helped me up and we jumped and giggled, trying to make one another bounce even higher. But I was much smaller than she was and ended up being bounced uncontrollably while I squealed with joy.

"Meghan!" a woman called from the front of the house. "I need you for a moment."

"I'll be right back," Meghan promised as she hopped down to the ground and ran to the front.

I jumped up high as I could and landed on my back, thrilling at how it didn't hurt a bit to fall on the bouncy black surface. Something rustled and squeaked. I turned on my stomach and looked toward the back of the house. A man in a gray suit was pulling open double wooden doors at the bottom of the house. If it was anything like our house, I knew they led to the crawlspace underneath. Scary things like spiders and huge brown camo-crickets lived in there, and I hated it even though Dad had told me they were more afraid of us.

I didn't believe him for a minute.

The man held a round piece of plywood upon which was a complicated pattern of bare copper wires strung around nails. It looked kind of like a drawing I'd seen in one of mom's picture books she kept hidden in her office. I'd found them when she'd left me with Dad one day and looked through them all, fascinated by the strange patterns and wondering what the odd words next to them meant. I knew how to read most things, but those words hadn't looked familiar at all.

Another man in gray trudged up the hill behind the first one who was now putting the plywood under the house. The two looked like identical twins. The other man had a thick cable with sharp alligator clips on the ends. The men looked normal but something was very strange about them. Their faces seemed to be set in stone because they didn't smile or frown or make any expressions for that matter. Even their sickly pale skin looked grayish. Something about that scared me, so I stayed very still and very flat on the trampoline, using the big tree next to it to stay hidden, curious to see why they were putting the plywood under the house and running the cables to it.

I thought back to the pictures in Mom's books, trying to remember which one looked like the pattern on the plywood. There had been the image of a shiny green shark monster next to it, I thought. Or was it the one with the big swirly pattern? No, that one had a picture of a huge red man next to it. This one was like a bunch of squares with a zig-zag running through it. Definitely the one with the green shark picture.

The man who'd gone under the crawlspace emerged, his gray suit covered with reddish dust from the dry clay underneath. A large black spider ran up his shoulder and across his face. I clamped both hands on my mouth in horror, but the man didn't make a sound. Quick as lightning, his hand plucked the spider off his face and dropped it to the ground. Then the two men started back down the steep hill. I waited until their heads vanished from sight and then got off the trampoline and sneaked to the edge of the decline, hiding behind some bushes.

A bright red machine sat at the bottom of the hill. The cables ran from the crawlspace and into it. One of the men jerked on a string, and with a thrum, the machine came to life, sounding a little like a lawn-mower. I heard a crackling noise like static popping off wool socks. Some squirrels in a nearby tree chittered, looked at the house, and then leapt down, dashing across the street. The sides of the house seemed to move. And then I realized the house wasn't moving—it was crawling with bugs.

"Gross!" I said, watching in disgust as spiders, crickets, and insects I didn't recognize squirmed, crawled, and buzzed away from the house, until the ground and air seemed alive with them. Thankfully, they didn't come near me.

I smelled a burning odor, like the time I'd stuck a hairpin into the electrical socket and blown out the kitchen lights. Light crackled through the crawlspace vents built into the bricks at the base of the house. A loud pop sounded and a sudden wind blew leaves and other debris against the house, forming a vortex at the door to the crawlspace.

Thunder exploded just as a blinding light flashed. Windows shattered on the house.

I stumbled backward, falling on my bottom.

And then I heard screams.

CHAPTER 12

*C*hills ran down my scalp like an army of ants.

"Mommy?" I yelled. Fear slammed into me like a wall and I wanted to run away as fast as my tiny legs could carry me. But my mom was in there. I had to help her.

I ducked to the ground as a broken branch whizzed past me, sucked into the crawlspace. All of a sudden I knew those men had done this. The green shark was going to eat my mom. I had to take the cables off the plywood. A strong gust of wind caught me as I stood and pulled me toward the house. I tried to slow myself, but the suction was strong enough to make me stagger on my little legs.

More screams and shouts emerged from the broken windows. I let the wind take me to the house, pressing against the brick and edging toward the cable draped over the doorsill. Closer to the door, the vacuum effect was much stronger but I didn't think it was enough to suck me in like the leaves. A green light glowed from the doorway. Someone was shouting. Strange black particles exploded and streamed from the doorway, only to vanish into the air.

I heard Meghan screaming for her mom. My mom shouted something as a deep rumbling voice chanted in a language sounding so very familiar to me I thought I could almost understand it if only I listened a little harder. But no matter how hard I tried, I couldn't grasp it. And then I realized I was only helping the monster by not pulling the cable. Disconnecting it would save everyone. It had to.

Squatting down, I reached for the cable. Gripped it. Jerked. Something gave and fizzled, scenting the air with a fresh wave of burning electrical parts. The chanting stopped. I'd done it! I'd saved everyone! I raced to the front of the house. And then I saw the red liquid splashed and streaked down the front sidewalk. My eyes followed it and found a woman. Meghan's mom. I ran to her.

"What happened? Where's Mommy?" I asked her.

"They must be stopped," she said. "But the others don't want to stop them. They don't want to..." her blue eyes glazed over and the last bit of color left her face along with her life. As the light left her eyes, I heard more shouting from inside.

Choking back the acidic vomit clawing up my throat, I rushed in as Mom, a thick ebony staff in one hand, hurled blinding black light at an oily green creature with a gaping maw larger than the rest of its shark-like body. The wooden floor was a splintered mess as though the creature had exploded up through it. What at first I thought were little red bumps clustered all along the monster's snout blinked and rotated, and I realized they were eyes, two of them much larger than the others. Mom hurled another pulse of glowing dark particles, but they only seemed to enrage the creature more than hurt it. Meghan had pressed herself tight into a corner, her face white and panicked. She screamed as the monster snapped its gaping maw at Mom, only to be rebuffed by another pulse of black light.

Then the creature's two big eyes swiveled toward me. The thing spoke, deep, guttural, and rumbling in the strange language. I wanted to say something back to it. Tell it to go away and leave us alone. But another part of me felt drawn to it. Felt sorry for it. It spoke again to me, and it seemed to be pleading. It wanted to go home, I realized. That had to be it. The men had made it come against its will. Deep in my heart I knew that's what it was saying. But I didn't know what to do or how to do it.

Its eyes hardened and glared at me as I stood there, mouth gaping, unable to speak to it or make it understand I *wanted* it to go home.

Mom saw it looking at me. "Run, Justin! Run!"

"Under the house, Mom! A piece of plywood. It needs electricity."

Her eyes narrowed. She turned and looked through the hole blasted in the wooden floor. I think she saw the plywood because she waved her staff at a nearby electrical socket, then said a word and aimed it down through the floor. Blue light arced from the wall socket, intersecting her staff and then shooting downward. A dark vortex formed. The monster's scarlet eyes seemed to soften. It looked at me once more, and seemed to bow before turning into a cloud of green smoke and vanishing into the vortex.

Mom jerked her staff up and the electricity stopped. She slumped onto the floor, sweat plastering golden locks to her face. Then she turned on her knees and threw up. A lot. I ran over to her and patted her back, my own stomach roiling and heaving.

"Mommy? Are you okay?"

She smiled and caressed my cheek. "Mommy's good boy. You're so brave. I will never let anything bad happen to you. I promise."

"I won't let anything happen to you because I'm a big boy now."

The smile on her face died as she saw Meghan in the corner and the trail of blood leading out the door. "Oh no. God, no." A tear trickled down her cheek. "Stay here for Mommy. Take care of Meghan, sweetie."

I ran over and gave Meghan a hug. She buried her face in my shirt and soaked it with tears. I noticed a piece of blood-soaked paper clutched in her hand. The writing was all but illegible. All but the last few characters: *ance 4311.*

Mom came back in, dragging the body of Meghan's mom with her. Then she came to me and took my hand. "Thank you for being a big boy, sweetie. Now Mommy wants you to sit still so I can make you feel better."

"But I feel good."

"Little boys shouldn't see certain things. And neither should little girls." She pressed a bloody hand to Meghan's forehead and said something. Meghan slumped and went to sleep. Before I could ask what she'd done, I felt Mom's warm sticky red hand against my forehead and darkness followed.

I JERKED and yelled as Meghan's older face appeared before me. She backed off, wiping her hand on her dress and then grabbing a bottle of hand sanitizer off the floor and applying it liberally.

"Did that really happen?" I asked. My heart thudded like a mallet and sweat dripped down my face. My muscles and joints ached with every little twitch, but I pushed myself into a better sitting position.

"Justin, my lamb, please be careful," Stacey said as I grunted and groaned with every move.

"Stacey, would you get me some water?"

She kissed my cheek. "Of course, darling." She got up and strode gracefully for the kitchen, all the while giving Ryland a glare. He smiled at her innocently—at least as much as any wolf in sheep's clothing would.

"Meghan," I said, "where did that green monster come from?"

"Hell."

"I may be demon spawn and all, but does a place like Hell really exist?"

"Think of it as a dark evil plane of existence where such creatures live." She shuddered.

"Did you see everything through my eyes?"

She nodded. "I never knew about the men or the pattern on the plywood. Your mom did a good job of suppressing our memories. I didn't even realize who you were until Ryland filled me in while you were unconscious." Another shiver ran through her body.

"How did the plywood thing work?"

"I'm no summoner, but I can tell you gateways can be opened with enough electricity and the proper pattern. They obviously opened it with a portable generator, and the pattern was fairly simple so the entity that came through was probably of a very low caste."

"And yet my mom couldn't seem to beat it."

"Even the lowest of the low are insanely strong...Justin."

I felt a smile on my face. "Thanks."

"For what?"

"Using my name instead of calling me a thing."

Stacey returned with a tall glass of water. I took it and gulped. My body tried to throw it up almost immediately so I clamped my mouth shut and fought back the convulsions until the water stayed down.

"Why do you hate spawn?" I asked Meghan. "Better yet, why is my kind universally despised?"

She frowned. "Not everyone hates the spawn. Vampires love their blood and consider spawn one of their few true adversaries in the politics of the Overworld. Lycans, you see, are too straightforward and lean toward action while sorcerers are mostly human and tend to distrust anything the others do."

"I can see that. But you didn't answer my question."

"Remember when I told you my father died two years before my mother?"

I nodded.

"He didn't exactly die. He made a bad deal with a spawn. It cost him his soul."

My forehead tightened. "Demon spawn can take souls?"

"They can feed on the essence and even damage a soul enough for all practical purposes to kill someone, but they cannot wholly consume it in human form."

"What do you mean?"

She shuddered. "Spawn are the earthly agents of Hell, or the dimension we call Hell. Their human forms are little more than vessels. From a very young age, I was taught the dangers of the Overworld. Taught to mistrust the vampires, to use caution around the lycans, and, at all costs, avoid the spawn."

"Must be what they teach everyone," I grumbled.

"For good reason. I learned. My father discovered his sister had cancer. While most skilled healers such as myself can heal such things, this particular cancer was resistant to all forms of treatment. He heard spawn blood could cure almost anything and made a deal with one such spawn should he help his sister."

I tried to stretch my cramped arm and grunted with the pain of it. "Was it anything like what I went through?"

She shook her head. "No, the procedure turned out to be far simpler, and his sister, my aunt, was cured with only two treatments."

"And then the spawn turned around and sucked out your dad's soul?"

"No, he was given a decade to set his affairs in order."

"So he damned himself to Hell to save his sister? That's horrible."

"His soul was not so much damned as it was consumed."

"You mean no afterlife or anything?"

She shook as sobs took her and tears streamed down her eyes. I wanted to give her a hug and comfort her as I had nearly ten years or so ago when the green creature had killed her mother. But I knew better. Now, I would only repulse her.

"Nobody knows for sure, and the spawn would not tell me no matter how much I screamed or begged for mercy."

I clenched my teeth. It was about all I could do without pain slicing into me. "Who was this punk? What was his name?"

She shrugged. "He only gave the name Vad."

"This Vad came to your house and killed your father in front of you?" My mouth hung open and I felt sick to my stomach.

"No, my father went to it and commanded us to remain home. My mom went nearly mad with grief. My Aunt Nancy, his sister, begged the spawn to take her instead, although she screamed and cursed at Dad once she found out the bargain he'd made."

"He didn't tell her?"

"No. But that's not the worst part." The tears stopped and her fists clenched tight around her teacup until it sprang from her grasp and clattered on the wooden floor. "I hired a seeker to find the identity of the spawn who struck this bargain. The seeker found more, so much more than I wanted to know. This spawn had allies, dark creatures I'd never heard of before. One of those had given my aunt the tumor. It was a regular con job this spawn ran."

"You've got to be kidding me," I said, feeling sick and dizzy and furious all at once. "This thing gave people cancer?"

"Yes." Her voice grew very quiet. "But I found its weaknesses. I caught it. And I tortured it to death."

My skin went cold.

Stacey's eyes widened and she pressed herself against me. "I do not mean to insult you," she said, "but you don't seem the torturing type."

Meghan's dull eyes met ours. "Sometimes you have to be a monster to deal with one."

"And, I think that's about enough," Ryland said, coming over and taking Meghan by the shoulders. "You're starting to scare your guests, sugah."

She shook her head as though clearing a fog, and a contrite lock passed over her face. "I'm sorry. I really am." She stood shakily. "I've become as bad as them, haven't I?"

"No you haven't," Ryland said. "Not by a long shot, hon."

Stacey gave Ryland a wondering look. "Did they neuter you when you were a pup?" she asked him with a wicked gleam in her eye.

He laughed. "You're a lively one, sweet thang." He looked her up and down. "I think I liked you better when you were naked, though."

Her eyes grew huge as her face glowed scarlet. "You met me at a rather low point in my life." She sniffed and leaned against me.

I groaned.

"I'm sorry, lamb."

"Meghan," I said. "I need to get on my feet. Do you have some kind of painkiller you can give me?"

She shook her head. "I don't think it's a good idea."

"I don't care. A painkiller, please. I'm sure I'll heal up just fine."

"You don't understand. I used a great deal of your blood and with it, the special blood plasma storing essence when you feed, to create the healing agent. Your supernatural healing relies on that essence, so even if you feed—" She shuddered and took a breath before continuing. 'Feeding won't help much until your blood plasma regenerates. That will take a day or two."

I thought of Dad. Of Elyssa. I didn't know what in the world Mom was up to or what to make of the strange dreams I'd been having. I knew one thing though: I had to get off my ass and meet Smith. I had to do it now and not waste another minute lollygagging in bed.

"Stacey, please move," I said, despite how good it felt to have her warmth pressed against me. I tried to tell myself it wasn't because she had such nice curves in all the right places and, when she was fully human, kissed really well. Elyssa would break me over her knee if she found out about that kiss.

"But Justin."

"No buts, girl. Move it."

She stood, worry creasing her brow. "Shall I help you?"

I shook my head. "No." My voice sounded gruff so I took another swallow of water and wrestled it down my esophagus as it tried to squirm back out again.

Every muscle felt like a heavy slab of raw pain as I gripped my left leg and swung it off the cot. I repeated the process with my right leg, using my arms to rotate my body with it, biting back the cries of pain best I could.

"Stop it, Justin, stop!" Meghan said, pleading, but not going quite so far as to touch me.

"No!" I pushed my hands against the cot frame, straining my legs as scorching agony exploded in every joint and muscle. The pain grew so blinding I didn't realize at first I was standing up.

Stacey took my arm as I wobbled. Ryland gripped my other, an amused expression on his face.

"You're one stubborn son of a gun," he said, his smile widening.

"More like a bloody fool," Stacey said, pressing her lips into a pout. "I try to care for you, my lamb, but you simply won't listen."

"Believe me," I said, panting with the strain of standing. "I want to lie down and go to sleep so bad right now, it's not even funny. But my dad is going to die if I don't meet Smith, unless Shelton comes up with something. And I don't plan on taking chances." I took a step and almost fell, held up only by Ryland and Stacey. I gritted my teeth and groaned at the pain of their touch against my sore arms. "Just give me a minute."

"Are you talking about Harry Shelton?" Meghan asked, her eyes going hard.

"Yeah. He's kind of a jerk, but besides my mom and you, he's the only sorcerer I know."

"And how do you know him?"

"He tried to capture me and my dad and bring us in for a bounty. Then he ended up helping me rescue my dad from a bunch of rogue vampires who kidnapped him for his blood."

She shook her head slowly as if jiggling her brain around would help her understand the situation. Even I had issues figuring out how in the world my life had come to this point. After a moment, Meghan went into the kitchen and returned with a cup. "Drink this," she said.

I gave it a suspicious look and sniffed. It stank like sewage. "You better not be putting me to sleep or I swear when I wake up I'll hug you and kiss you until you barf."

Her eyes went wide as she leapt back from me, her wand held defensively. She took a breath to calm herself. "It's only a painkiller."

"Woman, you need to calm down. I won't give you spawn cooties, I promise."

Stacey and Ryland both laughed while Meghan narrowed her eyes at both of them. "Don't mock me."

"I'm not," I said. And then I remembered something from the memory Meghan had cleared for me. "That writing on the bloody scrap of paper. What did it mean?"

"I don't know. My mom..." She took a deep breath and closed her eyes for a second. "She was giving it to Alice. The information on the paper was why your mother came by that day. She seemed to think it was very important."

"What did it say?" Stacey asked.

"It was like the last three letters of a word and ended in 'ance' with the numbers four, three, one, one." I grimaced at a fresh onslaught of burning tingles in my legs.

"Maybe code for a spell?" Meghan said.

I tried to shrug and failed miserably. "Maybe you'll remember something else. Heck, maybe I will. I hope so. In the meantime, Meghan, I want to thank you for helping Stacey. Thanks for everything." I held out a trembling hand.

She stared at it for a long moment before swallowing visibly and grasping it. "You're welcome, Justin." She let out a deep breath, her next words coming in a rush. "But there's something you should know about Shelton."

"You know him?"

A scowl turned her pretty face into a mask of anger. "My seeker discovered Shelton also worked with the spawn who devoured my father's soul."

CHAPTER 13

"What?" I would have fallen over if not for the steady grips on both my arms. "What else do you know about him? Is he a con artist?" My dad was alone with him. What if Shelton had really been the one to tag him? What if he was playing us for fools? A wave of fear overcame my anger.

"The connection he had was tenuous, but enough to link him not only to my father's murderer, but to other bad elements in the Overworld community."

"He sounds rather nefarious," Stacey said, quirking an eyebrow. "How interesting."

"'Interesting' isn't the word I'd use," Ryland said.

"I don't know how deep the connection goes," Meghan said. "But be careful."

I groaned. I wasn't sure if I should rush back to Dad or go on to meet Smith. I tried to reach for my cell phone, but the pain in my arms and the bad angle from Stacey and Ryland's grips on my arms made it impossible. "Can you get my phone from my front right pocket?" I asked Stacey.

A mischievous grin spread on her face.

"Come on, this is serious," I said. She seemed abashed which surprised me since I didn't think she ever felt ashamed about much of anything.

She withdrew my phone and handed it to me. I dialed Dad and got his voicemail. I tried him again, not wanting to talk with Shelton. For all I knew he could lie to me about whatever I asked.

Dad answered. "Justin?" Static crackled in the earpiece.

"Hey, Dad, how are things going?"

"Can't hear you well. Bad reception." Or at least that's what I think he said as the connection faded in and out.

I repeated myself in loud slow words.

"Shelton...computer...blocking spell. Going...and feed," I heard through the static.

I almost sighed with relief. "Okay. I'm going to meet Smith soon."

The connection hissed again. "...careful, son."

"I will." I hung up and Stacey tucked my phone back without even trying to feel me up.

"Things okay?" Ryland asked.

I nodded. "Well as they can be, all things considered."

My limbs tingled, feeling a bit numb—the effect of Meghan's painkiller, I hoped, as opposed to worse alternatives. I took a tentative step and wasn't met with another dose of hurt so I took it as a good sign. Meghan handed Ryland car keys.

"It's to my Prius in the driveway," she said. "Please bring it back in once piece."

"You don't have to," I said, although I *really* wanted to ride in a car as opposed to having Stacey give me a piggy-back ride. How humiliating would that be?

"An ecologically-friendly sorcerer," Ryland said with a grin. "A woman after my own heart."

She smiled, almost shyly. "I want to help you and your mother, Justin. I don't want my mother's life to have been lost in vain."

"Maybe you can dig up more on Shelton?" I said.

"Perhaps I could." She paused, seeming to wrangle with a decision. "I'll talk to the seeker I hired. Maybe Ryland could call me later and let me know what you find from Smith."

"Do you know if my mom was working on some hardcore spells with your mom?"

"They did spend many hours together, though most of the time they met with other people. Unfortunately, I wasn't allowed in their meetings."

I got Stacey to release my arm so I could pull the flash drive with Mom's spells from my pocket. "Copy these files and take a look. I need to find out what these spells do, but Shelton said they're missing a lot of variables."

She retrieved her tablet computer and copied them in seconds before handing the flash back to me. "I'll look, but I'm not much at deciphering spell code outside my area of expertise."

"I wouldn't let anyone else know about them," I said, thinking of the murderous intent the spells seemed to have. "Just in case."

She nodded. "I'll be careful."

We left. I managed to hobble to the car and get in without much help from the others since the painkiller seemed to have helped. But I wasn't going to be running marathons anytime soon.

Stacey stared at the car for a long moment, and even longer once Ryland slid in behind the wheel. "Perhaps I'll meet you there," she said.

"You afraid of the big bad wolf, sugah?" Ryland said with an amused grin.

"I'm afraid my delicate nose couldn't handle your stench."

Ryland laughed.

I sighed. "Stacey, please get in the car. I want to talk to you."

She crossed her arms and pursed her lips, all the while giving Ryland a distrusting look, but finally got into the passenger seat. "I suppose I can make a sacrifice for you, my lamb."

Ryland pulled out of the driveway and headed toward Trader Mike's. Very little traffic was on the road at this early hour, but it was already past six and the number of cars would be increasing exponentially before long.

"What was it you wished to discuss, dear?" Stacey asked, turning her body to face me.

"When the hellhounds attacked, did you notice anyone else with them?"

"I had very little time to react and even less time to see beyond the immediate threat. Nightliss warned me first. She told me she happened to be near your home and saw strange people rummaging through your house and some of them were coming our way."

"Nightliss saw this? Did she mention anyone with red hair?"

"She had little enough time to warn me the strange men were trespassing on us. Marmalade and Dots rushed to meet them, and I thought for sure they would scare the men away." She took a deep breath as a large tear rolled down her cheek.

"Is Nightliss okay?"

"I don't know. She dashed away, warning the others and that was the last I saw of her."

"She was warning the other cats?"

"Of course. Why would she not?"

Our conversation reminded me of the unpleasant news I needed to tell her. "I'm afraid a lot of your friends died. I pulled several bodies from the rubble."

More tears rolled down her cheeks. I wanted to hug and comfort her, but my lack of energy and the size of the car made it difficult. "We need to bury them. They do not deserve to be left out as food for crows."

"We'll need help to clear them from the rubble," Ryland said. "And there's no time for that now."

Stacey glared at him. "As if you care a bloody whit about them, wolf. I'm sure you're content to let them rot."

"Stacey, that's not fair," I said. "He helped me dig through the rubble. He killed one of those hounds. Why the hate?"

Ryland gave Stacey a sideways glance. "I'll help you bury your dead, sugah."

"I don't want your filthy paws anywhere near them!"

At that point, I was certain I should have let Stacey meet us at Trader Mike's. This was like the time when a friend's dog had tried to make buddies with a cat, only to have his nose clawed every time he got too close. I wasn't sure if the cat was scared of the dog or simply hated it. If ever there were two types made to hate each other, it had to be lycans and felycans, although I'd hoped their human sides would have won out at some point thanks to, oh, I don't know—brains, maybe?

"Are you certain you're not a female dog?" Ryland said.

"How dare you even insinuate I'm one of those filthy things? I do not eat my own feces."

"Good lord, people." I said, trying to throw my hands into the air but only managing a shrug in my weakened state. "Apparently it was a horrible mistake on my part to think two mostly human people could put aside their differences long enough to help me out." I felt like sniffing in disdain, but was too tired to try. "Ryland, why don't you just go back to Thomas? I'm well away from his property now and obviously not an immediate threat to his daughter."

"I told him I would see you home and I intend to do just that."

"Yeah, except my home was overrun by hellhounds earlier today. I don't have a home right now."

"I also need to return Meghan's car at some point—"

"Then return it. I'll catch a cab."

"I'd be happy to carry you, my lamb," Stacey purred.

"And there is that," I conceded despite the indignity of it all.

Ryland sighed and pulled over, parking next to the curb in front of a row of small shops. "We're here," he said.

I glanced out the window and spotted Trader Mike's two stores down from us. We were near Grant Park, just a little way from East Atlanta Village and not far from where two of my friends, Ash and Nyte lived, although I'd never actually been to their homes. Thinking of them reminded me of school. It also reminded me of football practice and the reason I had to be there. The principal, vice principal, head coach, and probably half the school staff were members of the Quarterback Club which, in my opinion, was the mafia of my high school, Edenfield High. If I didn't want anything to happen to me or my friends, I had to win games for our football team. Otherwise, Principal Perkins had warned me unpleasant things might happen to my "devil-worshipping friends." Apparently, that's what Goths were in his eyes.

In less than an hour and a half, school would be starting. I didn't see how I was going to make it in time. Maybe I could just show up for practice. Not that I'd be able to do much except lay around and groan pitifully.

"I'd like to get to the bottom of this mystery," Ryland was saying. "I can help you."

I didn't answer right away because I wasn't sure what exactly *was* the best thing to do. True, I needed help, and Ryland was a Templar. But I didn't want to suffer through him and Stacey going for each other's throats. On the other hand, I didn't want to make Stacey leave. I considered her a friend and felt obligated to help her recover and bury her dead.

"A wolf is bad enough, Justin," Stacey said. "But a Templar wolf is even worse. How could you trust him?"

"As if he could trust a felycan," Ryland growled.

"You two are going to drive me insane," I said. "I get it, okay? I totally understand the cats versus dogs thing, but I don't have the luxury of watching the train wreck happen. I need steady support I can depend on until I recover, and that means one of you has to go." I looked at Stacey and opened my mouth to speak.

"Surely you can't mean me!" she said. "How could you?"

"I was about to tell you to stay, for crying out loud. Can't you give me two seconds to talk?"

"But you were looking at me after you said—"

I waved away her concerns, or rather flopped my arms around a little bit as I tried. "You're my friend. I know you and, despite your oddities, I trust you." I turned to Ryland. "You, on the other hand, work for Elyssa's dad, a man who obviously wishes I did not exist."

"My loyalty is with the Templars, not one man."

"And I think you're a good person, from the little I know of you. Maybe we can become friends someday." I shrugged. "Stranger things have happened, believe me. But right now I can't have you two getting into pissing matches all the time. I need to know we're on the same page."

"I can tolerate her if she agrees to behave," Ryland said, a lopsided grin on his face.

"So wolfy wishes to play," Stacey said, her eyes narrowing to amber slits, lips sliding up into a playful smirk. "I can ignore his jibes, Justin. If that will help you."

"This is worse," I said. "Now you're both gonna go all passive-aggressive instead."

"I swear to help, not hinder," Ryland said.

"And I will not let his body odor affect my judgment," Stacey said with a sniff.

I had a sudden sense of déjà vu all over again. The universe had a decidedly wicked sense of humor.

And my life depended on it.

CHAPTER 14 - ELYSSA

*E*lyssa turned the Harley down the twisting maze of alleys and backstreets until her GPS told her she was in the right vicinity. Few working street lamps lit the place but her night vision negated the issue. The real problem was she'd been so hungry and tired when she and Justin had left earlier she wasn't sure which of the doors in this wretched foul-smelling alley was the one to Shelton's hidden lair. The GPS on her phone wasn't pinpoint accurate and the tall downtown buildings made getting an exact lock on her position even more difficult. She parked the Harley behind a nearby dumpster and surveyed the line of similar doors before setting out to find the correct one.

She felt like an idiot for losing her focus. Normally she'd memorize an area and be able to find it again, but this time she'd missed crucial details. She almost smacked herself on the forehead the same way Justin did to himself every so often. The way he did it was adorable.

"Good god, did I really just think that?" she said aloud as she dodged trash cans and cardboard boxes, some with bums sleeping inside, and tested each of the metal doors in the back of the old building. This was no good. She pulled out her phone and called Justin. She'd wanted to surprise him but that little plan was down the tubes. The phone went to voicemail after a couple of rings.

She hit redial and got the same result. Worry gripped her chest. Had something happened? Was he okay? Then again, Shelton's hideout was underground. Maybe the signal down there was bad. She had only a couple of bars of reception herself, again, thanks to the tall buildings. The logic still didn't allay her fears so she picked up the pace, jogging and jerking hard on each door. Some opened but revealed completely different interiors than the one she remembered, namely the nasty mattress in the corner.

One of the doors opened in the alleyway across the road from the one she was in. Shelton stepped out followed by David, Justin's dad, their faces visible beneath a dim street light. Relief numbed the worry and she took a deep breath. They closed the door behind them. She wondered if Justin had stayed inside, or if he might already have gone to meet Mr. Smith. The clock on her phone indicated she still had another hour before the store opened but it would make sense to get there early. In any case, it would be a good idea to check in with Shelton and David just to make sure.

Just as she took a breath to call out to them, a shadow detached itself from the mouth of the alley opposite her. She focused her eyes on the figure and realized it was a man dressed in black. A mugger maybe? She wouldn't be surprised. He was in for a shock if he tried to mess with those two. Elyssa tagged along behind, waiting for him to make a move. She slid a silver starlet from her knapsack and pressed her thumb against the power trigger should she need to disable the man quickly.

The starlet looked a great deal like a standard ninja throwing star except for the thick center housing the magic-driven power supply. The tines were thin and needle-like as opposed to razor sharp blades. It was meant to disable, not kill, and the spell on the power supply could be adapted on the fly depending on the target. In this case, a simple electric shock should suffice.

Justin would probably think he'd died and gone to heaven if he knew she had these things. She smiled at the thought and smiled even more when she remembered the Kings and Castles tourney. She'd found herself so caught up in the fun of fighting with foam weapons she'd won the game for his team. Of course, after celebrating the win she'd almost killed him when he slipped up and revealed he was an incubus—demon spawn. The smiled faltered and she felt ashamed. Her parents had trained her to react to danger. To never question her training. If she hadn't known Justin at all before discovering he was a spawn, what would she have done? Would she have killed him? Apprehended him?

He really was a good man. A strong person. But he needed someone with better planning skills to keep him out of trouble and Elyssa was, of course, the proper choice.

The shadowy figure continued to tail Shelton and David for several blocks but never made a move. She was certain by now they were in no danger of anything so mundane as a mugging. But a chilling thought occurred to her. What if the man was following the tracker? What if he was an assassin? She picked up her pace and closed the gap.

The two men reached an Irish pub and stepped inside. Their shadow followed. Elyssa was surprised the place was open so early, but noticed a big sign in the window proclaiming the proper Irish breakfast they served each morning.

She pulled her coat tighter around her, hoping no one would notice the night camo underneath. Even so, they might mistake it for gym attire. She slipped inside and seated herself per the sign up front, just behind several old men at a round table in the center. Elyssa assessed the small, dim interior. She noted Shelton and David sitting at a booth in the far back. The laughing group of elderly men blocked a direct line of sight so she could duck and not be seen if either of her targets turned to look.

A man dressed in dark jeans and a black shirt emerged from the bathroom and approached Shelton's table. Elyssa adjusted her position so she could see the expressions on the faces of the two men. She prepared herself to whip out a starlet and fling it should things go south in a hurry.

"What can I get you to drink, honey?" asked an older female waitress with a southern twang as opposed to an Irish lilt.

Elyssa peeled her attention from her targets for a split second. "Um, a water to start with please? I'm waiting on someone, so I won't order anything else until they get here."

"Sure thing, sweetie." The waitress walked away.

David was talking to the third man, his face a mix of emotions. He didn't look pleased but he didn't look threatened either. Shelton seemed to be slightly concerned but not to the point of danger. Elyssa felt with her senses to see if she could detect anything indicating whether the third man was a man at all or something different. But none of the men at the table gave off vibes suggesting they were anything but normal, and the men at the center table were talking so loud she couldn't filter them out and eavesdrop on the conversation at David and Shelton's table. Just because she couldn't sense anything supernatural about them meant nothing. Nearly every super had a way of masking their presence when they didn't want to be noticed.

A nearby seat creaked. Elyssa jerked from her focus and almost flipped her own chair over backwards with shock. A figure wearing a dark hoodie sat in the chair right next to her. She must really be slipping tonight to let someone sneak up on her.

"I'm sorry, that chair is taken," she said.

"Yes, it is," a sensuous female voice replied.

Elyssa glanced down at the woman's attire—tennis shoes, designer jeans, and the nondescript hoodie. The clothing did not fit her voice. "Who are you?" She tried to see inside the hood, but it was drawn down low and shadow covered the features.

Elegant hands with smooth young skin and an amazing manicure reached for the hood and eased it back. Golden hair the color of summer sunshine spilled out in gentle waves. Rich hazel eyes warmed the gaze of the fair-skinned woman and made Elyssa feel distinctly ugly by comparison. But there was something familiar to this face. To the eyes. The conclusion had her reaching for a sword that wasn't in its usual place.

"I see you know what I am, if not who," the woman said, her voice soothing and smooth as warm honey.

"You're spawn."

"We prefer the term Daemos."

"And a member of House Slade."

"Very good. Bonus points if you know my name." She smiled and cute dimples formed alongside her rosebud lips.

"Yeah, no extra credit for me today," Elyssa said, readying a starlet under the table and wishing she had a sword or even a knife handy. She'd been in such a hurry to get out of the house she hadn't retrieved proper weapons.

"I am Daemas Anae-Vallaena Slade," she said flashing her dimples again. "But everyone just calls me Vallaena." Her accent was complicated, roughly Italian, perhaps, and she rolled her r's. Then again, entities that lived for centuries or more often changed quite a lot from their original state.

Elyssa remembered some bits of the spawn naming convention from school. Daemos for males, Daemas for females, and they considered 'spawn' a derogatory term. Neither Justin nor his dad seemed to mind it, but that was probably because they were no ordinary spawn. "Anae" also had some meaning—something to do with position within a family. Elyssa couldn't remember and it didn't matter.

"You obviously know what I am as well."

"I do indeed, Elyssa, daughter of Thomas, House Borathen."

Elyssa tried to keep surprise from registering on her face or in her eyes. "We don't go by houses."

"Ah, yes, and such a shame to lose sight of one's titles and honors."

"What do you want?"

Vallaena's dimples vanished as a slight frown replaced the smile. "It is such a disappointment humans have lost the ways of good conduct and manners as well." She sighed. "It should be no surprise to me, I suppose, though I try to deal with humans as little as possible."

"Except when you need them for feeding."

"Oh, that requires very little talking, I assure you, and manners of a different kind come into play."

Elyssa didn't want to know. No spawn she knew of had been charged in the death of any humans for feeding, but the Templars weren't omniscient and the spawn were powerful and secretive. God only knew what crimes hid behind this woman's ancient eyes. And they were most definitely ancient eyes.

"Again I ask you, what do you want of me, Daemas Anae-Vallaena of House Slade?"

The other woman's eyes lit with delight and her dimples returned in full force. "Templaras Elyssa, Dhampyras, of House Borathen, I wish to negotiate terms for the surrender of your mate to my protection."

Elyssa's mouth dropped open. "My mate?"

She nodded. "The Castratae known as Justin Case."

"The what?"

"Ah, perhaps you were not taught proper Daemos stratifications."

"You mean your caste system?"

Vallaena shook her head. "They are not castes, simply designations indicating the import of one's title. I am Anae or first order of House Slade. Only the Paetros or Maedras are above me in position, and there are only three other Anae in my house."

"And what's Castratae?" It didn't sound good whatever it was. The thought of eunuchs came to mind thanks to its similarity to "castrate".

"It is unfortunate your mate is considered such, but surely it is his father's fault." She glanced across the room as Shelton and David spoke to the strange man. "It means 'outcast'. It means you have no house and are considered the lowest of the low."

"Yeah, definitely a caste system. You should Google it."

"I mean it as no insult to you, Templaras."

Elyssa's phone rang. She pulled it out and saw it was Justin. Vallaena touched her hand. "Can you return his call in a few minutes? I would ask you to hear me out first."

Elyssa had to admit one thing. Vallaena was nothing if not polite. But her designation as Anae meant this woman knew how to survive spawn politics. That meant she was extremely dangerous and far more experienced than Elyssa's handful of years. And speaking to Justin in front of this woman would be a terrible idea. Any little thing Elyssa said could give away too much. She slid the phone back into her pocket. "Who's the man speaking with David?"

"Such information is beyond the confines of our discussion, I'm afraid."

"Is he with you?"

Vallaena shook her head. "In some ways, but not in others."

As if that made any sense. "Is he spawn?"

A patient smile drew up the corners of the other woman's face. "As I said, details of such a nature are beyond the confines of our conversation. I would ask we return to the subject at hand. As first mate of Justin, I would do you the honor of asking permission and your help in securing him as my ward. I can assure you he would be well protected."

"From what? The way I understand it he needs protection from your kind. And I can tell you right now in no uncertain terms I will never betray him to you." She also wanted to add a few other less polite terms but the inquisitive Templar part of her brain wanted to squeeze the woman for more information.

"This would be no betrayal, Elyssa. You would deliver him to safety from those who wish him harm. Dark forces gather and it is in our best interests to shield him."

Elyssa folded her arms. "Now you're just being mysterious. I need something concrete to go on. For all I know you just want to brainwash him while he's still new to the community. Or maybe you want to get rid of him. I know how your kind is about inter-species breeding."

Vallaena shuddered delicately and pursed her lips as if she'd just tasted a lemon. "If you knew anything about our inner politics, you would know how distasteful it is to even speak with Castratae. I believe, however, this situation can be redeemed and your mate's status can be raised a notch. Perhaps even to Denae should he work hard to earn it."

It was Elyssa's turn to shudder. "Not to be impolite, but you people are disgusting and your politics belong to the dustbin of history. I won't do anything to help you. In fact, I'll do everything I can to keep Justin out of your hands."

"What if we were to offer rescission?"

"Of what?"

"The death mark upon that." She nodded toward David, a look of revulsion on her beautiful features.

"You're the ones who put out the hit?"

"I did not, no. Nor do I know who did or believe it originated from our house. But we are very good at finding information. We could find

the party responsible and arrange terms for a rescission of the contract."
She raised an eyebrow. "What do you say now?"

"Still no."

Vallaena sighed and gave a sad shake of her head. Men at the center
table had been eyeing her for some time now though most of them
looked well past their prime years, not to mention overweight and out
of shape. One took out a comb and touched up his comb-over, as if it
did any good. But Vallaena's beauty trapped their gazes, captivating
them like flies in a glue trap. A column in the middle of the room kept
David and Shelton from seeing her, and Elyssa was certain the woman
purposefully arranged it just so.

"Is there anything I can say to change your mind?" the other woman
asked.

A frown tugged at Elyssa's face. "Tell me why he's in danger. I want
specifics. If you're so concerned about his well-being, help me protect
him." It seemed unlikely the woman had specific dangers in mind and
was hoping to scare her into cooperation.

"I wish I could give you specifics but our information is rather nebulous at this point."

"Nebulous information somehow indicating Justin is in danger?"

A hint of uncertainty crossed Vallaena's face. Elyssa wasn't sure if the
woman meant to do it or if the question really had dislodged a nugget of
honest emotion.

"He is in danger. I'm sure of it."

Elyssa's senses prickled. She looked up in time to meet David's
burning glare from only a few feet away. He bared his teeth and
clenched his fists as he stared at Vallaena. The other woman followed
Elyssa's gaze.

She sighed. "I think this will be rather unpleasant."

CHAPTER 15

*S*tacey woke me with a gentle nudge. "I think your Mr. Smith is here."

My eyelids stuck together, or maybe it was that I craved sleep so badly they just didn't want to open. But the urgency of contacting Mr. Smith pried them open and gave me enough energy to pull myself into a sitting position in the back seat of the car. I didn't remember going to sleep. The last thing I remembered was Stacey leaving the vehicle to go for a walk, and Ryland doing the same thing shortly thereafter.

They seemed to be competing for the gold star of good behavior, but I wasn't handing out any gold stars or smiley faces until my dad was safe from assassination. At that point they could let the fur fly for all I cared and beat each other silly. I sat up, massaging the god-awful cramp in my neck which just wouldn't go away. My super-recuperative abilities could take care of such things in a hurry. I hoped my blood regenerated fast so I didn't have to put up with feeling like crap for much longer.

The store wasn't open yet, but a medium-sized guy with pale skin and dark brown hair was sitting on a bench outside, a *Popular Magic* magazine open in his hands. I rubbed my eyes and looked again, because I'd never heard of this particular magazine. My eyes wandered instead to Stacey. She'd cleaned up and was wearing black yoga pants and a long-sleeve pink workout shirt which hugged her every curve. Ryland wasn't in the car. I noticed him across the road, leaning against a building, his eyes locked on Stacey. He caught my gaze and looked away.

"Where'd you get new clothes?" I asked Stacey.

"Our gym is nearby, lamb, so I ran over and cleaned up. I rent a permanent locker there."

"How 'bout you put your hotness to work and go find out if that's our Mr. Smith."

She beamed, her face flushing. "I would be delighted." She turned and left without even trying to squeeze something sexual from my compliment.

Yep, she was definitely going for a gold star.

Ryland strolled across the road and put his head in the car window. "Least that woman has some use."

"You think she's cute, don't you?"

He snorted and scratched one of his mutton chops. "Yeah, right." His eyes drifted to Stacey as she sauntered her way toward Smith, hips swaying, arms swinging.

I tore my eyes off her rear end and noticed Ryland was still looking at her as she reached Smith and started talking with him. Smith gawked at her chest, his big nose and thick glasses joining forces to put the 'n' in 'nerd'.

"Kid ain't got a chance," Ryland said.

He might be a wolf at heart, but even he couldn't deny Stacey was a spectacular-looking woman.

I pulled myself to the door and reached for the handle. Even with the door unlatched, my muscles felt like useless lead weights. "Give me a hand?" I asked Ryland.

He walked around, opened the door, and hauled me out with one of his muscular arms. I was jealous of his good health. My formerly puny arms had sprouted muscle over the past few weeks, but it was all decorative at the moment. At least the pain hadn't returned. I limped toward Smith under my own power, pulling out my phone and checking it on the way. My heart raced when I saw a missed call from Elyssa. I must have been conked out when she called.

Redialing her sent me to voicemail after five rings. I hoped she was okay. She had to be fine. Her father's Templar compound was probably one of the safest places to be. I doubted she would see much active duty for a while after my little encounter with Thomas. I tucked my phone away as I reached Smith's bench and took a seat next to him.

"—and a protein shake will give you extra energy," Stacey was saying. "Within a few months I think you could definitely put on some muscle."

"Giving workout advice?" I said with a smile. It was probably the last thing I'd expected her to be talking about.

"This is my friend, Justin," Stacey said.

Smith tore his eyes off Stacey and glanced at me. "Oh, hi."

"TP sent me," I said.

He flinched, looking at me with wide eyes. "TP Shelton?"

I nodded.

"I haven't heard from him in—hey did you send her over here to distract me?"

"Did it work?"

"Of course it worked. What straight male wouldn't fall into those beautiful amber eyes and feel his heart beat a little faster at the sound of that musical voice?"

Stacey's fluttered her long eyelashes. "Oh, do go on, Mr. Smith."

He took her hand and kissed it. "My dear, I cannot believe they would so callously use such an angel."

"Who are you?" I asked. "The Casanova of the nerd community?"

"He's so charming," Stacey said with an appreciative sigh.

Smith winked at her before turning back to me. "So, TP sent you. What does he want?"

"Actually, I'm the one in need of help."

He held up a hand. "Best if you don't say anything else just yet." At that moment, the storekeeper unlocked the front door and flipped over the 'Open' sign. "Let me grab my comic." Smith vanished inside.

"I like him," Stacey said with a purr.

"Figures, all it would take are a few pretty words in that empty head to impress you," Ryland said.

Her eyes widened. "How rude."

I glared at Ryland but he already looked abashed.

"Sorry. I'm kind of grumpy this morning."

"Maybe you should go home and clean up. I'll bet Thomas is wondering where you are."

"I'm good," he said, giving one armpit an experimental sniff.

Stacey wrinkled her nose. "Really, now, that's just disgusting."

"I'm sensing conflict again," I said, feeling more like an arbitrator than a teenager who was going to be late for school.

Several minutes passed and I wondered if maybe Smith had scooted out the back door. Panic shoveled a fresh load of worry into my heart and I realized I'd made a horrible mistake by not asking Ryland to cover the exits.

Ryland seemed to notice something was wrong, probably thanks to the sweat beading on my forehead as I tried to think of what to do next. "He's still in there, if that's what you're worried about."

"You see him?"

He nodded. "He's buying a comic now."

I sighed in relief and wiped my forehead. Stacey wandered a few doors down from us and was looking with interest at a dress shop displaying steampunk outfits and dresses with designs straight out of the Victorian Era. Seeing as how she was born around that time, it probably made her feel nostalgic.

"Can you keep an eye on Smith?" I asked Ryland.

"Sure thing."

I pushed myself up and hobbled down to Stacey. A black dress with laces, frills, and all sorts of accessories was on display in the window. "You like it?"

"It reminds me of home," she said. "Those dresses were rather uncomfortable in comparison to what passes for a dress code these days, but it's a bloody shame everything is so informal." She smiled at me. "I do so miss the days when everyone dressed up for a proper to-do."

"Like a party?"

"Oh yes. Going to a ball was one of my favorite things in the world."

"I hardly know anything about your past. I'd like to hear about your younger years."

Her smile faded. "My childhood doesn't make for a wonderful story, Justin. In fact it's rather grim."

"So you'd rather not talk about it?"

She took my hand in hers. "I believe I would tell you. If only because you are the closest thing to a true friend I have in this lonely world."

"Don't talk like that. Maybe if you play nice, you can be friends with Shelton and Ryland." *Hey, it could happen.*

A giggle burst from her lips. "You're such the optimist, dear. If the world worked the way you see it, we'd be living in a fairy tale."

"Jeez, I'm not that delusional am I?"

"No, my lamb, just idealistic."

I glanced back at Ryland. Smith had just walked out of the store. I turned to Stacey again. "Are you trying not to get along with Ryland? It seems like you two keep saying stuff just to annoy each other. It's almost like you want him to hate you and vice versa."

Stacey looked at Ryland. "Wolves and felines do not mix. I've had nothing but trouble with wolf packs and I don't expect that to change."

"He's not with a pack."

"Ah, a lone wolf. They are a rare type, but the instincts are still there."

"Have you ever considered you two might be more alike than you think?"

Her eyebrows rose. "Another fairy tale?"

"You're a loner. You have your companions, but none of them are your true equal. Ryland's a loner too. From the way his story sounds, he's not much for pack politics."

"I prefer to determine my own fate inasmuch as it is under my control."

"He's kind of the same," I said, hoping I wasn't completely misjudging a man I'd only just met. Sure, he was with the Templars, but the story of him leaving his pack instead of taking leadership made me think he wasn't much for politics either. Of course the Templars might be consumed by rules and simpering politicians for all I knew.

"I know you just want me to be friends with him, Justin. You're a sweet person—"

"Ugh, don't call me sweet, girl. You want to completely ruin my dangerous rep?"

She smiled and took a deep breath. "For you I will try."

"To be friends with him?"

"To be civil. Please do not expect more than I can deliver, my knight in shining armor."

"That's all I'm asking, Stace. I'll ask him to be more civil too. The comment about you having an empty head was totally uncalled for. You may be pretty, but you're no ditz. In fact, I think you're a lot smarter than you let on sometimes."

Her mouth fell open and she drew in a delighted breath. "You know just how to make a woman feel good, you dear thing."

"Yeah, I'm a real charmer. Come on." With that, I made my way back toward Smith.

"I'm having a dilemma," Smith said as he dithered outside the comic book store.

"Why?" I asked.

"I'm sure Shelton told you I'm something of a conspiracy hound. And I don't usually take strangers to my house."

"How about bags over our heads or blindfolds?"

He laughed. "Are you kidding? People would freak out if they saw me leading a group of people with bags over their heads, and I don't doubt for a second your friends here could sniff out the route even blindfolded."

"So what do you suggest?"

"Let's grab some coffee down the block. You tell me what's going on and we'll go from there."

We walked down the street to Java Hippo and grabbed an outside seat next to a kerosene heater. I noted with a bit of nervousness we weren't too far from the warehouse-styled lofts the rogue vampires who'd kidnapped my father called home. Stacey sat across the table from Smith and I sat next to him while Ryland remained standing and leaned against the black metal railing bordering the dining area. A young girl with tattoos on her arms and a green bandana on her head took our order.

"Do you have a computer with you?" I asked.

Smith nodded and pulled a tablet out of his backpack with a flat icon in the shape of an orange emblazoned on the back. A stem with a single green leaf protruded atop the orange, and a strip of the peel was gone. It looked a lot like the one Meghan had been using, and reminded me of the familiar Apple logo. Suppressing a stream of questions about his odd tablet, I handed him the flash drive and waited for him to retrieve the spells on it. He had a spell program like Shelton's so it displayed the spell script pretty much like it had on Shelton's computer. Smith blew out a whistle.

"Wow. Who wrote this?"

"My mom, I think."

He gave me a look from the corner of his eye. "I suppose I should have found out a little more during the intro stage but it's never too late to be polite. Who exactly is your mother?"

I hesitated, unsure how much I should tell him. Then again, this guy seemed pretty tight-lipped. "Alice Conroy."

His mouth dropped open. "It's you."

I nodded. "Uh, yeah, it's me all right."

"You and your father have some hefty bounties on your heads."

"Tell me something I don't know."

"There would probably be a lot to tell."

I chuckled. "I'm sure. Can you reverse engineer this code?"

He touched two fingers to one of the question marks where a rune should have been and spread the fingers apart. The view expanded into a mind-numbing array of gibberish. He scrolled through it for a few minutes, muttering to himself. "This thing doesn't play around." He looked at me. "This spell is designed to kill en masse. It would require a hell of a lot of power and some DNA from the affected parties, so it wouldn't be easy by any means." He shook his head. "But it could wipe out an entire species."

"Do you mean supernatural species?"

He scrolled back and forth through the lines of code for several more minutes before answering. "If I had to guess, I'd say these missing runes relate to the traits of a specific super." He closed one spell, opened another. Checked it, and moved to another spell. "Each one of these is aimed at taking out a different type."

"Which ones?"

He shrugged. "I won't know without figuring out the missing runes. Every super has a weakness so you'd have to supply a rune exploiting the weakness."

I slumped, pressing a hand to my forehead as a wave of depression settled into me. "Just when I think things can't get worse, I find out my mom wants to commit genocide."

"I'm sorry. I wish I could say different." Smith pursed his lips. "I should probably reverse-engineer the thing before we jump to conclusions though."

A female voice from behind me interrupted my pity party. "Hey bro, sorry to bother you but I need some cash."

Stacey's eyes shot wide and a hiss escaped her lips. Ryland shot up from his casual position against the fence, his eyes locked onto something behind me.

I turned and looked into the eyes of a girl I knew. Not just a girl, a vampire. And not just any vampire, but one who'd not only helped kidnap my dad but tried to kill me and Elyssa.

CHAPTER 16

Felicia the geek-chic vampire sucked in a breath the second she saw my face. Her eyes expanded until the whites of her eyes were huge against crimson irises. She turned to run but Ryland had her almost at the same time Stacey vaulted over the table and twisted the vampire's arms behind her back.

"What the hell are you doing to my sister?" Smith said once he turned around enough to see what was going on.

"Felicia is your sister?" I asked, shock nailing me in the stomach.

His face crumpled when he saw the panicked expression on Felicia's face. "Oh crap, sis. Please tell me you didn't do something even more stupid than going vampire."

"It wasn't my fault!" she said, wriggling uselessly against Ryland and Stacey. "Maximus made me do it."

The waitress came out of the restaurant with our coffee, saw Felicia. Instead of looking alarmed, she groaned. "Felicia, who'd you piss off now?"

I gave Smith a look. "Does your sister know where you live?"

"Do you think I'm stupid?" he said. "My little sister is about as trustworthy as a crack addict."

"I heard that," Felicia said.

"I'm sure you did." Smith turned to me. "Mind telling me what she did?"

I glanced at the time. Making school today was going to be impossible. I was too weak for football practice anyway. "I hope you have some time."

"Plenty."

Stacey and Ryland pinned Felicia between them on the bench opposite of me and Smith. She wriggled and squirmed, but she might as well have been boxed in by concrete.

"Just keep still you bloody little fool," Stacey said when Felicia tried to bite her, fangs extended.

"Or I might show you what biting really is," Ryland said from the other side, his eyes flashing wickedly, upper and lower canines lengthening with dark menace.

Felicia gulped and slumped, defeated.

With her settled down, I told Smith all about his sister's complicity in my dad's kidnapping, though I started more or less from the beginning. I told him how Shelton tried to bag us in an alleyway so he could claim the bounty only to have Felicia and a group of vampires jump us and make off with my dad. How me and Elyssa, Stacey and Shelton had rescued him, fought off a horde of vamplings, and captured a few vampires for bounty to the Red Syndicate, the ruling body of the vampires. He looked absolutely incredulous by the end of the story.

"I always knew TP was an ass, but he really went off the deep end with the bounty hunters stuff." Smith turned to Felicia. "And you! Kidnapping is bad enough, but who in the hell is creating vamplings? Maximus? Does that poser have a clue what he's doing?"

"He's got plans, Adam." Her brow furrowed with zealous sincerity. "He wants to help all of us and offer immortality to anyone who deserves it."

Smith pounded the table. "Dammit, you stupid girl." He seemed ready to lay into her with a sermon, instead pulling off his glasses and pinching the bridge of his nose. "What do you plan to do with her?"

Felicia's surprised gaze shifted to me, though she kept her mouth shut.

I raised an eyebrow. I really hadn't planned on doing anything with her even if she was a vicious little brat who'd sicced a bunch of vamplings on me and Elyssa. It wasn't like I could turn her in to the Templars. I didn't know much of anything about the supernatural community either. But maybe I could use her to get Smith to trust me more.

"I'd be happy to leave her with you once we're done here."

Smith shook his head. "I don't want anything to do with her anymore, especially after hearing what you've told me."

"How can you say that?" Felicia asked, tears brimming in her eyes. "I'm your sister."

Smith clenched his teeth and glared at her, a thousand unspoken words passing between them. I had no idea what their history was like, but it couldn't be good. He took a deep breath and seemed to calm before looking at me. "I feel as though I owe you something for the ordeal my sister put you through."

I almost blurted back that he didn't owe me a thing for the bad behavior of his sibling, but I really wanted his help. Maybe he would have helped me anyway, but a little insurance couldn't hurt. "If you can help Shelton remove the tracker from my dad and figure out these runes, that would totally rock."

"You got it." He looked at Felicia for a long moment. "Where is the Templar you mentioned? Can she maybe lock up my sister for safe-keeping?"

Felicia lunged across the table at him fangs bared and hissing, barely making it halfway before Ryland and Stacey jerked her back. "Don't you dare, Adam. I swear to god I'll kill you if you make them lock me up again."

He threw his hands up in the air. "Make them? Make them? I had nothing to do with the last time. You did that all on your own. But Maximus has brainwashed you to the point you don't even think for yourself anymore. It'd be doing you a favor."

Now that Smith mentioned it, I'd love for Elyssa to toss Felicia in Templar prison complete with a pretty orange jumpsuit. Unfortunately, I wasn't sure when I'd see Elyssa again after the disastrous meeting with her father. Just thinking about it sent my heart plunging to the bottom of Depression Bay. It made me want to hurt somebody. And if I'd had my strength right then, the 'somebody' would have been Felicia. On the other hand, Ryland could probably take her in, though I hadn't told Smith the werewolf was a Templar.

"We can take her with us to Shelton's hideout. I'm sure there's something we can do to hold her in the meantime."

Smith nodded and pulled out what looked like a brass smartphone. Once I looked at it closer, I realized it was a regular smartphone modified with a steampunk theme.

"Shelton told me you don't use a cell phone or email," I said.

Smith chuckled. "I don't have any one phone number or email address. It took me a long time, but I wrote a spell allowing this device to spoof other phones at random."

"So the number you use changes each time," I said. "Wow, now that's cool."

"More like freaky," Felicia said. "In case you didn't know, my brother is a total nut-job who thinks there's a conspiracy behind everything. He even thinks someone in the Conclave killed our—"

"Shut it, Felicia," Smith said, smacking the flat of his palm on the table.

"What's the matter?" she said in a whiny mocking voice. "Don't want them to know how crazy you are?"

He took a deep breath and calmed himself. "I may be a conspiracy nut, but I'm not crazy."

I looked at Felicia. "Do yourself a favor and stop trying to tick off your brother. Otherwise I may ask Stacey or Ryland to knock you out."

"I might even do it myself," Smith grumbled.

I looked around and noticed more people coming into the restaurant. It was time to get a move-on. "We should go to Shelton's now."

Smith nodded. "Meet me at your car. I need to grab a few things from my place."

"How in the world are we going to fit everyone into the back of that sodding Prius?" Stacey asked.

Good question.

We made our way out of the restaurant, Stacey and Ryland pressing Felicia from each side. Felicia, for her part, looked defeated and slumped visibly between them. Even if she did break free, either of those two could catch her in an instant, and considering how much wolves and panthers relish the hunt, the takedown would probably get nasty.

"Should I follow Smith?" Ryland asked me as the sorcerer split off from us and went between two shops.

I shook my head. "No. Let the man have his privacy. Besides, if his hideout is anything like Shelton's we couldn't get in without a magic wand anyway."

"It would still be a good idea to know where it is," Stacey said.

I gave the two of them a look. "You two just agreed on something? Amazing."

Ryland grinned at Stacey.

She blushed and gave me a cross look. "Really, my lamb, must you ruin things with such a crude observation?"

Felicia, for her part, looked completely out of it. Her head was down, pigtails flopping on the sides. With the short plaid skirt, knee-high socks, and the geek glasses, she looked like a Catholic school girl who'd gotten busted for hacking computers. I wondered why she wasn't cold considering it wasn't much above freezing at the moment, but neither Stacey nor Ryland seemed all that affected by the weather, either. Maybe I'd been as blissfully and supernaturally unaware of the cold before donating most of my blood to Stacey.

At least I wasn't dragging like before. My body still felt loaded down with bricks but Meghan's pain-killing tea was still doing the trick.

We reached the car. Ryland had to drive—I didn't trust myself behind the wheel—and we needed someone strong in the backseat with Felicia. That left Stacey. She pushed the vampire into the backseat from one side while I climbed in on the other, sandwiching her between the two of us. Felicia didn't know I was in a weakened state, so hopefully she wouldn't try anything.

I closed the door and leaned back, my eyes wanting to close again and not open for a good eight hours or so.

"I'm sorry," Felicia said.

I opened my eyes and looked at her. "Kind of late for apologies."

"I know." She hung her head and bit her lower lip. "You just don't know how things are under the Red Syndicate. They rule everyone with an iron fist, and all the initiates like me are treated like dirt. Maximus makes us feel important. He wants to help people, not enslave them like the masters do."

"The masters?"

"Yeah, the vampire governors. They make rules and live like kings while the rest of us have to do whatever they tell us. It's really unfair."

"Maybe you should have thought of that before becoming a vampire."

"Maximus saved me. I was in a really bad place in my life. He gave me a purpose and a family."

Ugh. I wasn't having any of this crap. Since when did a vampire help anyone? Granted, I only knew what I'd seen in the movies, but this girl was full of excuses. "I'll bet your brother and parents were happy to find out about your new family."

She sniffled and a tear trickled down her cheek. "My parents are dead."

I congratulated myself on not feeling bad for making a girl cry. On the other hand, I felt bad about her parents if it was true. Of course, all I had to do was ask Smith when he got back.

"I'm sorry."

"Why do you think Adam is so loony? He thinks it was a conspiracy reaching all the way up to the Overworld Conclave." A bitter laugh escaped her lips. "As if those idiots could agree on anything, much less conspire to kill a couple of no-name people at the bottom of the rung."

"Why aren't you a sorceress?" I asked. "Obviously your parents were part of the arcane community seeing as how your brother practices magic."

She pulled off her glasses and wiped red-rimmed eyes. "That's just it. My dad was a big-wig in the magic community but my mom was just a nom. Adam got all the abilities in our family." She sniffed and wiped her nose. "I was just plain old me. A nom."

Stacey handed Felicia a tissue. "That's no reason to nick somebody's father, dear."

Felicia blew her nose loudly into the tissue. "I know, I know. I didn't want to do it, but Maximus told us how evil spawn are and how we'd be doing everyone a big favor by keeping one prisoner."

I narrowed my eyes. "Did Maximus put the bounty on my dad or me?"

She shook her head. "No. He didn't even know about you two until Mortimer found the bounty online and showed it to him. Maximus was certain about spawn blood being the answer to his issues."

Her answer brought up another thought which promptly kicked me in the guts. "Those vamplings...my god, they were people. He killed those people trying to turn them and you and the others helped him. How can you live with yourself?"

Her eyes widened to the point where I thought they'd fall out. "What do you mean he killed them? He didn't kill anyone! He said they died because they were too weak to undergo the change. He gave them a choice."

"Don't give me that crap. You said he knew about his problem with turning people. His attempts to make them into vampires killed them and created those zombie things. That makes it his responsibility."

"But they all went willingly! Maximus is the one who turned me and Mortimer and several others. He said he needed your dad's blood to be more potent so the weak people could survive as well. He wants immortality available to everyone, not just the privileged few."

I shook my head unable to make sense of it. It wasn't like I knew a damned thing about vampires or how turning worked. Either Maximus was lying to them, or Felicia was willing to protect him at all costs. Probably both.

"Ain't no way Maximus turned you if he made vamplings," Ryland said. "You either can or you can't, and it sounds like he can't."

"How would you know?"

"I'm a Templar."

Felicia's round eyes grew wider though her face couldn't get any paler, being a vampire and all. "Are you going to kill me?" Her voice was a small frightened whisper.

Ryland showed her his teeth. His silvery eyes gleamed with the promise of things worse than death.

"Ooh," Stacey murmured, her face full of something like awe. She shook her head when she noticed what she was doing and blushed like a school girl.

Either the werewolf didn't notice, or he pretended not to. "Vampire, I know all about vampiric turning. Only one of potent blood and focus can enable the virus to make the change happen. Anyone lacking either will unleash a vampling infected with a contagion the likes of which you've never seen."

"Then how did he change me?"

"Give me your finger, girl."

"Are you going to bite it off?"

He grimaced and shook his head. "You kidding me? Vampires taste as bad as hellhounds."

Her lower lip quivered but she held out a pale finger to him. He pricked it with a silver dagger, pulled from under his ninja camo. She shrieked at the unexpected blade, but he held her finger fast and touched a bit of parchment paper to the dark black blood welling on the tip. Felicia sucked on her finger when he let go.

"Why does silver hurt so bad?"

Ryland ignored her as he mumbled something, pulled a lighter from his pocket and set the paper ablaze. It burst into a white flame, the paper vanishing instantly and leaving strange symbols hovering in the air which faded to nothing within a few seconds.

"What was that about?" I asked, clearing the afterimage of the brilliant flash from my eyes by squeezing them shut.

He tucked the lighter away. "It's a blood test. Her blood is clean of infection and points to a vampire of just over two centuries old as her blood master."

"Nobody in the uprising is that old," she said. "Maximus is just over a hundred and fifty."

"And that's way too young to be a blood master." Ryland wrinkled his forehead. "Hell, two-hundred is too young, so whoever did it must have some special blood, or been turned by one of the ancient masters."

Felicia knitted her eyebrows. "Maximus claims he was turned by an ancient master."

Ryland snorted. "Yeah, well he claims a lot of stuff, this Maximus idiot. And he's obviously lying. I'll bet he has someone there who's turning people for him. People he wants to live through the process anyway."

"When you say blood master, does it mean that vampire can control you?" I asked.

"It depends. From what they taught us at the Academy, the old masters have a lot of control over their brood. How much control is anyone's guess."

The passenger door opened and Smith climbed in. He saw Felicia's red-rimmed eyes. "Don't fall for the teary-eyed act. God knows I gave her enough money before figuring out that little game of hers."

Felicia gasped. "I'm your sister. Why would you say such mean things about me, especially to strangers?"

Smith laughed. "Considering your reputation and what you did to them, I don't see how their opinion of you could be any lower."

Ryland pulled into traffic and headed for Shelton's. He sniffed the air through his open window, his eyes casting about, ever watchful. The sun just barely lit the sky on the horizon, but gray clouds threatened to make it a gloomier day.

That's when they came from the shadows. A lot of them.

Vampires.

CHAPTER 17 - ELYSSA

*E*lyssa had been expecting a fight. Maybe even a couple of deaths resulting from the fight. After all, David had looked ready to tear off Vallaena's head. Instead, the man he and Shelton had been speaking with came over and threw himself between them, speaking urgently in a language Elyssa didn't understand. David's coiled muscles relaxed ever so slightly, but the look on his face betrayed the violence lurking behind his thin façade. He nodded and followed the man back to the other table.

"If you will excuse me," Vallaena said, and followed him.

Elyssa allowed her breathing to return to normal. If a fight had broken out, she wasn't sure what she would have done. David was Justin's father, but as a Templar she couldn't go around cutting up other spawn because of a family feud. She also desperately wanted to find out who the mystery man was.

"Well, lookie who's here," Shelton said, coming over a few minutes after Vallaena left her sitting there pondering her thoughts and wondering what to do next.

"Have a seat, Shelton," Elyssa said, gesturing to a chair across from her. "I think we need to have a little conversation."

"Oh, is the weather really nice?"

"Don't play coy." She leaned across the table as he dropped into a chair. "Who's the man you and David were talking to?"

Shelton waved his hands palms out. "Hey, you want to get me hurt? You'll have to ask those two. I ain't stepping hip deep into that pile of trouble."

"The three of you were chatting away for quite a while before David came over. I want to know what's going on."

Shelton waved the waitress over and ordered another coffee. "You want anything?"

Elyssa shook her head. "No. And stop avoiding the questions."

After the waitress left, Shelton rested his arms on the table and grinned. "How 'bout you tell me what you and Rapunzel were talking about over here?"

Elyssa leaned back and crossed her arms. "It doesn't concern you."

Shelton's smile widened. "Well, how about that? You got your business, and I got mine. If David tells you, then it's his decision."

A dull ache rose in her temples and Elyssa realized she was clenching her teeth and her fists against the desire to leap across the table and hammer the truth out of Shelton. Justin had been right not to trust the man. She got up and walked across the room to the original table where Shelton had been sitting. David, Vallaena, and the other man occupied it now.

She pulled up a chair and sat down while the others watched her.

"I think it just as well she knows," Vallaena said to the mystery man. "She's just as instrumental as the others." The man turned and repeated what she'd said to David.

David's face was already red but he spoke to the man. "You don't even know the full truth of it. It's just a fairy tale."

Again, the mystery man repeated the words to Vallaena.

She shook her head. "It may well be, but if we don't find out more, we won't be prepared."

"What in the world is this about?" Elyssa said. "This has to be the dumbest thing I've ever seen. Are you not speaking to David because he's Castratae and you're Anae?"

Vallaena raised an eyebrow. "Perceptive, Templaras. I must use an intermediary lest I soil my honor."

Elyssa looked at the third man, looking for some hint as to what he might be. "Is he Daemos?"

"Yes, and a Denae. He is not of House Slade, however, and is not a person of interest to you or anybody else." Vallaena sighed. "Young curiosity is so troublesome. Tell him who you are, Denae."

"I am Daemos Denae-Nyles Kalamander. I am a ward of Daemas Anae-Vallaena Slade sent here by my father to strengthen the blood of our two houses and to do the bidding of all my ward commands me."

"I thought you told me he wasn't your man," Elyssa said, her tone accusing.

"You asked if he was with me, not if he was my man."

"And you interpreted the meaning of my words however you saw fit. Thanks for reminding me why people never trust spawn."

Nyles paled. "She has insulted you, Anae. Shall I—"

Vallaena held up a hand. "She is not of our kind, Denae, and not to be held to our standards." Her dimples appeared alongside a small grin. "Since I determined you would probably be unwilling to help bring Justin under my protection, I thought it wise to ask his father as well."

"And I told her no way in hell," David said, his eyes on Elyssa. "Knowing her, she's probably got a dozen other irons in the fire as well." He leaned back in his chair. "She also didn't tell you I met with Nyles because he claimed to have information about my wife Alice. Apparently it was a lure to draw me into this meeting."

Elyssa pshawed. "My father always told me to take the number of overt actions by a spawn, multiply it by a hundred, and the answer would be a closer estimate to the truth."

"Every action is a thread, Templaras," Vallaena said. "Every reaction and decision along the thread is another branch to be explored, another avenue to take. I know people who believe the direct path to a goal is the shortest, but my years of life have taught me a great deal. If the direct path is through stone, why not ask a mason to chip it away?"

"Or dynamite to annihilate it," David said, looking at Nyles.

"Why are you convinced Justin is in danger?" Elyssa asked. "Give me some reason besides the lines you were feeding me back at the table."

"It's nonsense," David said. "My dear sister believes there's a conspiracy—"

"Not a conspiracy, a foreseeance," Vallaena said, her eyes burning bright. "A possible interpretation of a future to come."

David gave her a shocked look which she returned while Nyles blanched.

Vallaena groaned and actually looked as if she might have just thrown up in her mouth. "I suppose I must do a cleansing after this conversation." She made a circular motion over her heart with her left hand and pressed the palm against her chest.

"Because you accidentally talked directly to your brother?" Elyssa wanted to slap them both silly. "Drop the stupid act and join this century, people." Before Vallaena could launch into another culture lesson, Elyssa spoke. "You said a 'foreseeance'. Do you really believe in those things?"

The other woman brushed a golden lock from her eyes and leaned forward. "No. Or at least not most of them. But this one may be coming true before our very eyes."

"Do you have a copy?"

"No. I don't even know the full text."

"You must be kidding me." Elyssa snorted. "All this fuss and you don't even know the full text?"

"Elements in the Conclave have kept this secret for nearly two decades. It was only by luck I learned of it."

Elyssa felt the urge to get up and walk away. This was a complete waste of time. Foreseeance was the official term for a prophecy, probably to make such a fantastical thing sound more realistic. In the old days, Templars had collected and researched prophecies, back before the Templar Scholars left the order because they abhorred the violent methods of the Templar Knights. It was all part of a plan to keep catastrophic disasters from happening. But according to history class, they hadn't stopped a thing because none of the prophecies came true.

And now, a very powerful spawn seemed convinced one of them was coming true. And that Elyssa's boyfriend was involved. Vallaena wasn't just some homeless guy with a cardboard placard warning everyone about the end of the world. She was someone who could make things happen. What if she decided to kidnap Justin since neither Elyssa nor David would give Vallaena permission to take him as a ward?

Instead of walking away, Elyssa needed to point this dangerous missile in another direction. Convince her someone else was involved

"Tell me what you know."

Vallaena looked at David. He nodded.

"Very well. The foreseeance speaks of a half-damned who must defend against those acting in the name of a dead prophet. This youth will make unlikely alliances and tame the hearts of natural enemies. But others will try to kill him before the Unmaking or the Remaking."

Elyssa was certain more than ever this woman had gone over the edge. Nothing in those words pointed at Justin. Unfortunately, there wasn't enough in what Vallaena knew for Elyssa to twist and redirect to some other poor sap. "Are you saying half-damned means half-spawn?"

"It is a common misinterpretation of our nature," she said, preening a lock of golden hair, "though we Daemos do not consider ourselves damned. In fact, we consider ourselves to be rather blessed."

"How can you be so certain this points to Justin? Surely there are a million other interpretations."

"Daevadius—David is already marked for death. How long will it be before Justin is marked and dealt with?"

Elyssa shook her head. "David's death mark is probably due to his ticking off the Conroys."

"What about Justin's friends?" Vallaena said, her eyes alight with fervent belief. "He is friends with a sorcerer, a felycan, and you, his mate, are a dhampyr and a Templar. The foreseeance speaks of 'unlikely alliances'. Surely the 'half-damned' and 'unlikely alliances' identifiers are enough to at least point to Justin."

"Why do you care? Even if it is about Justin, why would someone as powerful as you give a damn?" Elyssa held a finger in the air. "Oh, I get it. You're afraid of losing your place in the world if this prophecy is right and the world is remade."

"My reasons are my own, Templaras, and I would not expect you to understand them."

"See?" David said. "It's nonsense. I think she wants Justin so she can control me, bring me kicking and screaming back into the family, much to the amusement of our father."

"Little brother," Vallaena said, the shame of addressing him directly turning her face red and giving her the look of one who has just eaten a very sour lemon. "You are a child straight from the loins of the Paetros and Maedras, as am I. This is a rare honor. Why would you shun your family so? Why would you ignore your duties as a Daemos?"

"Because I'm not one of you," he replied in a gruff voice. "And I never will be."

Nyles bowed his head to Vallaena. "May I speak, Anae?"

"Yes. Speak freely since I have already soiled myself by speaking to the lowest of the low."

"Thank you." Nyles looked at Elyssa. "Before I was sent as ward to House Slade, I also heard whispers of a foreseeance, though the rumors were quickly quashed by the Conclave's representatives in my country."

"You're from another country?" Elyssa furrowed her brow. The man had a strange accent of his own, but he didn't look overtly foreign.

"I am from Spain, although the Conclave does not divide itself by the same boundaries the mortal world does."

True, the Overworld Conclave didn't recognize geographical boundaries, only the different supernatural nations and species comprising it. It was up to each nation to arrange its representatives, confusing as it was. But each region still had its elite, House Slade being the most powerful spawn house in North America.

She steepled her fingers and peered over them. "You're saying the same exact foreseeance was given by a different individual in your part of the world and mysterious conspirators within the Conclave hushed it up."

"From the research I have done for Anae-Vallaena, this has happened in other parts of the world as well. At least two other times," he said, holding up the same number of fingers.

"And yet word still hasn't gotten out?"

"Whoever is preventing this from becoming public knowledge is very powerful."

That did it. Elyssa slapped her forehead and mumbled a couple of choice curse words under her breath. "I don't want to offend you, Vallaena, but this is crazy. Has it ever occurred to you maybe you guys have lived so long you're bored and are looking for shadows in the dark?"

Sadness or possibly regret filled Vallaena's eyes. "I had hoped we could come to some peaceful solution. Unfortunately there are others who wish to possess Justin or who will hope to possess him once they discover what he is."

The door to the bar burst open and a man with olive skin and black hair flashed to Vallaena's side. "We must go, Anae."

Worry flashed across her face. "Who is it, Ali?"

"Minions, Anae. Hellhounds."

"Are you the one who sent hellhounds after us?" David asked, face boiling with rage as he jerked to his feet and sent his chair skittering to the floor behind him.

Ali scowled and reached for a gun. Vallaena shook her head. "I have already soiled myself by speaking to him, Ali. I will cleanse myself later."

The man bowed. "As you say."

Vallaena turned to David. "I'm afraid it was not I who sent the hellhounds. Rather, it was yet another whose honor you soiled by your foolish actions."

David's face paled. "No, not her."

Vallaena nodded sadly. "Yes. Your betrothed."

CHAPTER 18

*R*yland cursed and hit the gas so hard, I heard the pedal thud into the floorboard. The Prius, not exactly a sports car to begin with, paused for a few seconds before deciding the driver really did want to destroy the environment by burning through the fuel it would take to accelerate at such a speed. In the meantime, a big male vampire with a leather trench coat and black shades zipped into the road in front of the car. Ryland slammed the brakes and my head thumped into the back of his seat.

"Just great," Smith said. "Looks like your almighty master is here to save you yet again."

"Let me go and I'll tell him not to hurt anyone," Felicia said, her sad voice turning triumphant.

The big vampire in the road smiled. Massive shoulders pressed against the large trench coat he wore and meaty pectorals strained the tight black shirt underneath it. His black hair was spiked six inches straight up and I had to admit he looked pretty badass. On the other hand, he was also the ass who'd ordered the kidnapping of my dad. Unfortunately, I could hardly fight my way out of a wet paper bag in my condition, much less take on a vampire of his age.

"How about you tell him to get out of the way and I won't hurt any of them," Smith said with a sarcastic smile.

Ryland looked through the rear-view mirror. "It'll be daylight in about five minutes and then your friends won't be much of a challenge."

Vampires didn't burn up in the sun, I'd learned, but it made them lethargic and gave them a nasty sunburn if they stayed out in it too long. I glanced over at the cloud bank to our left and wondered if it would nullify the sun issue.

Smith stuck his head out of the window. "What do you want?"

"Release my faithful from your bonds and I shall let you live," Maximus said in a deep booming voice.

He sounded really reasonable, I thought as his command echoed in my head. "Hey, that's a good idea," I said, trying to open the rear door. But it wouldn't open and I realized the child safety locks were on.

"Don't let his voice cloud your mind," Stacey said. "Bloody vampires and their mind games."

"A trick?" I asked, still trying to open the door by pressing my shoulder weakly against it.

Stacey leaned across Felicia and gripped my chin in her hand. Her amber eyes darkened, seeming to form a vortex sucking me into their depths. I felt myself falling, falling, falling into the bliss of her gaze. Reality faded in a warm fuzzy haze. Then she slapped me so hard I saw stars.

"Ouch!"

"Sorry, my lamb, but it was the fastest way to snap you out of it."

I realized I no longer had the desire to let Felicia go. In fact, I was ready to get out and beat the snot out of Maximus—although extreme physical violence from my end was hardly in the cards right now since my arms had the strength of wet noodles.

"Get ready to gun it," Smith said to Ryland.

"It'd be faster if I pushed," the lycan grumbled.

Smith uttered a few nonsensical words, held a metallic-looking wand out of the car window, and then twirled it skyward. A brilliant halo of light surrounded the car, bathing everyone outside in intense white rays without affecting those of us in the car. The vampires freaked, running and screaming as red blisters formed on their skin. Maximus howled and ran for the shade as well.

"Maxi, don't leave me!" Felicia shouted as Ryland gunned the car forward.

Smith leaned back in his seat and groaned. Sweat glistened on his forehead.

"Was that hard?" I asked.

He wiped his brow. "Difficult? No. But the effort and energy of something so bright really takes it out of me. I knew I should've brought my staff. It has a stronger generator."

I turned to Felicia. "Maxi, huh? Let me guess. He likes to take advantage of the females he 'saves'". I made air quotes in case she didn't catch the sarcasm.

She sniffed and stuck her nose in the air. "I wouldn't expect a man to understand. You saw how sexy he is. How powerful. What lucky girl wouldn't do anything for a man like him?"

"He's a user. Guys like him are a dime a dozen, especially at my school." I thought about Nathan Spelman and his cadre of football-playing cronies. I shuddered at the thought of going back to school and seeing him again. True, Nathan and I were no longer at war, but that didn't mean we were friends.

"There is no one else like Maximus."

"You're delusional," I said. "Ryland could kick his ass and eat him for breakfast."

Ryland cast one of his wolfish grins over a shoulder and looked Felicia up and down, like sizing up a piece of meat. "You're cute, vampire, but stupid."

"Hey, watch it—oh never mind," Smith said. "I have this instinct to protect my sister, but you're right. She is stupid." He shook his head. "Such a damned shame, too. She was top of her class until…"

"Thanks for piling on, jackass," Felicia said.

"Until your parents died?" I asked.

His head snapped around to face me. "How did you—?" He looked at Felicia. "Oh. I guess she told you all sorts of stuff while I was gone."

I shrugged. "Some."

He rubbed a hand down his face. "Just great. I hardly know you people and you already know I have a crazy sister and a crappy childhood. I hardly know a thing about you."

"I don't think any of us have a pristine past," I said, although my childhood had been pretty darned good up until my mom left, my dad went over the edge looking for her, and I found out I was demon spawn. "I know you want to be mysterious and all with your conspiracy stuff, but nobody here's gonna crucify you for your past."

"Unless he's a murderer," Ryland said, quirking one side of his mouth into a lopsided grin as he weaved the car through traffic.

"Yeah, there is that," I said.

Smith offered a wan smile. "You ever heard of the Nosti family?"

I shook my head. "No."

"I believe I remember hearing of them," Ryland said.

"Keeping up with families is not something I do," Stacey said.

Smith stared out the car window and pushed his thick glasses up his nose. "My dad was kind of a big deal in the sorcery community. He was on the Arcane Council, he taught advanced classes at the Academy, and he was well-liked. My mom was just a nom even though she was the daughter of another powerful couple in the arcane community."

"Like the Conroys?" I asked.

"Not quite that powerful, but pretty far up the chain."

I wondered just how powerful my mother's parents were.

Smith glanced at his sister, disappointment etched into his face. "Felicia, believe it or not, was head of her class in a nom school. I think she was on track to pass me up when it comes to brains."

Felicia gazed fondly at her brother but quickly looked down at her hands when she saw the look on his face.

"She didn't go to an arcane school?" I asked, trying to figure out the bits and pieces of the magic community from what he was saying.

"No. Besides, we all go to a more or less normal school until we're ten. It helps us fit in with the noms. Then we start our arcane training. Most can't tap into their abilities until around ten or eleven anyway. When I was eighteen and Felicia was thirteen, our parents were found dead in an alley, supposedly mugged."

"Someone mugged a sorcerer?" I asked, thinking if his father had a chance, he would've magicked his way out of it.

"Not bloody likely," Stacey said, an eyebrow raised in disbelief.

"My thoughts exactly," Smith said. "The bodies were moved after they were killed. The Arcane Inquisitor's office said it was a matter for the normal authorities and refused to get involved, while the police detectives who were involved encountered only bad luck and dead ends."

"What about the Templars?"

"They were prohibited from intervening by the Arcane Inquisitor."

"That does sound fishy," I said.

Ryland grunted. "It ain't all that fishy. Every major faction has its own version of the police to settle internal matters and they don't want the Templars in their business if they can help it. They only call us in when one supernatural group mixes it up with another."

"But the Inquisitor didn't know who killed the Nostis," I said. "What if it was a vampire?"

"They were shot in the backs of their heads," Smith said, a grim tone to his voice. "If another super did the job, they did it with mortal instruments to make it look like a normal crime."

A sob erupted from Felicia. She bent over, hands pressed to her eyes as tears dripped down her cheeks. Smith put a hand on his sister's head for a brief moment before pulling it away and sighing.

"Did you ever find out anything?" I asked.

"Some dead ends. I know my dad was meeting with a woman, but I never could find out her name. I sometimes wondered if he might be having an affair." Smith shook his head. "But he just didn't seem like the cheating type."

"This is tragic," Stacey said, resting a hand on Felicia's back. "And your sister went off the deep end after the murders?"

Felicia shot her a tear-stained look. "I'm not the one who went off the deep end."

"Yeah," Smith said, ignoring her. "I had enough inheritance to get my own place. Felicia moved in with me. But I was so wrapped up in my own investigation I didn't realize what she was going through." His lips tightened and it looked like years of guilt suddenly climbed onto his shoulders. "Then one of her teachers called me and asked if she was sick, because Felicia hadn't been at school for a week." Anger flashed on his face. "When I tracked her down, she was doing meth with some loser dropout and his buddies in a trailer park. I wanted to kill them all."

"Will you shut up," Felicia said, wiping away her tears. "Stop talking about me like I'm not here."

"That's the problem," Smith said. "It's almost like you're not here. Like the Felicia I knew died a long time ago."

"Good god," I said, looking at Felicia. "You were doing meth? How old were you?"

Her bottom lip quivered and fresh tears threatened. "Sixteen."

Smith's lip curled up in distaste. "It got worse. I became obsessed with finding my parents' killer. And Felicia just did her own thing until one day one of her boyfriends came by, banging on the door and crying like a baby. When I opened it, he had my sister in his arms." He sucked in a breath as his voice caught. "I thought she was dead."

Felicia took her brother's hand in hers and gripped it. "I'm sorry, Adam. I couldn't take the pain anymore. Maybe it would've been better if you'd just let me die."

Smith shook his head. "And lose the last family I had?" He dropped her hand and looked away. "I guess you have your own vampire family now."

"You're my brother and I still love you," Felicia said, her face red and soaked with tears.

Stacey handed her another tissue.

"You don't love anyone except yourself," he snapped back. "If you cared at all about me or the memory of our parents, you'd stop doing stupid crap and make something of yourself."

"Well, I'm sorry I wasn't born with any useful abilities, Adam! I'm sorry I was the useless nom. I wanted to be something special. Why else do you think I accepted Maximus's offer?" She blew her nose with all the gusto of a drama queen just as Ryland took a sharp corner, rocking Felicia into me.

I cringed away from the well-used tissue.

Smith blew out an exasperated breath and swatted her excuse with a wave of his hand. "If even half of what Justin told me is true, about vamplings and kidnapping, then the price of his 'gift' was too high. It wouldn't even be so bad if you'd done a single worthy thing with your abilities. Instead, you've only made things worse."

Ryland pulled the car to a curb and hit the brakes hard enough to send everyone flailing against their seatbelts. "We're here," he said.

No kidding!

Smith got out of the car quick as he could and stormed away, fists clenched. I couldn't blame him. His sister was a hot mess and brain-washed besides. On the other hand I knew why he still wanted to help her and protect her. She was his only family. It was the same reason I wanted my mom back and why I wanted to rescue my sister. They were my family and I had to do everything in my power to help them. Not that I was doing a great job of things right now.

Stacey pulled Felicia from the other side of the car, but I didn't think we had to worry about her running. The grief in her red eyes and slump in her shoulders spoke of defeat. But a tiny part of me understood why she'd turned vampire. If I had an older sibling who inherited all the family abilities and I had nothing, I'd probably be jealous too. And if some hot curvy vampire woman offered me supernatural strength and immortality, I'd probably take it.

I looked at the line of iron doors in the alleyway, trying to remember which one was Shelton's. They all looked the same. Then I noticed the column of smoke pouring from a building down the road. I saw several distant figures rush around a corner and head our way, running like their lives depended on it.

CHAPTER 19

"*I*s that Elyssa?" I asked, unable to make out who it was since my supernatural vision was still on the fritz.

"It's her and several others I don't recognize," Ryland said.

"Those are frickin' hellhounds," Smith said, gripping his wand. "Son of a—Felicia, get inside now!" He flicked the rod at one of the iron doors and it burst open with the loud ping of metal.

Ryland gripped my arm. "I have to help them, Justin. Will you be okay here?"

I felt absolutely useless, staring at the figures down the road. "Yeah."

"What do you want me to do?" Stacey asked as Ryland and Smith raced down the road.

I looked at Felicia who was huddled against the brick wall near the door her brother had opened. Dim sunshine filtered through the clouds and it seemed to be affecting her.

"Will you help them, Stacey? I think I can manage Felicia for now." Truth be told, I really didn't care if she ran away at this point. I had much larger fish to fry and the vampire chick wasn't on the list.

Stacey regarded the girl for a moment. "Do not trust her for one moment, Justin."

"I won't," I said as I peered down the road to see what the situation was.

She nodded and blurred away in a streak of blonde and pink. I clenched my fists though I hardly had the strength to call the act 'clenching'. The urge to hobble down the road as fast as I could was almost unbearable even though I'd only be a liability.

Elyssa. I wanted to make sure she was safe. I wasn't fit to wipe a hell-hound's nose in my state.

"I know the feeling," Felicia said from the shade of the building. She didn't seem eager to enter the dilapidated old building Smith had opened for her and I didn't blame her, considering the rank odor drifting from inside.

"What feeling would that be?"

"Feeling useless."

"How do you know what I'm feeling?"

"Something's wrong with you or you'd have been the first one down there. And it's killing you that you can't help."

She might be a world-class bitch who'd almost murdered my girl-friend, but she wasn't stupid. "Yep. So if you're gonna run, you might as well do it now."

She squinted at the weak sunlight and shook her head. "I'm done with running."

I crossed my arms. "Twenty minutes ago you were ready to run to Maxi-poo."

"I love him. He's so amazing, you can't believe it."

"Are you sure he didn't brainwash you with his voice trick?"

"He would never do that," she said, anger rising in her voice.

"So run back to him. Skedaddle like a good dog. I'm sure Maxi will be happy to have you back." I shook my head and left her in the shade, hobbling down the road a bit for a clearer view of the battle. From what I could tell, Ryland and Stacey had shifted forms and were facing two of the hounds. Shelton and Smith were shooting the third one with what looked like crazy white beams of light while my dad unleashed a flurry of blows against a fourth. A woman with a mane of golden hair stood next to Elyssa. Between them lay a body, and it wasn't moving.

"Maximus was hired to kidnap you," Felicia said.

I spun. "What?"

"I overheard someone offering him money for your capture."

I walked over to her, wanting to grip her shirt and jerk her to her feet, but realized I was more likely to face plant on the filthy alley floor in my current state. "Who? Did you see them?"

"No. But that's why we were following the sorcerer. That's why we were ready for you."

"But you took my dad."

"Maximus didn't care who we caught. He wanted a spawn so he could increase the potency of his blood. He's obsessed with it."

"Obviously. Did the person who hired him say why they wanted me?" This struck me as odd considering my dad was the one with the death mark. Why would anyone want me?

"I have no idea."

The brick wall to our right exploded in a shower of red dust and fragments. Felicia shrieked. I stumbled back, barely catching myself against the wall before I fell down. Yellow eyes glowed in the dust and moved toward us as a rumbling growl gave me a pretty good idea what owned those eyes. A massive hellhound, black as night and scary as hell, emerged from the dust and stared straight at me. The thing was big as a mule and looked like something out of a dog catcher's worst nightmare. I couldn't run. I couldn't hide. The damned thing would just tear straight through the walls of the nearby buildings. When it growled, its black muzzle quivered and thick saliva drooled from black razor-sharp teeth. I thought a regular dog's breath stank. The humid rankness coming from this creature's mouth rivaled a rotten omelet stuffed with raw sewage.

"Leave him alone," Felicia said, jumping in front of me and holding her hands out to the sides as if flailing her arms would make her skinny little self look threatening.

"Don't get in its way," I said. "You won't even slow it down."

"I can deal," she said, a bit of snark entering her voice.

The clouds had further obscured the sun, but her skin was already turning pink.

"Why do you want me?" I asked the hellhound. "Tell me who sent you."

It didn't seem to understand a word I said, or else it was ignoring me. I was so sick of being chased. So damned tired of not knowing what was going on. And the worst part was they kept attacking the people I cared about!

The hellhound advanced. Felicia ran at it. Ebony canines snapped. She punched the hound right in the nose. It yelped. Growled. Lunged at her. She punched its nose again and it backed off, hackles bristling, massive head low, muscles coiled. A deep rumble in its throat vibrated the air.

"I used to be a dog-sitter," she said, not looking back at me. "Some of them were nasty aggressive and this was the best way to deal with them."

"Great. I guess you're the dog whisperer, vampire edition."

The hound lunged. She jumped back, but the sunlight slowed her reflexes. The creature batted her aside with a huge paw. She smacked against the iron door with a loud clang, knocking her senseless. The hound went for the kill, its savage teeth primed to rend Felicia to bits.

"No!" I screamed. Agony slammed twin spikes into my forehead. My skin seemed to swell. The beast inside me raged. "Don't harm her!" I shouted. Or I tried to shout those words. Instead, my voice came out deep and guttural and in a language I didn't recognize. Or did I?

The hound froze in place. Turned to me, its eyes full of understanding. Or maybe it was just hungry. It cocked its head to the side like a confused puppy and whined. I didn't have a clue what to do next. I tried to remember what I'd said and how I'd said it, but whatever brain cells I'd just used were back on vacation.

Then the massive hound perked up its ears and looked toward the hole it had smashed through the brick wall. It gave me another curious glance before vanishing into the rubble.

I ran to Felicia…well, sort of. I actually limped to her and eased myself to my knees by bracing an arm against the brick wall. She moaned. Her right arm was bent at a grotesque angle and the right side of her face was purple.

A trickle of blackish blood dripped from her nose. I had no idea if she was going to die or heal. The sun managed to poke a ray through the cloud and touched her face. The skin pinked, turning to red within seconds.

Weak as I was, I knew I had to drag her into the hole left by the hound and get her out of the sun. Dragging my own body was hard enough, but I had to do this. I slid my arms under hers and pushed my feet against the pavement. We inched toward the hole. Her skin where the sun hit it was going from red to purple. I pulled off my shirt and covered her face. But I couldn't do anything about her bare legs or hands. I hoped the damage wasn't permanent.

Inch by bloody inch I dragged her into the shadows. Cold sweat drenched every pore and my breath came in shallow ragged pants. But she was in. She was safe. I heard shouts from outside and panic swelled like acid in my throat. Was Elyssa okay? I didn't know if any of my friends had been hurt and I couldn't move to check.

"Oh my god!" Stacey said from somewhere outside.

Rapid footsteps echoed off the alley walls and then the outlines of several people stood in the hole where the wall had once stood.

"I'm here," I croaked, barely able to form a syllable.

"Justin!" Elyssa was there, hands pressed to my face, lips kissing me. "What happened to him?" She pressed me to her soft chest. "Justin, talk to me. Are you okay?"

"I'll die a happy man if you keep my head right here," I said in a hoarse whisper. "This is heaven."

She laughed. "Playing injured just to get some TLC?"

"Not exactly playing, no."

"What's wrong with you? Why aren't you healing?"

"Long story," I said with a groan, trying to get up but discovering every muscle in my body hated me for what I'd just put it through and was taking a siesta. "A lot happened while we were apart."

"He saved my life," Stacey said.

"What? You'd better tell me what's going on," Elyssa said, steel in her voice. I forced a smile. "I will. Promise."

"What happened?" Smith said as he knelt next to Felicia.

"Is she okay?" I asked, forcing each word out like a lead weight. I was so tired. I just wanted sleep.

"Let's get them inside," Shelton said. "We should be safe for now."

"What about *her*?" Elyssa asked, the steel in her voice razor sharp.

I tried to look around to see who she was talking about, but I was fading fast and could hardly turn my neck.

"She might as well come too," Shelton said. "It's best we sort this friggin' mess before figuring out what to do next."

"And you're qualified to make this decision because?"

"Because it's my damned hideout and I want to know what in blazes is going on here."

"I'm kind of curious too, TP," Smith said. "This is quite the crew you have here."

"It ain't my crew, Geronimo. It's his."

"Justin's?"

"You think I'd piece together a group of misfits like this?"

"Just get us inside, Shelton," Elyssa said in an exasperated voice. "He needs attention."

"Maybe I should get Meghan," Ryland said.

"Who?" Shelton said.

"Meghan Andretti?" I heard Dad ask.

Ryland replied. "You know her?"

"I know of her. Alice mentioned her before. Said she's a very gifted healer."

"She is."

"Then get her, please!" Elyssa said. "Just do it now!"

"I will," Ryland said.

Someone picked me up. I smelled Elyssa all around me and knew she was cradling me in her arms like a baby. I felt really embarrassed but used the opportunity to press against her soft curves anyway.

She laughed softly. "We never finished where we left off."

"I know," I said, dredging a little extra strength from somewhere. "Darned hellhounds and assassins don't want us to deflower each other." A warm tear splashed on my arm. "Don't cry, babe, it'll be okay." I took a deep breath. "Who's the blonde woman?"

"Someone who cares about your future, Justin," said a strangely accented female voice from nearby.

Elyssa's body tensed. "Will you just leave him alone?"

"He'll be fine. He is Daemos."

Whatever that meant. "Just when I think I have answers, it gets more mysterious," I said, and then I must have passed out.

DARKNESS GRIPPED my ankles and pulled me from my bed. I clawed at the floor, my fingernails breaking against the polyurethane coating on the hardwoods, leaving a streak of crimson blood. I turned on my back to see the shadow hands gripping and pulling me. Dragging me toward the light.

Wrong way, Justin! A voice echoed in my head or from somewhere around me. I couldn't tell.

"They're dragging me!" I grappled for the doorframe, getting both hands on it as my feet went around the corner of my bedroom doorway, my stomach still resting on the jamb. It took every ounce of strength just to hold on. And then the shadows wrenched my body out the door. Still, I hung on. I looked toward my feet, toward the blinding light at the end of the corridor. A dark shadow stood there, cane in one hand, a tall top hat filling in the space above his head and below the entryway.

I looked in the opposite direction and saw absolute pitch black. In the black stood a white feminine outline.

I am your light in the dark, said a voice from my memory, *your dark light.* Or had that been a dream too? Wasn't this a dream? It felt terrifyingly real.

After doing some quick calculations in my head, I decided the light in the dark seemed a little better than the dark in the light even if neither made sense to me. I strained with all my might, pulling away from the light and straining for the dark. The shadowy hands slipped from my ankles little by little and suddenly I was free. I catapulted toward the light, my body floating free, weightless as if in space.

And then the hallway burst apart around me, splintering into shards, and I was on my knees in front of Meghan's mother. Life had left her eyes but a groaning whisper emerged. I held my ear to her mouth. Listened hard. But her dying words made no sense.

Images flashed in my mind and I saw the bloody scrap of paper. A number on it. An angel with Elyssa's face whispering a number in my ear. Meghan's mother saying the number with her last breath. That number, what did it mean? Why was it so important? I had to find out what it was.

Someone had to know what forty-three eleven meant.

CHAPTER 20

a beautiful woman with silky blonde hair gazed down at me. I wanted to touch it, feel it between my fingers. "Are you the angel?" I asked weakly.

"What the hell are you doing near him?" Elyssa shouted.

The woman moved from view and glass shattered.

"That was an antique lamp, dammit!" Shelton shouted.

"Are you okay, Justin?" Meghan's face appeared above me.

"What are you doing here?"

"Ryland brought me back. You strained yourself. Almost killed your fool self trying to help that...that vampire girl."

"Is she okay?"

"She's fine. A little sunburned, but her bone breaks and bruises are healing quickly now that she has blood."

"Blood? Whose blood?"

Meghan smiled. "Elyssa gave her a blood pack."

"You're friendlier now than you were before." I tried to sit up, but my abs felt like they were on fire.

"I'm coming to grips with you," she said. She looked at something across the room and her face hardened. "But not with her."

I turned my head to look, but the pillow blocked my view. "Who?"

"Your aunt."

"My aunt? Who? How?"

"Maybe your father should explain. In any case, I gave you more painkiller brew. Your blood count is rising, though more slowly than it would if you'd get some sleep."

"But I just woke up."

"Whatever state you were in just now, it wasn't sleeping."

Fragments of the dream flickered through my mind. The numbers. I had to find out what they were. "Can you prop me up?" I asked.

"Not a good idea."

"Please. I need to speak to everyone."

She sighed. Reached for me and hesitated a moment before visibly steeling herself. Then she pulled me upright and adjusted the cot I was on so it locked into place. Shelton's hideout was a madhouse and he looked like a patient. His hair was frazzled and his eyes were wide and frenzied. Elyssa glared at the blonde woman from across the room where Ryland and Stacey held my girlfriend in place. A smashed lamp lay in the middle of the floor. Smith sat on a couch, his sister Felicia leaning against his shoulder, her face weary and pale, but not as bruised as I remembered it.

Another man lay on the ground, a pillow under his head, and I couldn't tell if he was alive or dead.

The blonde woman looked at me, her hazel eyes full of urgency. I looked past everyone and saw Dad back inside the metallic circle in the other room. He sat on the edge of the bed and smiled at me. I smiled back.

"You know how to throw a party," I said to Shelton.

He gave me an incredulous look, eyes full of panic. He probably didn't know what to do with this crowd any more than I did.

"Justin!" Elyssa said, struggling against Stacey and Ryland's grips. They looked at each other and nodded, letting her go. She rushed to my side, knelt, and peppered my face with kisses. "You were shouting and trying to move after you passed out. Were you having nightmares?"

I shook my head and was gratified I could actually shake it, even if my neck muscles felt like I'd borrowed them from a two-day-old corpse.

"I need everyone's attention," I said. Since everyone was already looking at me—well aside from Shelton who was staring at his beloved antique lamp—it wasn't hard to gain the undivided gaze of everyone in the room.

With all the attention focused on me, I felt nervous. The dreams I'd had were crazy. Surely they were bits and pieces of memories my mom had hidden from me, and my mind was just replaying them in bizarre fashion while I slept. Maybe I wasn't going crazy, though it sure felt like it. For all I knew, my brain couldn't handle the overload of blurred memories and was compensating for them by giving me insane dreams. On the other hand, even if I was going crazy, these people might be able to help me. Or at least make sure I found proper care.

So, I went for broke. "I've been having these insane dreams. Dreams about being little and seeing strange stuff, but more importantly, I keep seeing these numbers in my mind. The numbers forty-three—"

Elyssa's eyes widened. "And eleven?"

My mouth hung open for a moment before I found the presence of mind to nod. "You were in my dream."

"I am your dark light? Or something like that?"

"What? How—how did you know?"

Elyssa's eyes went wider. A lock of black hair fell across her face and I wanted so badly to touch it, tuck it behind one ear. But I didn't have the strength to do it. She looked around the room at the others. "It was a dream! Just a dream."

Although I was surprised, I wasn't shocked or anything. Having led a normal life up until a month or so ago only to endure an odyssey of epic proportions and discover all the weirdness existing right under my nose, dream sharing seemed kind of minor. Judging from Elyssa's reaction, it wasn't so minor after all.

"So the fact we experienced a similar dream is not a normal occurrence, I take it?"

"There are types who can do it," the blonde woman said, "but mostly those who cannot." She smiled at Elyssa. "Do you believe me now?"

Elyssa shook her head. "So what? We had a similar dream. It doesn't prove anything."

"About what?" I asked.

The blonde woman took a few steps toward us. "Far enough," Elyssa said in a low, threatening voice.

The other woman stopped and smiled. "Justin, I am Vallaena, your father's sister. Your aunt."

"What, none of that hierarchical first of house stuff you lectured me about?" Elyssa said. "You're not making yourself dirty by talking to him?"

"I have already sullied myself by speaking to my brother. It is of no further consequence if I speak to Justin."

I was confused. Obviously these two had spoken before and not become BFFs. From everything I knew about my dad's family, this woman could be a very dangerous and unscrupulous person. But she seemed kind of nice to me. And she was way too hot to be my aunt.

"All right, you're my aunt. What do you want from me?"

"I want to protect you, Justin."

"In case you hadn't noticed, I already have a badass ninja girlfriend. What else could a guy need?"

Elyssa smiled at me just before tossing a *see-I-told-you-so* smile back at Vallaena.

Vallaena didn't seem to notice. "It's very important we protect you, Justin. There are indicators you are a person of import. You may be the key to preventing a disaster from occurring."

"You gotta be kidding me," Shelton said. "Who brought Nostradamus with them? Are you talking about a foreseeance?"

"I am," Vallaena said.

Shelton rubbed his hands together. "Let me get some popcorn. This ought to be good."

Blue fire flashed in Vallaena's eyes. "Do not mock me, magic man. You hide behind lies and half-truths, earning money from other people's misfortunes, and have no right to cast judgment on me."

Shelton's mouth dropped. "Who—"

"I know all about you Harry Shelton. I know about Aerianas. Unless you wish me to elucidate further, you will keep your mouth firmly closed."

I hadn't known Shelton for long, but considering his abrasive and uncaring nature, it amazed me anything could turn his face white and render him speechless—well, except for his beloved antique lamp. Elyssa had also gone very still as she watched Vallaena, but I couldn't see her face to know if it was a wary kind of stillness or if she saw something in my dear aunt's face that gave her serious doubts. Vallaena's tone sent a shiver down my back as well. I caught a faint whiff of something, a sweet smell lingering with the odor of burnt tires. But it didn't stink, not in the way it should have. Instead, a part of me liked it.

Vallaena turned back to me in the shocked silence of the room. All eyes were on her. Then Dad caught my eye and shook his head ever so slightly. I guessed he was telling me not to trust her. Or maybe he just thought she had bad manners.

"Back to the subject at hand," I said, trying to grin and possibly lighten the funereal tone of the room, "even if I'm supposed to prevent a disaster, what do you want from me?"

"I am the first of House Slade. I wish to officially take you under my protection."

"She wants to do it before Kassallandra has the chance," Dad said.

"Uh, who?" I asked trying to figure out how to spell such a fancy name.

"Your father's betrothed," Vallaena said with a wicked little smile.

"She's the one who attacked us at the restaurant," Elyssa said. "She's the one sending the hellhounds."

"Flaming red hair?" I asked.

Her eyebrows shot up. "How did you know?"

"I caught a glimpse of her hair back at the house when all this mess started."

"This mess, as you call it, started long before this," Vallaena said.

"Kassallandra wants to put me under her protection?" I said. "She has a funny way of doing it."

"Anae Kassallandra also wishes to exact a measure of revenge on your father for abandoning her and..." She shuddered and looked like she was about to become ill. "Marrying and mating a human."

"Is she his sister too?" Dad had told me some nasty things about spawn breeding. Men were rare and had to mate with a lot of females to keep the bloodline going, even if it meant doing it with their own family members. I didn't want to think about how many uncle-daddies or aunt-mommies were in this family.

Vallaena shook her head. "She is from another house and young like your father, Daevadius, and also a direct descendant of the patriarch and matriarch of her house. The marriage was to unite the firsts of our houses by blood."

So Daevadius was Dad's real name? It sounded cooler than David though a lot more pretentious.

"She's leaving out the good part," Dad said. "Not only would I mate with Kassa, but also her mother and sisters while she would mate with my father and brothers."

"Gross!" Felicia said about the same time others chimed in their exclamations of revulsion.

Meghan heaved and I was sure she'd just thrown up in her mouth. I knew I felt like doing it.

"Why bother with marrying?" I asked.

"It is a formality," Vallaena said. "And before the rest of you judge us, you should know our blood is not weakened by a small genetic pool. We operate on a completely different level than those of human stock."

"In other words, your crap don't stink," Ryland said with his trade-mark wolf grin.

"I didn't come here to engage in a symposium on Daemos breeding rituals," Vallaena said. "Justin, if you accept my protection, then Anae Kassallandra will have to go through proper political channels to get you."

"Either way you cut it, it sounds like prison to me," I said, shaking my head. "I'm not interested. Why don't you use your power to stop Kassa instead?"

"Her power comes from House Assad. I cannot force her to stop. And since you are considered Castratae, there is no political solution unless you ask for asylum."

I really wanted to get up and pace, think about this crazy situation, and come up with a great idea to get out of it. Unfortunately, I wasn't as good at getting out of messes as I was at getting into them. That was why I had Elyssa. She could usually reach into her pouch and pull out a tissue, a candy bar, a sword, or whatever the situation called for. But she didn't have her pouch with her at the moment.

"I need to heal and think," I said. "But I've got to say this foreseeing thing sounds pretty thin."

"The number you and Elyssa spoke of, forty-three eleven."

"Yeah, what about it?"

"That is the name of the prophecy. Foreseeance four-three-one-one."

CHAPTER 21

My mind flashed back to the scene after the green demon had killed Meghan's mom. I saw the bloody scrap of paper in Meghan's trembling hand. Her current self in the here and now looked down at her own hands as if seeing the same thing, as if suddenly recalling something terrible she'd forgotten. I knew the exact feeling. Elyssa's hand tightened on mine.

"Let me see this foreseeance," I said to Vallaena. "I want to read it for myself."

"I don't have it," she replied. "I explained to Elyssa that every variation of it which has been spoken and recorded has vanished over the years."

"Sounds like a conspiracy," Smith said.

Felicia groaned. "Oh crap, not this again."

"Conspiracies exist!" He threw his hands in the air. "Why are you so opposed to the idea?"

"Can't you just let our parents rest in peace?" Felicia jerked herself off the couch, face red. "Not only did I become an orphan, but I lost my brother because he's so damned obsessed." She stormed away, though not far since the hideout wasn't very big.

Smith looked embarrassed. "People conspire all the time. I mean, who wouldn't want to at least find out who murdered their parents?"

"Who were your parents?" Dad asked.

"The Nostis."

"Phillip and Maryann?"

Smith nodded. "You knew them?"

Dad shook his head. "I remember Alice talking about them."

"I remember Phillip and Maryann," Meghan said. "They met with my mom sometimes."

"Did they meet with my mom too?" I asked.

"I think so. Like I said, my mom didn't allow me into her meetings and I think she might have blurred some of my memories."

"What was the date the green demon attacked us?"

Meghan furrowed her brow. "I couldn't say exactly. Though the memory is pretty clear now, some details are still blurry."

I concentrated, trying to recall something, anything that would give me an indicator of the date. I'd been fairly little at the time. Seven, maybe eight? It seemed about right, because Mom told Meghan's mother, Sandy, that she was pregnant. It amazed me how clear some of those details were now, as if the horrible event had just happened yesterday. If my sister Ivy was almost eleven now then, yeah, my age guesstimate would be about right.

"How old were you when your parents died?" I asked Smith.

He looked up from his tablet computer and took a moment before answering. "Eighteen."

"Roughly five years ago?"

He nodded.

Utilizing the power of math, I figured the attack on Meghan's mom had happened nine or ten years ago, four years before the murder of the Nostis. Were the two incidents connected?

Smith ran the numbers as well. "Four years is a long time to wait if they were trying to wipe out your mom and her acquaintances," he said. "Why not all at once?"

"Might look too obvious?" I couldn't think of another reason, though

I felt certain some diabolical mastermind out there could figure it out in a second.

Dad arched his eyebrows. "Wait a minute, Justin. Are you saying you, Meghan, and your mother were there when Sandy Andretti was killed?"

"Yeah." I was willing to bet there were a lot of things Mom hadn't told Dad. "She blurred it out of my mind just like she did all the memories of her pregnancy."

Shelton's eyes lifted from the floor. "You have a sibling?"

My heart did a double-thump as I realized I'd just let the proverbial cat out of the bag. Ivy's existence supposedly wasn't widely known and I'd purposely not told Shelton about her due to his low-trustworthiness factor. And now the room was practically brimming with people who didn't know, and at least one in particular I didn't want to know: Vallaena.

"A sister. How interesting," Vallaena said as my eyes met hers. "Daevadius has been a very busy man, I see."

"Don't you even think about going after her," Dad said.

Vallaena didn't turn to face him. "Perhaps we have more to talk about than I thought."

The look on her face sent a chill coursing through my back. I was almost glad the Conroys had Ivy. Even Vallaena wouldn't have an easy time taking her from them.

"If you even think about going after my sister, you can forget ever having my cooperation." I tried to keep the tremble of anger from my voice. Or maybe it was fear. This was the first time I'd met one of my father's family face-to-face, and while she seemed surprisingly nice, I knew it could all be a mask hiding the demon beneath.

"Your sister need never come into the equation should you take my offer," Vallaena said, sweetening the offer with a dimpled smile. "There is far more at stake here than you realize."

I had plenty more to add to this conversation. But not here. Not now. There were too many people, some of whom I didn't know well enough to trust just yet. Hell, I didn't even know if I could trust Shelton.

"A sister?" Shelton shook his head. "Damn. Talk about keeping secrets. All the research I did on you two and I never caught a whiff."

"I hope you're talking about research before you tried to kidnap us for the bounty," I said.

He narrowed his eyes. "What else would I be talking about?"

Smith tapped on his tablet and grimaced. "I made a timeline a while back. I added Sandy's death to it, but I don't see anything else in my data connecting her death to my parents'."

"Well, it's a start." I sighed and looked at the unconscious figure still resting on the ground. "Maybe someone can clear up one mystery for me. Who's the dude on the floor?"

"He is my Denae, Nyles," Vallaena said, offering another dimple-cheeked smile. "My bodyguard, Ali, was going to evacuate us, but the attack came too soon. Still, he managed to hold them at bay so we could escape."

Great. Another spawn. "Was anyone killed?"

"No." She motioned her head toward the exit. "Ali is guarding upstairs, however, in case of another attack."

"Hard to believe after all that ruckus. The bar looked like a warzone."

"I do not think Kassallandra wished to kill anyone." Vallaena's gaze found my father where he sat glumly on the bed inside the metallic circle on the floor. "But if her hounds could have captured your father, I am certain a little torture would have been in order."

Shelton had the nerve to chuckle.

"I've got some bad news," Smith said as he puzzled over something on his tablet. "I don't think I can remove the death mark. At least not easily. And even if I did remove it, it wouldn't stop the assassin from finishing the job."

I wanted to grit my teeth. Clench my fists. Stomp around and yell. But a sigh was all I could manage. "Are you saying there's nothing we can do to stop my dad from dying?"

"This is Underborn's mark." Smith pushed up his glasses and frowned. "You might be able to buy off a normal Guild hit, but this guy operates differently than the rest."

"Well, yeah. His fee is astronomical," Shelton said with a wry expression.

Smith crinkled his face. "Yes, and no. He, she, or whoever Underborn

169

really is doesn't charge money. His payment is the most precious treasure of the contractor."

"Talk about a vague notion," Elyssa said. "What if it happens to be money? Then you have to give him your life savings?"

Smith nodded. "Something along those lines."

"How do you know so much about him?" I asked.

"When you're digging for answers about murder, the Assassins Guild is a good place to start." Smith sighed and leaned back into the couch. "I found out a lot of things I didn't want to know and came very close to a personal meeting with Underborn himself."

"Dangerous," Ryland said in a low, almost admiring voice.

"Yeah." Smith took a deep breath. "I went to the meeting place, a ramshackle little bar in the Grotto. The summons told me to pick the table in the far end and to take a seat facing the wall. It also told me not to look back."

Shelton snorted. "I'll bet you were about to crap bricks."

"Oh yeah," Smith said, sweat breaking on his forehead. "I don't know how long I sat there expecting a dagger in the back at any minute. After a while, a man with a missing arm sat down to my left. He asked me if I was Adam Nosti. His question surprised the hell out of me because I thought I'd been really clever, keeping my identity secret. Then he told me to look at him, so I did, thinking the whole time it meant a death sentence because I was sure this guy was Underborn, and nobody knows what he really looks like. But instead of seeing a stranger, I recognized the man."

"You knew him?" Shelton asked.

"Not so much knew him as knew *of* him. It was Aston Beaumont."

Shelton's mouth dropped open. "The guy who won the Arcane Tourney all those years in a row?"

"That's the one. He told me to take a good look at him, and just sat there for a minute like I was supposed to take in every detail. He looked rough. Unshaven, bloodshot eyes, and that damned missing arm. Then he gave me a scrap of flash paper and left."

I didn't have a clue who Aston Beaumont was or where this was going, but it was interesting. "He didn't tell you anything else?" I asked.

Smith shook his head. "I looked at the paper. It said 'Aston gave up his treasure to destroy his better. Should you continue to seek the truth, it will be your sister who loses that which she values most.'"

"What does that mean?"

"Aston was an amazing sorcerer," Shelton said. "One of the best, until he lost his arm in an accident." He held up a hand to keep my next question at bay. "When we practice magic, it's just like playing baseball or anything else—we get used to using a certain hand. Sure, I can switch it up, but unless you're ambidextrous, you'll lose some power and focus."

"So Underborn took his arm, his most valued possession."

"Yeah. That year there was a new kid on the block named Folder Reeves. He was a friggin' prodigy. Everyone expected him to be the next Aston Beaumont. Except he died in an accident two weeks before the Arcane Tourney."

"And Aston lost his magic arm as the price," I said. "I'll bet he didn't win first place."

"Nope. Matter of fact, he came in dead last by a long shot."

Shelton whistled and gave Smith an accusing look. "Man, now there's a story you could've told me over coffee."

"No way in *hell* was I gonna talk about that encounter to anyone. It took me a year to stop looking over my shoulder every two minutes. I didn't have a clue what Felicia valued most, but I didn't want Underborn to take it."

"You're kidding me, right?" Felicia said in a scornful tone.

"Maybe your boyfriend, Maximus?" Smith said. "On second thought, maybe I should've let Underborn wipe that skid mark off the planet."

Tears pooled in Felicia's eyes. "You're such a stupid bastard!" In one smooth motion, she pushed herself from her sitting position on the floor and stormed into the bedroom, slamming the door behind her.

"That son of a bitch, Maximus," Smith said, punching his palm with a fist.

"Men are so daft," Stacey said. "You bloody fool. Your *life* is her greatest treasure, not that mental vampire, Maximus. You're the last family she has on this Earth and you've wasted years ignoring her so you could solve your parents' murders. And look where it's gotten you."

Smith went white as her words sank in. I felt surprised myself because I sure as heck hadn't seen that one coming.

"You have quite a way with words, Stacey," he said. "You're obviously as intelligent as you are beautiful."

She blushed and blinked her eyes quickly as if trying to figure out why he wasn't yelling at her for her bluntness. "You are too kind, sir." A smile lit her face. "But if you're looking for more advice, I suggest you go apologize to your sister and start things down the right track from here on out."

"Wait, a minute," I said. "What about my dad? What about the death mark? Can't we do anything?"

"I've isolated the frequency for the tracker," Smith said. "The circle won't be necessary to cut it off any longer. But the only way to stop the hit is to appeal to Underborn."

"And offer him my most valued possession?" I cast a worried glance at Elyssa.

Smith got up and tucked his tablet into a wide pocket inside his dark overcoat. "I have no idea. Best I can do is tell you how to initiate contact with him. Then you're on your own. That's just how he works."

"It's not worth it, son," Dad said, his face screwed up in anger and misery. "Block the tracker and I'll put good use to whatever time I have left."

I wanted to argue with him. Tell him we'd find a way. But I couldn't promise anything right now. I was tired as hell and in no shape to do a damned thing. Smith gave me a sympathetic look as he went into the bedroom to talk to his sister. Stacey looked from my father to me, her eyes glistening. Vallaena looked troubled, but I didn't think for a moment she'd shed a tear for my dad.

"I must go for now," my aunt said, as Nyles staggered to his feet. He looked like a truck had run him over. Considering how much punch those hellhounds were packing, that probably wasn't far off the mark. "We have a great deal to discuss, Justin." She came closer despite Elyssa's nasty glare and lowered her voice. "I need a decision in one week. Otherwise, I will be forced to pursue other options."

"Turn myself over to you or you'll go after my sister? Is that it?"

"I am not alone on this. There are...other parties involved who desire your cooperation, but above all, your safety. I hope you see my plan is for the greater good."

"As in your good," Elyssa hissed. "You want to ensure you stay in power."

Vallaena raised a blonde eyebrow. "I make no secret of my desire to keep the status quo, Templaras. Please, consider the offer."

"I'm not accepting anything right now," I said, giving her my most heartfelt glare. "But we need to discuss these 'others', and I want to see the bigger picture. There's a lot going on that you're not saying."

Her dimples showed again. "Of course." She straightened and motioned Nyles toward the exit. "I hope to hear from you soon, nephew."

"You heading out, Blondie?" Shelton said, joy practically dancing in his eyes, probably because part of the circus was leaving his house.

"I am."

He headed out the door, giving her a curt motion to follow him. She gave me one last gaze, as if trying to divine what choice I would make before following the sorcerer out.

Anxiety hammered my heart into a solid heavy lump in my chest the moment she was out of sight. I wanted to throw up and kill the person responsible for this mess, and not necessarily in that order. Elyssa pressed a hand to my cheek and kissed me on the lips.

"We're not going to let this happen," she said in low tones. "We'll find Underborn and stop him. I promise you, we will stop this." Her hand tightened on mine. "And I'm going to shove Vallaena's threats back down her demon-infested pie-hole."

The burn of tears hit the backs of my eyes and I took a deep breath to ward them off. Now was not the time to get sentimental and turn into a pansy in front of everyone.

Meghan came to my cot and gave Elyssa a cup of something. "Justin, you need to sleep. This will help you."

Much as I wanted to argue and stay awake to figure out what to do next, I realized she was right. Until I regained my strength, I was useless to everyone. I nodded as Elyssa gave me a querying look. "Don't let me sleep too long," I said.

"I'll be right beside you, hot stuff." She winked. "Maybe I'll even break me off a piece while you're out of it."

"You did not just say that," I said, a smile overcoming the melancholy tug on my facial muscles.

She smiled and leaned down until I felt her warm breath on my ear. "I think I just did." Her teeth nipped my earlobe.

A shiver of pleasure went through my body and almost made me forget the room was full of other people. Not that I could lift a hand to make good on the friskiness. "You'd better watch out once I'm feeling better."

"Not only will I be watching out, I'll be looking forward to it." Her full lipped smile made me want her so badly right then; I wished I could sweep her off her feet and kick everyone out of the place. Instead, I leaned forward and sipped the brew Meghan had prepared until the sweet-tasting mixture was gone.

Elyssa curled up next to me, our faces just inches apart, and squeezed me. She backed off, her eyes wide. "You might be weak, but something is still working."

I tried to smile but sleep dragged me down and away.

CHAPTER 22

I woke up alone and in the dark. Panic took me full in the chest and I jerked off the cot, flailing and hitting something soft with my knee. I went down face-first and landed on a bed. An empty bed, from the feel of it. I felt for the other side and touched something. A pillow, maybe? I moved my hand over it and realized it wasn't large enough to be a pillow. It felt almost like skin except it wasn't warm as it should be. Then I found a knee and recoiled in horror. Had they dropped a dead body in the bedroom with me?

I stumbled back away and felt the edges of the bed, frantically making my way around it and to the light switch while my night vision strobed off and on like a bad florescent light. I flicked the light on. Felicia's still form lay there, her eyelids fluttering as the light hit them. She pushed herself up on one elbow and gazed at me groggily.

"You're awake?" she asked.

I looked down at myself. "Uh, looks that way. Why am I in here?"

"They figured it was too noisy out there. I came in to get some shuteye myself since Shelton won't let anyone sleep in his bedroom."

"Vampires need to sleep?"

"Duh. Remember when you broke into our home? All the cots and beds?"

As if I could forget anything about that awful night. "Guess I ruined your game of Dance Revolution, huh?"

"Dance Central, actually."

I shrugged. "Didn't mean to."

She pushed her petite body into a sitting position, the movement quick and graceful. "Supposedly, older vampires don't need much sleep and normal sunlight doesn't hurt their skin either." Her eyes softened and she looked down. "Thank you, by the way."

"For what?"

"You saved me from a freaking hellhound, that's what! I guess it must have knocked me out." She looked up. "How did you stop it from killing me?"

I thought about it and still had no idea. "I told it to stop. I guess all my yelling and screaming confused it."

She laughed. "Maybe I should've screamed instead of punching it in the nose."

I couldn't keep a smile off my face at the memory. "I should thank you for saving me. That was crazy brave smacking that monster in the schnauzer."

Felicia reached over and took my hand in hers. I realized her hand wasn't warm as it should be, but it wasn't cold either. It felt soft and normal to me, though I wasn't sure why she'd taken my hand.

"I'm sorry, Justin." A tear glistened in one eye before making a slow journey down her pale cheek and past her crimson lips. "I'm a horrible person for letting those vamplings almost kill you and your girlfriend and for helping to kidnap your father. I just thought spawn were these really evil creatures, you know? Maximus told us all these terrible stories about your kind, so I thought we were doing something good."

I patted the top of her hand. "It's okay. I mean, it's not okay to kidnap people and try to kill them, but somehow we all made it out of there alive."

She nodded. "I thought the felycan was gonna kill us. When I woke up later on the floor, I couldn't believe I was still alive." Her wide eyes looked at mine as more tears tracked down her face. "You had every right to kill us for what we did."

176

"Well, I didn't, thankfully, or your brother might not have been so willing to help me out." A part of me wanted to be nice and tell her I forgave everything. Another part of me stirred with anger and resentment. But I didn't totally blame her. I placed most of the blame on Maximus's shoulders. I'd settle that score one day soon.

"How did you change?" she asked.

"Change?"

"Into that demon thing."

I remembered being cornered by the vamplings. I'd just taken Elyssa's essence and thought I'd killed her so I could fight them off. And then I'd lost control and raged. Manifested into my spawn form, annihilated the vamplings, and chased the vampires until I somehow had managed to barely control the beast and turn it back around so I could save Elyssa.

"I don't know and I don't care to do it again," I said.

"I'm never messing with another spawn again. I thought Maximus could be scary, but you guys are effing terrifying."

I laughed, although I knew she was right. And I was only half spawn. "Are you done with Maximus?" I asked. "I have to agree with your brother. Your almighty leader is only going to get you into worse trouble."

She nodded. "I want to leave him, but I obviously have a problem with addiction whether it's drugs or sexy, hot vampire men. Ever since becoming a vampire, drugs don't really affect me much because of the healing factor, so I was able to go cold turkey. Drinking blood was the next big rush. You can't imagine how alive it makes you feel. And sex while feeding is even more amazing."

"Uh, TMI, Felicia. Really didn't want that image in my head."

She laughed and kissed me on the cheek. "Too bad you're taken."

I suppressed the urge to flinch from her kiss. *Yeah right. Me and Felicia? Not gonna happen.* She was cute, but the girl had serious issues.

"I've been wondering," I said. "Why didn't the vamplings attack you and the other vampires?"

She shrugged. "They'll attack anything, but if there's hot blood, they go straight for it. Most of us can mask our presence, too, using compulsion, but it's really hard for us younger vampires. This cute Italian guy, Raphael, was bitten when he tried to sneak a drink of your dad's blood." Her eyes looked down as if talking about the crime heaped fresh shame on her. "We had to lock him in the crypt with the vamplings because the virus infected him and turned him into one. His screams were just horrible."

"But a vampling bit Elyssa and she didn't turn."

"Really?" Felicia's eyes widened and met mine. "She would've shown symptoms by now. They're freaking nasty."

"Is there a cure?"

"Supposedly, if a master vampire feeds you his blood shortly after infection, it'll kill the virus. But we don't have a master vampire we can ask." She shuddered. "Poor Raphael. He was really good at Dance Central, too."

A spark of panic shot into my body. I had to ask Elyssa if she was feeling okay.

"I guess you must be feeling a lot better," Felicia said.

It hadn't occurred to me I'd been bumbling around the room under my own power. A grin lit my face. "Hellz yeah." I patted her hand again and let go. "Guess I better go visit the troops."

"I'm going back to sleep. I haven't had a decent day's sleep yet and I'm bushed."

I turned off the light and slid out of the door. Elyssa sat at a small table, her side to me as she talked to Meghan. Smith and Shelton were doing something with Dad—hopefully blocking the tracker. Ryland and Stacey were nowhere to be seen.

I strode to Elyssa. Meghan looked up at me. Elyssa turned to follow her gaze. Her eyes brightened when she saw me and she got to her feet. I engulfed her in a bear hug. I kissed her cheeks, then pulled her against me for a real kiss, one hand pressing against the small of her back while my other hand smoothed her hair back from her face. When we came up for breath, I noticed Meghan's bright red face.

"Get a room," Shelton said with a snort.

I ignored him and stared into Elyssa's sparkling violet eyes. "Man, that felt good."

"It was kinda fun when you were helpless," she said, a glimmer of amusement in her eyes. "I could do anything I wanted to you."

"Where are the others?"

"Stacey said she needed to attend to a few things, and Ryland said he'd escort her in case more hellhounds showed up."

"Oh, I'll bet she loved that," I said with a laugh. "Those two are like oil and water."

"I think he gets off annoying her. Stacey was making fun of his haircut on the way out."

"And nothing more from Vallaena?"

Elyssa shook her head. "No. But I really don't like the way she gave you a time limit."

I rubbed the back of my neck and sighed. "Seems everyone is giving me deadlines these days." My conversation with Felicia popped to mind, so I pulled Elyssa across the room and toward the tiny kitchen. "I had a discussion about vamplings with our favorite vampire girl."

"Felicia?"

"Yeah. She told me vamplings can infect vampires with their virus and actually turn them into one of those zombie things."

"And you're wondering why I haven't tried to eat your brains?" Elyssa said with a grin.

Some of the panic sparking through my system eased when I saw her grin. "Yeah."

"Templars have immunity to most supernatural viruses. The Divinity gives us a few useful perks."

"The Divinity?"

"Yeah. Nobody knows exactly who or what it is, but it's the power source and central core that makes Templars what they are. It can make noms immortal, give them preternatural abilities, and all that, so long as they can pass the Cho'kai."

"The show what?"

"It's a trial all recruits have to pass before becoming a full Templar. If they fail, the Divinity strips them of their gifts and they have to wait a year before they can reapply as a recruit."

"A trial—like doing a hundred pushups and low-crawling through electrified mud?"

She laughed. "Nobody knows. The trial takes place in the chapel and nobody ever remembers a thing about it. That's pretty much the way any interaction with the Divinity is."

"Even your father doesn't know?"

She shook her head. "Not even the Templar Synod, our ruling council, knows, and some of them have been around since before the Roman Empire."

"That's freaky." All sorts of possibilities drifted through my head, most of them having to do with Star Trek and glowing balls of light that killed people or gave Captain Kirk an inexhaustible libido. "Is this thing sentient?"

She nodded. "Yeah, but on a level that makes us look like monkeys."

"We're barely smarter than monkeys without a super being to make us all look dumb." I thought about Nathan and bullies like him and shuddered. The human race was chock full of dummies.

"Speaking of dumb things," Elyssa said with a sideways look and a wistful smile, "Meghan told me what you did for Stacey." Her smile faltered and she looked down. "You scare me to death sometimes, Justin."

I squeezed her to me. "I scare myself. Look, she's my friend. I had to do something to help her."

"Just like when you leapt into the back seat of the truck to protect Katie?"

"She would have died."

"Do you have some kind of a superhero complex? Do you want to get killed?"

"Yes, I do have a complex, and no, I don't want to die. At least not until I've had my way with you, and then I'll die happy."

She blushed. "Don't talk that way. We're going to have a lot of fun before I let anything bad happen to you."

"I could kick Felicia out of the bedroom."

Elyssa laughed. "There is no way we're engaging in hanky panky with your dad, Shelton, and everyone else right outside the door."

"Yeah, that would be kind of icky."

"And Shelton's probably got cameras in his rooms."

"Nasty!"

After our laughter died down, I looked at Smith as he worked away on his tablet computer. The urge to pepper him and Shelton with questions was strong, but I didn't want to interrupt their work. At the same time, I wondered if keeping Dad on lockdown might not be a better idea than letting him loose again. He was just as good at getting into messes as I was.

A knot of worry rolled around in my stomach, followed by sharp stabs of anxiety. Dad was going to die unless I somehow convinced Underborn to call off the hit. That meant I had to find the guy. Which meant I had to ask Smith how to contact him. I already knew what my most precious treasure was and I'd rather die than let Underborn take Elyssa from me.

"You've got that look on your face," Elyssa said.

"What look?"

"The one meaning you've recovered from your last near-death encounter and are about to head out for the next round."

"I need to talk to Underborn."

Meghan, who had walked to the kitchen for more tea, gasped. "Are you crazy? Smith's story was bad enough, but I've heard more and worse about that scum." She took a seat on the brown leather couch against the nearby wall.

"I'm not going to sit around here waiting for that jackass to kill my dad."

"Instead, you're going to rush off and let him kill you too," Elyssa said. She shoved me away. I still didn't have all my strength back and toppled backward onto the couch. Wide-eyed, Meghan scooted away from me without spilling a drop of her tea.

"If it was someone you loved, wouldn't you do the same?" I asked, pushing myself into a less-awkward position.

"What if it was me running off to see him?" she asked. "How would you feel?"

"Angry and scared as hell of losing you. But I'd also know stopping you would be impossible, so I'd go with you and beat the crap out of anyone who tried to hurt you."

A rueful chuckle burst through her frown. "This is by far your worst idea *ever*." She face-palmed and shook her head. "When do we leave?"

"Soon as I figure out how to contact the guy."

"Are you going to tell your dad?"

"Oh, hell no." I watched as Dad patiently endured the attentions of the two sorcerers while they poked and prodded the tattoo on his neck. "But I need to ask Smith how he contacted Underborn." My stomach growled.

Meghan shuddered. "I think you need to feed, Justin." She pulled out her wand. "May I run a test?"

I nodded.

"It might hurt just a bit," she said, focusing her gaze on my arm and speaking a word.

A needle-like sensation pricked my arm, but it was nothing compared to what I'd felt during Stacey's procedure. A globule of blood emerged from a pore in my skin, forming a half-inch crimson sphere which drifted toward Meghan. A shimmering shield materialized around the sphere, glowing golden and warm. The sphere spun faster and faster until it was a gold and red blur in the air. When it stopped, the red in the blood was separate from a bluish substance with a glow of its own.

"Spawn blood plasma," Meghan said, her eyes full of wonder. "It radiates energy. Very few arcane healers have the chance to study spawn physiology because your kind are so secretive."

"Is it really that much different than humans'?"

"The blood plasma certainly is. I noticed it when making the transfer to Stacey. I'm almost certain this is where your body stores the psychic essence you take from others."

I noticed she didn't shudder that time, maybe because the scientific part of her mind was overriding the part nurturing her hatred for spawn.

"What are you looking for?"

She said a word and a spark of amber light pierced the sphere. After a moment, tiny numbers and symbols appeared in the air next to it, hovering for a moment before Meghan waved a dismissive hand. The entire thing flashed bright, leaving only a tiny spray of mist where it had been.

"Your blood levels are very close to nominal," Meghan said. "But the energy level in your blood plasma is running low, no doubt due to the recovery effort. You should replenish it."

"You don't seem grossed out by it right now."

"Oh, I am, but I'm becoming better at forcing back the urge to vomit. At least spawn feeding isn't as repulsive as drinking blood."

"Gee, thanks," Elyssa said. "Wish I didn't have to but it's not like I have a choice."

"I'm sorry, Templar Borathen. I didn't mean to imply—"

Elyssa held up a hand. "It's fine, Meghan. And please don't get all formal on me. I know how my dad is, but I am most definitely not him."

"I imagine he must be very upset about your connection to Justin."

I laughed. "Upset is hardly the word I'd use." I gave Elyssa a puzzled look. "That reminds me; I thought you were in big trouble. Your parents didn't ground you for life?"

"Oh, I just had a mother-daughter chat and then went looking for you."

"That easy?"

She smiled. "Of course."

Meghan gave her a dubious look. "Is there something going on I should be aware of?"

"Justin met my parents." Elyssa's lips trembled as she tried to smile. "Things didn't go so well."

"I can imagine," Meghan said. "After the Thunder Rock disaster, your father probably hates spawn as much as I do—present company excluded, of course, Justin."

Elyssa's gaze sharpened. "You know something about Thunder Rock? As far as I know, he's never told anyone what really happened there, aside from the Synod. And he's the only one who survived."

"I don't know the details," Meghan said, "but your father and I once had a discussion about spawn when I joined the Templars."

"Was this after your own father's death?" I asked.

She nodded. "It was one of the reasons I joined. To fight evil."

"What did he tell you?" Elyssa asked, curiosity blazing in her features.

"Only that he felt he and I were kindred spirits since we had both suffered evil at the hands of spawn. Beyond those few words, he didn't go into specifics. If he had, I'd tell you. He did say he'd detailed everything in his journal and wanted me to write down my own story in great detail so he could present a case against the spawn at some point in the future."

Elyssa snorted. "As if the Conclave could do anything about them."

"Typical," I said, my chin tight. "Spawn I don't even know tick off your dad and now he hates all of us."

Meghan's lips flatlined. "I'm afraid my story is just one of many. Believe me, after my father's death I looked for other stories like mine, and there are a lot of them."

My stomach growled again and I suddenly didn't feel like discussing the shortcomings of my relatives. "I think it's time to feed." I looked at Smith. "I'm going to talk to him and find out how to contact Underborn. Then we can go."

I strolled to the room with the metallic circle embedded in the floor and watched for a moment as Smith ran a program on his tablet. Red words flashed on the screen and I figured it didn't mean anything good.

"Part of the tracker is blocked," Smith said, "but not all of it. I think it's using a backup frequency."

Shelton grunted. "Makes sense. I'll run the scanner again since we have the first one locked down. Maybe we can identify it."

"Hanging in there?" I asked Dad.

A bored expression weighed down his face. "Barely." He looked back at Elyssa as she shoved stuff into a knapsack. "You two going somewhere?"

"I need to top off the old tank, if you know what I mean."

"You and me both." His eyes settled longingly on the exit.

I glanced at Smith. "I need to ask you something."

"Fire away."

"Umm, it's kinda personal, about your sister."

His forehead scrunched with confusion. "Why don't we step outside, then?"

Dad and Shelton had confused looks as well.

"It's not what you're thinking," I said.

"Hey, I don't blame you, man," Shelton said. "She's kinda hot. I'd be all over that."

"Hey now, that's my sis—ah dammit," Smith said. "Why do I get so protective? Not like there's anything left to be protective of."

Shelton barked out a laugh. "She's still your sister. Guess you'd be even worse of a brother if you didn't stick up for her."

"Yeah, yeah, TP." Smith shook his head.

He led me to the exit, uttering a word or two, and waiting for the stairs to form. Then we walked up to the ground floor where the resident mattress greeted us with its moldy aroma and a cheerful array of colorful stains. Elyssa came up a second later.

"What do you really want?" Smith said. "Obviously, you have no interest in my sister."

"I think she may be coming around," I said, then cleared my throat nervously. "We, uh, had a little conversation after I woke up. She apologized about her bad behavior—the kidnapping and attempted murder stuff."

He looked unimpressed. "She's come back before with the contrite apologies, tears, all that jazz, only to circle right back around into a worse situation. I don't think this time will be any different."

"Not with that attitude," Elyssa said. "Act like a big brother and maybe things will work out. Drop the conspiracy obsessions."

"I can't," he said. "I have to find out what happened."

"You're hooked on solving a mystery, and she's hooked on whatever fills the void where your attention should be," Elyssa said.

Smith grinned. "You must be related to Dr. Phil."

I laughed.

Elyssa glared at the two of us and we shut up.

"By the way," Smith said, pulling out his tablet. "I found out some even worse stuff about those killing spells you gave me to analyze."

I had almost forgotten about the wretched things. Almost forgotten my mom apparently wanted to murder a lot of people. "How can mass murder be worse?"

"I wrote spell analyzing routines that deciphered several runes. My tablet isn't very fast so I uploaded some of the spells to my server. It has a more robust version of Arc OS running on it."

"Is that like the magic version of Windows?"

"Exactly. It's just a computer operating system which uses science and arcane elements together."

"I can't believe you guys created your own operating system. Can you play video games on it?"

"All right, geeks," Elyssa said in a weary tone. "Enough with the nerd talk. What's up with the spell?"

"Ah, yeah," Smith said, the smile vanishing from his face. "What you have is a group of spells, each one dedicated to a particular use. You remember how I told you these spells are made for killing en masse?"

I nodded.

He pulled up a spell on his table. "This one could wipe out every vampire in a hundred-mile radius."

CHAPTER 23

"One little spell can wipe out thousands of supers just like that?" I was aghast at the possibilities.

"It's not just a 'little' spell," Smith said. "In fact, to pull this off you'd need massive amounts of power and exceptional skills to focus it properly. At its lowest level, you could kill vampires in your immediate vicinity. If you chained together with several exceptional sorcerers and an arcane generator on a ley line, you could nuke every vampire within a thousand miles."

"Holy crap." I tried to wrap my head around the sort of power he was talking about, but I still didn't have much of a frame of reference or the time to dig into too many specifics. "Shelton showed me how you can use computers for complex spells. What's to stop just anyone from executing this spell and running it?"

"Unless they know exactly how to focus it and possess the willpower to back it, either nothing would happen, or they'd burn out." Smith zoomed in on one of the runes. "These custom runes are like nothing I've ever seen. They're so intricate and dense it must have taken years just to craft each one."

"Sounds like you're impressed," I said. "You do realize your sister would be killed if anyone cast this spell, right?" I glanced at Elyssa. "Would it hurt dhampyrs?"

He shook his head. "I'm not sure. It might kill dhampyrs or it might simply clear the vampire genes out of their system and leave behind only their human side."

"This spell could make me normal?" Elyssa said, her eyes sparking with interest.

"Define *normal*," Smith said.

"Don't even think about it," I told her. "I love you just the way you are." She smiled, but I could sense the lingering doubt.

"What does this rune mean?" I asked, pointing to the one he'd zoomed in on. It looked like a swirling ladder carved with tiny inscriptions, almost like DNA.

"You've got to understand—a lot of what's in here is over my head. Whoever made this understands the fundamentals of what makes a vampire a vampire. A vampire is made partly from the focus and will of a master vampire, a virus in the bloodstream, and magical energy. These bind together and change the individual person, morphing them from a standard human, to a being with different digestive needs, denser muscles, and much thicker blood to support such a system."

"Sounds like you understand it pretty well," I said.

He winced. "Part of my dismal attempts to see if I could reverse Felicia's transformation without killing her."

"I assume you didn't figure it out?"

Uncertainty flashed across his face. "I don't know what I figured out. I needed to test my theories, but couldn't bring myself to kidnap a vampire. I didn't want to kill anyone." He looked down at the rune. "This single rune has all the scientific and MDNA—i.e. magical DNA—of a vampire spelled out." He scrolled over to another rune, this one in the eerie shape of a reddish skull with a stake through the temple. "This is the killing rune. It unravels one tiny part of the force binding the MDNA together, causing a backlash, killing the subject."

"What enables it to kill on such a wide scale?" I asked.

"That would be a factor of energy, focus, and will—same with any spell. But the human body can only funnel so much energy before it burns out."

"What if someone grabbed hold of a huge radar dish or power pole and did it?"

He laughed so hard it took him a minute to answer. "Oh, man, you come up with some funny ideas." He took a breath and forced away his grin. "It doesn't work that way. Even if you're using an arcane generator to power a staff, your body has to be able to handle the feedback and power flow in order to drive it through your focus."

"The focus being the staff?"

"Right. Focus, power, and will, are the three fundamentals of sorcery."

"And the other spells are probably tooled to kill other supers?"

"That would be my guess." He tucked the tablet under his arm.

I banged my fist against the crumbling plaster wall and grunted. A sprinkle of dust drifted from the ceiling. "I can't understand why my mom wants to kill all those beings. Has she totally flipped?"

He held up a finger. "Ah, I meant to tell you. I don't think your mother wrote these spells."

My mom might not be a murderous lunatic? Hope blossomed in my heart. "Why do you say that?"

"Your mother is not only a genius, but one of the most powerful sorcerers in this day and age. These spells are beyond even her skills." He scratched the back of his neck. "Hell, I couldn't name anyone in the arcane community capable of writing them."

I'd heard some good things about my mom, but Smith practically revered her. I should have been happy, knowing my mom was all that and a bag of chips. Instead, jealousy darkened my feelings, knowing Smith knew more about my own mom than I did. I wanted so much to question him about her, but the urgency to confront the Underborn problem prodded me in the ribs and told me to get a move-on.

"What you're saying is some lunatic wants to kill off a bunch of supers because he's a hater."

"This stuff is light-years ahead of us. It's almost like an alien race gave us blueprints to stuff we could hardly conceive."

189

"Doesn't seem so far out of reach," I said. "I mean we can sequence DNA with computers. What's to stop someone from decoding magical DNA?"

"You ever play video games?" Smith asked.

Elyssa groaned. "Don't you have something else to ask him, Justin?"

I held up my *give me a moment* finger to Elyssa. "Yeah, why?"

"Programmers create a virtual world using computer language, complete with rules like gravity and so forth. Our universe operates the same way. Science is man's way of using the existing laws of physics to make things happen. Magic is our way of tapping into the programming code of physics to make things happen."

"Like the Matrix?"

"Except in this case, there is a spoon and you can make it bend by editing the laws on a tiny scale."

I really wanted to take Shelton up on his offer to teach me all this magic stuff since he'd told me I might have inherited some of my mom's mad skillz. But now was definitely not the time to embark on a secondary education. Still, I felt so much better knowing my mom was not a mass murderer. But nothing so far explained *why* she had these spells. Was it part of some research? The more I found out about my mom, the more I realized how little I knew of her. She might have raised me, but she was almost a complete stranger to me otherwise.

"I do have another thing to ask you," I said uneasily. "I want to contact Underborn."

Smith nodded. "I just emailed you instructions. But it won't be easy."

"What?" I said, surprised. "You're giving it to me just like that?"

He nodded, an amused expression creeping over his face. "I'd do the same thing if I were you." Pain and sorrow erased the amusement from his features. "I just hope you have better luck than I did."

"He'll have me," Elyssa said, flashing a confident grin.

Smith nodded grimly. "Whatever you do, follow the instructions exactly."

"Or we'll die?"

"Nah, most likely you'll just never make contact."

I shook his hand. "Thanks for everything, man. I can't tell you how much I appreciate it. Especially putting up with Shelton."

He laughed. "He's not all bad once you get past his serious character flaws." Smith winked. "Good luck." He turned and went back down the stairs, flicking his wand behind him and closing the entrance.

Elyssa and I looked at each other for a long moment. Then I pulled her in for a long deep kiss. It was so much nicer not feeling the pressure of everyone's eyes on my back when I made out with my girlfriend. Her hand wandered down to my butt and squeezed.

"Want to try out the mattress?" she asked, looking at the abomination.

I shuddered. "Much as I want you, there's no way I'm getting close to that disease-riddled monstrosity. It might eat us." I checked the email on my phone and found a message from one Buzz Masterson, Smith's latest randomly selected email account, waiting for me.

It read:

1. *Go to The Laughing Dog in the Grotto.*
2. *Purchase a Mr. Nutter's Angel Biscuit.*
3. *Go to Grotto Park.*
4. *Sit on the northeast bench facing Orange and MagicSoft.*
5. *Wait. Wait some more. Keep waiting.*

P.S. You can eat the Angel Biscuit if you get hungry.

"AN ANGEL BISCUIT?" I said, scratching my head.

"I guess you've never been to the Grotto, have you?" Elyssa said.

"What is it, a shopping mall?"

She smiled. "It's time you found out."

We walked down the trash-strewn alley toward the road. I'd grabbed more cash from my duffel bag so we could take a taxi. Running wasn't really an option for me just yet, at least not until I fed and let my body recover. Voices echoed from around the corner and one of them had a familiar British quality to it.

"You really are a filthy animal," Stacey said.

"Very filthy," came the reply. It was Ryland, judging from the southern drawl.

Elyssa and I stepped around the corner. Stacey stood on the sidewalk, arms crossed and gaze stern as she stared Ryland down. He leaned against the wall, one foot pressed against the brick, his demeanor cocky and confident. And something was very different about his face, but I couldn't quite place it.

"What are you guys doing?" I asked.

Stacey started, nearly jumping out of her skin. "Good lord, Justin. You just about gave me a heart attack."

"Seriously? You didn't hear me or sense me coming from a mile away?"

"I was somewhat preoccupied, thank you very much, sir." Her face flushed pink.

"We're keeping a lookout," Ryland said. "Seems quiet for now. After the whoopin' we gave those hellhounds, I doubt Kassallandra will be making another move soon."

"You guys made a great team," Elyssa said. "The way Ryland drew their attention so Stacey could flank was like watching art."

I glanced at Elyssa and saw she was deadly serious. In fact, she looked kind of jealous, maybe because she couldn't turn into a panther. Which, come to think of it, would be totally badass.

Stacey flushed red. "No, we do not make a *team*, nor could we ever. Wolves and panthers do not hunt in packs."

"I got it!" I said snapping my fingers. "You shaved your mutton chops."

Ryland rubbed a hand over the bare skin where the long sideburns had been. He looked a lot better and younger without those nasty things. "Yeah. Decided it was time for a change."

Elyssa looked from Ryland to Stacey and back, a slightly wild look entering her eyes. "Uh, well, we're off to the Grotto. We'll be back soon."

Ryland pushed himself off the wall. "I got Meghan's Prius around the corner. We can be there in twenty minutes."

Elyssa shook her head. "Don't bother. Justin and I will be fine."

"Sugah, I ain't about to let you go wandering off by yourself after what we've been through. Your dad would kill me."

Elyssa put a hand on Ryland's shoulder and looked him in the eyes. "I'm sorry, Ryland. We can't bring anyone else along for this."

"But—"

"No buts."

"Surely, I'm coming too," Stacey said, stepping closer to me. "I owe you my life, lamb, and I don't intend to let you run off to the slaughter."

"I'm going to meet Underborn," I said. Shocked silence met my little admission. "I can't risk that he won't meet with me if I have a whole gang tagging along. Please, don't follow us or try to keep us from going. I have to do this for my dad. I have to try."

"What an absolutely disagreeable idea," Stacey said. "Then again, planning has never been your strength, has it, dear?"

"I'm a doer, not a thinker," I said. "Now promise me you'll stay here and keep an eye on things."

Stacey made a mewling noise and a black streak dashed from across the road and up to her.

"Nightliss!" I said, picking up the little black cat and petting her. She purred and rubbed her face against mine. "I've missed you, little girl." I'd been certain she'd lost her life with the other cats.

"She found me while we were pulling bodies from the rubble of my former abode," Stacey said, a tear in her eye. "I was so worried about her."

"She's so brave," I said, scratching behind her ears. I held her up and kissed her nose. "Aren't you just the bwavest kitty in the world!"

Nightliss's ears flattened and her eyes narrowed, as though I'd gravely insulted her.

Stacey sniffed. "She's not a child, Justin."

"I'm sorry," I said, putting her down after one more kiss on her cute little nose. "I got carried away."

Ryland laughed as Nightliss ran up his leg and perched on his shoulder. She gazed at him with her serious green eyes, and then sniffed his hair. Apparently she liked the odor because she rubbed her cheek against his face and purred.

Stacey looked aghast. She mewed. Nightliss looked at her and made some really bizarre noises that hardly sounded like kitty talk. Stacey's mouth dropped in disbelief. "Well, I never," she said.

"What did you say?" I asked.

"I'd rather not talk about it," Stacey said. She gave Nightliss a withering stare before looking back at me. "Nightliss informed me she would be most agreeable to accompanying you and providing some assistance."

"Great," I said, remembering how Nightliss had saved my rear end during my dad's rescue. I looked at the little black cat. "You ready to go?"

She leapt the short distance from Ryland's shoulder to mine and settled down.

"I guess so," Elyssa said, giving Nightliss a strange look. "That is one smart cat."

Stacey hugged me. "Good luck, my lamb. Please do be careful."

"Don't die or your father *will* murder me," Ryland said, his tone deadly serious as he tossed Elyssa the keys to the Prius.

"I don't plan to," Elyssa said.

We walked down the street and found the Prius parked behind a dumpster.

Then we went to meet with an assassin.

CHAPTER 24

*O*n the way to the Grotto, we stopped for food and so I could recharge my supernatural batteries. Fifteen minutes later, we were back on the road, headed for Buckhead, one of the ritzier parts of town.

"Is the Grotto a big restaurant?" I asked as we reached Phipp's Plaza, a real uppity mall full of stores catering to folks with more money than sense.

Elyssa grinned. "Just wait. You'll like it."

She pulled into the parking deck and, ignoring the big green arrow pointing toward the mall parking spots, headed straight for a concrete wall to the right.

"Watch out!" I yelled, bracing for impact as we...went straight through the wall.

Elyssa laughed so hard tears of mirth leaked from her eyes. Nightliss flattened her ears and glared at her.

I released my death grip on the door handle and growled. "You punk."

"That was so totally worth it," she said between laughs. "It's an illusion so the noms won't find this place."

"Lovely."

As I recovered my wits, Elyssa wended the car down a dark spiraling ramp with rough-hewn rock walls on either side. Ten minutes later, we reached a cavernous underground garage rivaling the shopping mall on the surface in size. Massive marble columns reached from the asphalt and vanished into the darkness hiding the ceiling. Elyssa found a parking spot right behind what looked like a mobster car from the 1920's. I saw everything from plain-Jane Toyotas to a sleek red Maserati and a purple Lamborghini. Seriously, anyone who had the cash to buy a purple Lamborghini had to have a spare million or so I could have. Odder vehicles sat in roped-off sections and stalls of their own.

Horse-drawn carriages, rickshaws, and even an old wagon with a mule awaited their owners. A team of sleek white Clydesdales whickered softly to each other, munching on grub from the feedbags attached to their heads. The mule brayed at the horses, its lips splaying out from large buck teeth. It was probably jealous. In a large wooden stall to the right, a team of camels rested on the floor, their legs folded beneath them as they contentedly chewed their cud. Nightliss raced from our side and, using the camels as stepping stools, leapt to the top of one of the stall dividers.

A large red circle with yellow stripes painted diagonally across it dominated the center of the huge garage. In the center of the painted area sat an imposing black arch mounted upon a shiny black slab of circular stone. It looked big enough to drive several semi-trucks through side-by-side, though I couldn't imagine what purpose it had sitting there aside from decoration. The material making up the arch seemed to twist and bend in a peculiar way, hurting my eyes when I stared at it too long, even though the arch itself was flawlessly curved.

"What in the world is this place?" I asked, unable to stop gawking at the menagerie and bizarre structure.

The thrum of electricity filled the air before Elyssa could answer. A klaxon went off with a harsh growl and the animals brayed, whinnied, and even bleated. Apparently there were goats somewhere behind the carriages. Lights embedded in the concrete around the perimeter of the red circle flashed on and an azure sheet of shimmering energy flickered into existence. The space in the center of the black arch flashed black, gray, and then white, alternating with ever-increasing speed until the electric thrum turned to a crackle.

I looked at Elyssa. She looked back at me and grinned, probably enjoying my complete befuddlement. Nightliss sat atop one of the carriages, ears flat and eyes narrowed. I couldn't blame her for not liking the racket.

"Look, or you're gonna miss it," Elyssa said, pointing back at the arch.

I looked just in time to see the area in the center of the arch burst into crackling black and white static before clearing. Instead of seeing the garage on the other side, however, I saw a rolling gray mist and what looked like the green foliage of a jungle. A massive emerald waterfall cascaded down a rocky cliff face where people swam in the crystalline water. In the center of the arch stood a big gray pachyderm, almost tiny by comparison. The elephant carried a large covered deck atop its back where three people sat with imperious looks, as if arriving via elephant was the only way to travel. Obviously, they hadn't seen the purple Lamborghini yet.

The huge animal stepped through the arch, coming from the jungle and into the garage, tracking mud and other debris across the circular slab. As it lumbered toward a large stall supplied with fresh hay, a boy raced from a small building I hadn't noticed before and took hold of a rein the elephant driver dropped down to him. The boy led the creature to what I supposed was the elephant unloading zone and stopped it next to a set of stairs.

One of the riders, a dark-skinned man dressed in vibrant clothes reminding me of something out of a Bollywood film about ancient royalty, stepped to the top of the stairs and helped a woman and girl step from the deck. The girl, who looked about my age, flashed me a bright smile as I stared dumbfounded at them.

"It's not polite to stare," Elyssa said, taking my chin in her hand and turning me to face her.

"Wh—what in the world is this place? What the heck is that arch?"

"This is the entryway to the Grotto, one of the major marketplace hubs of the Overworld. The Obsidian Arch is a gateway connected to others like it across the world. It can transport people almost instantly from one place to another if they have the money."

"You have to pay to use it?"

"Yeah. The Arcane Council has a monopoly since they're the only ones who know how to activate and use them."

"No buttons to push?"

She smiled. "No, silly."

"How does it do that? Does it fold space or create some kind of quantum gateway?"

"Someone's been watching too much Star Trek."

"It's so cool," I said, walking toward the arch.

Elyssa grabbed my arm to keep me from stepping inside the circle. "You don't want to do that."

"Why not?"

"When the arch is activating, it apparently makes little cracks in our realm that could drop someone in the Gloom if they're not careful. And then you need a sorcerer to come drag you out before you're lost forever."

My skin went cold. "The Gloom?"

"Yeah. It's kind of like an in-between place buffering our reality from the demon plane and other nasty places. I've never been there but I know Templars who have. You don't want to know the sorts of creatures who try to sneak into our world." She shuddered. "Hope I never have to leave this plane."

"Unbelievable," I said in a whisper. Despite being a demon spawn, I still found it hard to conceive such a thing as a demon plane existed, much less other worlds or realms.

"I think it's creepy," Elyssa said with a grimace. "Our world is hard enough to worry about without wondering if someone's gonna figure out how to open a door demons can walk through at will."

"It sounds like a mess," I said watching as the elephant riders stepped through a pair of large wooden doors up ahead. The faint strains of music and people talking filtered through the doorway. "Maybe we should go on in."

Elyssa smiled wistfully. "I was kind of hoping an ostrich rider would come through the arch."

I laughed at the image in my head. "I'll take the Lamborghini any day."

As we made our way toward the door, the boy who'd led the elephant to its stall gave me a cheerful grin and bowed. "G'day, guvnah!" His cockney accent sounded straight out of Oliver Twist.

"Hi," I said, trying not to laugh. I nodded toward the elephant. "What happens when the thing drops a load of poo?"

A sad look replaced his cheerful smile. "A lot of bloody shoveling, sir. But that's what Rachel is for."

"You get a girl to clean up the mess?"

He laughed in the high-pitched way kids do and pointed at the mule. "That's Rachel. She pulls the dung wagon."

I wondered what the normal people shopping in the ritzy mall above would think about having a poop wagon and a mule right under their noses.

The boy pulled open one of the dark-stained wooden doors for us as Nightliss appeared from nowhere and brushed against my leg. "Enjoy yourselves, guvnah and young miss!"

Elyssa ruffled the kid's hair and smiled. "Thanks."

We stepped through the door and into bedlam.

People scurried everywhere along a shop-lined cobblestone street from an era long past. The shops were crafted of marble with roofs of a greenish slate, though further down I could see buildings of rougher stone varying wildly in color. Some of the stores were connected while others stood apart. One nearby shop stocked old-style female attire that looked like a complete nightmare to put on. A black velvet-looking affair complete with gloves reminded me of the Goth dresses Elyssa favored when she went to school. Nightliss scrambled atop my shoulder and made herself at home, her green eyes darting this way and that at the myriad of sights and sounds.

"Is this where you shop for clothes?" I asked Elyssa.

She snorted. "No way. This street is Golden Way which pretty much describes how expensive these stores are. I prefer Under Alley, personally. Great character and some cool little stores that won't rip you off."

"You're telling me the Grotto is like a town with streets and all?" I looked up and saw sunlight filtering through clouds. My mouth dropped open, probably for the millionth time in the last ten minutes.

"Think of it like an old-school outdoors mall."

"But we're underground. How can I see the sun?" I looked left and right for the cavern walls that should border the place but couldn't see past the buildings.

"We're not exactly underground. We're in a nexus."

"So we're not really underground?"

Elyssa touched her chin in a thoughtful manner before answering. "Think of this place as being mostly on Earth but partly in another plane."

My eyebrows climbed my forehead. "You just lost me."

"I don't know how it works." She shrugged. "Someone told me this place shares space with another plane of reality which is why you have the sky even if technically we're on Earth. If you walk far enough, you'll hit an invisible wall which keeps you from going any further."

I peered at the sky, looking for any hint of an alien landscape. "You can see more of the other place it shares space with?"

"No, just gray mist."

I nodded and looked for the edges anyway. "Sounds like we're in a bubble."

"That's as good an explanation as any I've heard." She motioned at our surroundings. "It's not like anyone else understands how this place works."

"Wait, so how did it get here? Who made it?"

Elyssa shrugged. "It was here already, just like the Obsidian Arch. A few buildings already existed—those are located in the historical district —but the rest was just empty space and people built up over time. There are others like the Grotto scattered across the planet, but only a few are this large."

"Isn't that kind of spooky? What if bad people or things made them?"

She pressed a lock of hair behind her ear. "Believe me, the Templars and Arcane Council studied these places and concluded whoever made them had an understanding of magic we've long forgotten."

"Like Stonehenge?"

She smiled. "No, that place really is just a collection of rocks."

"That's kind of a disappointment."

We walked down Golden Way and I followed Elyssa through small twisting alleys and along smaller streets lined with what looked like houses, restaurants, and other stores. Though the place wasn't exactly bustling with life, I saw all sorts of supers. A group of vampires were having their teeth whitened at a shop claiming to have the best teeth-cleaning spells in the Overworld. Several young sorcerers emerged from a shop, flourishing velvety new robes, the girls wearing yellow, purple, or pink, and the boys mostly in black. A pack of what Elyssa told me were lycans sat in front of a restaurant, gnawing on huge haunches of meat, their rowdy conversation echoing up and down the street.

Everything about this part of the Grotto had an old world appeal, from the cobblestones to the carved wooden placards above the quaint shops, to the live music from people playing what looked like lutes, pan flutes, bulbous guitars things, and even a crazy-looking nut job prancing around with bongo drums and an oboe strapped to his chest.

"This place is like Disney World without all the snot-nosed little kids," I said. "I think I like it."

Elyssa grinned. "It's pretty quiet here today but it gets crazy around the full and new moon."

We turned down a street absolutely packed with booths and stores. Every nook and cranny seemed to be filled with merchants of all sorts, yelling and shouting about their wares. One woman was selling exotic purple snakes. A man with a turban sold flutes he claimed would charm any animal. There was even a joke shop. I couldn't help myself and swung inside, staring at the wild array of items.

I found a box of spider marbles, guaranteed to cover anything with illusionary creepy-crawlers when one was broken, and grabbed a few. "How much are these?" I asked the thin-faced proprietor behind the counter.

"Barter or tinsel?" he said.

I had no idea what he meant. "Barter for what?" I asked.

"Anything which might be of use. I always need more ingredients for my products."

"I don't have anything like that on me," I said. "What's tinsel?" All I could think of was the silvery stuff people put on Christmas trees.

"It's Overworld currency," Elyssa said giving the shopkeeper an apologetic smile. "He's kind of new to all this."

"Do you take dollars?" I asked, showing him a twenty and feeling kind of stupid for assuming an international marketplace like this would take normal money.

"Of course!" he said with a big smile. "I just need to figure out the exchange rate." He pulled out a tablet computer—I wondered if any sorcerer worth his salt didn't have one—and pulled up a website named "Moogle" which showed him a tinsel was trading for just under a buck.

I ended up buying a bag of the spider marbles for about twenty bucks and walking out of the shop a very happy man. I couldn't wait to test them out at school.

"You realize we might have to run for our lives in a little while?" Elyssa said, her eyes bright with amusement.

I shrugged. "I gotta live just to try this stuff out."

She laughed. "Maybe we should send it to the exit so we can pick it up later."

"You can do that?"

She nodded and, taking my hand, guided me to what looked like a large black mailbox. She stapled the bag shut and then spoke to it. "Justin is a dork."

"Hey, I'm no dorkier than you are."

A giggle escaped her lips. "That's the passcode to unlock the bag when we leave." She dropped the bag into the mail bin and closed it.

"Someone picks it up and takes it to the exit?"

She nodded.

"I love this place," I said. "We're definitely coming back." And I absolutely had to go over that joke shop from top to bottom. It was a gold mine.

Her hand tightened on mine. "I'm glad. I'll have to show you a couple of my favorite restaurants."

"We can finally have a real first date," I said. "I saw a playhouse earlier. Maybe dinner and a play?"

"That would be so nice," she said, her eyes growing soft. "Oh, and next month is Unification Day."

"What's that?"

"Every year they celebrate the founding of the Overworld Conclave and the Obsidian Arch is free to use. People come from all over the world, they have fireworks, a big festival, everything. We should definitely go."

"Heck yeah!" My body tingled and for a moment, I forgot all about my dangerous mission, about my dad, my missing mom, and the sister I'd never met. Just when I thought the supernatural gig couldn't get any cooler, I found something else to surprise the heck out of me.

Elyssa's eyes glowed with amusement and in that moment, I loved her more than ever.

"You're getting a really far-off look, Justin," she said with a big smile.

"Yeah, just fantasizing."

She looked up and down the alley we'd just entered, then pressed me against a wall and smothered me with a passionate kiss. "Fantasizing about that?"

I nodded dumbly then pulled her in for another kiss, spinning us around and pressing her against the wall. Our breathing grew heavier and I felt the clawing of my inner demon as it sensed the building excitement.

"Blasted kids these days," muttered a young-looking guy as he walked past.

"That dude couldn't be more than a few years older than we are," I said, laughing.

"Never can tell with supers," Elyssa replied. She grabbed my hand and led me out of the mouth of the alley and into a huge square. Nightliss was already sitting there staring at an amazing sight.

At each corner and side of the square stood gargantuan marble statues facing the center where the likeness of two planets dwarfed everything else. The faces on the statues were intricately detailed. In the corner nearest us stood the statue of an old man wearing a flowing robe and clutching a staff in one hand. Inscribed upon its large square base was a golden crescent moon cradling a silver star beneath which were words written in a language I didn't understand.

The next statue was of a beautiful woman, her marble hair carved with such minute care it truly seemed to flow across her shoulders and down to her waist. Upon her head rested a jeweled crown and rings decorated each finger on her detailed hands. A drop of red liquid falling into a crimson ocean had been carved into the pedestal, standing out in sharp relief to the otherwise pale marble of the statue.

Each of the other statues was much the same—white marble with a colored symbol carved into the large square base. The next one I noticed sent a shiver of apprehension through my body. Across the way and to the left of a large arch stood the statue of a man with lips so full and hair so long it made him look more beautiful than handsome. Aside from a fig leaf to preserve his modesty, he was nude, his body lean and well-muscled. Two large horns curved up from his forehead, jutting above narrowed eyes that seemed to bore into my very soul. He held his arms out, fingers splayed and palms facing each other, as though he wanted to grip the massive planets in the center of the square. A carving of a blue snake curled around a skeletal tree adorned the pedestal.

"I assume these statues are representative of the supers in the Overworld," I said, repressing another violent shudder as I turned away from what had to be the statue of a spawn.

"This is Founders Square." She brushed the scene with a stroke of her hand. "And these are the founders."

We walked around the towering globe in the center. It looked like Earth sheathed in a delicate shell of crystal. Etched into the surface of the crystal were more symbols I didn't recognize, each one casting a bluish glow.

"Amazing," I said, staring up at it.

"The symbol of the Overworld," Elyssa said, arching her neck. "Ezzek Moore, the dude with the staff," she said pointing at the robed statue, "said the Overworld Conclave is the delicate harmony protecting the world from anarchy and chaos. Or something like that. I didn't pay as much attention in History as I should have."

As we walked around the Overworld statue, I realized it eclipsed another effigy standing on the opposite side of the huge arch from the devil-horned spawn. I felt my eyes bulge. An angel with furled wings looked heavenward, hands splayed palms-up in supplication. The face was every bit as beautiful as the spawn's, though I couldn't tell if the angel was male or female.

"Angels?" I said, adding an exclamation mark to my question.

Elyssa laughed. "Yeah, that statue threw me for a loop when I saw it for the first time. My history teacher told us the artist who built these statues made the angel out of a sense of religious piety. But some purists say there were angels involved in crafting the Conclave."

My heart sank like a rock to the bottom of a river. "I guess that means there is such a thing as being damned."

Elyssa squeezed my hand. "If there's anything I've learned, it's that all things are possible. Demons come from their own realm, so why not angels? And if any religion is true, I don't see why even spawn can't be saved."

I tried to smile but it took effort. "Maybe heaven is hell for a demon spawn."

She chuckled. "You have a really jacked up way of looking at things sometimes."

"Give me enough time and I can rationalize anything if it'll make me feel better." I winked.

I felt like I could stand there all day gazing at the magnificence those statues represented, but Elyssa pulled me toward a small exit leading to a curving alley barely big enough for two people to walk side-by-side. Nightliss dashed ahead of us. My mind kept wandering back to the statues, namely the spawn and angel. Did angels really exist? Maybe there were supers old enough to remember or know.

Elyssa stopped and I bumped into her. We stood on yet another road, this one filled with a patchwork of uneven brick pavers and rounded stones. A rusty set of train tracks ran in the center of it, and I saw a red trolley trundling down the rails away from us, stopping every so often before vanishing around a corner to our left. I vaguely remembered seeing tracks in other parts of the Grotto as well. It made sense to have some form of transportation—this place was big as a town and not everyone had supernatural stamina and speed. I still hadn't recovered much of mine yet, despite topping off the old incubus tank earlier, but at least my feet weren't aching.

"There you go," Elyssa said pointing across the road.

I followed her finger and found a gray stone building. Attached to the front was the massive stone head of a dog, its tooth-lined maw curled up in a wicked smile. Inside the muzzle I could see a door leading inside.

We had reached the Laughing Dog.

CHAPTER 25

*M*y stomach turned sour and my nerves jangled like loose leaden coins in my guts as I stared at the gaping maw ahead of me. "That place sells Angel Biscuits?"

"Among other things."

The gaping dog head looked ready to devour anyone who stepped inside it but I needed a Mr. Nutter's Angel Biscuit, whatever the heck that was. I crossed the street and stepped onto the red stone tongue leading inside the mouth and up to a wooden door. I opened it, and a cozy pub complete with a roaring fire in one corner and haphazardly arranged wooden tables, greeted me. A few patrons sat at the bar, drinking what looked like beer and making quiet conversation.

"Greetings and salutations, friends!" said the chubby rosy-faced bartender, shattering the calm with his overenthusiastic manners. "What can I get for you?"

We stepped up to the bar since the restaurant portion was completely empty.

"I'd like an Angel Biscuit, please, and a bottled water."

"You mean Boggle water?" he asked.

"No, as in a plastic bottle of water."

He looked a bit confused. "Like the ones noms have in their stores?"

"Uh, maybe just the Angel Biscuit then."

"We just got in a fresh batch of Bloody Benjamin for the lady," he said beaming at her. "And you, sir, might enjoy a nice tankard of our Hale Hell Ale."

A shock ran through me as I realized this guy seemed to know what we were on sight. Or was he expecting us?

"A Bloody Benjamin does sound good," Elyssa said.

"Just the Angel Biscuit, please," I said, trying to smile over the worry playing skip-rope with my guts.

"Sure thing, friends," the man said, his smile cheery as ever. "But please stop back by and try out some of our new drinks, each one catered to your specific delights."

I widened my forced smile. "Sounds great!" *Now get my biscuit already!*

He went to the back and returned a moment later with a small to-go container. "We don't get a lot of orders for these. Mr. Nutter's Devilish Doughnuts are usually more popular. Then again, I suppose the Angel Biscuits are supposed to be a healthy alternative." He chuckled and shook his head like he couldn't believe anyone would want such a thing. "That'll be a quarter tinsel, please."

"Uh, you take American dollars?"

"But of course," he said, and tapped his chin for a moment before rounding the cost to a quarter.

I dropped a quarter in his hand, thanked him, and we left. "Where do you get tinsels?" I asked Elyssa.

"The Overworld Merchants Bank, usually."

"Why the heck can't they just use Euros or dollars or something that already exists?"

"You might as well ask me why dollar bills are green. I have no idea."

I thought back to the joke shop merchant. "And what's Moogle?"

"MagicSoft's answer to an internet search engine."

"Except it has Overworld stuff too."

"Yep." Her eyebrow quirked in amusement. "Orange has its own version named Tangerine."

"Oh, that's cute," I said, rolling my eyes. I opened the box the bartender had given me and found what looked like a very flat doughnut inside. It appeared to be made of several different grains. I sniffed it but it didn't have much of an odor. "No wonder people like the Devilish Doughnuts," I said, closing the box. I checked the list of things we had to do to find Underborn. "Where's Grotto Park? And where's Nightliss?"

An answering meow came from my feet as Nightliss appeared from wherever she'd been and hopped back onto my shoulder.

Elyssa smiled and petted the little cat. "Grotto Park is a few blocks over." A bell dinged in the distance and a trolley came into view down the road. "Want to take the trolley?"

"Sure."

Although I didn't see a driver in the front window, the trolley slowed as we waved it down. We were the only two people on it, and the number of people in the streets seemed to have dwindled significantly from just an hour ago. After riding along the winding streets for a few minutes, Elyssa stood up.

"We just need to cut through a couple alleys and we'll be there."

The trolley slowed as we stood up and waited for us to hop off before it sped up again.

"Do they have cameras on those things? Some dude remotely controlling it?"

Elyssa gave me a perplexed look involving two raised eyebrows. "After everything you've seen, you're still looking for a techie answer?"

I felt stupid for having asked. "Guess I'm not as used to all this as you are."

She smooched me on the cheek. "You're so cute when you're confused." Her eyes rolled. "Ugh, how do you do this to me?"

"Do what to you?"

"Make me get all lovey-dovey and gooey like some hormonal teenager."

"You are a hormonal teenager. Aren't you? I mean, you're not really a hundred years old are you?"

A giggle escaped those perfect lips of hers and her eyes sparkled like violet stars. "No, I'm really your age. Guess I'll have to tell you the sad story of how my family came to be sometime."

"I'd really like to hear it."

"It's such a tragedy," Elyssa said, pressing the back of a hand to her forehead and feigning a dizzy spell.

"You make me feel warm and gooey inside," I said, my own heart beating hard with desire.

Nightliss hissed and jumped off my shoulder, her claws digging in along the way.

"Ouch!" I said, watching the little black cat as she dashed down an alley. "Wonder what got into her."

"Probably saw a mouse," Elyssa said as she pressed herself to me and kissed me long and hard. When she pulled away, I gripped her tighter around the waist and held her there, my other hand gently brushing against her lips, her fair-skinned cheeks. I kissed her neck and drew in her scent—a mix of oil and leather, and something deep, mysterious, and all her.

"Is it so bad feeling gooey with love?" I asked after a moment or two of silence.

"I'm just not used to it." She sighed. "It's why I resisted you so much at the beginning. Maybe it's what kept me away when I found out what you are." She pressed her hand to my chest. "I don't like feeling so vulnerable. Like something could take you away from me at any moment. It was so hard when we were apart no matter how hard I tried to hate you."

My throat tightened at the memory of those terrible days. "I am still a little worried, though."

"About what?"

"The bad side of me. Whenever things heat up between us, I feel it trying to get out. I don't know if I'll be able to control it when...um, we you know."

"We'll figure it out when the time comes. In case you hadn't noticed, I didn't have any issues fending it off last time."

"Yeah, my throat remembers. Oh, and so does my butt after you flung it across the gravel parking lot."

She laughed. "Good times, huh?"

"The best."

I kissed her again before letting go of her waist and letting my hand drift down to catch hers. All I really wanted to do was keep her sweet lips pressed to mine and make out until all the stars in the universe winked out. Unfortunately, I couldn't afford to be so greedy since Dad was living on borrowed time.

We entered yet another of the winding alleys in this maze of a place, following the curve through an archway. Doorways lined the walls, each one apparently leading into a residence or maybe the backside of a shop. A large door ahead where the alley made a ninety-degree turn opened. A man in a gray business suit exited, his silvery hair slicked back like some businessman from the 1950s. Behind him emerged several more men, each one dressed the same, each one with silvery hair.

Despite the coloring of their hair, I would never have mistaken him or the others for old men because they looked middle-aged and their hair shimmered with whatever gunk they used to keep it in place. As my gaze took in their faces, I realized they all looked remarkably similar. The last man exited the door and closed it behind him, standing with the others and staring at me—at us—across the couple hundred feet in between.

Elyssa stopped as abruptly as I did. I backed up, keeping my eyes on the men ahead. The thud of hard-soled shoes pounding the cobblestones sounded behind us. I spun and saw more of the gray-suited men dropping from the top of a three-story building to our left. Each one landed without a grunt or any hint of exertion. They straightened from the impact of landing flat on their feet, eyes focused on us. There were now six of them to either side. And they all looked identical down to their expressionless faces.

"How strong are you feeling?" she asked.

I clenched my fists, testing. "Not very."

She looked at the sides of the alley. "We could hop back and forth, maybe get to the top of the building they jumped from."

"You probably can, but I can't."

"I'll carry you."

"You're so sweet."

One of the men pulled out a black tube and pressed a button. Something silvery flashed toward us. Elyssa shoved me aside and ducked. Two tiny darts pinged against the concrete alley wall above her head. She moved toward me. Stiffened and groped for her back. Then she dropped to her knees, eyes wide with shock, and slumped to the ground.

"Elyssa!" I screamed and scrabbled across the ground to her. I found a silver dart embedded in her back and plucked it out. "What did you do to her? What do you want?"

Did these men work for Underborn? Trying to contact him had obviously been a huge mistake. The gray men didn't answer. Didn't utter a word or a sound. They advanced on me like a squad of silent uncaring assassins, arms hanging unnaturally by their sides. I dug deep into my exhausted body, searching for any hidden wells of strength. Lifting Elyssa was a chore. I'd grown accustomed to everything feeling light but she felt like a sack of bricks in my arms in my current condition. There was no way I could dash past these people, much less haul my unconscious girlfriend with me.

I looked back toward the door where the first of them had emerged. They walked toward me, faces neutral and calm as though they'd just stepped out for a Sunday stroll. The other group advanced in much the same way. No matter how many questions I hurled at them, they never once opened their mouths to answer. One of them raised a black tube and aimed it at me. This was it. I couldn't hope to dodge those darts.

A patch of black dropped from the three-story building where the second group of gray men had come from and landed behind them. Silver flashed and the man nearest the back dropped wordlessly as his head rolled from his shoulders, face as emotionless as ever. The gray men turned, swords appearing in their hands, and met the figure in black. They moved so fast their swords were a blur, but the black figure met them all with graceful cuts and dodges. One of the gray men streaked toward their attacker, slashing downward. Sparks flew as the sword met concrete. The figure in black had already run up the wall and flipped behind him, severing the gray man's head with a quick slash of the sword just as his feet hit the ground.

I realized with sick fascination not a single drop of blood came from the severed stump of the neck. What in the name of Scooby Doo were these things?

The other group of men rushed us. I grabbed Elyssa under the armpits and dragged her with all my might back toward the alley exit, a hundred yards and an eternity away. I was going so slow I might as well have not been moving at all. The black figure struck the head from the last gray man in the second group and turned to face the others. I felt so helpless. So damned useless. Anger churned like hot lava in my chest. What good was I, weak like this?

I propped Elyssa against a wall and pulled knives from the sheaths on her thighs. Those bastards weren't going to take me down without a fight. My fists clenched tight around the hilts and my stomach roiled as fury burned like a heat wave from my center to the tips of my toes. It felt like a pulse hammering in my head, the pain ratcheting up as my anger grew. I yelled out a war cry and charged.

The first gray man I reached swatted me like a gnat and I flew back, slamming against the wall and rolling. Blood dripped from my elbows where I'd skinned them. I roared and pushed myself back up. Agony stabbed into my forehead but I ignored the pain and rushed the attackers again. A gray man staggered back soundlessly as the black figure delivered a solid roundhouse to his face. I leapt, both daggers extended, and stabbed them into his back. The man didn't so much as grunt as both blades cut deep into his flesh. Then he reached around and grabbed me.

Twin chisels seemed to slam from inside my forehead and I felt my clothes tighten against my skin. I was manifesting, spawning into my demon form but I didn't care. I would do anything to protect Elyssa. Strength poured into me. I gripped the gray man's head and twisted. It made a sick popping noise and ripped off. I threw the head at another attacker. The black figure whirled and sliced the other man's head off before my projectile reached him. The last two gray men split up, one coming for me.

"Come get me," I said, my voice deep, guttural, totally inhuman.

He did. I swung a fist and connected, sending him flying back against a wall.

"I'll teach you," I said in the deep voice, "to mess with me!" The last part came out in my normal, much punier voice and I felt all the strength leave me like air from a balloon as the gray man hurled himself at me, the neutral face never changing its expression once.

I slumped to the ground as my knees gave way. The gray man flew over me and crashed into the wall. Cracks spider-webbed in the concrete where his head hit. Before he could get back up, the black figure blurred across the few feet separating them and slashed downward, sending the gray man's head plunking onto the concrete. When it hit the ground, a tiny compartment opened behind his ear and a globe of light floated from within, sparkling, sputtering, and eventually flickering out, leaving a cold gray lump of what might have been clay.

Two nubs, no longer than the tips of my pinkies, lay in my lap. I looked closer and realized they were teensy tiny little horns. Apparently I didn't even have enough strength to go ape-feces on these guys and completely manifest. I was useless. So damned useless.

"Are you okay?" asked a deep male voice.

I turned and looked at the black-garbed figure. He wore baggy black pants, a sleeveless billowing black shirt, and a hooded cloak shrouding his face. A black cloth covered his features from the nose down and dark sunglasses prevented me from seeing his eyes. His bare arms rippled with muscle, joining to his torso with thick, rounded shoulders. This dude was buff. He reached down a hand which I gripped, and pulled me to my feet then rushed over to Elyssa's side and checked her head and her pulse.

He drew in a sharp breath. "She'll be okay."

"Who are you?" I asked.

His head turned toward me. "I'm on your side, spawn." His voice was low and ominous and I got the impression having this guy on my side wasn't necessarily a good thing.

"Why?"

He regarded me for a moment. "Because I have to be."

"Not because we're besties?"

"It is my duty. Nothing more, nothing less."

"Just because you're dressed in black doesn't give you the right to talk all mysterious. The way you handled that sword—" I shook my head as an image flashed into my mind's eye and I realized something.

I knew who this man was.

CHAPTER 26

"You're the one who saved me from the moggy, aren't you?" I said to the man in black, wishing I could see more of his face and gauge his reaction. The first time I'd gone to Stacey's hideout, one of her monstrous house cats incapacitated me and was about to use me as a pincushion when a flash of black and silver had beheaded the creature. My guardian angel, I'd called the mysterious figure. And this had to be him.

He stood and faced me. A month or so ago he would have towered over me, but I'd sprouted like a weed since then. If I was just over six feet, this guy was somewhere around six feet, five inches. Maybe more. I'd grown some muscles since then but where I was lean, he was thick as a bull. As we faced each other, I could practically feel his glare through those sunglasses.

"I did." His voice was deep. Almost too deep and unnatural.

"Are you stalking me?" I almost shuddered at the thought. "What in the hell is going on? Are you with the Templars?"

His covered eyes regarded me for several seconds. "I cannot say."

"Can't or won't?"

"Can't." He folded his arms. "And won't."

Frustration stoked the embers of my earlier anger though I was too tired to do much. I looked at the bodies of the gray men. Not a one of them was bleeding, but some sagged like melting wax. "What are those things?"

"Golems."

The term rang a bell though I didn't know right away what it meant. "What else can you tell me? Why were these things trying to kill me? Why are you following me? I'm sick of being in the dark, especially when it puts her in danger." I motioned toward Elyssa.

He stiffened, fists clenching as though I'd just mortally insulted him. I could tell it cost him something to relax. "They were not here to kill you, only to capture you. As for the rest of your questions, suffice it to say some entities wish to take you off the board while others want you to remain. I am on the side of the latter, but I won't be around to help you every time the others make a move. I suggest you use greater caution in the future. Perhaps employ your felycan and sorcerer companions to assist you." He nodded his head toward Elyssa. "Keep her far from you if you truly care about her."

"My girlfriend is pretty badass," I said, "but those things knocked her out first. Otherwise she would've kicked their gray butts back to wher-ever they came from and you could've hung around on the roof eating corndogs or whatever the heck you were doing up there." I glanced back at the bodies for a moment and turned around in time to see a patch of black cloak as it vanished atop the roof of the three-story building. "Come back and visit any time," I shouted after him before cursing soundly under my breath.

Guardian angel? Check. Crazy insane, highly unstable guardian angel? Double-check. But aside from knowing he was built like a brick outhouse I didn't know a thing about who he really was or who he was working for. I had a feeling it all boiled down to stupid Foreseeance 4311, though. I checked Elyssa's pulse. It beat strongly, but she wasn't stirring. I locked her arm over my neck and shoulder and struggled to my feet. Carrying the dead weight of a human was tough without super-natural strength, and Elyssa had a robust figure packed with dense muscle.

"I help," said a female voice behind me.

217

I yelped and almost dropped Elyssa, staggering backwards and into the wall in an attempt to keep my balance.

The pretty young girl from the forest stood there, except this time she wasn't as naked. A simple green dress covered her tender bits down to about mid-thigh. From there down, her feet and legs remained bare and white dust covered her toes.

"Who are you?" I asked for probably the thousandth time that day.

She smiled, displaying pearly white teeth and walked to me, her hands touching my face and looking into my eyes like I was a wondrous thing to behold. "I help." Her voice was sweet and, if I had to use a ten-dollar word to describe it, mellifluous. For some reason, I trusted her without question. In my gut I *knew* she wasn't going to whip out a knife and disembowel me.

"Thanks."

The girl positioned herself on Elyssa's other side. Where Elyssa was tall, fair-skinned, and muscular, this girl was short, petite, and olive-toned. But she had no problems holding up my girlfriend. If anything, she had an easier time of it than I did even if Elyssa's feet were dragging.

I turned to head back to the street but the girl shook her head and pointed toward the sharp turn in the alley ahead. Right at the door the gray men had emerged from.

"You want to go to the park?"

She nodded.

So we headed on, though my stomach knotted and twisted at the thought of another group of golem dudes attacking us. As we passed the last of the gray men's bodies, I noticed it was dissolving into a puddle of gray sludge, leaving behind nothing but the suit. From the little contact I'd had with the things, the flesh had felt real, though it was hard to remember now in the fading heat of battle. The one whose head I'd ripped off had felt flesh-like, but the way the head had popped off like a doll made me shudder in revulsion. Vamplings. Hellhounds. Golems. Seemed there was no end to the kinds of monsters out to kill or capture me.

"Where do you come from?" I asked the girl.

She smiled shyly but said nothing.

"Lovely," I muttered. "Well, at least you're nicer than mystery man."

She beamed at me.

After a couple more turns we reached a large marble-paved round-about bordered by five-story buildings, curved and molded in designs that didn't seem physically possible. These buildings looked modern— no, futuristic—and were spotless. One building was stark white with stainless balconies and appeared to be made from shiny glowing plastic. Another was a checkered black reminding me of carbon fiber. I felt my pie hole hanging open as the woman and I carried Elyssa through a sprawling park, green and lush, in the middle of the roundabout.

Hardwood trees similar to maples towered above the glade while well-manicured hedges bloomed with flowers of more colors than the paint section of a hardware store. We moved Elyssa to a bench made of the checkered black material and set her down. I remained standing and gaped at the amazing scenery. The buildings looked like apartments, each one of unearthly design. as if a series of architects had tried to outdo the last one. Ordinary items like bicycles and flower pots on the balconies added a surreal touch. Designs like this were the last thing I expected after touring the old-world areas.

On the opposite side of the park, I saw a blue sign proclaiming *MagicSoft* affixed to a building made from what appeared to be liquid glass. People walked up shimmering stairs and beneath an arching entrance. Just across from it was a stark white sign with an orange on it, identical to the ones I'd seen on Meghan and Smith's tablet computers. I sighed in relief, happy to finally be in the right area.

"You like?" the girl asked, startling me from my reverie.

I nodded. "Very much."

She smiled—it seemed like the thing she did most. And she did it very well.

I looked at her dark olive skin, the slight slant to her eyes and wondered where she was from. Maybe she didn't speak much English. At least one thing was sure. "You're not a woodlander are you?"

Her large eyes blinked and she tilted her head slightly to the side.

"You know, like a wood nymph."

She shook her head. "No."

Her accent wasn't what I would consider Asian, but she definitely had some kind of a weird lilt to her speech.

Elyssa groaned. The girl looked at her. Her smile faltered and flattened. She looked at me and the smile returned, lighting her features with happiness. A sweet sigh escaped her lips. "I go." She pecked a kiss on my nose and giggled, covering her mouth with a hand like a shy teenybopper on the first date. With that, she bolted away in a flash, vanishing into the same alley mouth we'd just come from. I gaped for a moment until Elyssa groaned again.

I pressed my hands to her cheeks, her forehead. "Sweetie? Can you hear me? Are you okay?"

One eyelid fluttered open followed by the next. "Huh? What?" She bolted upright, hands going for the knives that were no longer in their sheaths. I'd left them embedded in the backs of a couple of golems.

"It's okay. You're safe."

Elyssa rose from the bench, staggered and pressed a hand to her head with a wince. "What did they hit me with?"

"No idea." I told her about the fight and the guardian angel mystery man.

"Did he have any tattoos or scars? Rings? Other jewelry or markings?"

"No, not that I could see. But his voice sounded weird. Like it was deeper than a normal voice."

"Disguised?"

I shrugged. "It didn't sound normal. Kind of reminded me of this toy android mask I used to have that made my voice sound like a nuclear space robot."

"Uh, okay." The corner of her lip lifted in a half grin.

"He was ripped. Huge arms and shoulders, a little taller than me—well, half a head or so—and he knew how to handle a sword. Those golems were inhumanly fast but they couldn't touch him."

She frowned, furrowed her brow. "There are a lot of blade masters in the Overworld, so that doesn't narrow it down much."

"What's the deal with swords anyway? What's to stop someone from whipping out an automatic rifle and blowing away a guy with a blade?"

She flicked a hand in disgust. "Guns are considered cowardly weapons."

"So? I'll bet there are plenty of bad dudes who don't give a crap about honor when it comes to fighting."

"There are also plenty of sorcerers who don't need guns," she said, rubbing her eyes and blinking them. "I've fought them as well and I'll tell you something: I'd rather face someone with a gun."

"I'd rather go without all the bloodshed. I'm a peacenik."

She laughed. "This coming from the guy who plays Kings and Castles."

"Yeah, but that's make-believe murder and mayhem."

Elyssa glanced at the MagicSoft sign and motioned toward it with her head. "Want to continue this little quest or go home?"

I was scared, no doubt about it. The golems had shattered any pretense of a pleasant outing, but what had I expected? I was trying to meet with the guy hired to kill my father. He might very well kill me himself.

"Let's do this."

She nodded and we walked across the park and sat on the bench facing the MagicSoft sign. A line of people wearing everything from jeans to suits and ties, to long flowing sorcerer robes stretched around the front of the store and vanished around the corner. The inside of the store, clearly visible through the odd liquid glass material making up the walls of the building, was packed. Several very tired-looking sorcerers stood behind a shiny metallic counter, talking to people and taking money. A poster on one of the windows showed a smiling man in fancy black robes holding a laptop computer in one hand. He wore thick rimmed square glasses reminding me of Smith a little bit, though this guy looked older.

Across the road was a very similar scene aside from the orange on the sign and the glowing white material of the building. The line of people waiting there looked very much like the one at MagicSoft. Every so often one of the people in the Orange line shouted an insult at someone in the MagicSoft line. Some of the banter was playful; some of it was downright mean.

Orange's posters featured a thin balding man with a goatee holding various devices. A tagline on the poster read: *Now you can compare Apples to Oranges!*

"What the freak is going on there?"

Elyssa raised an eyebrow and shrugged. "Must be some new release I guess. Orange and MagicSoft are super-competitive and their tablets and smartphones are pretty popular."

"Good lord. I guess there's an Overworld equivalent for everything."

She took my hand and squeezed it. "I know it must all seem crazy to you. I grew up in this world so it's not such a big deal to me. I've been here tons of times, some for shopping and having a fun day out with my mom." Her eyes grew distant and welled with emotion. "But I guess that's done now." She pressed a hand over her eyes and took a deep breath.

I hugged her. "It'll be okay, babe. We'll work this out somehow."

She nodded and kissed me on the cheek but I noticed her eyes were already dry and she'd forced her face back to neutrality. "Yeah. Maybe pigs will fly, too."

I chuckled. "Hey, I'll bet Shelton could make it happen."

A smile broke through her steadfast façade. "I'd like to see that."

I opened the cardboard box and sniffed the angel biscuit again before pinching off a piece and nibbling it. It tasted like roasted almonds. "Hey, this thing isn't half bad."

Elyssa took a bit herself and nodded. "Nutty."

"Well, it is Mr. Nutter's Angel Biscuit." I nodded at the posters on the MagicSoft and Orange windows. "Who are the guys in the posters?"

"That's Thaddeus Crumble, the guy who founded MagicSoft, and he," she said, nodding at the Orange poster, "is Enias Glover, founder of Orange. They used to be partners at one point before splitting up to do their own thing."

I gestured at the MagicSoft poster. "I'll bet he got a few wedgies in school."

"Even if he did, I'm sure he's more than made up for it," Elyssa said. "He's one of the richest people in the Overworld and that's saying something considering how many centuries some of the older members have had to collect their fortunes."

"He still looks like a nerd. Especially with those square glasses."

"I think the glasses are rather stylish," said someone with a haughty British accent from behind us.

I twisted so quickly in the bench I fell off it and onto my butt. Elyssa, meanwhile, sprang away from the voice, her hands held in a fighting pose.

"Did I startle you?" asked the very short man standing several feet back from the bench. His voice was much deeper than I would have expected from someone so short—he barely reached up to Elyssa's waist. But he wore a dark green suit with a silky sheen and a funny little red bowtie. He wore his auburn hair combed neatly to the side. Long sideburns stopped well short of the mutton chops Ryland had favored, and a prominent nose gave his small face far more gravitas than his tiny stature should have carried.

Just as I was about to ask who someone was for the millionth time that day, the small man smiled and said, "I am Phissilinth. If you would be so kind as to follow me, I'll show you the way."

What the hell kind of name was Phissilinth? I wanted to ask. His name was longer than he was. But my stomach clenched and folded itself into a tiny ball of anxiety when I realized this guy was going to lead me to Underborn. Elyssa seemed to realize the same thing and relaxed a bit though she still stared at the tiny man with caution.

"Don't you need to blindfold us or something?" I asked.

He chuckled. "No, no, good sir. You'd never be able to find the place I'm taking you unless we wanted you to." A wicked gleam entered his otherwise jovial eyes. "And even if you did, you'd never survive to tell of it."

CHAPTER 27

*M*y legs tried to turn and carry me as far away from Phissilinth as possible, but the shame of running from him, even if he was a highly qualified midget assassin, caused my ego to revolt and prod the coward inside to go with the little man. Aside from the one crack about killing me if I ever did find their hideout, Phissilinth sounded like a very pleasant British chap. Short as he was, he didn't walk with the same waddle small folk usually did, instead keeping the limber stride of a very agile child.

"Don't let his size fool you," Elyssa whispered as we walked behind our guide. "I get the feeling anyone who thinks he's easy prey ends up dead."

"The same thought occurred to me," I muttered. "He's probably like the British version of Yoda without the bad grammar."

"This way, please," Phissilinth said, leading us to a nondescript brown door set in one of the many alleys leading away from Grotto Park. He gripped the brass handle on the door—it was several inches above his head—and twisted it open.

After a moment of hesitation, I stepped into a small marble foyer where antique chandeliers hovered overhead and dark green-and-purple striped wallpaper covered the walls. A burgundy-carpeted stairwell led up to a small dimly-lit balcony. Elyssa stood to my side, her eyes searching every square inch of the place.

"How are we *not* supposed to find this place?" I asked her under my breath. "It's right off the stupid park, for goodness sake."

Phissilinth shut the door behind us and, removing an old-style skeleton key from his pocket, locked it. My ego suddenly joined hands with my cowardice and they fell like heavy jagged rocks into my midsection, weighing me down with a feeling of doom. Had he brought us here to kill us?

Elyssa looked up the stairs then back to Phissilinth who stood next to the door, counting quietly to himself.

"Well?" she asked. "Are we going to stand here all day or—"

Phissilinth held up a hand to quiet her, then slipped the skeleton key back into the lock, twisted it again. The door unlocked with a click. He opened it and my eyes bulged. Instead of seeing the alley we'd come down and the park beyond, a grim stony passageway greeted us with a belch of dank mildew-scented air. Flickering neon lights attached to the wooden support beams in the corridor bumped up the creepy factor by a bazillion.

"How? Where? What?" I couldn't form a complete sentence.

"As I said, my lady and gentleman, there is very little danger of you stumbling across our humble abode." He stepped through. "If you'd continue to follow me, please."

I looked sideways at Elyssa. She wore a dull expression as if she'd seen this sort of thing too many times before. Maybe she had, being a Templar and all. Considering what she'd told me about the Gloom and other planes of existence, being a Templar sounded more adventurous than the Peace Corps.

I took her hand and stepped through the door. Phissilinth shut it behind us and locked it again. As if to show us that, yes, his precious little key was magic, he unlocked the door and opened it to reveal a blank stone room that seemed to go nowhere.

"Will that key take you anywhere?" I asked.

"This is just a copy of the Master Key," he said. "It can take you quite a few places, but the Master Key can take you just about any place there's a door."

I really wanted to get into the hows and whys of magic keys. Could he use it on doors without locks? What about folding doors, car doors, or the toy doors on a Barbie playhouse—not that I had one of those, mind you, but darn it all, I wanted to know! But the little man tucked the key away and led on while I kept my curious mouth shut. Besides, my mind had more pressing concerns weighing on it—like how to survive what was to come.

Then something occurred to me and I smiled.

"What are you thinking?" Elyssa asked.

"I just figured this all out," I said. "Well, not the magic key part or the guardian angel part, or even the strange mystery girl part, but something important."

"Spit it out then."

I cupped my hand over her ears like a kid telling a secret. "The little guy is Underborn."

She tilted her head to the side, looking the little man over, probably sizing him up and deciding if I was right. It made sense to me. We'd probably reach a room somewhere then he'd take a seat, proclaim his real identity, and then murder us after having a good laugh.

I shuddered.

After a few short minutes we reached a large stone room with a roaring fireplace against one wall to chase the damp chill from the air, and a large round wooden table with about a dozen or so seats around it. Several brown leather couches sat in a triangular formation with a rich oriental rug spread out on the floor between them all. A stout oak coffee table covered with magazines and books took up the space between the couches.

"If you'd take a seat, please," Phissilinth said, motioning his hand at the couch. "Would you like some hot tea and biscuits while you wait?"

"Are they poisoned?" I asked. "Are you going to kill us?"

He chuckled. "Murdering guests would make for dreadful manners, sir. Please make yourself at home and my lord will be with you in a few moments."

Elyssa sat down and picked up a *Cosmopolitan* from the table. "Hey, it's a current issue." She showed me the cover.

"What kind of assassin keeps Cosmo on the coffee table?" I said, looking over the stack. I found a copy of *Popular Magic* and flipped it open to an article demystifying the reaction between Mentos and soft drinks.

Though the noms have their own "scientific" explanations, we've discovered their theories only partially account for the volcanic reaction between The Freshmaker and tasty carbonated beverages. How? Because Mentos were created by one of our very own Overworlders who added his own magical twist to the candy. How else do you think young people miraculously come up with great ideas to crash parties, recover lost soccer balls, and land that hot young lady after eating one of the delicious candies?

"What are you so engrossed in?" Elyssa asked, bending over the magazine.

"I want a subscription to this magazine," I said. "You should see all this cool stuff they do in here."

She raised an eyebrow. "You're going to be a magic nerd aren't you?"

I nodded enthusiastically. "Holy crap, they did a test of flying carpets in here." I looked at her. "Flying carpets! They exist!"

"I wouldn't trust my life to one of those stupid things. They're still magic-fiction as far as I'm concerned."

"What do you mean? Haven't they been around since Arabian Nights?"

"That's a fairy tale, silly." She giggled. "Yes, things like flying carpets and brooms and all that nonsense have been around for ages but the Conclave banned all means of obviously magical transportation so the noms don't freak out."

My heart sank. "That sucks."

"If you're really set on zipping around on a magic carpet, there's a guy in the Grotto who rents them out."

My heart soared. "Why didn't you say so in the first place, woman? We could've been flying all over the place instead of walking."

"I didn't think about it. And I don't trust those flimsy things either."

I rubbed my hands together. "Man, I hope Underborn doesn't kill us. I really want to fly on a magic carpet."

Elyssa squeezed me and kissed my cheek. "You're so sexy when you giggle like a kid."

"Yeah, yeah," I said. "A kid in a candy store. It's really gonna suck if he does kill us." I pressed a hand to my forehead as gravity popped a hole in my happy balloon. "All I want is to enjoy life, not feel like me or the people I care about could die at any moment."

"We have each other," Elyssa said, leaning her head on my shoulder.

I shifted so I could see her better and stroked her cheek with the back of my hand. A lock of black hair came loose from behind her ear on cue and waited for me to put it back in its place. But this time, I left it as my heart swelled with such emotion my eyes got a little misty. "I don't know what I'd do without you, my pretty ninja girl."

Her eyes softened and a gentle sigh escaped her lips. "How do you do this to me?" She laughed softly. "Boys never made me feel like this before. I never cared. But you do something to me and none of the rules apply anymore."

"It means the world to me I can touch your heart in a way nobody else has."

Her mouth opened slightly as she regarded me with a wondering expression. "Do I touch you the same way, Justin? Do I affect you more than Katie or Stacey or any other girl?"

I gripped both her hands in mine and pressed them to my chest. "Anything I felt before you was a candle compared to the sun. A whisper to a hurricane." I chuckled. "See, you even have me going all poetic on you and I suck at it."

She pushed me against the armrest of the couch and lay atop me. "It's perfect. It's beautiful." Her lips met mine and fire spread down my neck, my chest, and the embers of my love roared into full heat.

I wrapped my arms around her and pulled her tight, pressing my lips, my tongue against hers, wishing I could take her all into me at once. Her hands ran up under my shirt, her fingernails raking against my bare skin all the way down to the small of my back. I shivered and moaned.

"Ahem."

We jerked upright and stared at the thin sallow man with a copper tray balanced on one hand.

"Sorry to interrupt, sir and madam, but I've brought you tea and biscuits," he said in a very proper British accent, similar to Phissilinth's. The butler—I assumed—placed the tray on a clear spot of the coffee table, moved some of the magazines to clear another spot, and set the table with napkins and utensils. "Would you like one lump or two?" He pointed to a tray with cubes of sugar.

"Uh...what?" I asked, my mind still very much on what Elyssa and I had been doing.

"We'll do it ourselves," Elyssa said, pulling her shirt back down over her flat stomach, her face bright red.

"Very good, madam. There is milk and cream as well. Should you need me, please pull the sash over there." He motioned to a silky black strand hanging from the ceiling with a brass ring tied to the bottom. 'I am Milton, at your service."

With that, he left the room with all the dignity of a person accustomed to the nuances of being a house servant, including love-struck teens tearing each other's clothes off on the couch.

I looked at Elyssa about the same time she looked at me. "Were we really about to do...uh, you know in Underborn's secret lair?"

Her lips tightened. "I'm going to be majorly ticked if we die before it happens."

"That's putting it mildly."

We stared at the tea then back at each other. At the tea again. Back at each other. Then we burst out laughing at the absurdity of the situation —at least I was.

"Just when I think life can't get any stranger—"

"He will see you now," Phissilinth said from the doorway.

Elyssa and I stood.

"I'm sorry, but Justin is the only person he will see right now."

"She can hear whatever he has to say to me," I said, not wanting to separate from her. If we were going to die, it would be together, not apart and alone.

"He was very specific—"

I sat back down. "She and I are in this together. You go tell him we're both coming." My nerves knotted so tight my hands tried to shake. I clenched my fists and jammed them under my legs. What was I doing? Underborn might be the only person who could stop my dad from dying but I couldn't bear the thought of leaving Elyssa alone out here. Things had been just peachy so far—tea and crumpets, and the polite Mr. Phissilinth, but it could all be a front and her life was the most precious thing to me in the world.

Phissilinth raised an eyebrow. "Then sir, you must leave. I will show you the way."

I shook my head. "I'm not leaving until he sees both of us. Tell him that." I jabbed my finger down toward the couch. "We're not leaving this spot."

"Justin, it's fine. Go see him," Elyssa said. "I'll be all right."

I shook my head. "No." I tightened my jaw and forced as much seriousness and determination into my expression as possible, hoping it didn't make me look mentally unstable. "Tell Underborn."

"I am not your servant to order around," Phissilinth said, his voice remaining calm and proper as ever. "You, sir, must either leave or get past me and tell him yourself."

Elyssa gripped my arm tight. "Don't do it," she hissed in my ear. "For god's sake, Justin, leave me and go by yourself."

I shook my head. "No, it might be a trick. They might do something to you after I leave you here alone."

"We're in his headquarters, for crying out loud. Do you think there's anything they *couldn't* do to us right now?"

"As long as we're together, we're strong."

I stood up and advanced on Phissilinth, knowing even if I had my full strength, this guy could probably whip my tail. But I had to see Underborn and I wouldn't leave Elyssa.

"Justin, no!" she said and put herself between me and the small man. Her hands pressed against me and shoved me back until she immobilized me against a wall. "I'm not letting you fight him. We'll either leave or you'll go in alone. I will be fine."

"She will come to no harm. You have my word," Phissilinth said.

"Fine, fine," I said holding my hands up in surrender. "I'll go in alone."

Elyssa directed a penetrating gaze into my own and released me. I walked across the room and over to Phissilinth. As he turned I grabbed him. Air exploded from my lungs as my back slammed into the floor. The small man's face filled my view. He was smiling.

"You're rather persistent, aren't you?"

"Uh huh," I said, gasping for lost air.

"He said you would do this. That it was your nature."

"Underborn?"

"Indeed." He held out a hand. I gripped it. "Up you go," he said, jerking me to my feet despite his small stature.

Good lord, the little man was strong. I bent over and took some deep breaths to fill my lungs. When I straightened, Elyssa gave me a concerned look.

"Are you okay?"

I nodded and she slapped me hard enough to make stars flash before my eyes. "Ow!"

"Never, never lie to me, Justin." Her voice was low and angry, but more than anything full of hurt. "How dare you lie to my face? You say you love me and then you serve me up a bald-faced lie and attack someone who could kill you in a heartbeat."

Shame constricted my throat and I looked away. I hadn't even thought about it like that. "I'm sorry."

"I made my choice, Justin. Respect me enough to abide by it."

I breathed hard to choke down the guilt and looked at her. "I'm sorry, Elyssa. Please forgive me for being an idiot."

She touched me tenderly on the cheek she'd slapped. "I forgive you for that all the time, my love. Don't ever lie to me again. Okay?"

I pressed her hand to my face. "Okay."

"If you'll both accompany me, he will see you now," Phissilinth said, the barest hint of an amused grin on his face, and walked through an open set of double doors and down the hall.

My forehead almost cramped from the confused look sprouting on my face. "But you just said—"

"Yes, of course. All in due time. All in due time."

Had it been a test?

Elyssa took my arm and guided me down the hall without another word. We passed through a long hallway lined by closed doors. Sounds emanated from behind the doors, all too muffled to make out, and I wondered what atrocities were hiding behind them. Portraits lined the hall, unfamiliar faces looking out from each one. Tiny brass labels had a name and a date beneath the portraits and I wondered if these were former members or victims of the Guild.

The hallway dead-ended at a single door. Phissilinth stopped.

"I will leave you here," he said. "Simply enter and close the door behind you." He turned and walked back down the hallway.

I took a deep breath to calm my frayed nerves, braced myself, and opened the door. Bookshelves lined the room beyond, and a large stone fireplace held a crackling fire. Elyssa closed the door behind us and we walked further inside what looked to be a library stretching on for several hundred feet.

"Greetings," said a voice containing no hint of an accent.

Elyssa and I spun to the right. A figure stood there, wreathed in the shadow of a support column blocking the light from the large chandeliers overhead. The figure reached out a hand and pulled the chain on a lamp mounted on the column. The light flickered on.

And I looked into the face of a man I knew.

CHAPTER 28

*M*r. Turpin, my English teacher, smiled warmly back at me. "I see you're staying on task, Justin."

My legs turned to goo and I almost butt-planted on the floor. Elyssa had a similarly shocked expression on her face, her mouth hanging open, eyes wide.

"But you're a nom. A high school teacher," I said.

"Yes, I am."

"And you're Underborn?"

"The one and only, Justin."

"Are you going to kill us?"

He laughed. "Why should I bother when there are so many others willing to do it?"

Cold fear wrapped itself around my midsection. I clenched my teeth and forced the fear away best I could, replacing it with anger. "You're the almighty Underborn? The one who put a bounty on my dad? I want you to leave my father alone and tell me who put the hit on him."

"Oh, is that all?" He walked to a small round table in the reading area of the library. "You two have a seat and we'll discuss matters."

I gave Elyssa an uneasy glance before pulling out a chair for her and then me.

"Good manners, Mr. Case," Underborn said. "You always were a smart student. Not like Nathan Spelman and the bullies he associates with."

Approximately one point three billion questions burst into my mind, each one begging to be answered by this guy, but I buried them all beneath the most pressing items. I folded my arms on the table. "What will it take to make you call off the hit on my dad?"

"I assume you know of my fees?"

"A little. Something like whatever is most precious to the buyer."

"Yes. That which they treasure the most. A rather simple arrangement."

"How do you even know what they value the most?"

"My associates are excellent at profiling and discovering such things." He steepled his fingers and smiled. It looked really creepy knowing he was a school teacher, for god's sake.

"And I assume you know what I value most."

He turned his gaze to Elyssa. I wanted to jump across the table and throttle him.

"In your dreams," I said, barring her with my arm as if it might stop him from looking at her.

"In this case, Mr. Case," he said with another oily grin, "Or should I say, Mr. Slade, the payment has already been met."

I jumped up from my chair sending it toppling over backwards and pressed my clenched fists against the table. "What did you do? What have you taken from me?" Fear and anger used my heart as a punching bag. I was two seconds from charging him.

"Calm down, Justin." He motioned me to sit. "I have taken nothing from you except your time."

I wondered if he had some magical way to suck years from me even though I was supposed to be immortal. "Time?"

"I placed the original bounty on your father. I also placed the tracker on your father and gave the information to certain parties of interest."

"You what?" My shout echoed in the room. A feeling of helplessness overcame the anger and I had no idea what I could do against someone like this. Against someone so underhanded and evil.

Elyssa gripped my wrist, probably thinking I was about to attack Underborn. "Justin, please sit down." She looked at me with pleading eyes. "Please."

Somehow, I found my chair, righted it, and took a seat. I ran my hands through my hair and gazed forlornly at the wooden table.

"I did this for good reason, Justin. I had to know what kind of man you are. How you would respond to certain stimuli. In effect, I tested you."

"Didn't I already pass your lousy English exams?"

He laughed. "Your dark sense of humor is one of the things I like about you, not to mention your ideas of justice and desire to do the right thing not just by you, but your friends."

"You've been psychoanalyzing me?"

"Consider this your trial for the troubled times which lay ahead, young man." He leaned back in his chair and crossed his arms. "While I find you a rather admirable subject, you're also lacking in important areas, namely strategizing. You tend to ram headlong into things without thinking first. This is why you and Miss Borathen are quite the package deal."

I glanced at Elyssa, confused. Her expression, however, changed to one of understanding.

"You see," he continued, "she shores up your weaknesses and plays off your strengths. Where you are the doer, she is the thinker, the planner. You two must stay together."

I gripped her hand. "I don't plan on letting her go anywhere."

"You must understand I'm not the only one who's aware of this. There will be others who want to separate you. They know how much you value each other and to what lengths you'll go to protect one another. They can make you do things you'd never do otherwise."

"You're an assassin. A killer. Why should you care about any of this?"

"For the very same reasons others care. Something ominous lingers on the horizon and all my information so far points to you as being pivotal in preventing the annihilation of life as we know it."

I laughed. Laughed until I wanted to cry. "Are you kidding me? More of this foreseeance mumbo-jumbo? Maybe you and Vallaena Slade should hook up."

"She can be one of your most powerful allies," he said, nodding. "But do not let her smother you. And whatever you do, don't accept her protection—at least not in the way she now imagines it. You need to cultivate her and others, use them for the fight to come."

I wanted to get up and leave. This was ridiculous. "All I care about is you removing the death mark from my father. I don't need that threat hanging over me."

"I will, but first you must convince him to marry Kassallandra."

"What?" I shouted. It was becoming a habit with this guy. "In case the almighty Underborn didn't know, he's already married to my mom, thank you very much."

He waved his hand as though swatting an inconvenient fly from the air. "Spawn do not recognize unions with humans. Your father's first task must be returning to his true family and raising his status from lowly Castratae back to Anae, gaining the power he should rightfully hold and uniting two major families through marriage."

"He would never in a million years betray my mom. He's obsessed with finding her and my sister, something I'm sure you know with all the fancy dossiers you probably have on us."

"He must. If the great families are split, there's little hope for the future."

"How about uniting the Slades to the Conroys?" Elyssa asked. "If that hurdle could be overcome, it might form an even better alliance."

I gave her a surprised look. She really was the thinker. "Yeah, what she said. We can find another way to unite my dear demonic family."

Underborn gave an adamant shake of his head. "Impossible. The politics of that unfortunate situation would never allow it to work." He stood up. "Let me show you something. Wait here." He walked to a nearby filing cabinet, shuffled through it, and pulled out a red folder. Walked back to the table and set it before him as he sat down. "This contains the little I know of Foreseeance 4311."

"You have a copy?" Elyssa asked, leaning forward to get a better look.

"I have fragments, lifted from the lifeless fingers of a courier who worked for the ones who wish to keep all knowledge of it out of the hands of the Conclave."

"Great, more of this garbage," I said.

"You know about your dark light, don't you Justin?" he asked.

A sliver of uncertainty crept into me. "How do you know about that?"

"Has it come to you in dreams or visions?"

"I had a stupid dream."

"We both did," Elyssa said. "I am his light in the dark."

Underborn nodded. "You are indeed, my dear. You will be with him when the end comes."

She gasped, falling back into her chair as if all the weight in the world had just been dropped into her lap. "Please tell me it doesn't mean—"

He shrugged. "As with anything related to foreseeances, there are many shifting variables and even more uncertainties. 'The end' could refer to a new beginning, death, or any number of other circumstances. I wish I could say for certain, but I do know that you must be with him at a critical moment or all may be lost."

I snorted. "Much as I'd like to be with her twenty-four-seven, there's the little problem of her parents."

"I'm well aware of that issue." Something seemed to flash in his eyes, though what emotion only Underborn knew. "Thomas Borathen has a long memory and a deep hatred for spawn. After Thunder Rock, I can hardly blame him."

Elyssa's eyes lit with interest. "What do you know about Thunder Rock?"

"I know far more than his official report says."

"How?" Her eyes narrowed. "Far as I know, he never told a soul what really happened there, except maybe my mom."

"What the heck is Thunder Rock?" I asked. "I remember you and Meghan talking about it."

"My father and thirty other Templars were ambushed by spawn

there. Everyone but him died. His official report was heavily redacted so nobody except him and the Templar Synod know what really happened."

"That's not entirely accurate," Underborn said. "I was there."

"You?" Elyssa said, eyebrows rising.

"You were just a little thing at the time," he said, smiling. "And I was known as Kevin Sorenson."

"You? Kevin Sorenson? My father's second in command died along with everyone else."

"Even I thought I was dead." His eyes took on a thousand-mile stare, looking right through us for a moment before coming back to the present. "Sometimes, I think I am."

"Considering what you do now, maybe you're dead inside," I said.

"Perhaps." He leaned forward, his dark eyes penetrating. "When you feel your soul being devoured while you lay helpless, it makes you realize there are worse things than death."

I grimaced and shuddered. "If your real name is Kevin, how did you come up with such a cockamamie name like Underborn?"

"Because, young man, in the depths of that quarry lake, far underground, I was reborn. I emerged from the encounter a new man with a new mission. The Templars represent the order that comes in the light. I am the order that comes in the dark."

"Details," Elyssa said. "I want to know exactly what went down that day."

"The short of it is this, my dear: A rogue spawn by the name of Vadaemos Slade was manifesting and absorbing souls from a number of victims, some supernatural, some normal. The Templars had jurisdiction but House Slade wouldn't cooperate. They claimed to be handling it internally. One of our very few spawn informants told us the rogue was hiding at Thunder Rock. We arrived in force—thirty-one of us. We were ambushed. Only Thomas Borathen and I survived, though I wasn't aware of the outcome until days after dropping into the depths of the quarry lake and awakening in Cahuinari National Park."

I racked my brain but couldn't remember ever hearing of the place. "And where is this park?"

"Southern Colombia."

"As in the country in South America?"

He nodded. "The very same."

"How did you end up there?" Elyssa asked.

"A question I have wanted to answer ever since," Underborn replied. "It took me quite some time to return to the States. The last thing I remembered was the agony as a crawler tore my soul from my body. I managed to pull myself into the lake somehow, and, gripping a large rock, let it drag me into the cold dark waters. I was certain I would never see daylight again. But death was preferable to having my soul devoured. Imagine my surprise when I woke up in the jungle."

"They ambushed you with crawlers?" Elyssa looked horrified.

"And other various demon spawn," he said. "It was quite a slaughter. It's no secret the spawn despise the Templars due to their holy origins and would like nothing better than to see them gone. I'm sure Thomas saw this as an act of war but he's been unable to return fire thanks to the Conclave."

Elyssa's face paled. "What did they do to the soulless, the husks?"

Underborn shuddered and leaned back in his chair, arms crossed tight against his body. "I don't know if they ever did anything about them. Thunder Rock was under quarantine long before the incident ever occurred and it remains a restricted area to this day."

I knew for a fact anything that could make someone like Underborn shudder had to be bad. "What do you mean by soulless?"

"Soulless are the husks remaining after the soul is gone," he said. "In most cases, the bodies simply go inert, wither away, and die. In other cases, what's left of the person goes quite insane. The problem with soulless Templars, however, is the bodies will not die. They may wither and lose muscle to the point of being skeletal, but so long as they have the blessing of the Divinity, the bodies are immortal, save extreme injury like beheading or blood loss."

"The spawn didn't eat the bodies?" I asked, resisting the urge to gag.

"I'm sure they mutilated the bodies, but shadow spawn gain no sustenance from consuming flesh," Underborn said.

"Shadow spawn? I thought you said they were demon spawn."

He nodded. "Shadow spawn are insidious creatures which can be summoned much like hellhounds, although they cannot keep a physical shape in this realm for long, whereas hellhounds can remain indefinitely."

"Why was this Thunder Rock place quarantined in the first place?"

"If you know anything about The Grotto, you know it was constructed long ago by beings with a far greater understanding of magical theory than we now have." Underborn motioned at the room around us. "This place exists on Earth and yet it also exists somewhere else. We don't know how or why, just that it does. The Obsidian Arch and its relatives were probably built by the same beings. Thunder Rock was a granite quarry until the Overworld Conclave realized deep beneath the quarry was a site very similar to the Grotto. For some reason, however, this site was left unfinished by its creators. The closer the noms got to the source beneath the quarry, the more they noticed the strange side-effects in reality. So the Conclave purchased the land, placed it under quarantine, and had the Arcane Council erase the place from collective memory with a dense shroud of spells."

"And that made it a perfect hiding place for the rogue," Elyssa said as something like understanding dawned in her eyes. "And it's also what transported you to Colombia. You must have stumbled into one of the arches."

Underborn nodded. "I've theorized as much but the last time I tried to enter, the quarantine shroud physically kept me out. I suspect Thomas had the Arcane Council place a barrier spell on top of whatever already exists there."

"This is all fascinating," I said, because it really was, "but how is knowing any of this going to help me win the blessing of Elyssa's parents?"

"What matters is not so much what we think we know about Thunder Rock," Underborn said, "but what you must prove about it that may win Thomas Borathen to your cause."

"Prove? Prove what? Sounds to me like you're the one who needs to dig into the incident, not me."

"Thomas believes spawn ambushed him and his people at Thunder Rock. So long as he has this belief, you will never gain his trust."

"Brilliant observation. What am I supposed to do about something that happened when I was just a kid?"

Underborn smiled. "I believe spawn had little if nothing to do with Thunder Rock. I believe they were set up."

CHAPTER 29

"You really think the spawn were set up?" Elyssa asked, her voice laced with disbelief.

Underborn nodded. "Someone wanted the Templars to blame them. To create an even larger rift in their already poor relations with your comrades-in-arms."

"And Elyssa and I are supposed to miraculously prove this wonderful theory of yours?" I shook my head. "We can't even get in. You said yourself there's a barrier there now."

"And this is where your remarkable skill at finding allies comes in," Underborn said. "You have befriended sorcerers who could get through the barrier. Use your resources, Justin."

"Friends are not resources," I said.

"We are all resources. Your friends are there to help you. Ask them and they will join your cause, I'm sure of it."

I shot a suspicious glare his way. "I get the feeling you're just using us to do your own dirty work."

"Oh, I won't deny it," Underborn said without a trace of shame. "I hope you succeed where I have thus far failed. But Thunder Rock can wait another day. First, you must take out the most pressing threats and then you can work your way toward peace with Thomas Borathen."

"Maybe we can wash your car and do your laundry while we're at it."
I stood up, wanting nothing more than to get out of this crazy man's
lair. "When will you remove the mark from my father?"

"I have no problems doing it right now, Mr. Slade. However, I do
have a few minor conditions attached."

I shifted uneasily on my feet. "Conditions?"

"You may be wondering why I'm at your school."

"Because you're a creeper?"

He smiled. "No, because of your old friend, Maximus."

My face warmed at the mention of that vampiric douchebag. "What
does he have to do with my school?"

"Miss Borathen is at the school for the same reason, whether she
knows it or not."

It was Elyssa's turn to narrow her eyes and cast a doubting glare at
the assassin. "How would you know about my assignment?"

He shrugged. "The same way I know about all sorts of things." He
leaned forward on the table. "You were assigned to keep an eye out for
vampires masquerading as students. What you didn't know was *why*
they were doing such a thing."

"Maybe because fifty-year-old vampires who look like teens want to
hook up with underage students." Her nose wrinkled in disgust. "Creepy
pedophiles."

My nose wrinkled too. "Nasty! I'll bet fifty is a low estimate. Imagine
dating some dude who's a hundred years older than you are."

Underborn folded his arms and leaned back. "Some vampires were,
in fact, doing that very thing. But that's not the real reason they were
there."

"Spit it out already." Elyssa said, eyes growing harder by the second.

"Maximus put them there. In fact, he has agents in several metro
high schools, not just here, but all over the country."

Elyssa's mouth dropped open and her eyes grew distant. "He's
recruiting from the student population?"

"Indeed."

"Maximus is a poser. A loser." I snorted. "He can't even turn people
into vampires."

"The average nom has no idea of vampire capabilities, blood potency, or other items on the checklist required for a successful transformation," Underborn said with a shrug. "Surely, you see the scope of his crimes. Recruiting is expressly forbidden by the Red Syndicate and the Conclave. It is even rumored that his activities aren't limited to the United States. The scope of his operation reaches far beyond that which someone of his humble standing in the Red Syndicate should be able to achieve. It points to another hand. A higher hand, moving him, utilizing him as a chess piece."

I crossed my arms and narrowed my eyes. "And what does this have to do with me?"

"You are to return to school and root out the identity of his moles."

"Who do I look like, Encyclopedia Brown?"

"No. You look like Justin Slade, the young man Maximus hates with a passion because you stole your father back from him. He believes spawn blood is the answer to his impotency."

I creased my forehead. "What, he can't get it up?"

Underborn chuckled. "I refer to his inability to turn humans into vampires. Your father was his golden ticket. If anything will draw out his minions, it'll be his desire to capture you."

"Why don't you do it?"

"My goal is to stop Maximus for good. But first, I need to discover who is turning his recruits into vampires, because it certainly isn't him. Once I discover who it is, we can eradicate his support and bring Maximus's fledgling revolt to a stop before it further weakens the Red Syndicate."

"Again, I ask, why do I have to do it?"

"I believe my cover is compromised. Even worse, so is my organization. I may be dead in short order unless I root out the traitor. And you, Mr. Slade, need a test run. You bring me the identities of Maximus's recruiters at your school, and I'll rescind the hit on your father."

"You'll do it now, or you can forget my help."

He raised an eyebrow and studied me. "I have no problem with such an arrangement. Do bear in mind, however, I can imprint another mark should you renege on our agreement."

I slammed both fists on the table and had to bite back the howl of pain threatening to erupt. The table was hard as a rock. "You threaten to kill my father to test me and get me to come to you so I can be your errand boy, and then have the temerity to call this an agreement?" I'd been saving the word 'temerity' for quite a while and was happy for the chance to finally use it in a meaningful way. "You, sir, are an asshole of the first order and I hope the traitor in your organization rams a sharp object up your bunghole."

Underborn laughed. "Mr. Slade, you are practically brimming with piss and vinegar. Let us both hope it translates into a winning solution." He handed me a slip of paper with symbols scrawled on it. "Give this to Shelton and Smith. They'll know what to do with it."

"Okay." I almost thanked him and mentally kicked myself. This was the guy who'd put me and my dad through all the crap in the first place. Just to test me! *Jackass.*

"Another suggestion, Mr. Slade. Your speed and strength will only get you so far. It is time for you to explore your arcane abilities. Harry Shelton would be suitable to the task of orienting you and placing you in a respected school once you are done with Edenfield High."

"Vampire recruiters aren't the only problem I have at my school, Underborn. Coach Burgundy and his pals still have a leash around my neck."

"Ah yes, their threats against your classmates. Their little old boys club is actually worse than you can imagine. Coach Burgundy, Principal Perkins, Sherriff Skinner, and Police Chief Amerson all graduated from Edenfield High back when Decatur was a sleepy little hamlet in the suburbs of Atlanta. They've been in power for this long because they're ruthless. However, I would be more than happy to help. Would you like—"

"No!" I shouted. "I won't have you murdering anyone, even if it's lowlifes like Burgundy and his pals. I'll take care of them myself."

Underborn's eyebrow arched. "I wasn't offering to kill anyone."

"Then what were you offering?"

"Their vulnerable spots. Children, wives, addresses. With very little effort, you could turn this around. Make them—how do you kids say it nowadays? Ah yes, make them your bitches."

"You're insane." I gave him my best look of wide-eyed disbelief. "I'm not stooping to your level." I had to admit, though, a part of me relished the idea of turning the tables on those rednecks.

He shrugged. "Very well. However, once you realize the fight ahead will require a little dirt on your hands, perhaps you'll see things my way."

"Not likely." But a part of me doubted my own words. To save my father, I'd had to put my girlfriend in danger. I'd had to ignore my missing mother and sister who were likely being held against their will by the Conroys. My demon side carried with it not just strength and sexual super powers, but an infernal rage which could transform me into a mindless killer. Was it really only a matter of time before I started down the dark slope Underborn had traveled? Before I decided it was okay to kill someone to protect my own interests? I'd wanted to kill the vampires who'd kidnapped my father at the time. But having met Felicia, I realized they were a brainwashed bunch. Killing them wasn't the answer. Taking Maximus out of the equation might be.

"Is there anything else?" Underborn said, rising from his chair.

"Remove all the bounties on his father too," Elyssa said, steel in her voice. "Wipe the slate clean, or I'll be sure my father finds out about you."

A sly grin crossed his face. "Excellent, bargaining Miss Borathen. The moment Mr. Slade has fulfilled our agreement, the bounties on his father will be rescinded."

I was really happy Elyssa had remembered that rather large detail—I'd practically forgotten about it. But I didn't like how happy it made Underborn after she'd threatened him. "Aren't you worried she'll tell her father?"

"If she does, I'm sure I'll find out about it. However, I doubt he'll believe the story, and even if he does, Thomas Borathen has little time to worry about me. In case you hadn't noticed, the Conclave is weakening. Internal strife and turmoil threaten to tear the delicate threads knitting it together. The Red Syndicate fighting Maximus's rogue organization on one hand and dealing with the Arcane Council on the other after one of their schools was attacked by vampires. The spawn and Templars are at each other's throats due to Thunder Rock, and even the spawn have internal conflicts thanks to your dear father Daevadius Slade and his rejection of Kassallandra Assad."

"Things are that bad?" Elyssa said, her eyes filled with shock.

"Indeed, Miss Borathen. Whoever is pulling the strings is masterful." He seemed more awestruck than worried, however, and I had the feeling he'd be more than happy to be on the other side.

What surprised me the most about everything he told me was how little I cared. So what if vampires and assassins and even my dear old demon spawn relatives were having issues? The world would be better off without them. "Dude, you've got issues." I took Elyssa's hand and headed for the door.

"Remember, Mr. Slade, your decisions may impact us all."

I LOOKED BACK AT HIM. "As long as you don't flunk me out of English class, I don't really care."

He stood and walked to the door, opened it. "Safe travels, Miss Borathen, Mr. Slade." With his other hand he held out the red folder he'd brought to the table. "Read this in your spare time. If nothing else, you may find it entertaining."

I stared at it for a moment. "It's not poisoned or anything is it?"

He chuckled. "Of course not."

I took it, shaking my head slowly. "An assassin English teacher. That's just wrong, man."

"I'll hold on to it," Elyssa said, and slipped it under her arm.

Phissilinth appeared from nowhere. "Shall I see them away, sir?"

"Please do," Underborn said.

Phissilinth nodded. "Very good, sir."

I glared at the small man. "Hey, that's not code for 'kill them' is it?"

"No, sir, I can assure you it is not."

We followed the small man back through the maze of hallways until we reached the door he had used his magic key on earlier. He stopped and looked at us. "Is there anything else you require before you return?"

"Yeah, I want you and Underborn to give up killing people and start a charity going door-to-door and selling cookies to raise money for orphans."

An amused grin formed on the small man's lips. "You may think we kill for money, sir. I assure you, we are not as bad as you think."

"If you're even half as bad as I think, then you're scum in my book." I smiled. "No offense."

"None taken, sir." With that, he twisted the key in the lock and opened the door.

An alley lit by tiny blinking lights waited on the other side.

I stuck my head out the door to make sure we weren't about to drop into a pit of spikes and tentatively tapped my foot on the cobblestones. After assuring myself nothing dangerous waited, we stepped through. The little man shut the door behind us and we were alone.

"Unbelievable," I said. "What a manipulative jackass. He's insane." I looked up at the blinking lights overhead and realized they were tiny lightning bugs. Their little abdomens glowed much brighter than the ones I remembered, casting a yellowish glow illuminating the place bright as street lamps.

"Underborn didn't tell us everything," Elyssa said as we walked toward the park. "He has other reasons for using you. I just wish I knew what they were."

I slashed a hand through the air. "Whatever his reasons, I don't care. Once I'm done with the recruiters, Maximus can rot in hell."

She squeezed my hand. "I wish he would."

We made our way to the Grotto's exit. Nightliss appeared from an alley and trotted up to us.

"Where have you been, little girl?" I asked, picking her up and stroking under her chin. She meowed a couple times but mostly purred. I was just glad she was okay. Otherwise, Stacey would probably kill me.

As we walked through streets lit by thousands of lightning bugs, I noticed crowds gathering at the pubs along the way, and a line of people waiting outside some of the fancier clubs and restaurants. A young vampire grinned at Elyssa as we walked past, his long teeth glistening. A pack of lycan teens howled with laughter as they rolled past at breakneck speeds on strange skateboard-like contraptions with large rubbery wheels.

I even saw a huge flying carpet as one soared low overhead, loaded down with goggling tourists.

"Are those noms on the carpet?" I asked.

"That might have been the Arcane Council's indoctrination tour—the one they give to noms who find out about the Overworld," Elyssa said.

It was almost too much to take in. Despite the weight of the world on my shoulders, the temptation to stop and smell the supernatural roses tugged on my sleeves a time or two. Once I'd cleared the death mark from Dad, maybe I'd bring Elyssa back here for a romantic night out. Heck, I might even trade some dollars for tinsel to make it look like I knew what I was doing.

When we reached the parking garage, I saw the young stable boy—or whatever his official title was—shoveling a huge mound of poo where the elephant had been earlier. He gave us a cheery wave as we passed by.

"Poor kid has a supernaturally cheerful attitude," I said. "Or maybe they drug him."

Elyssa laughed.

"Sir, don't forget your purchases," the boy hollered.

I snapped my fingers. "Ah, yes. Almost forgot." I walked to a nearby table where a number of packages sat, many of them identical. "How do I know which is mine?" As if in answer, what looked like a holographic image of my face popped up above the paper bag from the prank shop.

"That's how," Elyssa said with a smile. "Now you have to say the code words."

I tried to take the bag but it wouldn't budge from the table. "You're really enjoying this aren't you?"

Her grin widened and she stifled a laugh. "No. Not at all."

"Ha, ha. Justin is a dork." The bag came free. "I ought to bend you over my knee for that one."

"Ooh, is that a promise?" She winked.

A blaze of heat ran up my tender bits. "God, I hope so."

We went to the car and took off. Thankfully, this drive was heart-attack-free. I texted Shelton while we were parking outside his hideout so he could open the stairwell and let us inside. Smith waited just outside the door to the grungy room hiding the secret entrance. His shoulders were slumped and his gaze seemed captivated by the brick wall across the alley from him.

"You okay?" I asked him.

He flinched and then realized it was us. "Not really."

"What's wrong?"

"It's Felicia. She's gone back to Maximus. God help us if she tells him where we are."

CHAPTER 30

I smacked a palm against my face and squeezed my eyes shut at the sudden onset of a headache.

"Stupid girl," Elyssa said. "How could she go back to him?"

Shame kicked a field goal with my stomach and celebrated by kneeing me in the gut a few times. I'd actually accepted her apology. Believed that maybe she really hated Maximus and had repented of her sins with him. Even worse, the leaden weight of depression in my chest made me realize I had actually started to like the girl.

Stupid me.

"I told you," Smith said, his voice heavy with sadness. "I love her, but I hate her. Sometimes I just wish she'd die and get it over with." He slumped back against the wall. "And then I realize it's my fault she turned into such a loser. I should've paid more attention to her after our parents died. I should have been there for her."

Elyssa stepped next to Smith and placed a comforting hand on his shoulder. "We all make decisions impacting those around us, but the choice ultimately lies with them, not us. You can't blame yourself. Just move on with your life."

He patted her hand and nodded. "Yeah. If only it was so easy." Then he took a deep breath and straightened, brushing an invisible bit of lint or something off his shirt. "Anyway, you're not here to give me counseling." He chuckled. "I have no idea why I'm suddenly spilling all my worries out on you guys. It's not like we even know each other that well."

"Bottle it up too long and it comes bursting out," Elyssa said. "Besides, I'd like to think we can all become friends. You seem a lot nicer than Shelton."

Smith laughed. "Shelton has his charms." He raised an eyebrow. "Man, I'm so busy feeling sorry for myself I forgot to ask whether you arranged a meeting with Underborn or not."

Elyssa and I looked at each other.

"We did a bit better than that," I said. "But I'd prefer to wait until we can tell everyone."

"Sure thing." He entered the iron door and waved us on. "Speaking of Underborn, we finally blocked that damned tracking spell from transmitting anything and, believe it or not, might be close to actually disabling it. We've been at it all day."

"Great," I said, feeling guilt creep into my voice. I hoped they weren't ticked off that all their work was for nothing.

We descended the stairs to the sounds of classical music and the delicious aroma of cooking food drifting up to greet us. I stepped inside and stared at Ryland, who was wearing an apron stating, *This is where the magic happens,* as he stirred a medley of veggies and meat in a large wok on the gas stove. He picked up a nearby glass of dark red wine, held it out toward us as if toasting our arrival, and took a big gulp.

Stacey sat in another corner of the room, a magazine in one hand and a glass of white wine in another. She beamed a huge smile as we entered and rushed over to squeeze me in a hug. "My lamb, you're back. You actually made it!" She pulled back then turned to Elyssa, giving her a peck on each cheek. "You kept him safe, didn't you, dear?"

Elyssa's face flushed pink and she seemed off balance by Stacey's enthusiastic greeting. "He needs a lot of babysitting," she said, an uncertain smile finding its way onto her face.

"Justin!" Dad rushed from the room where they'd been keeping him and smothered me with a bear-hug. "Son, I—I can't believe you did something so stupid! I've been worried sick."

"I had to tell him," Stacey said without a hint of shame. "He was rather worried when you were gone so long."

"I'd like to say I'm sorry," I told Dad, "but I'm not. I spoke to Underborn."

Shelton emerged from his bedroom, his eyes underscored by dark circles. "What the hell is going on—Justin?" He rubbed his eyes and looked at me again. "I take it you're not a ghost?"

"No. Underborn has better things to do than kill me." I handed him the scrap of paper the assassin had given me. "See if this helps with the tracker."

Shelton unfolded it and stared at the symbols for a moment before laughing. "Smith, look at this."

"At what?" the other man said.

"Read it and weep, buddy. I told you if we tried your method it'd trigger the failsafe and burn his body to ash."

Smith gazed at the scrap of paper, rotating it for a moment before snorting. "You were looking at it upside down."

Shelton snatched the paper again and looked at it. "No I wasn't! I'm right!"

Smith laughed and slapped him on the back. "Don't get all sensitive, TP. We definitely would have burned his body to ash."

"Jackass."

"Will this fix it?" I asked.

"Yeah, in about five minutes," Shelton said. "Guess it's a good thing we didn't try to totally remove it."

"Yeah, thanks for not burning my dad to a pile of smoldering ashes." I looked at Dad. "Well, what are you waiting for? Go get the mark removed."

Dad looked at the floor, his eyes tight. "Son, I don't know what to say. I feel—"

"Hey," I said, smacking him on the shoulder. "Don't worry about it."

His eyes met mine and I could almost see something like shame in his. "Okay."

He followed Shelton into the room with the metallic circle in the floor and dropped heavily onto the bed.

Elyssa took my hand and led me away from the others. "You need to have a talk with him, Justin."

"About what?"

"He's feeling a lot of guilt right now. He thinks he's failed you."

"How do you know?"

"I can see it in his eyes. He's tried so hard to get your mom and sister back but instead you've had to bail him out twice. I may not be a man, but I know how the ego works, and his is hurting right about now. How would you feel if you were in his position?"

I gave her words some thought and realized with horror she was right. I'd feel like crap if I couldn't keep my family safe. Even worse, I still hadn't done a thing to help my mother or sister. Dad's problems had tangled me up so much that reuniting with the rest of my family had fallen to the bottom of a long list. But now it was over. He was no longer marked and we could rescue Mom and Ivy together. Once I took care of Underborn's task.

"You're about to do something really stupid," Elyssa said. "Again."

"Huh?"

"It must be about finding your mother and sister."

"Are you sure you can't read minds?"

"Your face is like an emoticon, Justin. Every time something pops into your head, your face either turns into a frowny, a smiley, or the far-off vacant look you have now which tells me you're planning—I mean about to leap headfirst into—something."

"A vacant look?" I glanced around for a mirror but didn't see one. "Great, now I know I look like a moron when I'm trying to figure something out."

She laughed and pecked a kiss on my nose. "I think it's cute." Her smile faded as she regarded me, curiosity burning in her violet eyes. "Now tell me exactly what's going on in that head of yours."

"Just like you said. I want to rescue my mom and sister." I glanced back at Dad. "I want to help Dad this time. Maybe things will work out better."

She nodded. "How about we gather some intel, draw up some plans, and maybe put a bit of thought into things first?"

I thought back to Underborn's comments regarding mine and Elyssa's strengths and how they complemented each other. He might be a backstabbing assassin but he had a point when it came to my girlfriend.

Stacey giggled and rested a hand on Smith's shoulder as he spoke with her near the stool where she'd been reading a moment ago. He pushed up his thick glasses and smiled. Not more than a few weeks ago, I'd had glasses like his. I'd also been shorter and quite a bit rounder around the middle than Smith, too. I glanced at my arms and rubbed a hand across my flat stomach. I'd come a long way physically, but what about mentally? I was still a nerd, no doubt about it, but what kind of a person was I turning into? Things had been so frantic I'd hardly had a moment to think about any future more than five minutes away. What if I ended up like Underborn said? What if I figured it was okay to black-mail or kill people to have my way?

I looked at my dad and thought about the rest of my family. I thought about winning the approval of Thomas Borathen, and an unwelcome dagger of ice twisted in my guts. What would I have to do for a normal life? Would I be able to keep myself whole, or would I even recognize myself by the end?

Elyssa squeezed my hand. "Earth to Justin, come in, Justin."

I smiled. "Sorry. I think my brain is short-circuiting."

"You're just now figuring that out?" She graced me with one of her rare giggles. "I'm going to search the Templar database to see if we have records on the Conroys. First thing we need to figure out is where they live and whether your mother and sister are there. I wouldn't doubt it if they keep her somewhere else."

"Sounds good," I said. "I'm going to rest. It's been a long day."

Elyssa came closer, pressing a hand to my forehead and looking into my eyes. "You do look pretty worn out, hon. Get something to eat and go to bed. We can't do anything until you're fully recovered anyway."

"I will." I kissed her and then walked over to where Ryland was cook-ing. "That smells really good."

"Thanks," he said in a surly voice.

"Are you cooking for everyone?"

"What does it look like?"

I dropped into a nearby chair. "Jeez, dude. The wine giving you a tummy ache or something?"

Stacey giggled again as Smith conjured a pair of flying kittens with tiny superhero costumes and made them fly around the room.

I chuckled. "Man, I'll bet the women eat that up."

Glass shattered. I turned and saw wine dripping down Ryland's hand and arm since his wine glass had apparently imploded.

"Are you okay?" I asked.

He growled and rinsed his hand in the sink, a deep cut in the flesh healing within a minute. "Peachy." He tossed a load of stir-fry into a large bowl and handed it to me across the kitchen counter.

I looked at him in confusion a moment longer before digging into the food. My taste buds rejoiced from the first mouthful. "Holy cow, Ryland, you can really cook." I chewed slowly, savoring the tangy sauce he'd used.

He turned away from me, apparently pouring another glass of wine. "Yeah." When he turned, his eyes locked onto Smith and Stacey.

Something in my stupid man brain clicked at that moment. I looked from him to Stacey. Each time she smiled or touched Smith, Ryland's scowl deepened. I had suspected he might have something for her but dismissed it as sheer lunacy. Since when would a wolf fall in love with a feline? Then again, they were mostly human, right?

"This might be none of my business," I said, "but if you like her, you should talk to her."

"You're right," he said. "It's none of your business."

"No wonder you've been sticking around. Isn't Thomas gonna be ticked you're not back yet?"

He shook his head. "No, because I'm spying on you and keeping an eye on his daughter."

A chill ran through my chest. "What have you told him?"

"Nothing of use." He turned his gaze to me. "I happen to think Vallaena is right about you." His top lip curled up, revealing an unnaturally long canine. "Much as I hate to admit it, I think something bad is coming."

I paused mid-bite. "You do?"

"Templar duty used to be pretty straightforward. A few rogue vamps, a lone wolf or two gone bad, sometimes even a black sorcerer who was up to no good. But ever since Thunder Rock, things have heated up. The Templar logs from the last few years are full of major incidents and the band of rogue vampires who kidnapped your father are just the tip of the iceberg."

"You're simply too much, Adam," Stacey said in response to Smith, her voice loud and clear from across the sizeable common room.

I could hear Ryland's teeth grinding. Stacey's eyes glanced toward him for a split second. She *knew* Ryland was getting ticked. Judging from the mischievous tilt of her smile, I had a feeling everything she was doing was calculated. It wasn't like I felt any more observant about women or anything, but my incubus instincts were kicking back in as my body recovered.

"You really like her, don't you?" I said to Ryland.

His eyes widened and he hurriedly gulped down the rest of his wine, turned, and went for the bottle.

I snorted. "Don't get all embarrassed on me."

"I ain't embarrassed. Just don't like talking about it."

"And how's that working for you?"

"Not so good."

I took another bite of the delicious stir-fry and regarded Stacey and Smith for a moment. "She's just flirting with Smith to egg you on. I think she likes you too."

Ryland grabbed a seat next to me and leaned over. "You think so?"

I nodded. "I'm an incubus, after all." I tapped my temple. "I know this stuff." Actually, I was applying another incubus skill, namely, bald-faced lying. I didn't know for sure Stacey liked him, but something in my gut told me she did.

"I guess you would, right? I mean, don't you guys have a sense for emotion?"

"Yep." I finished the last bit of stir-fry and set the bowl on the counter next to my seat. "Do you feel weird at all that she's a felycan? I mean, can the wolf-cat thing work out?"

He shrugged. "I've never felt like this so I don't know."

"What do you mean you've *never* felt like this?"

"I've been with women over the years. Even loved a few of them. But this girl—" he shook his head and gazed adoringly at Stacey. "She lights a fire in me. Drives me crazy, too. Sometimes I just wanna pin her against the wall and shut her up with my lips."

My face grew warm and I took a gulp of water to cover my embarrassment. I'd felt that way about Elyssa a few times for sure. At this point, I really didn't know what to tell him, so I went for broke. "So why don't you? Maybe that's what she wants you to do. You're both Alphas of your own packs. So act like an Alpha and take charge."

He leaned back in his chair, arms crossed and gazed with a thoughtful expression at Stacey. "All or nothing, huh?"

"Ryland, you're a wolf. Since when does a wolf not take what he wants?"

He smacked the bottom of his fist into the palm of his hand. "You're right, Justin. I've been wussing out over this girl for too long."

"Hell, yeah, Ryland. Man up and carpe girl."

"Carpe girl?"

I shrugged. "Yeah, you know. Carpe diem? Seize the day?"

He burst into laughter. "Seize the girl?"

"Exactly."

The door to the other bedroom opened and Meghan came out, yawning and rubbing her eyes. Smith did a double-take and offered some parting comment to Stacey before making a beeline to Meghan. Stacey slinked over to us like a cat on the prowl, the roll of her hips hypnotizing, and I wondered if she weren't part succubus.

"Keeping the dog entertained, my lamb?" Stacey said in a purr.

Ryland got up and walked back around the kitchen counter. "You hungry, or did you just come over here to insult me?"

A languid smile curled Stacey's generous lips. "Someone is rather sensitive this evening."

Ryland poured himself some more wine.

"Adam is very charming, Justin. Did you see the flying kittens?"

"Kind of hard to miss," I said. "Nice trick, I suppose."

Ryland leaned back against the fridge and looked across the room, his eyes lingering on Smith and Meghan.

"How was the stir-fry, Justin? Can the dog cook?"

Ryland's face darkened but all he did was take another swig of wine.

"Carpe girl," I said and stood up.

"What?" A puzzled look furrowed Stacey's forehead.

Ryland's look turned glum. What was going on with him? He couldn't really be shy, could he?

"The stir-fry is amazing," I said. "You should grab some."

"Perhaps I will," she said, stepping into the kitchen. She reached for a bowl on the shelf behind Ryland, her body brushing against his. Poor guy. She was toying with him like a cat with a mouse at this point.

Stacey took the bowl and set it on the counter. "I'll be surprised if it's palatable. You know the sorts of things dogs eat."

Ryland blurred into motion. Grabbed Stacey by the shoulders. Spun and slammed her against the kitchen wall. Her eyes widened with shock as his lips met hers. She struggled, hands pushing at him but he overpowered her, pressing the length of his body against hers.

I wondered if I'd made a horrible mistake telling him to go aggressive as Stacey squirmed and shoved. I backed away, my face heating with uneasy embarrassment.

Then, out of the blue, Stacey gave a contented sigh as her arms encircled Ryland, pulling him tight. She ran her leg up his and he growled deep in his throat. My embarrassment reached new heights. I spun on my heel and walked across the room to Smith and Meghan.

"What's wrong?" Meghan asked the minute she saw me. "Your face is bright red."

"I'm kinda tired. Probably gonna hit the sack."

"You want to help me set up a perimeter?" Smith asked Meghan. "I love how you tie off your wards. You're so neat about it."

"You really think so?"

"Heck yeah. I'm hoping I can learn a thing or two by watching you."

Meghan's face brightened with the compliment. She bounced a little on her heels, clasping her hands in front of her and giving them a shy look. "I'd love to help."

One thing was for sure. Smith was a natural flirter. I said goodnight to Dad and found Elyssa in the smaller of the two bedrooms, fiddling around with her smartphone.

"I hope I didn't just upset the balance of the universe or anything," I said, "but Ryland just kissed Stacey on my advice."

Her eyes widened. "No way."

"Yes way."

"I knew Ryland had a thing for her. But I had no idea Stacey liked him."

"Apparently so."

"So, dish! I want to hear everything."

I chuckled and gave her the rundown of events. She ate up the details like a woman reading a trashy romance novel. "I'll bet you enjoy reality TV."

"You have a problem with that?"

I shook my head. "Of course not. What could be more fun than watching other people make train wrecks out of their lives?"

She nodded. "Exactly."

"And to think I always figured you for the low-drama kind of girl."

She yawned and stretched. "That's me, all right. I let other people live out the drama so I can enjoy it."

I took off my shoes and shirt and lay back-down on the bed. My limbs felt like dead weight. "I'm so tired all of a sudden."

Elyssa lay down sideways, leaning on her elbow and traced my newly chiseled—and formerly buried in chub—abs with her fingers. "Are you trying to tempt me?"

I pulled her on top of me and kissed her. "Any way I can."

She smiled. "I researched the Conroys, but haven't come up with anything actionable just yet. A little more time and we should have something to go on."

"You're so hot when you go all Sherlock Holmes."

She pecked my nose and smiled, then slipped off me and leaned on her elbow again as her smile faltered. "What are you going to do about school? About Nyte and Ash?"

I blew out a long sigh. I hadn't thought about our mutual friends much over the past couple of days, but it was time I started. Coach Burgundy was probably wondering where I'd vanished to and his threat against my friends hung heavy on my conscience. In a nutshell, he'd told me if I didn't play football, bad things could happen to my friends. Elyssa and I didn't have much to worry about, but Nyte and Ash were mortal and vulnerable. And if Maximus truly had allies at the school, he might tell them to go after my friends. Maybe kidnap them or worse.

"I'm sick of threats hanging over my head. I think it's time we go back to school and take care of Maximus's goons. Maybe we'll figure out how to handle Coach Burgundy and his thugs too."

My phone rang, scaring the crap out of both of us. I pulled it out of my pocket and looked for the caller ID but it came up as blocked. Could it be my mom again? I answered.

"Justin, it's Felicia," Smith's sister whispered. "Something terrible is about to happen."

CHAPTER 31

"*F*elicia? Why did you go back to Maximus? Smith told us about it and—"

"Quiet!" she said. "Listen to me. I came back to spy on Maximus for you. He's up to something big. Something nasty. I'm trying to find out more."

My stomach clenched. "And he took you in, no questions asked?"

"I told him you kidnapped me, which is technically true. He hates you with an unholy passion. Ever since you busted out your dad, he's been trying to find you."

"Felicia, I really appreciate you doing this. It's very brave, but you should come back to us, to your brother. If Maximus finds out what you're doing, he'll kill you."

"He won't. I know what I'm doing."

Famous last words. "Please. Come back."

"No!" she hissed. "I've got to go. I'll let you know as soon as I have something. Just be careful. Maximus has eyes all over the city looking for you."

The line went dead.

"Crazy stupid girl," I said.

Elyssa shook her head in disbelief. "I heard everything."

"What do we do?"

"Tell Smith for one thing. Then we play it by ear."

"Aren't you supposed to be the planner?"

She shrugged. "I can't think of everything."

I slipped back into my shirt and went into the common room but Smith and Meghan were gone, probably outside setting wards on the perimeter. Shelton was still busy with my dad, and Stacey and Ryland had also vanished. Looking at Shelton reminded me of our earlier argument. Elyssa had been certain he was hiding something from me and it occurred to me what it might be. But now wasn't the time to confront him. I was so tired I could hardly see straight.

I went back into the bedroom and found Elyssa wearing a pair of short-shorts and a black tank top. Her curves pressed against the fabric, offering a tantalizing preview of what treasures they concealed. I stopped dead in my tracks and gazed for an awestruck moment before remembering something I'd wanted to ask her earlier. "You packed enough clothes for school?"

She looked up from fluffing her pillow. "Since when have I ever gone anywhere unprepared?"

"Yeah, yeah, stupid question, I know." I slipped out of my clothes and into a pair of shorts from my duffel bag while Elyssa made appreciative comments and wolf-whistles. My face burned by the time I hopped into the bed.

"Aw, are you shy?" she said, snuggling up to me under the covers.

A certain part of my body reacted immediately to her soft warmth.

She giggled. "Ooh, something's not shy."

"That's not under my control," I said, trying to think about baseball, chess, or even Coach Burgundy to banish my embarrassing situation.

"I wish we didn't have people with preternatural hearing outside the door," she whispered, a pouty frown tugging at her face. Her lips found mine as she pressed harder against me.

My inner demon slammed against its cage and I pulled away breathing hard. "That's it. I'm getting us a hotel room."

She rolled her eyes. "How romantic. Maybe you can get us one of those places that charges by the hour."

"As if this place is more romantic?"

"It's naughty for sure."

"Not with my dad in the next room." A yawn cracked my jaw.

"Poor baby. You must be exhausted."

I snuggled against her and decided cuddling with Elyssa was better than anything else in the world. "I am." My heavy limbs seemed to sag even further against the bed.

She kissed me on the forehead. "Goodnight, sweet prince."

I SNAPPED AWAKE JUST before six in the morning. The alarm on my cell phone hadn't blared its morning greeting yet so I switched it off. Elyssa lay on her right side, facing me and breathing gently. She looked so beautiful asleep. Technically, she looked beautiful to me all the time, but there was something about the peaceful serenity of her sleeping face that reclaimed the lost innocence being a Templar had stolen from her.

My finger reached out to trace her cheek. Her hand snapped painfully tight around my wrist and she sprang to her knees, the other fist cocked and ready to fly.

"Good morning?" I said uncertainly.

Her wide eyes went back to normal. She released my wrist and offered a sheepish laugh. "Sorry. Reflexes."

"What in the world was that? A ninja wakeup assault? Your parents must have done evil things to you while you were asleep."

She shuddered. "Templar training is not kind. Although the Divinity grants supernatural gifts to noms and preternaturals alike, you have to hone those skills razor sharp."

"You and Underborn spoke a little about this Divinity being. He said people blessed by the Divinity can't die."

"Not of starvation or thirst or natural causes. We can still die by plenty of other means as you should know."

My mind flashed to the cave where I had almost lost Elyssa. Where I'd almost killed her by draining her essence. I remembered seeing the light in her eyes flicker out and a knife seemed to twist in my heart. Somehow, I'd pushed essence back into her and brought her back.

"Do you remember being dead?" I asked.

She shook her head and got up, heading for the shower. "I—I don't remember a thing. I don't think I was dead anyway, just very close to it."

The way she stumbled on her words made me wonder if this was the truth. But why would she lie about such a thing? "Is there something you're not telling me?"

She pulled clothes from her knapsack and smiled reassuringly. "Why would you think that?"

I blurred from the bed and gripped her shoulders. Stared deep into the ultraviolet glow in her eyes I had almost snuffed out. "I remember someone telling me to never lie to them. Ever. Hiding something counts as a lie, in case you're wondering."

A large tear welled like a shimmering crystal and tumbled slowly down her fair cheek. "Please don't make me say it," she said, another tear falling down her other cheek. "If I don't say it, it won't come true. It was a dream. Just a dream." Her voice faded to a whisper.

"Saying or not saying something won't make it any less true, my love." My own eyes burned as salty tears tried to force their way out. Seeing Elyssa like this swelled my heart with tenderness and pain.

"When I was...dead or unconscious, this beautiful blonde woman came to me. The way she carried herself reminded me of a queen. And she wore this fake angel outfit, with white wings and a wire halo. Everything around me was black as pitch except for this huge marble slab I was sitting on. The woman glowed pure white." Her brow furrowed and she shook her head.

"What?"

"I don't know. It's just—her glow would dim and look kind of orange, and then it would come back. I don't know if it matters, but it was so strange. So surreal." She looked at me. "A dream, right? I mean it was so loony and all."

"Did she say anything? Say why she wore an angel costume?" I didn't see what about this made her so sad.

"She told me you would die. She said our love was never meant to be."

A trap door opened under my heart and it dropped like a rock into an abyss. "Hopefully it was just a dream." I smiled—fake as a three dollar bill—and kissed her. "I wouldn't worry about it."

She pressed her face to my chest, wetting my skin with her hot tears. "I won't let it happen, Justin. I won't."

More than anything else, I wanted to believe my fierce warrior girl could prevent it from happening. But deep inside I knew it was wishful thinking. And keeping her close to me might spell out her death warrant. But I was feeling greedy. Selfish. If I was going to die, I wanted to spend every last minute with her. I knew such wishes weren't possible either, but I planned on being with her as much as I could until whatever happened, happened. Screw Foreseeance 4311.

I kissed her on the forehead. "Where did we put the folder Underborn gave us?"

"I tossed it."

I felt my eyes expand. "You what?"

"I took the sheets from it and folded them up. Easier to carry."

"You enjoy giving me heart attacks."

A smile broke through her tears. "You're too easy." She withdrew several folded sheets of paper and flattened them on the bed. "Are we going to school or looking at this, because I need to get ready."

"Yeah, we're going to school," I said. "We'll figure this thing out later."

I glanced over the sheets of paper. One was a list, the others filled with rambling sentences. Despite my doubts, I was curious to go over them at length, so I refolded them and jammed them into the pocket of the jeans I planned to wear. I spotted the crumpled shopping bag from the Grotto as well and slipped a few of the spider marbles into a pocket, just in case I had the chance to bust one over Principal Perkin's head.

Elyssa headed for the bathroom, stopped, and winked as she closed the door behind her. I slipped on a shirt and shorts and went into the common room. Dad stood at the counter, cooking some breakfast.

He looked up from the bowl of eggs he was beating and smiled. "Feeling better?"

"Yep." I touched the back of my neck. "How's the mark?"

"Gone." His arm blurred with speed as he whipped the eggs into a froth. He set the bowl down and dipped some bread into it. "French toast?"

My stomach grumbled. "Heck yeah. Make some for Elyssa, too?"

He chuckled. "I hope you guys were careful last night."

I quirked an eyebrow. "Obviously we were or we wouldn't have made it back in one piece."

An amused smile tugged on his lips. "No, I meant *careful* in there."

Atomic heat spread from my face and worked its way into my chest. My eyelids parted like the Red Sea. "Nothing happened." I shuddered. "Not to be mean, Dad, but it's not something I want to talk about. Not with you, anyway."

"There's nothing wrong with *it*, son. I just want you to be responsible. There's nothing better than a healthy sexual relationship."

I fended off his words, shoving the air with my hands. "Gross, Dad! Don't even start talking about the 's' word." His words made me think of him and my mom and—I tried to think about Coach Burgundy's purple-veined face again. Something about his ugly mug overwhelmed all sorts of unpleasant thoughts. Maybe I could use his face to banish hellhounds.

Dad laughed. "I understand how you feel. And I won't bring it up again unless you want me to."

"As in never."

"You want bacon?"

I nodded, eager to be off the current subject, though the thought of mom dampened my mood a bit. I walked around the counter and put a hand on Dad's shoulder as he set bacon in a pan. I could see his thoughts had wandered the same direction as mine from the grim set of his face and the sadness in his eyes.

"We're coming up with a plan to get Mom and Ivy, and you'll be included," I said. "Promise me you won't go Rambo on us again in the meantime."

His fist clenched tight, cracking his knuckles with loud pops and he stared forlornly at the bacon. "Maybe you shouldn't include me." His shoulders slumped and it seemed all the air just went out of him. "I'm a failure, Justin."

"Don't say that."

"I'm a failure. Twice now I've almost been the cause of your death. Once with the vampires, and now with the damned Underborn." He leaned back against the counter and rubbed a hand down his face. "I've hardly been a father to you since Alice left."

"Don't you for one minute blame yourself for this mess," I said. "If it wasn't for Elyssa, I'd probably be dead now. She's the one who helped me rescue you. She's the one who comes up with inventive ways to keep me alive." I slapped him on the shoulder. "We're men of action, Dad! There's nothing wrong with that at all. And once Elyssa comes up with a brilliant plan, we'll have Mom and Ivy back in no time. Heck, maybe we'll even get Shelton to set us up with one of his fancy hideouts."

"I'm gonna what?" Shelton said, sitting up from the couch where he'd apparently been dozing.

Dad laughed the way someone does when they're trying not to cry. I knew exactly how he felt. "I'll wait," he said. "I promise. No more heroics on my part."

I held out my hand. "Shake on it?"

He gripped my hand firmly and gave it a shake. "What's on the agenda today?"

I grimaced. "School."

His face went from amused to confused in a heartbeat. "Why? Isn't that a dangerous place to go right now?"

"I have a few loose ends to tie up." I didn't dare tell him Underborn required it of me.

"Can I help?"

"I'm afraid this is all on me."

"No heroics though, right?"

I grinned. "Nope. Just straightforward bedlam."

Shelton staggered over, his eyes bloodshot and hair sticking out in a dozen different directions. "Coffee," he groaned.

Dad poured a mug full and handed it to him.

Shelton sipped it and moaned. "Heaven."

I chose that moment to look at him and say, "By the way, Underborn says hello."

CHAPTER 32

S helton stopped mid-sip and closed his eyes as if hoping when he opened them again, I'd be gone. Since I didn't know any disappearing tricks yet, I was still there when he opened them.

"That son of a bitch." He shook his head slowly. "He told me to keep my mouth shut and then he goes and tells you, huh?"

His reply confirmed what I'd been thinking even if Underborn hadn't said a thing about it. "What amazes me is how much you went through to see his little trial to the end."

"I didn't know it was a trial. Not at first. When someone like Underborn tells you to do something, you do it."

"And you didn't give a crap what happened to us."

"Not before I knew you." He blew on the steaming coffee and pulled up a stool.

"You're saying Shelton was in on the bounty from the beginning?" Dad asked. "Everything we've been through was a test?"

"I'll let you explain, Shelton," I said, hoping to hear a few details he might otherwise leave out.

"I posted the bounty for Underborn. He told me I'd have first dibs on bringing you in."

"Did he tell you where to find us?"

He shook his head. "No, I found out on my own." He pursed his lip for a moment. "At least I think I did. Who knows? Maybe Underborn planted information for me to find. In any case, he tooled me just like he tooled you."

"When did you know what Underborn was up to?"

"Right after the Maximus ordeal, Underborn contacted me and asked me if I was interested in more money. When I told him no, not if it concerned you again, he got a bit more persuasive."

"He threatened you," Dad said.

Shelton nodded. "You don't say no to an assassin." He turned to my dad. "By then, he'd already marked you. Told me if I gave a crap, I'd play along and things would work out just fine."

"And you believed him?"

"I didn't know what else I *could* do. It didn't matter if I believed him or not. I just figured it'd be safer for me—and everyone else—if I did what he told me to do and kept my fingers crossed."

"Was Smith part of the plan?"

His head shook adamantly. "Hell no. I got him involved. Hoped he'd be able to get the mark off. Maybe Underborn wanted me to figure it out. I don't know. He didn't fill me in on the details. Maybe I was there as a safety."

"Was anyone else involved?"

"Not that I know of, but that doesn't mean anything. Underborn is a master at manipulating his targets and getting them to the destination he wants them to reach. He told me killing is less than one percent of assassination."

For some reason, the next question I wanted to ask stuck in my throat. I hadn't realized how much the answer might mean to me. Shelton was selfish, rude, and abrasive as cheap toilet paper on a chapped ass. He enjoyed calling people names and cursing like a sailor. But despite his rough edges, I kind of liked the guy. He seemed to do what he said he'd do even if his own interests came along for the ride in the front seat.

So I asked the question anyway and knew I'd get a blunt and possibly honest answer. "Are you really my friend, Shelton?" My voice caught on the last part of the question and I looked away, ashamed I'd let emotion creep into my throat.

Shelton set his coffee down and gave me a hard look. "Do you think for a minute I'd put up with all this hullabaloo, gone through all the damned trouble to keep your dad safe, and let the friggin United Nations of the Overworld camp out in my hideout if I wasn't your friend?" He gripped his coffee and took a swig.

I put a hand on his shoulder and squeezed. "Thanks."

He patted my hand. "Yeah, yeah, now get your damned hand off me. We're best pals, okay?"

"Justin?" Elyssa said.

I turned to face where she stood in the bedroom doorway. "Yes?"

"Better get ready for school."

"Yes, mother."

Her withering glare sent Shelton and my Dad scurrying for cover.

I showered, tossed on some jeans and a T-shirt, and somehow even remembered to put on deodorant. Dad gave me a worried look and a hug on the way out. Shelton escorted us up the stairs.

"If you want back in, make a circle, focus on where the stairs should be, and break the circle while thinking, 'Make it so'. That should give you enough juice to trigger the charm," he said as we prepared to go.

"'Make it so?' Like Picard on Star Trek?" I asked, unable to stop my smile. "Shelton, you're a bigger nerd than me."

He ignored the jibe and handed me a set of keys. "These go to my pickup in my garage. Don't dent it."

"Thanks, Shelton," I said.

He whispered something and the brick wall across the alley folded up like a garage door, revealing an old Dodge pickup, obviously lovingly restored and cared for.

"Not a dent, cowboy."

I tossed the keys to Elyssa. "There. Now you can blame her."

Elyssa's eyes brightened like she'd just been given a shiny new toy. Shelton groaned. She hopped in the cab and started the engine. It rumbled deep and throaty like a racecar, and I wondered what sort of modifications it had under the hood. Elyssa pulled out of the garage and took it nice and easy until we hit the interstate. Then an evil grin spread across her lovely lips and she gunned it.

As we pulled into the back parking lot of the school, it seemed so unreal. It had only been a few days since I'd been there, but it felt like years. I saw familiar faces getting off a bus. Saw Nathan and his football buddies striding into the school like they owned the place, and Randy Tosser and his gaggle of nerds following behind the jocks at a discreet distance.

"You ready for this?" Elyssa said, eyes brimming with uncertainty.

"Nope. But let's do it anyway." I kissed her and slid off the bench seat of the pickup. Neither of us had our schoolbooks with us and I felt naked without my full-to-bursting Lord of the Rings backpack slung over my shoulder. I took Elyssa's hand in mine and we walked toward the school.

"Oh my god, you're back!" Elyssa and I both jumped as Katie emerged from a car and raced toward us. She gripped me in a hug. "I thought you'd died or something horrible. And I couldn't remember how to get back to those magical stairs."

"That was for the best," I said. "Believe me."

"What happened after I left?"

I extracted myself from her grasp and said, "That story could take a while."

Katie's eyes darted around the parking lot. "Things have changed around here in the past couple of days, Justin. Or maybe I just know what to look for now. I think there are vampires at our school. There's this group of strange kids who keep to themselves and don't talk to anyone else. They have their own table at lunch, too."

"And what exactly makes you think they're vampires?" Elyssa asked with a smirk.

Katie scrunched her forehead and gazed upward, like she was trying to look inside her brain. "The ones whose faces I could see wear hoodies all the time, their skin is really pale, and their eyes have a reddish tint although I think some of them started wearing contacts."

Elyssa rolled her eyes. "You're sure they aren't just Goth or emo?"

"Dangit, Elyssa, I'm trying to be helpful here. No need to patronize me." Katie folded her arms across her chest and gave my girlfriend a hurt look.

I headed for the school with the two girls in tow. "Point them out to us, Katie, and we'll know for sure." A lump of ice formed in my stomach. The mention of hoodies definitely reminded me of the mystery people who'd watched me at football practice a week or so ago. These might be the vampires Underborn was talking about or they might be albinos who wore hoodies to protect their delicate skin.

Yeah right.

We entered the school and hooked left into the gymnasium. As the gentle roar of conversations met my ears, a strange sense of not belonging crept up my spine, as if everyone here were somehow so different from me I could no longer fit in. I glanced around the huge room, catching a few surprised stares from other students when they noticed me. A shock of unnaturally bright red hair hooked my questing eyes as I spotted Nyte. Ash, shorter and Asian, sat next to him. Nyte's eyes widened when he saw us. He nudged Ash and the two of them stood and waved. I grinned like an idiot and waved back. A mixture of relief and happiness warmed me from the inside out as I saw they were okay, untouched as yet by Coach Burgundy and his thugs.

"You're alive!" Ash said, giving Elyssa a big hug.

"More or less," she said, her bright smile filling her eyes with radiance. "We were feeling under the weather."

"That's an unfortunate side effect of having a significant other," Ash said. "It's much easier to spread disease and germs."

"Nice," I said. "Way to kill the romance."

Katie leaned around Elyssa's taller frame to make herself visible. "Hi, I'm Katie."

Ash's eyes went wide and his complexion went from olive to white. "Hi," he said, his voice almost a whisper.

"Hey," Nyte said, waving uneasily.

"Something wrong?" I asked the two of them.

Nyte shook his head while Ash started playing with his smart phone. Elyssa's grin grew even bigger. I motioned Katie to sit between me and Ash since I felt certain putting her next to Elyssa was only asking for trouble. Ash's fingers froze on his phone and sweat broke out on his forehead.

"Dude, are you feeling okay?" I asked.

He nodded.

"You look so much better without the Goth stuff," Katie said. "Although I think it was wrong of the principal to say you couldn't wear it. That's definitely against the First Amendment."

"It's an unlawful abrogation of our rights," Ash said, finally finding something he could talk about without his voice shaking.

"I think you're right," she said, her eyes a bit uncertain. She leaned toward me and whispered, "Do they know about the vamps?"

I shook my head and glanced at Elyssa whose super hearing had picked up the question as well. I leaned toward her. "Should we keep them in the dark?"

"Telling them isn't an option, Justin."

"But Katie knows. Why shouldn't we tell our friends?"

"It's dangerous knowledge." She glanced at Ash as he carried on a conversation with Katie about repressed rights. "Members of the Overworld are forbidden to speak about it to noms."

"So it's like Fight Club?"

She smiled. "Yeah. First rule of the Overworld: You do not talk about the Overworld. Same goes for exposed noms. We need to get her into the Arcane Council's program ASAP before she slips up."

"Her and me both," I said. "I still don't know crap about the Overworld and I'm tired of asking questions about every little thing."

Katie nudged me. "Over there." She pointed to the bleachers on the opposite side of the basketball court, all the way at the back where almost nobody sat except a huddled group of three people wearing a mix of black or gray hoodies.

"Looks like a convention," I said, trying to peer at the faces obscured by the hoods.

"Bunch of weirdoes," Nyte said.

"They're entitled to wear their garb of choice," Ash said to Nyte. "How can you be so judgmental?"

Nyte shrugged. "I like having double standards."

As my eyes roamed the bleachers, they found Nathan and his gang across the gym from us. He and his buddies were looking my way. My supernatural batteries had apparently recovered from the thrashing Meghan had given them because I could make out the frown on Nathan's face. He was probably wondering why I was sitting with my real friends as opposed to him and his gang. While he and I weren't exactly friends—and I could never see myself trusting a bully like him— he probably expected me to change colors and go from nerd to jock. Wasn't going to happen.

"What do you think of the hoodie crew?" I asked Elyssa.

"Obviously, they're wearing hoodies." She shrugged. "I don't understand why anyone would want to go back to high school unless they're a masochist."

Because they're recruiting teenagers who think vampires glitter and drive Volvos, I almost said. But I didn't want Katie more involved than she already was.

"If they're you-know-whats, shouldn't we be able to sense them?"

She turned to me. "Remember how you learned to mask your presence from vampires when we rescued your dad?"

I nodded.

"They can do the same thing. Predators use camouflage to their advantage."

The bell rang. Ash and Nyte hurried off to class while the rest of us took our time, waiting for the hoodie crew to head for class so we could take a closer look.

"Aside from fangs, how can we tell what they are?" I asked Elyssa.

"Red eyes and a pale complexion are two indicators, but vampires can use compulsion to make people see what they want them to see."

"Why the hoodies, then?"

"Because they can't use compulsion on so many people at the same time or they'd pass out from exhaustion. Older vamps wouldn't need hoodies. I've seen those who could push compulsions on crowds all day and never break a sweat."

"Well these losers look like the Mark Zuckerberg fan club."

She chuckled.

Our people of interest finally moved out. By this time our group and theirs were the last ones in the gym and I felt very conspicuous loitering about. We headed out the doors and took up a position across the hall so we could see them as they emerged.

"What do you think you're doing?" said a familiar voice from behind us.

We turned to see the vice principal, Ted Barnes, glaring at us. "Get your butts to class."

I stifled a few choice curses but moved out along with the others and headed for homeroom. I walked Elyssa to hers which turned out to be Katie's as well.

"We'll have to hunt them down," Katie said. "Maybe corner one of them in the bathroom or something."

"I'm not trapping anyone in a bathroom, much less following them in there," Elyssa replied with a grimace.

"Yeah, no need to go Homeland Security on them," I said.

I pecked Elyssa on the cheek and made my way to homeroom, my mind consumed with what to do if the hoodie crew were Maximus's people. As if worrying about vamps wasn't enough, I also had to figure out how to quit football without Coach Burgundy wreaking havoc on the academic careers of my friends, namely Ash and Nyte. So far, I'd failed to come up with a way to solve the dilemma other than lifting the coach's fat butt off the ground and slamming him against a brick wall. Unfortunately, even a violent beat down wouldn't serve as a final solution since Sheriff Skinner and Police Chief Amerson were also in cahoots with him. Underborn's information about their good-old-boys' club filled me with apprehension. Killing the entire rotten bunch of them was out of the question. Just because I could do it with ease didn't make it right. I'd never killed anyone before. There had to be another way.

"Look who decided to show up for school." Jenny Matthews pointed me out to Annie Holmes as I entered the room and took my seat in front of them. The two girls were close friends with Katie though I didn't understand how anyone could put up with them. I had no doubt they'd both grow into bitter old shrews and make whoever they married miserable. For all I knew, they were certified members of the Over-world, classification: wicked witches.

"Brad's been looking for you," Annie said.

Jenny smiled. "Ooh, I think he wants payback."

"Brad Nichols?" I asked. I'd hardly given the guy a second thought since our big fight when he'd humiliated me in front of the entire school, although I'd somehow managed to knock him out. Thoughts of him dredged up bitter memories and a hard knot of anger lodged itself in my stomach. Katie had been dating Brad at the time but I'd kissed her while we were studying one night. The next day, he'd punched me in the stomach when I arrived at school.

"The one and only," Jenny said. She squeezed my bicep. "But I don't think you have anything to worry about."

I pulled my arm away and sighed. Katie and Brad were no longer an item since my newfound popularity had catapulted me from zero to hero in the eyes of the jocks, nerds, and the vast majority of girls it seemed. The spotlight of popularity was the last thing I needed considering the dark secret behind my football skills. Supernatural abilities were the only reason I could play the game and survive. The old me would have been squashed like an insect. Ignoring Brad seemed like the best thing to do, should I run into him.

The bell finally rang and I dashed out of the room. On my way to History class, I saw Alan Weaver and Cindy Mueller making out next to the lockers. He saw me and gave me a thumbs up. I forced a smile and dodged around them. I'd hooked the two of them up during a disastrous test of my incubus abilities, nearly causing a pornographic scene in Calculus.

Just down the hall, a familiar face regarded me from the doorway of his classroom. Mr. Turpin, aka Underborn, curled one corner of his mouth into a lopsided smile. A chill washed over me. I returned his gaze, a part of me wanting to grab him and bodily hurl him out of the building. No doubt he was watching and waiting for me to fulfill my bargain. If vampires could use compulsion to disguise themselves, it was going to be hard to identify Maximus's recruiters. Then again, they really might be the group with hoodies. I had to check them out pronto.

After History I was headed for Biology when I spotted one of the hoodie crew stepping inside a bathroom. I figured it was a good a time as any to take a surreptitious peek at the face beneath the hood and hope they didn't notice me peering sideways at them from an adjoining urinal.

Gross.

I peeked inside the door. A white cinder-block wall shielded the inside from view so I stepped in and edged to the corner. The cold presence of something not quite human abruptly revealed itself to my supernatural radar from less than a foot away. A pair of hands shot out from the other side of the wall, pulled me all the way into the bathroom, and slung me against the stalls. The partitions rattled and groaned with the force of the impact.

Three hooded figures regarded me from across the bathroom. The shortest of the three lowered his hood and grinned as the shock of recognition registered on my face.

"Mortimer?" He looked hardly older than a kid, frozen in time after being turned into a vampire.

"So, you know my name." He seemed pleased as punch by his notoriety.

"I remember that you whine a lot too." He'd been with Felicia when the vamplings had attacked Elyssa and me while trying to save Dad. I clenched my teeth as anger surged through me. Felicia and I might have made up, but this kid was fair game, even if he looked ten years old.

The next figure lowered his hood. I recognized the face, but didn't know his name. He'd been there too. But when the third person lowered his hood, my face went slack with disbelief and horror stole my voice.

It was Brad Nichols.

CHAPTER 33

"*B*rad?"

He smiled as his canines extended into sharp fangs. "Where have you been, Case? I've been waiting for you."

"When did you become a vampire?"

"Maximus recruited me after he heard about our scuffle. He told me about your unfair advantage and told me he'd level the playing field."

"By turning yourself into a stupid vampire?"

"Vampires are cool!" Mortimer shouted. "A lot better than dumb spawn are."

"Yeah? I'd like to see you seduce a woman, pipsqueak."

"You think spawn are the only ones with seduction abilities?" He shouted back. "I can have any woman I want."

My face twisted into a grimace. "That's just gross, dude. You look prepubescent."

Mortimer launched himself at me with a high-pitched war cry but Brad hauled him back by his hoodie. The three vampires looked paler than noms, and they were definitely wearing colored eye contacts to disguise the red tint of their irises. It seemed to me that hoodies made them more conspicuous—all except for Mortimer, of course, who could barely pass for a freshman unless they glued a goatee on his chin.

Brad cracked his knuckles and smirked. "Maximus wants you, Case. Big time. But before we drag your sorry ass back to him, I plan on getting a little payback."

"You want to fight again? Seriously?" I sighed and gave myself a face-palm for good measure. "You attacked me in the parking lot, threw me in mud, a frozen water puddle, and then tossed my favorite knit cap into the bushes. And you're the one who wants payback?"

"You knocked me out in front of everyone and made me look weak!" He pounded a fist against his chest. "I have a rep to protect and I'm not letting a stupid nerd like you ruin it."

I looked to the third vampire who, to this point, had remained silent. "What's your say in all this? You one of Maximus's pets too?"

He pointed to himself and looked around for a second, his eyebrows arched in confusion. "Who, me? Uh, my name's Mick. I'm just here to help them."

"Where are Lauren and Tammy?" Mortimer asked Brad.

"How should I know? They were supposed to be here by now."

It occurred to me that now might be the time to find out who Maximus's recruiters were. Obviously, Brad had been recruited by someone. "So, you're the ones recruiting students for Maximus?"

"Mick, Lauren, and Tammy are," Mortimer said jutting his chin out proudly. "I help out at the middle school."

"Sweet baby jeebus!" I couldn't believe my ears. "Middle School? What kind of sick perv is your leader?"

"Oh, he doesn't get them—"

"Shut your pie hole, dumbass!" Brad yelled. "He's just stalling for time."

"Mortimer, you idiot!" Mick shoved the smaller vampire in the chest. "Why the hell would you give him everyone's names?"

Brad narrowed his eyes. "How does he know about the recruiting in the first place?"

"I told you there's a friggin undercover Templar here," Mortimer said, sputtering. "Besides, what does it matter if he knows their names?"

Armed with the information I needed, it was time to make a graceful exit. "I don't have time for this crap. I'm out of here." I stepped toward the door. Brad sidestepped and blocked my path, his hand reaching out to push against my chest. "Not so fast, Case. I think it's time I tested out my new muscles."

"Are you out of your mind?" I said, grasping at straws. "We can't have a fight where noms might see us."

"Noms?" he asked.

"Yeah, normals." I glanced at the other vampires. "You haven't told him about nom-noms or the Overworld rules yet?"

Mortimer looked abashed. "We haven't had time to fill him in on much."

"Nom-noms like the Cookie Monster?" Brad asked.

I gauged the space between him and the door. One hard shove ought to give me room. But what if they chased me down the hall? "Yeah, it kind of sounds like 'normals' but since a lot of supers feed off normals, they call them noms."

Brad laughed. "Oh, that's good! I like that one."

I pushed his hand off my chest. "Wonderful! I'm so glad I could add joy to your life today. I guess they also haven't told you we can't show our supernatural abilities in front of noms? It's against the Overworld rules."

He shoved me in the chest again. "I don't give a squat about rules, dweeb. Fight me now or I'll hunt down your nerd friends and beat the crap out of them."

"Actually, he is right about the rules," Mortimer said to Brad. "It might be risky doing it here. Maybe we could stuff him in the trunk of the car and take him back to the compound."

Mick crossed his arms and nodded. "Maximus told us to get him if he showed up, Brad. I don't think he'll be happy if we attract attention with a fight."

"I'll do what I want!" Brad roared, his eyes rolling insanely until only the whites showed. He shoved me with an insane burst of strength. I slammed against the back wall, my back cracking the disgusting green hospital tiles.

I picked myself up off the floor, a queasy feeling bubbling in my stomach as the veins on Brad's face darkened, lacing his skin with black webs. Mortimer backed away.

"What the hell is wrong with him?" I asked as Brad doubled over, clutching his stomach.

"Oh Christ," Mortimer said. "This can't be happening!" He stumbled for the exit, only to meet a vicious backhand from Brad, crashing him through a toilet stall. The sound of shattering ceramic preceded a trickle of dark blood-stained water from beneath the warped partition. The preadolescent vampire staggered out, blood dripping from the back of his head. "Brad, you've got to listen to me—"

A ghastly bubbling noise erupted from Brad's mouth, and then he puked, spraying the bathroom tiles with a black foul-smelling goop. I gagged and held back a vomitous mass of my own, as I tried to skirt past the reeling vampires. Brad recovered at the last instant and blocked the exit with his arms, his lips speckled with dark blood. I backed off, unwilling to get within range of his arms. A hard lump in my jeans pocket gave me an idea.

Reaching into my pocket, I withdrew one of the spider balls and threw it overhanded. It smashed to bits against Brad's hard head, poofing into a cloud of dust and...well, apparently that was it. If I survived the raw anger blazing in Brad's eyes, I planned to beat the bloody crap out of the guy in the joke shop because the joke, apparently, was on me.

Something pattered to the ground followed by another barely audible thump. The bits of dust were expanding and sprouting into creepy crawlers of all sizes in a rapidly increasing chain reaction.

Mortimer was the first to scream as an army of small spiders paraded around on his arms. The black smudge of dust where the marble had impacted Brad's forehead transformed into a camel spider the size of his face. He swatted it away with a hysterical scream and raced out of the bathroom, the sounds of his maniacal flight fading into the distance.

Mick, however, gave Mortimer an eye roll and merely brushed the spiders climbing up his legs. "You think I'm afraid of spiders?" he said.

Strength and fury flooded into my muscles. "I really don't give a crap." With that, I blurred toward him. Delivered a left hook to his face. He ricocheted off the wall and splatted face-first into Brad's puke.

Mortimer, meanwhile, ran in frantic circles, sweeping his arms and blood-soaked hair as the spiders had their way with him. I took the respite and, dodging around Mick as he sputtered and pushed off the floor, raced from the bathroom, Mortimer's yells echoing behind me.

My hands trembled as I ducked into Biology. I took my seat as the teacher pulled a huge corn snake from the aquarium in the center of the room while lecturing about poisonous and harmless species. A lone eight-legged escapee from the bathroom, a spider the size of a tarantula I hadn't noticed, crawled up my back and perched on my shoulder. A girl in a neighboring desk loosed an ear-shattering scream, apparently noticing the hitchhiker the instant I did. The spell must have worn off at that moment because the spider flopped off my shoulder in a final death spasm, tumbled to the floor, and promptly collapsed into a pile of fine dust.

The rest of the students jumped at the scream, several other girls and Andy Dudowitz adding their own shrieks to the mix. The teacher let out a disgusted yelp as the corn snake loosed the considerable volume of its bowels on his polyester pants. I felt as rattled as the poor snake which the teacher quickly put into its aquarium so he could clean the white snake feces off his lovely brown pants. My stomach twisted and my heart pounded at the thought of Brad, now a vampire maniac, going berserk in the school. He'd looked like someone about to flip their lid, but I didn't know what I could do about it. And the fact no less than three vampires were here to take me kicking and screaming to Maximus didn't make me feel any better, either.

I had to get word to Underborn ASAP. I also had to warn Elyssa. And Katie. And Nyte and Ash. Ugh. This day was turning out to be a lot more complicated than I'd thought.

The intercom speaker buzzed and a squeal of feedback pierced my eardrums and sent everyone's hands racing for their ears.

"Mr. Rogers?" said the mousy voice of the Principal's secretary, Agnes Wright.

Our teacher looked up from rubbing the smelly mess off his pants and at the speaker. "Yes?"

"Please send Justin Case to the front office. That is all." Another shriek of feedback preceded a loud click as the intercom went off.

A chorus of "oohs" and "uh-ohs" filled the room as the other students looked to me, faces filled with the kind of joy which only comes from other people's suffering.

"Yeah, yeah," I said, and groaned through clenched teeth. What the fudge was this about?

I left and made my way to the front of the school, eyes alert for any hint of hoodies or other vampiric lurkers. A cute girl appeared around a corner and smiled at me. I didn't recognize her, but smiled back. Then she grabbed my arm and jerked me down the adjacent hall, pressing me against the wall.

"Hello, Justin," she said, her voice sickly sweet.

"Another one of Maximus's cronies, right?" I jerked my arm loose and backed away.

"We're not cronies," said another female voice behind me, this one low and seductive.

I turned so I could see the vampire chicks to either side. Their skin looked normal, and they weren't wearing hoodies. Everything about them looked so ordinary that I never would have guessed they were vampires. Neither was overly gorgeous or stood out from the typical female population which made them perfect for fitting in.

"No hoodies for you?" I said.

"Girls know how to apply makeup," the first girl said, and made a pouty face. "Brad refused to let us touch him up."

"Which one of you is Lauren?" I asked.

"How do you know my name?" the second girl asked.

"I just met Brad and his buddies."

The vampires looked at each other, displeasure carving scowls on their faces.

"Idiots!" said the first girl, presumably Tammy.

"I think you two should get the hell out of this school before I report this to the Templars."

Tammy laughed. "As if they'll listen to you."

"What the Sam Hill is going on here?" came a shout from the end of the hall. I almost cried with joy at the sight of Ted Barnes and his shiny bald head. He glared at the two girls. "This is the second time I've caught you two out of class. You'd better git right now or so help me I'll send you straight to Ms. Foreman for an after-school detention you'll never forget."

Lauren's eyes practically caught fire behind the contacts she wore. "This isn't over, Case," she hissed as she and Tammy left.

"Now get your butt in gear, Case!" Barnes yelled.

I followed him the rest of the way to Principal Perkins's office, my heart pounding at an alarming rate and sweat covering my palms. I'd probably die of an anxiety attack before Brad had another shot at me. Instead of dropping dead, I found Coach Burgundy flirting with Agnes in the front office while Barnes continued to the back.

Burgundy's eyes narrowed to puffy slits on his porcine face when he saw me. "And there he is, the famous Mr. Case."

Principal Perkins emerged from his office with Barnes in tow. "Ah, our esteemed Mr. Case." He looked at the vice principal. "Keep an eye on things for me, Ted. This won't take long."

"Him again, Mr. Perkins?" Agnes said and made a tsking noise. "They really need to bring back capital punishment to teach these kids respect."

"I think you mean corporal punishment, sweet thing." Perkins gave her a yellow-toothed grin.

She batted her eyelashes and fanned herself with an index card. "You're so smart, Mr. Perkins," she said breathlessly. "That's why you're the boss."

A distant hammering sounded in my ears and it took a moment for me to realize it was my heart. "What's going on?" I asked.

"Just follow us, Mr. Case." Perkins headed out the front door.

The last thing I wanted to do was meekly go along, but I wasn't sure what else to do at this point.

Coach Burgundy held open the door and motioned me out. "Get a move-on, boy."

I stepped outside and followed Perkins down the sidewalk as it looped around the back of the building and toward the practice fields and the workout rooms. I took a deep breath to calm my nerves. We entered the football locker room adjacent to the state-of-the-art weight room. Voices and laughter echoed from within and curiosity edged out some of the anxiety.

"...about as useful as tits on a boar hog," said a man with a redneck accent, much to the amusement of whoever else was in the room with him as evidenced by another round of hooting laughter.

As we rounded the center bank of lockers, my curiosity ran away and hid. Sheriff Skinner, Police Chief Amerson, and a thin strange man with bony cheeks and a gaunt face waited inside. Two tall, heavily-muscled men with buzz-cuts stood quietly in opposite corners of the room, their eyes scanning me.

"Gentlemen," Perkins said, nodding to the group. "As you can see, the errant Mr. Case has returned to us." He swung shut the heavy metal door and slid a bar across it.

At a motion from Chief Amerson, one of the burly men approached and frisked me, removing my smartphone and keys from my pockets, not bothering to take the harmless-looking spider balls. He opened the back cover of the cell phone and removed the battery, then set it on the bench next to the sheriff. Next, he looked under my shirt and patted down my legs. "He's clean," he said in a calm professional voice, and returned to his corner.

"All that and no flowers?" I said, trying to keep the tremble of anger from my voice. "What's going on here?" A part of me roared with inner fury, demanding I coat the room with their blood. It shocked me to hear a part of myself demand such slaughter, no matter how justified it might be. *I'm not a killer.*

Sheriff Skinner sat on a bench and rested his elbows on his knees. "Rumor has it you left your house and ain't been back in days, boy. Now you show up out of the blue and ask *us* what's going on?" He chuckled without an ounce of humor. "We got a real simple question for you, boy, and I suggest you answer it fast and honest."

Goosebumps crept up my arms as a chill settled onto my skin. I tried to speak but my voice suddenly felt very dry. Did they know about the hellhounds? About what I really was? "What's the question?" I said, finally able to get words out.

"My man has seen a lot of people in suits around your house. He also told me your front door was kicked in." The sheriff sat upright and stared me in the eye. "You been talking to the FBI, boy?"

Relief thawed my frozen joints and I had to suppress a grin. They didn't know anything. They must have seen the hellhounds in their black suits and mistaken them for the feds. "No, I haven't."

Sheriff Skinner glanced at the Chief Amerson who shook his head.

"In law enforcement we deal with liars like you all the time, Case." He stood and planted himself inches from my nose. "Spit out the truth or things are gonna get ugly real fast."

"I'm not lying. Besides, you guys might have the local law in your back pocket, but we're right next to metro Atlanta. It's not like we're some isolated redneck town in the middle of nowhere you can run like your own little kingdom. You do anything to me or my friends and I promise you I *will* take things to the FBI."

Skinner smiled. "See, that's where you're wrong, boy. You might try taking things to the FBI. You might even get them to believe you. But if things go bad for us, it'll go doubly worse for you and your friends. We know where you live. We know who your friends are and who you care about. We know how to hit you where it hurts."

"You people are insane," I said as doubt gnawed at my confidence. "This can't possibly be just about winning football games or betting on them."

He chuckled. "The money ain't bad, boy, but we discovered something else that made us a whole hell of a lot more interested in you. We know you've been juicing. In fact, when the results from your blood test came back, they were clean. All except for a few strange things the doc here noticed." He motioned at the gaunt-faced stranger.

A chill crept up my back. When I'd given the school nurse a blood sample, I hadn't known what I was. In fact, I'd been unfamiliar with my new abilities and it had only occurred to me the next day giving them blood was a bad thing. But by then it had been too late to stop it.

"I only discovered how unusual your blood is by accident," the doctor said, his eyes darting nervously between me and Skinner. "When I spilled an acid solution and contaminated your blood sample, your blood literally soaked up the acid like nothing had happened. I tried applying heat to your blood and yet the cells adapted and regenerated. I've never seen anything like it."

"Maybe I just have a great immune system," I said, knowing full well he wouldn't believe me.

The doctor shook his head. "No, that's not it." He placed a finger under his chin, his earlier nervousness seemingly drowned out by the thrill of scientific discovery. "There are minute traces of chemicals in your blood I can't quite identify, but they bear striking similarities to steroids."

Probably demon hormones, I thought. But I couldn't tell them that. "I think you got my blood sample mixed up with someone else's, or else the acid mutated the cells."

"I've seen you in action, boy," the sheriff said. "I can tell you're holding back when you play. We want to know what you're taking and where we can get it."

"You want me for my steroids?" I almost laughed. "Planning to juice up the other football players?"

He chuckled. "Why would we do that when we could sell the stuff for millions to the right organizations?"

"The compound you're using is virtually untraceable," said the doctor. "I could win the Nobel Prize for such a discovery."

I groaned. "Bad news, fellas. I'm not injecting myself with anything. I'm clean."

A flash of black caught my eye and I saw Nightliss slinking across the tops of the lockers against the far wall. She had something in her mouth. Something black and shiny. She vanished behind a wall strut, deep in shadow.

"I think we're using too much stick and not enough carrot," said Principal Perkins. "Mr. Case, how about if we included you in the proceeds? We'd be willing to make you an equal partner."

"Hold on now," said Amerson. "We didn't agree on nothing like that."

Skinner pursed his lips. "Perkins may be right. What do you think, Case?"

"I told you. I'm not taking steroids. I'm not taking drugs. I'm clean. The doctor made a mistake."

Amerson pounded a locker with the bottom of his fist. "I say we make an example of one of his friends." He gripped me by the shirt, his cigarette-stained breath nauseating to my supernatural sense of smell. "You don't appreciate the things we could do to make your life miserable, boy. One word from me and one of your friends vanishes into another unsolved mystery."

Heat pulsed into my face and fury roared through my veins. I clenched my fists tight to keep myself from slamming this bozo against the lockers until his body turned to mush. The reasonable nerd in my head grabbed my demonic fury by the arm and told me killing this man wouldn't guarantee the safety of my friends. It would only make me a murderer. More than anything, I needed Elyssa's brain to sort this out.

"Leave my friends out of this," I said, my voice tight with anger. "Take my blood, do whatever you need to do to find this steroid you're talking about but leave my friends alone."

Amerson slammed me against the lockers. "Son, you've got about ten seconds before I have my men teach you a few new things about pain."

Principal Perkins pulled the police chief off me. "All right, Jim. You've made your point. But I'm starting to believe Mr. Case here might be telling the truth. Why else would he offer up his blood?"

"Because he's protecting someone," Amerson snarled. "Or else he's got plans of his own."

Skinner tilted his head to the side and regarded me for a moment. "I'm inclined to agree with Lee on this. I think the boy would give up a drug before offering his own blood for testing." He looked at the gaunt-faced doctor. "What do you think, Doc?"

"It will take some time—perhaps a great deal of time—but I could probably isolate the chemicals and formulate something. But I'll need a properly equipped lab."

"Jim, didn't your lab boys just get a big upgrade from the state recently?"

Amerson's lip curled into a snarl as he stared me down, but he nodded at the question. "Yeah. State of the art."

Perkins clapped his hands. "Well, there we go. Problem solved."

Sheriff Skinner pursed his lips and regarded me for a moment. "Just to make sure Mr. Case understands how serious we are, I think we should enact our insurance policy." He pulled out a radio that appeared to be separate from the one he wore clipped to his lapel and clicked down the receiver. "Status?"

"Gold," a voice whispered back.

"What the hell are you doing?" I asked.

"Don't worry, son, we're not going to harm any of your friends—not directly at least. Consider this a test."

"A test of what? I told you'll I'll participate. What's going on?"

"Your girlfriend, Elyssa Borathen, I believe? She's about to lose a parent to a tragic run-and-gun robbery. I'm sure you'll be there to comfort her, though, won't you?"

My heart almost stopped. Could they kill Leia by shooting her? She was a dhampyr but for all I knew a headshot would be just as deadly to her as anyone else. I didn't want to find out. "Don't. Please don't do this. I told you I'll do everything you want."

"Maybe we shouldn't do this," Perkins said. "No sense in antagonizing the boy further."

"I say we show the little punk we don't screw around," Amerson said, his voice a low growl. "It'll save us time in the future."

"Mr. Case, I truly regret having to put you through this, but believe me, it'll help us all sleep better at night knowing you're fully on board." Skinner's lips curled into a self-satisfied smile.

"Stop!" I screamed.

The burly men pulled out guns and trained them on me. I didn't care. I couldn't let them do this.

"Status?" Sheriff Skinner said again.

"Subject exiting building. On approach. Green in ten seconds on your go."

The sheriff nodded.

My muscles coiled as rage coalesced into murderous intent. I would stop him. Remembering the spider balls in my pocket, I reached for them. Gripped them, and prepared to launch them. I'd probably take a bullet for this, but it was my only chance.

Sheriff Skinner pressed down the radio button to reply.

A frenzied, almost inhuman voice roared from outside, "Open up, Case! The big bad wolf is home!"

CHAPTER 34

*S*kinner released the radio button and stared at the metal door. "Who the hell is that?"

A sick feeling wormed its way up my throat, dispersing my rage. Despite the animalistic anger in the voice, I recognized the owner. Brad Nichols.

Something slammed against the door. The metal hinges groaned and two fist-sized dents formed. Mr. Perkins leapt back with a shout of dismay, his kettle belly jiggling. The two heavies in the room trained their guns on the door instead of me.

"I can smell your blood," Brad said, his voice groaning with sick anticipation. "Let! Me! In!" He slammed the door with each word. Concrete flecks sprang from the wall where it held the metal hinges. The bar across the door bent a little with each impact.

"Get over here and help me," Brad screamed at someone—probably Mortimer and Mick.

Another impact shook the wall and the cinderblocks crumbled around the edges. With a loud twang, the lock bar sprang out of the grooves holding it, whistled through the air, and embedded itself in a nearby locker.

I looked behind me and saw everyone but Principal Perkins aiming a gun at the door as it swung slowly open, warped hinges groaning with the effort. A foot lashed out. The hinges shrieked and broke. The door slammed against the lockers on the back wall. Bounced and collided with one of the benches across the room. Everyone, including me, jumped.

Brad shuffled into the room and a collective gasp rose from the assembly. Blackened veins pulsed and stood out against his pale skin. He'd apparently shed his contacts because his irises pulsed an angry glowing red. His fangs dripped dark crimson trailing down his chin and onto his shirt.

"What the hell?" I said backing away.

Mortimer and Mick walked in behind him. Mortimer's neck hung at terrible angle but he didn't seem to notice. His and Mick's marble-hued skin showed signs of dark-veined corruption.

"Help," Mortimer said in a feeble gasp. "Help."

"Shut up," Brad said, backhanding the smaller vampire across the room where he crunched into a metal shelf. Brad licked his lips and grinned at me before singing in an insanity-laced falsetto voice, "Found you, Case. Time for payback."

I didn't know who shot first, but I threw myself to the floor as all hell broke loose. Guns exploded from all sides. Brad flashed behind the lockers. Bullets sparked off the metal. Mortimer took a dozen hits to his small frame. He shuddered at each impact and collapsed on his back. Mick ducked and blurred away in the same direction Brad had gone.

Someone screamed like a girly-man. I rolled onto my back as Brad's pale black-veined hands wrenched at the head of one of the heavies. The loud crack of a snapping neck filled the air. More guns fired. Brad blurred across the room and leapt on the back of the next heavy. Sank his fangs deep into the man's neck. The stricken thug fired the gun over his shoulder, missing wildly as blood spurted from the holes in his neck. Guns clicked on empty. The sheriff and gang scrambled for more clips.

I took my chance and sped out of the wrecked door, colliding with Elyssa as she arrived from the other direction. We rolled across the grass and landed in a heap against a chain-link fence.

Screams and shots echoed from the locker room.

"What in the hell is going on in there?" she said, springing to her feet and pulling me up.

"Bad stuff. Why are you out here?"

"I heard the gunshots and left class. I just knew you had to be involved somehow." She glanced at the time. "Good lord, Justin, it's not even lunchtime yet. What did you do?"

"Brad Nichols is a vampire, but he's totally messed up. The hoodie gang? That's him and his buddies." I pointed back at the locker room with a shaking arm. "He's in there killing the sheriff, the police chief, the principal, and Coach Burgundy."

Elyssa's mouth dropped. "What? Oh my god, we have to stop him!"

I gripped her shoulders. "Something's wrong with him. He's got black veins all in his skin and he's gone nuts."

She gasped, her mouth wide. "He's a vampling."

"He's not quite as mindless as a vampling, but he's well on his way to being one. Brad told me Maximus turned him."

"Idiot!" Elyssa slapped the back of a hand into the other palm and grit her teeth. "What's he thinking, turning people and then cutting them loose?" Her eyes tightened as more screams erupted. "We have to end this madness, but I don't have a sword on me."

"If he's a vampling and he bites any of them, they'll turn, right?"

She nodded and headed for the locker room. "We can't let the infection spread."

A gunshot popped and a single wail of terror ended abruptly. I had the feeling we were too late. Brad staggered from the locker room, black blood oozing from several wounds, none of which seemed to be healing. He lunged toward me but fell well short as his legs gave out, and dropped to his knees.

"Screw you, Case," he snarled. Blackened veins pulsed in his skin and he groaned in pain, hands grasping his face as he writhed and shuddered. "Make it stop. Make it stop! Tell them to shut up, shut up. Shut up!" His pleas ended in a frantic scream.

Something popped. Brad shuddered as blood poured from a hole in his throat. Then he fell forward in a heap. Sheriff Skinner stood in the doorway, one hand clutching a bloody wound in his shoulder. Then he saw me and Elyssa and he turned the gun on us.

"What in god's name was he, Case?"

"You wouldn't believe me if I told you."

Red rage flushed Skinner's face as his lips curled back into a terrible snarl. He had the radio still clutched in his other hand but wires dangled from the cracked plastic casing. "I guess killing your little girlfriend's mother wasn't enough." He aimed at Elyssa and squeezed the trigger.

Time seemed to slow to a crawl. Elyssa had frozen at his last sentence as her mind probably processed the horror of what he'd said. I dove at her as the gun exploded. Pain ripped into the side of my neck, a white hot burning sensation tearing a long scream from my throat. We hit the ground. I ignored the pain. Rolled to my feet and charged as Skinner aimed his gun at me and pulled the trigger. This time, nothing happened. His bullets had run out. So had his time on this earth.

I rammed him with my shoulder, driving into him with ferocious force. His body smacked against the side of the concrete building and I could have sworn I heard every bone in his body crunch just before he slid to the ground and into a jelly-like heap of flesh.

Elyssa fumbled through her pockets. "A phone. I need a phone." I raced inside the building and grabbed mine from where the sheriff's men had left it, doing my best to ignore the broken bodies and spattered blood painting the walls. The muscle where my neck joined the shoulder ached with an intensity that nearly overwhelmed my senses, but I pushed it aside. Elyssa's mom could be dead or dying.

I raced back outside, put the battery in the phone, and turned it on. Elyssa took it and dialed a number. After several rings, a woman's voice answered. I eavesdropped with my super hearing.

"Mom?" Elyssa said.

"Elyssa?" Leia's voice was filled with relief. "Where have you been?"

"No time for that now. Someone is trying to kill you."

"You mean that idiot with the gun in the parking lot? I knocked him out and cuffed him. He's a sheriff's deputy, of all things. What's going on? How did you know about this?"

"I—I don't know exactly. They were trying to kill Justin and—"

A long sigh sounded. "Honey, I love you, even after what you did to me. Don't you think it's time to end this childishness and come home?"

A tear trickled down Elyssa's face. She wiped it away angrily. "Mom, I love you. Goodbye." She ended the call and stared at the phone, her eyes red with grief.

A sick gurgling noise rose from Brad as he struggled to rise. The life was gone from his eyes, but not from his body. I shuddered as his zombified remains jerked and went into spasms.

"Help me," came a gasp as Mortimer, his body riddled with bullets and head dangling to the side, emerged from the building. "Please. End it."

Elyssa gasped and backed away. "Brad infected them. We can't leave these bodies like this. We have to burn them."

The school bell clanged and within seconds, students poured outside and into the back parking lot as teachers led an exodus toward the far gates leading off the school property. Sirens sounded in the distance.

"Someone else must've heard the gunshots," I said. "They're evacuating the school. How are we going to burn the bodies here?" I glanced at the nearby buildings and bleachers. Everything was made of brick, concrete, or metal.

"I may have a solution," Underborn said as he appeared from behind the building. He whipped out a long silver blade and sliced Mortimer's head clean off, ending the pleas of the suffering vampire. I gagged and fought back the nausea clawing up my throat.

Underborn patted me on the back. "It would be best if you saved that for later."

I threw up anyway.

He sighed. "I have quicksilver, Elyssa. Would you be so kind as to help me administer it?"

"Real quicksilver? Do you have enough?"

"I raided a Templar armory some time ago and keep a supply in my vehicle at all times. I'll be right back." He raced away at supernatural speed and returned moments later with several six-inch darts. He handed Elyssa several. "Since I don't have a dart gun handy, simply jab the victim with the dart and depress the plunger on top just like a hypodermic needle. That should do the trick." He handed one to me. "Are you up to it?"

I nodded and took one from him. The burning sensation in my neck had subsided by now. I hoped the bullet hadn't lodged inside my healing flesh. Unfortunately, time was too short for me to worry about it. "How is this supposed to work if they're dead?"

"Quicksilver feeds on the infection in the blood. Whatever you do, don't get any on you. It can have rather adverse effects on supernatural blood."

His words failed to reassure me, but I took my dart and went to Brad's struggling form. I pressed his body down with one foot and, choking back another gag, stabbed the dart into his back and pressed down the plunger. Wormy black veins squirmed like parasites beneath his shredded T-shirt. The black suddenly gave way as silver flashed through them, devouring the darkness. Tiny mercurial tendrils raced across the blood on his shirt and arced from his shirt to nearby globs of blackened blood on the ground.

Brad's body convulsed. I jumped back as the black blood oozing from his bullet wounds flashed silver. Within seconds his body lay still. The silvery substance seemed to lose its form as whatever it fed on was consumed and evaporated from his wounds, leaving behind a mess of coagulated but otherwise normal-looking blood.

Elyssa and Underborn treated the other bodies and what was left of the sheriff with the other darts. I remained outside, unwilling to see any more of the aftermath of Brad's rampage. Something rubbed against my leg. I leapt into the air with a shout only to realize it was Nightliss. The black shiny thing I'd seen earlier dangled by a cord from her mouth. She dropped it at my feet. I picked it up and realized it was a small recorder of some sort.

I clicked play and heard the sheriff as he threatened me earlier. "Who gave you this?" I asked her, looking around for Stacey. She meowed and purred as I scratched behind her ears.

"Time to go," Underborn said as he and a very pale-faced Elyssa emerged from the building. "Unfortunately, I don't have any dissolution matrix or I'd get rid of the bodies altogether. The quicksilver has taken care of the vampling infection, but we don't want to be anywhere near this scene when the authorities, such as they may be, arrive."

He'd get no argument from me. I scooped up Nightliss and the three of us dashed across the football field, hurdling the tall chain link fence at the back. We ran the heavily wooded perimeter of the school, using the bare trees and bushes to hide us the best we could until we were able to blend into the tail end of the evacuating student body.

Mortimer's tortured face and broken neck flashed into my mind and my stomach roiled. It was one thing to fight anonymous vamplings but something far more horrible to watch people I knew devolve into mindless zombie creatures even if they were complete jerks. Killing them—well, I didn't want to think about that part. *It's not murder, it's self-defense,* I thought. But the images were seared into my brain.

What happened when Maximus recruited hundreds more like Brad? Were we looking at the zombie apocalypse thanks to this world-class asshole? His recruiters didn't have a clue what Maximus intended. If Felicia was any indication, they thought he had a cause. But the truth seemed pretty evident to me. Their fearless vampire leader only cared about his own power and glory. Everyone else was just a tool. Someone had to stop him. But why did Underborn want me to do it? I had more important responsibilities.

"There are two more vampire recruiters in the school," I told Underborn. "Lauren and Tammy."

"The freckled girl with dark brown hair and her blonde friend?"

I thought back, recalling their features and nodded. "How do you remember that?"

He tapped his temple. "Someone in my line of work remembers all the little details." He pursed his lips. "They did an excellent job of masking themselves. I would never have guessed."

"I've fulfilled my part of the agreement," I said. "Clear the bounties and leave my father alone."

"Done," he said, pulling out his smartphone and tapping on it. "I've sent a message to my person who works the bounty boards. His name will be removed by the end of the day."

One huge weight lifted from my chest. But another remained, a stubborn lump of stress that wouldn't go away until I forced it to. "You need to stop Maximus," I said. "He's just going to keep doing this over and over again until we're overrun with vamplings. Even if you get rid of his recruiters, it won't stop him from sending more. It won't keep other schools safe."

Underborn nodded but I could have sworn I saw the hint of a smile playing at the corners of his mouth. "Just as I told you, Justin."

"You *knew* this would happen," I said in a growl. "Did you engineer everything? Did you arrange it so Maximus would infect Brad, you sick son of a bitch?"

He shook his head. "I had nothing to do with this remarkable turn of events, although I must admit I was toying with the idea of arranging something similar which would force you to engage Maximus."

I stopped dead in my tracks, Elyssa halting beside me. We both stared at the man, me with a mix of horror and rage.

"What kind of monster are you?" Elyssa said, beating me to the punch.

"I am a man of necessity, my dear. One who will do what it takes to make sure our world as we know it survives."

"Maybe you didn't hear me," I said, resisting the urge to attack the assassin in full view of the other students. "I said *you* need to do it. Maximus isn't just my problem. What he's doing will affect the Overworld and noms alike."

Underborn resumed a steady march behind the other students, and we followed. "I've already explained why I cannot involve myself. My hands are tied. But the information you've given me will point me toward the vampire who is turning people into vampires for Maximus since he's obviously incapable of it himself."

His statement jarred a memory loose. "Ryland tested Felicia, one of Maximus's people. She told me that he'd personally turned her. But Ryland's test pointed to a vampire over two-hundred years old."

"Interesting." Underborn folded his arms. "I must test the blood of these female recruiters of his and see if the same blood master turned them as well. Such information will certainly narrow things down." He peered through the crowd a moment before turning back to me. "In the meantime, I suggest you think about ways to personally take care of Maximus."

"I'm done with your games. You take care of him."

"No doubt you wish to find your mother."

I feigned surprise. "Your powers of deduction are legendary."

He returned a tight smile. "You'll never reach her, you know. Not without my help."

"This is the part where you tell me to go after Maximus in exchange for that information, right?" I slashed the air with my hand. "Forget it. I'll figure it out on my own."

"You can be a rather obstinate young man." Underborn shrugged. "Have it your way, but know my information could greatly shorten your search. All you need do is take care of Maximus and his mysterious benefactor."

"You put a hit on my father just to 'test' me," I said making air quotes, "and then forced me to do more dirty work for you."

"I am the archer, and you are my arrow, Mr. Slade. I see nothing wrong with a little inducement."

I ground my teeth. "Has anybody told you you're insane?"

"Not to my face, no." He smiled. "Mr. Slade, you've helped immeasurably. By aiding me, you are helping yourself. Removing Maximus from this complicated equation will help you even further and possibly expose his accomplice. Do I need to write this down for you, or can you reason out the ramifications yourself? "

I bit back a smart response and replaced it with another. "In case you've forgotten, I'm brand-spanking new to this while you've been doing it for who knows how long. So don't patronize me and don't expect any favors, either. What I do, I do for those I care about, which is a hell of a lot more than you can say about you. "

"My reasons are my own, Mr. Slade. In any case, I suggest you keep a low profile for the time being. There will be many questions over the next few days and, considering the corruption in this despicable little community, a political catharsis shortly behind. You will not want to be caught up in this scandal."

Nightliss meowed as if to remind me of the recorder. I pulled it out and showed it to Underborn. "Good thing I recorded everything that happened in the locker room."

Surprised flickered on his face and vanished almost before it could register. "Interesting foresight, Mr. Slade. I'm surprised they didn't search you." He gave me a meaningful look. "I assume nothing we've discussed is on this recorder."

I tucked it away and recommenced walking well behind the other students as the long line trundled across the school campus and across the nearby highway. "You think I'm dumb enough to record us and then show you the recorder?"

"In that case, might I suggest you make several copies?"

"I already planned on it." Actually, I hadn't, but I wasn't about to give him the satisfaction of knowing a cat had thought things out better than I had.

Elyssa poked a finger into a hole on the front of my shirt next to my neck. She grabbed my arm and looked at my back. "Oh my god, Justin! Were you shot?"

I'd almost forgotten about my wound in the panicked minutes following Skinner's attempt on her life. "I guess so. Did it heal?"

She inspected my skin, pressing a hand to my back and chest. "Looks like the bullet made a clean exit." Her eyes softened. "You took a bullet for me."

"Did I earn brownie points?"

"Uh, that's off the brownie points scale, even if you can heal fast." She quirked an eyebrow. "I'll have to get creative with my rewards."

Heat flushed up my neck as my imagination ran wild. I quickly reigned in my erotic thoughts because I wasn't finished grilling Underborn just yet. "What's quicksilver?" I asked him. The only quicksilver I knew of was mercury. If killing vamplings was that easy, I'd carry the stuff everywhere with me.

He stepped around a car parked at the curb, his eyes on the disorderly line of students ahead. "Think of it as a deadly supernatural poison."

"So a dart of the stuff could kill me or Elyssa?"

He shook his head. "No, such a small amount would severely sicken a vampire or dhampyr. For you, it would do far less damage. At least a pint is required to kill a full-grown subject."

"But the vamplings—"

"It has a far different effect on them due to the infection in their bloodstream. For some reason, quicksilver has a violent reaction to the vampling virus, making it highly effective at eradicating the infection."

We reached the four-lane road bordering the high school and crossed, heading for a large church parking lot across the road. "Where do I get this stuff?" I had a feeling Maximus wasn't through making vamplings. Sick dread coiled in my stomach as I thought about the potential damage the vampling virus could do if unleashed on an unsuspecting population.

"It's extremely hard to find anywhere. Ancient alchemists were said to have the knowledge to manufacture it, but now all we have are rare geological deposits and the few Templar repositories which still have meager stocks." He raised an eyebrow. "As a matter of fact, there were known deposits of this substance located at Thunder Rock."

Nyte, Ash, and Katie appeared from the throng of students as we reached the church parking lot across the road from the school. Ambulances, fire trucks, and police cars roared past and screeched onto the school grounds while others lined up across the highway to barricade the closest intersections from traffic.

"What happened?" Nyte asked, peering across the road.

I looked at him and shrugged. "Don't know."

Katie's knowing green eyes met mine. I returned a look which hopefully got the message across for her to zip it.

As I turned back around to face Underborn so I could grill him on a few more items of interest, my gaze locked onto a face that trapped the breath in my throat. I couldn't move. I couldn't think. Standing across the parking lot from us, my mom looked at me for several long seconds before turning and walking away.

CHAPTER 35

I didn't dare take my eyes off her for fear I'd lose sight of her blonde hair in the crowd of students.

"I'll be right back," I said and pushed my way through the dense throng.

"Where are you going?" Elyssa said.

"Wait here," I said my eyes locked on the figure with golden hair.

I cleared the huddled masses and broke free. Across the large parking lot, my mom stood next to her car. Not caring if people saw me or not, I ran faster until the soft treads of my tennis shoes sounded like the staccato rhythm of a crazed drummer against the asphalt. She leaned against her car and watched me approach, making no move to leave.

Fifteen feet or so from her, I slowed. Her blue eyes gazed at me as cold and emotionless as the stony look on her face. She pulled a white wand from her jacket pocket and made a circular motion with it. I took two steps more and bounced off an invisible barrier.

"Close enough," she said, her voice tight with anger.

"Mom? What's wrong?" I probed the invisible barrier but found no edges to it. "Why are you blocking me?"

"I want you to deliver a message to David."

"To Dad? Your husband?" I pounded my fists ineffectually at the solidified air. It flexed and bent, absorbing anything I could throw at it. I gave up and returned her glare. "Who are you? You're not Mom."

She ignored my jibe and continued. "Tell David to stop coming after us. Our marriage is over and I never want to see him again."

Her words sank like a dagger into my midsection. I cried out at the pain and felt tears simmering behind my eyes. "What?" I pressed against the barrier. "Mom, what are you talking about?"

"From now on, my family consists of me, my daughter, and my parents. You, him, and your demon blood are to stay away from us. If I hear of either of you trying to find us, I'll formally request Templar intervention. Do I make myself clear?"

I leaned against the barrier for support and felt the hot sting of tears as they broke through the dam and ran down my face. "What's wrong with you, Mom? Why are you doing this?" Someone had to be controlling her, or else this was an illusion. This was not the woman who'd raised me. "Who the hell are you?" I shouted and pounded against the invisible wall. I stumbled forward, almost face-planting on the asphalt when the barrier abruptly dissipated.

She walked to me and her expression seemed softer, less angry. "I *am* your mother." She pressed a hand to my forehead and whispered something in a language I didn't understand. A tingle gathered at her fingertips and worked its way down my head and through my body. Her voice lowered to a whisper. "I'm sorry, Justin but it has to be this way. Give David my message, please." She kissed my forehead. "I have no choice." Fear blossomed in her eyes. "No choice." With that mysterious statement, she turned her back on me.

"What were you trying to warn me about when you called me? You said, 'whatever you do, don't,' and I lost the connection."

She answered without turning around. "The same thing I just told you. Whatever you do, don't try to find us, Justin." She wiped something off her face. Slid into her car and left.

I tried to move, tried to follow her. But whatever she'd done to me had locked my muscles in place, and all I could do was follow her car with my eyes until it vanished from sight. Elyssa appeared before me moments later, eyes wide with alarm. She patted my face and spoke to me, but it was several minutes before my muscles responded to commands and I could speak past the suffocating pain lodged in my chest.

"What happened, Justin? Who was that?"

I sucked in a breath to overcome the agony burning in my heart and scanned the area. Before I could ask which way the car had gone I felt a sudden release of pressure in my head and a vivid memory burst through my mind's eye.

Riding in a car down a long winding driveway toward a mansion on a hill. Children laughing at a birthday party. Chocolate cake. Mom, standing in the corner of the room, alone with another person I can't see. Talking. Arguing. Her shoulders tense and then slump. She turns toward me and I catch a glimpse of the other person's face. A man's face. He smiles. But the smile has no kindness to it. It's the smile of a person who enjoys pulling the wings off flies or torturing animals for sport. A terrible feeling nearly overwhelms me as I stare into that very familiar face. If he had his way, I would be that tortured animal.

"Justin?" Elyssa's face snapped into view.

I yanked my head back, wobbling on my feet as I played the memory back a few times, trying desperately to remember the man's face. Why did he look so familiar? "Where did she go?" I asked.

"Where did who go?" She looked around, her forehead creased. "Who were you talking with?"

"My mom." The words caught like steel barbs in my throat and it was all I could do to keep back the furious tears threatening to break free. I was so angry I could hardly think straight. I wanted to destroy something. Take the Conroys and break them, one over each knee. I didn't even know what they looked like, for god's sake. My only memory of my grandfather was the horrible recollection of him coming and taking away my baby sister.

Elyssa's eyes lit with excitement. "She came to see you? What did she say?" The joy in her eyes flickered out when she saw the sorrow branded on my face. Her mouth dropped open a fraction and understanding drowned the joy on her face. "Oh, Justin, I'm sorry. I thought—"

"She told me to deliver a message to my dad. She doesn't want either of us in her life anymore and she'll call on the Templars if we try to find her."

Disbelief washed across her face. "Are you kidding me?"

I shook my head and squeezed my eyes shut for a moment. "At first I thought it wasn't her. That it must be a trick. But then she touched my head and somehow I knew it was Mom. No one was controlling her." Had she released the strange memory? Or had her mere presence triggered it? "Right after she left, I had another memory return."

She inhaled a sharp breath. "Tell me."

I explained it, though it seemed hard to express the details in words. "I saw the man's face so clearly the first time, but it's harder now."

Elyssa snapped her fingers in my face, startling me. "Eye color?"

"Gray."

"Hair?"

"Silver. Slicked back."

"Glasses?"

"Yeah, he had on round spectacles." As if those few ingredients were enough, the man's face came back in vivid clarity and I ground my teeth at the sight. I knew where I'd seen his face before. "Remember the gray men I told you about? The golems?"

She nodded.

"They look exactly like him."

Elyssa rocked back on her heels, her eyes thoughtful. "This means something, Justin."

"Mr. Gray is an asshole?"

"Your mother helped you." She grasped my hand. "She helped you! This exact memory returning now is not coincidence."

I ran my other hand through my hair and growled. "She just told me to get the hell out of her life."

"Maybe she didn't mean it. Maybe she can't say what she wants." Elyssa touched my forehead as if she could touch the memory itself.

"She gave you a gift to hunt down your enemies. Mr. Gray might know how to save your sister."

I took her other hand in mine and squeezed as the hope dangling by its fingertips from the cliff of doom in my heart reached up another hand and took a firmer hold. "Maybe you're right." I swallowed a lump in my throat. "I hope you're right."

"What are you going to do?"

"Tell Dad and figure it out from there, I guess." I looked back at the milling mass of students. "I just don't understand why she's doing this. The day before she left she told me she'd love me even if I hated her. It's almost like she knew she'd be doing something terrible. Like she'd planned all this a long time ago."

Elyssa pressed my hand to her heart. I looked into her eyes and felt the pain and anger melt away. The tight band of pressure across my chest eased. I drew in a breath and squeezed back. No words were necessary in that perfect moment. I knew she wasn't just standing next to me. Elyssa was *with* me, a part of me I could count on more than anyone else in the world.

The love I felt for her right then swelled in my chest until I thought I would burst. I hugged her and buried my face in the soft strands of her black hair. I drew in her soft sweet scent, the smell of leather and oil and something else. Maybe it was just the shampoo she'd used that morning, but it made me think of her.

"What do you want to do now?" Elyssa said, pulling back and regarding me with a soft expression. "Your father is free and clear and it doesn't look like the good old boys will be blackmailing you anymore."

That was a really good question. Dad would want to go after Ivy and Mom. But there was a lot on the proverbial plate. What Underborn had said about Thunder Rock and about the instability of the Conclave struck a nerve with me for some reason. I wondered if getting to the bottom of Thunder Rock would clear up relations between Elyssa's father and me, or if it was just wishful thinking. But how could I possibly hope to solve something that happened before I was born?

No matter what Mom said, I had to find her and Ivy no matter the consequences. It was time to plan. Thunder Rock could wait. Mr. Gray awaited somewhere. Probably right in this very city. Dad might know where the mansion in my memory was. He and I would confront the evil bastard and find out why he was sending his puppet minions after me. I gazed at Underborn. He probably knew exactly where I could find this man. But his price was too steep. Maximus deserved a painful death, but I wasn't the one to do it. Let the master assassin handle it. I'd find Mr. Gray without his help.

I let my gaze drift toward the crowd of students. "Mom doesn't want me coming after her, so you know what that means."

Elyssa returned a knowing smile. "Naturally you want to go after her. Maybe the mansion from your memory is a hint. Maybe she really wants you to find her."

I nodded and felt hope gain a firm hold on the cliff of doom. "One hopeless quest down, a million more to go."

"I'm in." She pursed her lips. "But remember what you promised about planning."

"I haven't forgotten."

She tilted her head slightly and stared deep into my eyes. "My god, you've changed."

I quirked an eyebrow. "Miss the bottle-bottom glasses?"

A smile brightened the serious look on her face. "Sometimes. I still remember the shorter chubbier version of you, thick glasses and all." She pressed her hand against my surprisingly firm stomach. "But don't worry, I won't stop liking you even with all these disgusting muscles you've put on."

I laughed. "Give me a few tubs of ice cream. Maybe I can get rid of them."

Her hand felt hot against my skin, even through the shirt. She pressed it flat and ran it up to my chest, her violet eyes searching mine. "How do you feel?"

"Oh, I have a little indigestion, probably from all the gore. Nothing a little Pepto-Bismol won't clear up."

She raised an eyebrow. "I'm being serious, Justin. You killed someone."

"I did what I had to do. He tried to kill your mom. He took a shot at you." My entire body tensed. "Yeah, I feel conflicted about it. But I had no choice."

"You're a lot more confident than you were. But you seem to think you're indestructible sometimes. With Katie and the truck, giving so much blood to save Stacey, and then taking a bullet for me." She touched the bullet hole in my shirt. "A few inches difference and it would have been a head shot. You could have died."

When she put it that way, I sounded like Rambo. Hell, maybe there was a part of me that acted on pure instinct. But I had learned one thing about myself. I would do anything for the people I loved. And Heaven help anyone who got in my way.

"If I have a chance to save someone I care about, I'll take it," I told her. "But especially for you." I caressed her cheek. "I'd do anything for you. If that means killing someone—" The image of Sheriff Skinner's crushed body, the way his eyes, wide and accusing, stared at me after I'd slammed him into that wall lingered at the front of my mind. I felt sick even if the monster deserved it.

"I can take care of myself, Justin." She said it without anger, without scolding me.

I nodded. "I know. But I want to be there for you even if you are my ninja girl." I pressed a hand to the small of her back and pulled her tight. Kissed her hard on the lips. "Are you ready to ride a white horse into the sunset now?"

She grinned and looked at the noon sun. "It's a little early for sunset."

"Who cares? I just want to find a nice safe place where we can be alone together."

"Oh, Mr. Slade? You planning to seek out my inner goddess?"

"Is that what it's called?"

She raised an eyebrow in a very sultry way and said, "Why don't I let you find out yourself?"

* * *

I HOPE you enjoyed reading this book. Reviews are very important in helping other readers decide what to read next. Would you please take a few seconds to rate this book by clicking a link below?

Rate on Amazon

Rate on Barnes and Noble

Rate on Smashwords

WANT MORE? Touch here for more books in the Overworld Chronicles!

BE among the first to know about new releases. Join my newsletter here!

FALLEN ANGEL CHAPTER 1

Police officers outfitted in black body armor burst from the back of a SWAT van and stormed my school, assault rifles held at the ready. Wailing fire trucks and ambulances zipped past while police cars screeched into blocking position across the roads leading into and out of the school grounds. Pandemonium reigned at Edenfield High.

And it was all my fault.

Well, mostly anyway. Elyssa and I stood at the back of the milling student body. We'd evacuated to a church parking lot across the road and had front-row seats to the three-ring circus. I didn't want to watch. I knew *exactly* what had happened and didn't want to think about it. People had died. I was responsible for one of the dead. Vampires, half-crazed by the vampling virus, had killed everyone else.

The face of Mr. Turpin, my English teacher, caught my eye as he met a group of the po-po in the middle of the road and spoke with them. "If only those cops knew who they were talking to," I muttered to Elyssa.

"He's a creep," she said, gripping my hand as her gaze found my target. "But he's also full of useful information."

Mr. Turpin, aka Underborn, was the most notorious assassin in the Overworld. But whatever information he had to offer wasn't worth it. "His price is too high." I let go of Elyssa's hand, trading it for her shoulder so I could pull her closer. Without her, I wouldn't have survived the past few days. Underborn had marked my father for death. When I tracked him down and demanded he rescind the hit, he admitted it had mostly been a ploy to lure me to him. To test me, as he put it. As a price for calling off the hit, I'd had to help him with a vampire problem at my high school. Now our institution of lower education looked like a warzone.

"What a mess," I said turning away from the school. Violent images flashed through my mind, a stark reminder of the death and destruction that claimed the lives of nearly nine people, one of them a former classmate. "Everything I touch seems to go to hell, and Underborn thinks I'm supposed to be a leader?" Stress wormed its way into my insides, abrasive and painful.

"Even the best leaders can't plan for everything." Elyssa pecked me on the cheek. "Just ask my dad."

I chuckled. "Yeah. I'd rather not." I'd be more likely to receive a sword through the guts than advice.

Elyssa's violet eyes met mine. "Underborn will want you to go after Maximus, instead of your mother and sister, won't he?" she said, phrasing it more like a statement than a question.

Maximus was actively recruiting high school students all over Atlanta—maybe even the entire country—to form a rogue vampire organization. I'd done my part, acting as Underborn's errand boy and now I needed to find my sister and mother.

"I know he's not done with me," I said as my mind churned through plans to force Underborn to tell me what I wanted to know. "But I need to be done with him. Unfortunately, he's the only person I know who might be able to help me find Ivy and Mom."

"If I can convince my father to mobilize the Templars against Maximus, maybe that will be enough."

I took my eyes off Underborn and turned to Elyssa. "You really think you can do that?"

She shrugged. "Considering everything we've been through, talking our way out of a situation instead of fighting has a certain appeal."

A smile died on my lips as I thought back to my last fight. Maximus was a vampire, true, but he wasn't old enough to turn others into his kind. Instead, the turning failed, leaving behind an undead creature with vampiric abilities and a highly infectious virus, which would kill and turn others into what those in the Overworld called vamplings.

Maximus had turned Brad Nichols and the result had been carnage.

"Your dad is too focused on taking down the spawn to care about a rogue vampire." I thought back to my disastrous meeting with her parents. To say Thomas Borathen despised my kind would be a huge understatement.

She brushed a lock of black hair behind an ear as a gust of wind dislodged it. "Underborn told us my father's feelings might change if we figure out who engineered the Thunder Rock massacre."

Thunder Rock. Before I was born, Thomas Borathen had led a group of Templars to apprehend a rogue spawn responsible for manifesting into demon form and consuming the souls of those unlucky enough to cross his path. Instead of finding a lone spawn, they'd encountered hordes of dark creatures from the demon plane. Only two Templars escaped that day: Thomas Borathen and Kevin Sorensen. But Thomas didn't know about the second survivor. In fact, my eyes were looking at the presumed-dead Templar right now—Underborn.

"Pshhhht. Yet another mystery our beloved assassin wants me to solve," I said. "It's a never-ending cycle. He'll always want me to do more while he dangles Mom and Ivy's location like a carrot."

Elyssa's eyes narrowed. "We can't just let him dictate terms for everything, Justin. I say we make him talk. Make him tell us where your mom is."

"Or where Mr. Gray lives."

She bared her teeth at the mention of the name I'd given the sorcerer who'd sent his gray-suited golems after me.

The pressure of eyes watching me prickled the hairs on my neck. It took less than a second to find the source. Nearly a hundred yards outside the police roadblock to my left, a blaze of red hair in the window of a parked limousine captured my attention.

Kassallandra.

The breath caught in my throat as the window on the car rolled up and the pale face vanished from sight. This wasn't good. Not at all. Dad's family, House Slade, had arranged a marriage between him and Kassallandra of House Assad. Except Dad had fallen in love with my mother, Alice, and run away with her. I was pretty happy with the outcome—being born and all—but hell hath no fury like a woman scorned, and Kassallandra was a demon spawn like my father. Her temper obviously matched her fiery hair because she'd sent hellhounds to track Dad down and fetch him like a human Frisbee.

But now she was here. Watching me. Why?

It didn't take long for my brain to connect the dots. She probably planned to use me to get to Dad. Time was running out for me to question Underborn. I gripped Elyssa's hand. "Think we could kidnap an assassin?"

Her eyes widened. "What?"

Agnes Wright, Principal Perkins's secretary, appeared through a break in the crowd. Her beady little eyes locked onto me. She jabbed a finger my way and spoke to two officers following close behind her.

"Oh, crap." I took an involuntary step back.

Elyssa saw Agnes leading the policemen our way and grimaced. "Did she see Principal Perkins and Coach Burgundy take you outside the school earlier?"

I nodded. "Ted Barnes was there too. They took me to the football training room just before Brad and his two goons burst in and killed everyone." Just thinking about the black veins racing up Brad's face made me shudder. The vampling virus had turned him into a half-dead lunatic with all the strength of a vampire. Perkins and his good old boys hadn't stood a chance.

Elyssa tapped her chin with a finger, eyes deep in thought. "If the cops ask you, tell them Perkins and Burgundy were telling you about scouts at the next football game."

"Scouts?"

"Yeah, college football scouts. Tell them they were tipping you off there might be scouts and that you could get a college scholarship. Then they let you go back to class and that's the last you saw of them."

"Yeah but what if these cops know about Perkins and the others blackmailing me to play football? For all I know the entire police department was in on it."

"If there's one thing I've learned about corruption, the big players hold the most valuable information close to their chest and only tell their underlings what they need to know. If they were planning to make big bucks by manufacturing supernatural steroids from your blood, there's no way they would've told anyone outside their little group."

I could have run away at supernatural speed and they never would have caught me. But if I did, the cops would assume I was guilty of something. Ending up on the FBI's most wanted list would be the perfect capper to a crappy day. So I swallowed the nervous lump in my throat and tried to act natural.

"He's right there, officer," Agnes Wright said, voice crackling with accusation as she and two local police officers closed in on me.

I almost gulped but somehow managed an innocent look of concern. "Who, me?"

"Yes, you, you rotten kid!" Agnes screeched.

"That'll be enough, Ma'am," said the officer to her right, a dark-skinned officer of medium build who looked like he wanted nothing more than to get the school secretary as far away from him as possible. He looked at me. "Justin Case?"

Technically, Justin Slade. I nodded. "Yes, officer?"

"Mind if I ask you a few questions?"

I managed a shrug. "Sure." Elyssa squeezed my hand as a jackhammer pulse pounded in my chest.

"I'll take him to my car," the officer said to his companion.

I looked toward the milling mass of students in the church parking lot then across the road to where the nearest patrol cars sat, blue lights flashing. "What's going on? What happened?"

He gave me a shrewd look as we walked toward the car, a look that made me think he could see straight into my soul and pick out every little lie. Once we arrived, he retrieved a metal clipboard from the front seat and wrote a few things down on the paper clipped to it.

"Where were you at ten this morning?"

"Biology class."

"And after that?"

"Uh, Ms. Wright called my class on the intercom and told me to go to the front office."

"And?"

"I went there and met with Principal Perkins and our football coach." That much was true.

He scribbled on his notepad. "What was the nature of the meeting?"

"They took me outside and told me some college scouts might be coming to our football game this Friday and if I played well, I might have a chance at a scholarship." Actually, they hadn't said much of anything until they'd gotten me inside the football training room where Sheriff Skinner, Chief Amerson, a doctor, and two goons with guns were waiting.

"Anything else?"

"They said they were proud of me, sir." The absurdity of that lie almost made me burst into hysterical laughter. Instead, they'd informed me the blood sample I'd submitted for testing as part of the standard procedure for joining the football team had returned very surprising results. They mistook my supernatural abilities for a miracle steroid which had transformed my previous loser self into an all-star athlete. To them, I'd looked like a cash cow worth millions and they planned to milk my blood of the imaginary steroid. Then Brad showed up and killed them all.

The officer scrawled my lies on his pad, stopped, and tapped the pen against his chin. "Where outside were you, exactly?"

"On the side of the school, kind of near the cafeteria."

"Did anything else happen?"

"No. I left them right after they told me about the scouts and headed back for class. Well, first I had to go to the bathroom because I was kind of nervous about the scouts thing and it upset my stomach something awful. Whew, let me tell you it took a few minutes to squeeze *those* demons out."

He cleared his throat and raised an eyebrow.

I wondered if I might have over-embellished the details. "Uh, yeah, let me think. Oh, and then I headed to class but the bell rang and I found out we were evacuating."

"Did you hear anything on your way back to class?"

I shook my head. "No. Just the bells."

He narrowed his eyes and stared at me for several seconds. "Are you sure that's what happened?"

"That's exactly what happened." It took everything I had to look him in the eye and keep a straight face. For all I knew everything in my posture and voice was screaming, "Liar!" I swallowed and asked, "What's wrong? Why did we have to leave the school?"

"I'd like you to have a seat in this car until I say you can go." He opened the rear door of the patrol car and motioned me in.

"Am I under arrest for something?" My heart was trying to burst out of my ribcage at this point, and it was all I could do not to run away at top speed.

"No, but I need to confirm your statement before I let you go back to your friends, okay?"

I nodded and got into the car. He shut it and walked across the barricaded road. Underborn met him halfway and drew him aside. My nerves splintered even further. No telling what the slimy, backstabbing assassin was saying.

I slumped in the seat and buried my face in my hands. I could kick the door off the hinges. Run away and never look back. My normal life was all but over anyway. With the sheriff and his co-conspirators dead, my friends Ash and Nyte would probably be safe from retaliation. But another part of me recoiled in horror at the thought of giving up on a life that, up until a month or so ago, had been painfully boring and normal. I'd been an overweight dyed-in-the-wool nerd with a hopeless crush on Katie Johnson, who I'd mistakenly believed to be the *one*. My life had revolved around live-action role-playing by way of Kings and Castles.

I shuddered at the memories, but still kind of missed being normal.

Cries and shouts of alarm reached my ears and tore me from my thoughts. I peered through the windshield of the patrol car but saw only the other car blocking off the high school entrance. I looked through the driver's window and noticed students scrambling deeper into the church parking lot in a panicked, screaming throng. One of the cops standing in the middle of the road pulled his sidearm and aimed at something behind me.

I heard the roar of a diesel engine growing closer. I twisted in my seat. The officer fired. Bullets pinged off the grill of a huge truck. It was yards away and charging straight for me.

FALLEN ANGEL CHAPTER 2

I screamed like a little girl at the same time I tried to twist and kick open the car door, but it was too late. With a crunch, the truck smashed into the side of the car. My head whipped back and slammed into the window. I flew across the back seat and, for a stunned moment, couldn't think straight. I flopped like a rubber chicken to the floorboard.

As my wits returned, I noticed a flat metal blade like the kind I'd seen on forklifts had punctured the door to my left. I glanced through the center grille separating the back seat from the front and saw another flat blade protruding through the front driver door. It had driven itself through the seats. The computer console in the center sparked and died.

The truck was a garbage hauler with a massive lift on the front for picking up industrial dumpsters and turning them upside-down over the enclosed truck bed. And this truck was roaring full speed onto the school grounds. The tires on the patrol car squealed and smoked as the truck plowed forward, pushing the car sideways. The high-pitched thrum of a hydraulic motor kicked in and the police car lifted off the ground, giving the tires some respite just before another chain-link fence loomed ahead.

I ducked against the door as metal fence poles clanged and screeched against the side of the car. The forklift continued lifting and the car tilted, throwing me against the door closest to the truck. When I peeled my face off the armrest and looked out the window, I came face-to-face with the truck driver—a gray man. He wore a gray business suit and wore his silvery hair slicked back. His gray eyes bore no emotion. He might be having the time of his life, smashing a patrol car with a person inside, but his face didn't have so much as a smile on it.

The lack of emotions wasn't surprising, considering he, she, or it, was a golem—a life-sized animated Ken doll sent by the mysterious Mr. Gray.

"Let me out of here you oversized blowup doll!" I shouted.

The truck rocked as it hit a concrete curb, tossing me around like a rag doll. The lift moved the car upward, perpendicular to the huge vehicle until I could see the rusted top of the cab through the window. I braced myself to kick out the left door, which, due to the angle of the tilted patrol car, I now stood on. Another jolt plunged my leg through the window.

The window seemed to be bullet resistant so it didn't shatter. Instead, my leg punched a jagged hole through it, tearing at my pants and ripping my skin. I gripped the back seat and pulled myself up. The ragged corners of the window further shredded the side of my name-brand jeans, probably making them more fashionable in the process. I kicked the door. But it was impaled on the fork lift and wouldn't budge. The lift rotated the patrol car until it was upside down and shuddered to a halt. I tumbled across the headliner. Through the side window, I saw four black leather shoes slam atop the cab as two more gray-suited golems joined in the fun. In unison, they kicked the car. Metal screeched against metal as the vehicle slid off the forklift and tumbled into the back of the garbage truck.

I yelped as the roof clanged against the truck bed, jarring every bone in my body. The roof of the patrol car crunched but held thanks to the stiff roll cage. The door nearest me pressed against the slick metal inside of the truck bed so I crawled across. Braced my back. Kicked the door. It shot off its hinges and gonged against the metal enclosure.

I crawled out. The gray men jumped atop the undercarriage of the patrol car. The truck, still roaring ahead, slammed against a large bump, flinging us into the air. I took advantage of my airtime and gripped the top lip of the truck bed, some ten or more feet above the bottom, and pulled myself up. Hands like iron clamped my leg. Yanked me down. I kept my hold on the lip. Another tug yanked my arms straight. Pain flared in my joints at the intense pressure. I kicked the gray man holding my ankle. The bottom of my shoe stomped his face. He didn't make a noise. I kicked him again and again. It didn't matter to him. He just kept pulling my leg.

"Let. Me. Go!" I shouted with each kick.

His partner joined him, gripping my free leg and tugging. My arms screamed in agony as my shoulder joints popped. My sweaty fingers lost their grip. I flew backward, crashing into the golems. Pine branches shrieked against the sides and top of the truck as we entered the wooded area behind the school. The rugged terrain rocked the stiff shocks mercilessly, tossing the two golems and me around like circus freaks at a yacht club. The patrol car skidded sideways on its roof, trapping one of the gray men in the corner while pinning my arms, legs, and chest against the cold metal of the sidewall. I gasped as it crushed the air from my lungs. Even worse, I had no leverage to push it off.

Golem two climbed back to its feet. Leapt atop the overturned car. Gripped my head. I braced as it twisted my head side-to-side, like it was trying to snap my neck. Somehow, I resisted, keeping my head straight. It increased the pressure. My neck muscles burned from the effort. I clenched my teeth so tight I thought they might crack.

It reared back a fist and punched me. My head gonged against the truck bed. Stars exploded. The golem gripped my chin and the back of my head and jerked. Just then, the truck lurched. Wood cracked. Pine needles and cones showered the truck bed. The car slid away, freeing me. Golem two lost his footing and slipped, twisting my head as he tumbled away. A bone cracked loudly in my neck. I screamed.

Pins and needles pricked my skin as blood circulation reached the places pinched off by the car. I wiggled my fingers. Looked left and right. Somehow, I was still alive. I felt my neck, expecting it to be dislocated horribly. Instead, it seemed to be intact.

"You jackass!" I leapt for the golem. Slammed into it. It clanged off the metal wall and landed face down. I jumped, knees first, onto its back. Gripped its hair and beat the head to a pulp against the floor until a shiny knob of metallic skull showed through the freakishly realistic fake flesh. I stood. Backed away from the disgusting mess. The first golem—who I'd forgotten—wrapped its arms around mine and lifted me off the floor.

Pulpy-faced McPulperson staggered to its feet like a broken doll and came for me. A blood-chilling howl sounded. Something clanged into the side of the truck, ringing it like a massive bell. The metal frame groaned. Leaned to the side. Toppled over and slid along the ground. The two golems and I ricocheted around the metal cage. My face connected with the lights on the police car. Everything spun. Blurred. Suddenly, I was free of the truck, sailing through the open air.

A tree caught me, its trunk slamming like a sledgehammer into my ribs. I heard a cracking noise and felt knives of bone pierce my vitals. I rolled on the needle-strewn forest floor in a blinding haze of pain, no breath left in my lungs for even a scream. Leaves crunched around me. I took a shuddering breath and looked up. McPulperson and his BFF dragged themselves from the truck where it lay on its side at the end of a long furrow of freshly ground earth and leaves. The passenger-side door of the truck screeched and flew twenty feet into the air, making a whistling noise as it flipped end-over-end before embedding itself into the ground twenty feet away. The driver pulled himself from the cab.

Why in the hell was Mr. Gray sending his toy soldiers after me? What reason could he possibly have for causing such a spectacle? I didn't have time to think about it. I had to move.

I rolled to my knees and staggered upright. Every movement sent fresh stabs to my insides, tiny daggers wielded by wicked little pain fairies, the evil kin of sleep fairies. My vision faded at the edges, dissolving into static.

"Stupid gray bastards," I muttered through clenched teeth.

Without a word, or even an indication that they'd heard or understood me, they blurred forward.

I turned to run and yelped with surprise at a massive, drooling muzzle inches from my face. A gigantic hellhound, tall as my chest, blocked my way. Two more hellhounds sprang from behind bushes on either side of me. I was boxed in. Dead meat. The golems didn't seem to care or notice. They rushed full steam ahead.

Since I couldn't fly, I stopped, dropped, and rolled. My broken ribs gouged my insides like a meat grinder. But it worked. The first golem, running too fast to adjust course on the slick forest bed of pine needles, tripped over me. Smacked face-first into Gigantor, the oversized hellhound.

The hound's jaws clamped around the golem's waist and bit it clean in half, teeth shearing through fake flesh and metal bones like tin foil. The other hounds pounced on McPulperson and pal, tearing them to tiny gray shreds. The torso of the first golem pulled itself toward me by its hands. It reached for my ankle. Gigantor sank its teeth into the arm and wrenched it off with a savage jerk of its head. Then it leaned down. Sniffed the still-wriggling golem and, almost daintily nipped off the thing's head and spat it out on the ground.

Good news: The golems were dead. Bad news: I was surrounded by hellhounds. In my current condition, I wasn't outrunning a pack of demonic hounds. So I opted for the next best thing. Sweet-talking.

"Good boy," I said, reaching a very tentative hand toward the hound's lean, almost Doberman-like head. I wondered how long, if ever, it would take my arm to grow back once this thing bit it off.

It bared sharp canines and growled a deep rumbling basso, yellow eyes burning.

I backed away. "Take me to your leader?" My voice sounded distant and thick. I wondered if my healing abilities were overwhelmed from the trauma I'd suffered.

A small black ball of fur darted between the massive hound and me. It hissed and spat, fur standing on end to make it look bigger than it was. I stared in horror as Nightliss, the little cat I'd rescued from a slobbering dog at a dumpster not so long ago rawred and advanced on the creature towering over her like a giant. How had she found me? What in the hell was going on? It was like watching a crazy, surreal dream unfold right before my eyes. Then again, it could have been a hallucination thanks to brain trauma caused by McPulperson punching me in the face.

The hound's growl turned into an uncertain whine and it backed away, shaking its head in confusion and glancing at its pack mates who still surrounded us.

"Nightliss, no!" I scooped her up and cradled her to my chest. "Are you trying to get yourself eaten?"

Nightliss glared at me with angry green eyes. She meowed and struggled against my arms, setting off more agony in my snapped ribs. I set her down, expecting her to run. Instead, her body seemed to melt and flow, expanding until a very familiar and very naked girl stared at me with those same green eyes.

ABOUT THE AUTHOR

John Corwin is the bestselling author of the Overworld Chronicles. He enjoys long walks on the beach and is a firm believer in puppies and kittens.

After years of getting into trouble thanks to his overactive imagination, John abandoned his male modeling career to write books.

He resides in Atlanta.

Connect with John Corwin Online
www.johncorwin.net
john@johncorwin.net

BOOKS BY JOHN CORWIN:

THE OVERWORLD CHRONICLES

Sweet Blood of Mine

Dark Light of Mine

Fallen Angel of Mine

Dread Nemesis of Mine

Twisted Sister of Mine

Dearest Mother of Mine

Infernal Father of Mine

Sinister Seraphim of Mine

Wicked War of Mine

Dire Destiny of Ours

Aetherial Annihilation

Baleful Betrayal

Ominous Odyssey

Insidious Insurrection

Utopia Undone

Overworld Apocalypse

Assignment Zero (An Elyssa Short Story)

OVERWORLD UNDERGROUND

Possessed By You

Demonicus

Coming Soon: Infernal Blade

OVERWORLD ARCANUM

Conrad Edison and the Living Curse

Conrad Edison and the Anchored World

Conrad Edison and the Broken Relic

Conrad Edison and the Infernal Design

Conrad Edison and the First Power

STAND ALONE NOVELS

Mars Rising

No Darker Fate

The Next Thing I Knew

Outsourced

For the latest on new releases, free ebooks, and more, join John Corwin's Newsletter at www.johncorwin.net!